HONOR BEGINS AT HOME

COURA

a novelization by

RANDY ALCORN

based on the screenplay by

ALEX KENDRICK &
STEPHEN KENDRICK

Tyndale House Publishers, Inc.
Carol Stream, Illinois

GEOUS

Visit Tyndale online at www.tyndale.com.

To learn more about *Courageous*, visit CourageoustheMovie.com.

TYNDALE and Tyndale's quill logo are registered trademarks of Tyndale House Publishers, Inc.

Courageous: A Novel

Designed by Dean H. Renninger

Edited by Caleb Sjogren

Library of Congress Cataloging-in-Publication Data

Alcorn, Randy C.
  Courageous : a novelization / by Randy Alcorn ; based on the screenplay by Alex Kendrick and Stephen Kendrick.
    p. cm.
  ISBN 978-1-4143-5846-8 (pbk.)
  1. Police—Fiction. 2. Fatherhood—Fiction. I. Kendrick, Alex, date. II. Kendrick, Stephen, date. III. Title.
  PS3551.L292C68 2011
  813´.54--dc22   2011020882

Printed in the United States of America

17 16 15 14 13 12 11
7   6   5   4   3   2   1

Randy dedicates this book to:

My precious wife, Nanci,
my wonderful daughters, Karina and Angela,
my excellent sons-in-law, Dan Franklin and Dan Stump,
and my beloved grandsons, Jake, Matt, Tyler, and Jack.
For each of you, my family, no man could be more grateful
to God than I am.

Alex and Stephen dedicate this book to:

Our wives, Christina and Jill—your love and support have
added momentum to our pursuit of God's calling on our lives.
You are an incredible treasure! May God continue blessing,
teaching, and drawing us closer together and closer to Him.
We love and need you desperately.
Sherwood Baptist Church—may the love you have for Christ
and each other continue to shine brighter with each passing year.
Keep praying, serving, giving, and growing. It has already been
worth it, but your greatest reward is still to come! May the
world know that Jesus Christ is your Lord! To Him be the glory!

CHAPTER ONE

A ROYAL-RED Ford F-150 SuperCrew rolled through the streets of Albany, Georgia. The pickup's driver brimmed with optimism, so much that he couldn't possibly foresee the battles about to hit his hometown.

Life here is going to be good, thirty-seven-year-old Nathan Hayes told himself. After eight years in Atlanta, Nathan had come home to Albany, three hours south, with his wife and three children. New job. New house. New start. Even a new truck.

Sleeves rolled up and windows rolled down, Nathan enjoyed the south Georgia sunshine. He pulled into a service station in west Albany, a remodeled version of the very one he'd stopped at twenty years earlier after getting his driver's license. He'd been nervous. Wasn't his part of town—mostly white folks, and in those days he didn't know many. But gas had been cheap and the drive beautiful.

Nathan allowed himself a long, lazy stretch. He inserted his credit card and pumped gas, humming contentedly. Albany was the birthplace of Ray Charles, "Georgia on My Mind," and some of the best home cookin' in the galaxy. One-third white,

1

two-thirds black, a quarter of the population below the poverty level, Albany had survived several Flint River floods and a history of racial tension. But with all its beauties and flaws, Albany was home.

Nathan topped off his tank, got into his pickup, and turned the key before he remembered the carnage. A half-dozen big, clumsy june bugs had given their all to make an impression on his windshield.

He got out and plunged a squeegee into a wash bucket only to find it bone-dry.

As he searched for another bucket, Nathan noticed the mix of people at the station: an overly cautious senior citizen creeping his Buick onto Newton Road, a middle-aged woman texting in the driver's seat, a guy in a do-rag leaning against a spotless silver Denali.

Nathan left his truck running and door open; he turned away only seconds—or so it seemed. When the door slammed, he swung around as his truck pulled away from the pump!

Adrenaline surged. He ran toward the driver's side while his pickup squealed toward the street.

"Hey! Stop! No!" Nathan's skills from Dougherty High football kicked in. He lunged, thrust his right arm through the open window, and grabbed the steering wheel, running next to the moving pickup.

"Stop the car!" Nathan yelled. "Stop the car!"

The carjacker, TJ, was twenty-eight years old and tougher than boot leather—the undisputed leader of the Gangster Nation, one of Albany's biggest gangs.

"What's wrong wichu, man?" TJ could bench-press 410 and outweighed this dude by sixty pounds. He had no intention of giving back this ride.

He accelerated onto the main road, but Nathan wouldn't let

go. TJ repeatedly smacked Nathan's face with a vicious right jab, then pounded his fingers to break their grip. "You gonna die, man; you gonna die."

Nathan's toes screamed at him, his Mizuno running shoes no match for the asphalt. Occasionally his right foot found the narrow running board for a little relief, only to lose it again when his head took another blow. While one hand gripped the wheel, Nathan clawed at the thief. The pickup veered right and left. Leaning back to avoid the punches, Nathan saw the oncoming traffic.

TJ saw too, and he angled into it, hoping the cars would peel this fool off.

First a silver Toyota whizzed by, then a white Chevy; each veered off to avoid the swerving truck. Nathan Hayes dangled like a Hollywood stuntman.

"Let go, fool!"

Finally Nathan got a good toehold on the running board and used every remaining ounce of strength to yank the steering wheel. The truck lost control and careened off the road. Nathan rolled onto gravel and rough grass.

TJ smashed into a tree, and the air bag exploded into his face, leaving it red with blood. The gangbanger stumbled out of the truck, dazed and bleeding, trying to find his legs. TJ wanted some get-back on this dude who'd dared to challenge him, but he could barely negotiate a few steps without faltering.

The silver Denali from the gas station screeched to a halt just a few feet from TJ. "Hurry up, man," the driver yelled. "It ain't worth it, dawg. Get in. Let's go!"

TJ staggered into the Denali, which sped away.

Stunned, Nathan pulled himself toward his vehicle. His face was red and scratched, his blue tattersall shirt stained. His jeans were ripped, his right shoe torn open, sock bloody.

An auburn-haired woman dressed for the gym in black yoga pants jumped out of the passenger side of a white Acadia. She ran to Nathan. "Are you okay?"

Nathan ignored her, relentlessly crawling to his truck.

The driver of the SUV, a blonde, was giving their location to the 911 operator.

"Sir," the auburn-haired woman said, "you need to stay still."

Nathan continued his crawl, disoriented but determined.

"Don't worry about the car!"

Still moving, Nathan said, "I'm not worried about the car."

He used the tire to pull himself up enough to open the back door of the pickup. An ear-piercing cry erupted from a car seat. The little boy let loose his pent-up shock at the sight of his daddy on his knees, sweaty and bleeding. Nathan reached in to comfort him.

As sirens approached, the auburn-haired woman watched Nathan with his little boy in the tiny denim overalls. This stranger wasn't blindly obsessed with a possession. He wasn't crazy.

He was a hero—a father who'd risked his life to rescue his child.

CHAPTER TWO

CORPORAL ADAM MITCHELL approached the heroic father who sat on the back bumper of an ambulance while a paramedic tended his bloodied foot. Shane Fuller, Adam's younger partner, matched him step for step. Two other deputies interviewed the women who'd stopped to help. The man held his baby close to his chest and ran a hand over the soft black hair.

Adam addressed the paramedic. "How about moving the child over there? Someone keep an eye on him while we ask this man some questions."

"No thank you," the father said. "I took my eye off him once; next thing I know I almost lost him."

Adam paused, running a hand quickly through his dark-brown thinning hair, then asked, "Can you describe the guy who stole your truck?"

"Black—dark like me. Huge biceps and a powerful punch." He touched his jaw gingerly. "Can't tell you much about his face, but I could describe his fist perfectly: hard as granite. Big gold ring. Late twenties, wearin' a big hunk of gold jewelry around his neck."

"Notice any other markings? Tattoos?"

"No, it happened so fast. I think he had on a black do-rag. But I had my eyes on the steering wheel. And the oncoming traffic!"

Shane squinted and rubbed at the bags under his eyes. "What about the driver of the getaway car?"

"Didn't see him. I was just thinking about my son."

"You're lucky you didn't get thrown on the road. I can't believe you got away with that crazy stunt."

"I was fortunate. Not crazy, though. What else could I do?"

"Why not let the police go after him? That's our job!"

"And what would that thug have done with my son? Tossed him in the bushes when he cried? I wasn't lettin' go of that wheel. Jackson is *my* job."

"You know you could have lost your life?"

"Yes, sir," he said, cradling the child in his arms. "But I couldn't risk losing my son."

Deep in thought, Adam stopped jotting notes.

The injured man said, "I was looking forward to meeting you guys under better circumstances on Monday."

"Monday?" Shane asked.

"Yeah. I start working with you next week."

Adam glanced at the notes he'd written earlier. "*Nathan Hayes.* I wondered how I recognized your name." He extended his hand. "Adam Mitchell. Pleased to meet you, Deputy Hayes."

"Shane Fuller."

"Good to meet you both," Nathan said.

"Why Albany?" Shane asked.

"Wanted to give my family a slower pace. Grew up here. Went to Dougherty High. Life in Atlanta wasn't a good fit for us."

Adam checked out Nathan's truck. "I own an F-150 myself. I know a good body shop. I'll write it down."

"Thanks."

The paramedic interrupted. "Done with that foot for now. They'll take care of you at the hospital. Need to get you inside. We can strap your kid's car seat in."

"I want Jackson where I can see him."

Adam looked at Nathan. "I'd say welcome back to Albany, but I hate to after such a rotten day."

"Well, my son's okay. So I still say it's a good day." He smiled at Jackson and continued rocking him gently.

From his squad car, Adam watched as the paramedics shut the ambulance door and drove away with the brave father and his child.

He pulled onto the road. "Would you have grabbed the wheel? And held on while you were getting beaten to a pulp?"

Shane Fuller turned and thought a moment. "Well, I can think of a few ways he could have died doing that. Crazy as it was, I guess he saved his kid's life."

"So would you have held on to the wheel?"

"Honestly? I don't know. Would you?"

Adam thought about it but didn't respond.

It troubled him that he wasn't sure of his answer.

Carrying several files from the sheriff's office, Adam entered his back door and gazed through to the living room's most prominent wall hanging, a sixteen-by-twenty framed photo with the autograph of one of the greatest Atlanta Falcons of all time: Steve Bartkowski. He nodded to Steve, his boyhood idol.

Adam walked through the hall to the kitchen, where his wife was finishing the dishes.

"Adam, it's 8:15! Where have you been?"

Victoria had *the tone*, so Adam gave her *the look*.

"Working on reports. Trying not to miss any more deadlines. Sorry about dinner." Just walked in the door and already he was engaged in self-defense. He barely registered Victoria's thick dark curls falling onto her new blue sweater. Sometimes, even after eighteen years of marriage, Adam was struck by how pretty she was. But tonight his wall went up, romantic thoughts evaporating.

"You missed Emily's piano recital."

Adam grimaced. "I totally forgot about that."

"We talked about it last week, yesterday, and again this morning. And you'd have known if you'd been home for dinner."

"It was a crazy day. Lots of important stuff going on."

"What's more important than your children?"

Adam donned his best nobody-understands-a-cop face.

Victoria bit her cheek, then softened her tone. "Emily asked if she could stay up till you got home." She paused, searching for words. "Dylan is out running. When he gets back, he's going to ask you about that 5K race again."

"And I'm gonna say no again."

"I tried to tell him that. But he's determined to change your mind."

The back door opened. Adam sighed. "And here we go."

Dylan Mitchell, a skinny, dark-haired fifteen-year-old wearing a sweaty black sleeveless T-shirt with red shorts, walked through the door, breathing hard.

Adam studied the junk mail in his hand.

"Dad, can I talk to you?"

"As long as it's not about a 5K race."

"Why not? A bunch of other guys are running in it with their dads."

Adam finally glanced up at Dylan. *When did he get so tall?*

"You're on the track team! You don't need something else to run in."

"They hardly ever let me run because I'm a freshman. I can't sign up for this race unless you run with me."

"Look, Dylan, it doesn't bother me that you like to run. But there'll be other races."

Dylan scowled, then turned and walked stiffly to his room.

Victoria wiped her hands on a dish towel and approached Adam. "Can I suggest you spend a little more time with him?"

"All he wants to do is play video games or run five miles."

"Then run with him. This race is just a 5K! What's that, three miles?"

"Three point one."

"Oh, sorry. That 'point one' would kill you?" She smiled quickly, attempting to defuse after detonation.

"You know I've never liked to run. Shoot hoops? Okay. Throw a football? Anytime. But he doesn't like what I like. I'm forty years old. There's gotta be a better way to spend time with him than torturing myself."

"Well, you have got to do something."

"He can help me build that shed in the backyard. I'm taking time off next week."

"He's gonna see that as your project. Besides, he'll be at school most of the time. With track practice, he doesn't get home until just before dinner, which you wouldn't know since you're seldom home by then. Adam, you really need to connect with your son."

"You're lecturing me again, Victoria."

She walked to the sink and threw in the hand towel. Adam wondered whether she was conscious of the symbolism.

"Hi, Daddy!" Nine-year-old Emily entered the kitchen and leaned against the counter, smiling at her father. With dark curly hair like her mom's, she was adorable in her princess paja-mas.

"Hey, sweetheart. Sorry I missed your recital today."

"That's okay." She peered up with wide, dark, elf eyes. "I messed up three times."

"You did?"

"Yeah. But Hannah messed up four times, so I felt better."

Adam grinned and tweaked her nose. "You little stinker!"

Emily giggled.

Adam rounded the kitchen island and embraced his little girl. That's how it was, Adam realized—this hierarchy of rela-tionships in the Mitchell home. Dylan was hard work with little payoff. Next came Victoria. He still loved her, but these days things were sweet one minute and sour the next. The sour parts often involved Dylan.

Adam wanted to *leave* the world's toughest job at the end of the day. He did *not* want to come home to it. But Emily was a delight. So easy.

"Emily's been invited to Hannah's birthday party."

"She has, huh?" He gave Emily a squeeze.

"Hannah's mom says she can take her home after school. But I told Emily she had to ask you first."

Emily spun like a gyroscope. Adam loved the delight she took in the smallest of things.

"Oh, please, Daddy! Please let me go! I promise I'll do my chores and my homework and . . . everything! Please!" Her smile was big, her dimples in just the right places, and her excitement lightened the whole room.

Adam asked Victoria, "Has she committed any crimes or misdemeanors lately?"

"No, she's been very good. She even cleaned her room with-out being asked."

"Yeah, but not by throwing everything in your closet, right, Emily?"

The little elf smiled sheepishly.

"Oh, all right. But you owe me a really big hug."

Emily squealed and stretched her arms. "Yes! Thank you, Daddy!"

As Emily threw her arms around Adam's neck, Dylan ducked into the kitchen to grab an apple. He stared at his father embracing Emily. His sister took center stage, as always. Dylan felt his teeth clamp together. *He always gives her whatever she wants. He won't even enter a race with me.*

Dylan knew he was invisible to his father, but he saw his mom looking at him. She usually noticed him. His father never did. Except to shut him down.

Dylan turned his back on his father and retreated to his bedroom.

He didn't slam the door. If he had, the house would have shaken.

CHAPTER THREE

MONDAY MORNING, Adam entered the kitchen at 7:10 and reached for the nearly full pot of French roast. *The problem with morning is that it comes before my first cup of coffee.*

Sundays were supposed to be restful, Adam knew, but yesterday had been tense. When Dylan didn't want to attend church, Adam had to insist, and Dylan pouted through Sunday dinner. Adam came down hard. So Victoria objected, and Adam told her that Dylan needed to grow up and stop sulking when life didn't go his way. Victoria was convinced Dylan and Emily heard their loud exchange. A frigid wind blew through the Mitchell household all that night.

Now Victoria sat at the kitchen table sipping her own morning coffee. Her weak smile told him she was still unhappy but probably wouldn't come after him with a steak knife.

He ate a quick piece of toast and a bowl of Wheaties, then went through the living room and paid his habitual homage to Steve Bartkowski. Steve was ageless. He demanded nothing of Adam and reminded him of his childhood fantasies. Back then, Adam dreamed of becoming a football player or an astronaut. As he pulled out of the driveway, he thought of the boys who'd dreamed of becoming cops and were now businessmen. Maybe when they saw him, they imagined Adam was living the dream.

Yeah, right.

A cop's job wasn't easy. So why did being a husband and father seem far tougher?

The usual buzz of conversation filled the muster room at the sheriff's office, punctuated by laughter as the deputies shared favorite stories they'd rehashed many times while they waited for their shift meeting to begin. The room was a white cinder-block box crammed with fourteen fake wood folding tables in two rows, a narrow aisle between, and a podium in front. No one could mistake it for an executive boardroom.

Still, the stark walls and camaraderie were a familiar solace, and when Adam entered the muster room, he felt more at home than he'd felt with his family yesterday.

Adam and Shane sat next to each other on uncomfortable black stacking chairs, as they had for the last thirteen years, Styrofoam coffee cups, notepads, and pens in front of them. Ahead and to their left sat twenty-three-year-old David Thomson, fresh faced, looking like a grad student playing cop. Ten other deputies, eight men and two women, sat around them, two per table.

Adam turned to Shane. "Hey, I'm grillin' steaks on Saturday. What are you gonna do about it?"

"I'm gonna come over and eat one. Maybe two."

"That's what I'm talkin' about." He leaned forward. "David, you've got no life. Why don't you come too?"

"I've got a life."

"Yeah? What are you doin' this weekend?"

"Uh . . . I'm, uh . . . Well, it depends on whether—"

"Right. See you Saturday." Adam and Shane laughed. David smiled sheepishly.

Sergeant Murphy—a stocky, savvy veteran—began roll call. "Okay, let's get started. First, Deputy David Thomson has survived his rookie year."

Applause broke out. Adam raised a hand for a high five. David grinned in embarrassment and raised his hand to acknowledge the praise.

"You know what that means," Shane said. "Now you can start using real bullets!"

Everyone laughed. Meanwhile a uniformed officer walked in the door, recognized only by Adam and Shane.

"Now I want to introduce you to Deputy Thomson's new partner, Nathan Hayes. He's joining our shift. He has eight years' experience with the Fulton County Sheriff's Department in Atlanta. But he grew up here in Albany. Let's welcome him."

The cops clapped for Hayes. He waved as he sat in the empty chair by David, then extended his hand to him.

"Unfortunately Deputy Hayes already had a run-in with a couple of our gang members. I'm sure you've heard the story. I don't know department policy in Atlanta, Hayes, but in Albany we recommend staying *inside* vehicles on the highway."

"I'll try to remember that."

"We have two new warrants today: Clyde and Jamar Holloman. Two frequent fliers who opened up a drug operation on the 600 block of Sheffield. I'd like both warrant teams to handle this one. Everyone else stick to your normal beats. Now the sheriff has something he wants to tell us this morning. Sheriff?"

A tall, sandy-haired man in uniform entered the room. From his haircut down, he looked like a Marine because he was one. His steely blue eyes seemed tired. Sheriff Brandon Gentry rarely made appearances in the muster room, so the deputies knew this must be important.

"An e-mail came across my desk I'd like to share with you. A recent study was done on the increase in violent gang activity. It says almost every case has something in common. Runaways, dropouts, kids on drugs, teens in prison."

Sheriff Gentry paused and checked the printout. "The attribute they share is most of them came from a fatherless home. That makes kids growing up without dads our worst problem and the source of a thousand other problems. The study shows when a father is absent, kids are five times more likely to commit suicide, ten times more likely to abuse drugs, fourteen times more likely to commit rape, and twenty times more likely to go to prison."

He eyed the deputies before he continued. "The study ends by saying, 'As fathers check out in increasing numbers, these percentages continue to rise, with escalating gang violence and crime.'"

The sheriff lowered the paper. "So maybe you're thinking, why tell us this, since by the time we face it on the streets, it's usually too late? The answer is what we've told you a hundred times—the divorce rate for cops is high. I know your shift work is hard. But the bottom line is this: when you clock out, go home and love your families. All right, you're dismissed. Get out of here."

The sheriff strode out, and the deputies rose.

"'Go home and love your families'?" Sergeant Brad Bronson snorted, addressing Sergeant Murphy. "In the old days they just told us, 'Round up the bad guys and do your job!'"

"Yeah, and most of us were getting divorces, including you and me. The sheriff's just trying to look out for the men. You might wanna show more respect."

"He's all hat and no cattle," Bronson said to Murphy, way too loudly. "He's been livin' too long in high cotton."

Adam sized up Brad Bronson, a piece of work if there ever was one. Six and a half feet tall, over three hundred pounds nonstrategically distributed, he was saggy fleshed, a giant marshmallow in pants, but still managed to intimidate. The hair that once grew on his huge billiard ball head had been rerouted out his ears. His forehead was the gray of smudged newsprint, some veins permanently broken from his history of head-butting uncooperative perps. Thick-throated and chinless, Bronson smelled of cigar smoke. The sergeant believed "too stupid to live" was a valid jury verdict.

Shane whispered to Adam, "There's a lot of gravity in this world, but Bronson uses more than his share."

"Well, boys," Bronson said with a growl, "I'll keep the streets safe while you take the ladies to the ballet."

"Where you headed today, Sarge?" Adam asked.

"The toughest part of town. 'Course, the toughest part of town is wherever I happen to be standin'." Even now, Bronson gave Adam his hundred-yard stare, the one that would have made Clint Eastwood in his prime melt like a salted slug. He cleared his throat, sounding like he was mixing cement.

Bronson acted tough, but Adam sensed more beneath the surface. In the twelve years Adam had known him, Bronson had been through two wives and had four children between them. Bronson constantly caused headaches for his superiors. He'd earned the particular ire of the public information officer, who repeatedly lectured him on his public demeanor and disdain for the media.

As the deputies made small talk on their way out, several shook hands with Nathan.

"Hold on," Shane told Adam, then went to talk with Riley Cooper.

Adam approached Cooper's partner, Jeff Henderson, forty

feet away, standing by his patrol car. Now a fifty-six-year-old veteran, Jeff had made a career of breaking in rookies, as he'd done with Adam seventeen years earlier. Last year, after their youngest son's graduation, Jeff's wife, Emma, had filed for divorce and moved to California to live near the older children and grandchildren.

Jeff's jaw was still chiseled, but his cheeks were fleshier and his blue eyes that used to flash bright seemed dimmer now. Adam reached out his hand. Jeff shook it, his grip looser than before.

"How are you, Jeff?"

He shrugged. "Can't complain. Wouldn't do any good if I did." His once-booming voice now seemed as weak as his handshake. Though he smiled, it appeared pasted on.

"How's Jeff Jr.?"

"Still alive, I guess. He hasn't spoken to me for a year. He and his sister side with their mother. Brent's at college now, hasn't been back."

"I'm sorry, Jeff."

"That's life."

"How's the stomach?"

"Sometimes it's okay, other times . . . feels like it happened yesterday."

"It" happened fourteen years ago when Jeff and Adam confronted a shoplifter fleeing a store. Jeff tackled him on the sidewalk, and the guy buried a blade deep in Jeff's stomach. It pierced his small intestine. He'd had two surgeries and unending therapy, but things hadn't been right since.

Time was supposed to heal Jeff, but it didn't. It just made him older. Some cops stayed fresh; many became shopworn. Jeff put in his time now, doing his job with less passion. He had another young partner, Riley Cooper, who was eager, as Adam had been. But Jeff didn't appear the energetic mentor anymore. He had so much to offer, yet he no longer seemed to offer it. Sadly, Adam thought, that wasn't just Riley's loss, but Jeff's.

Whether it was the ongoing pain or the trauma of the stabbing, the Jeff that Adam had known years ago and the one he knew now weren't the same guy. At first, Emma had been the model cop's wife, standing by her man, trying to help him. But he wouldn't let her. One day thirteen years ago, Adam went to pick up Jeff at his house. Before Adam got to the door, it opened. Jeff came out in a fury and slammed it behind him. Emma called out the window, "Stop blaming your family! We're not the ones who stuck that knife in you!"

Adam had never forgotten that awkward moment. Neither had Jeff, though he never let on.

Jeff peered at Adam as if through a fog. "Your family okay?"

"Yeah. You know, the usual stuff. But we're fine."

Jeff nodded. To Adam they seemed like two old men on the front porch in their rocking chairs saying, "Yessir" to each other with nothing to talk about. He thought of inviting Jeff fishing or to a ball game. But if they couldn't keep a conversation going for five minutes, why shoot for hours?

"Ready to go, Adam!" Shane called as Riley Cooper, sunglasses donned and full of strength and youthful enthusiasm, approached Jeff's car.

"Later, Jeff," Adam said.

"Later."

As Adam walked toward Shane and his car, he thought about the sheriff's encouragement to leave his work behind him when his shift was over. How many times had he been told that? A hundred? How many times had he actually done it? A half dozen?

Now Adam Mitchell had to serve arrest warrants on a couple

of those fatherless young men the sheriff talked about. And if he wasn't careful, they could make Adam's kids fatherless too.

Seventeen-year-old Derrick Freeman made his way from the train tracks toward Washington and Roosevelt. Tall and slender, he was dressed in a purple plaid shirt with a black Volcom tee underneath and long black denim shorts. He approached an abandoned warehouse, cell phone to his ear.

"I can't do that right now, Gramma! I'll be home later." His jaw clenched. "I don't know when. I'm gonna take care of that later. Bye. I said *bye*!"

He crammed the phone into his pocket and peered into a shadowy building.

Big Antoine, TJ's right-hand man, spoke out of a dark corner. "Hey, man, why you talkin' to yo gramma like that?"

Derrick squinted. He saw Antoine leaning against a concrete pillar, wearing a camo do-rag and closely trimmed goatee, dressed in an Army shirt. Torn-off sleeves emphasized bulging muscles. He slowly and deliberately skinned an apple.

"Tired of her naggin' me. I'm gonna do what I wanna do, man."

"Ain't she takin' care of you?"

"She workin' all the time. I take care of myself."

The way Antoine used the knife on the apple made Derrick's nerve endings crawl. He wondered if someone with that same kind of knife had put the two scars on Antoine's right cheek.

"So you ain't got nobody? Well, little wannabe, you better be sure you ready to do this. It ain't no game, man."

Derrick took a few steps closer, eyes still on the rotating knife scalping the apple. "Tell TJ I want in. I'm ready."

"You *think* you ready. TJ's gonna check you out. Watch out, man. TJ's a beast."

Derrick hesitated, then blurted out, "Is it true the Waterhouse kid died when he was jumped in?"

Antoine stared. "Got a little rough. Stuff happens. That kid was weak. TJ don't mess around. He's gonna make you prove yo'self."

Derrick sucked in air, stuck out his chest, and tried to deepen his voice. "Then I'll just prove myself."

"Good. Just remember . . . I warned ya."

CHAPTER FOUR

ADAM DROVE with Shane toward southeast Albany, with Nathan and David behind them. Adam pressed the number 2 on his speed dial to reach Victoria. "Listen, a truck with the lumber's coming soon. Tell them to pile it next to the driveway, okay?"

Adam felt the phone buzz and pulled it away to read the screen. "Hey, Victoria, the sheriff's calling. I gotta go. Love you. Bye."

Adam pushed the button to connect. "Hello, sir. Yes. Headed right there."

Shane pointed left to indicate the turn.

"Yes, sir. We did that. Thank you, sir. Love you. Bye."

Shane gaped at him wide-eyed.

"Oh no, no, no!" Adam stared disbelievingly at his cell.

Shane snorted. "Did you just tell the sheriff you loved him?"

"I can't believe I said that. Should I call him back?"

"You gonna tell him you *don't*?"

Adam grimaced as Shane picked up the car radio. "693c en route to the 600 block of Sheffield. Reference 10-99."

"10-4," the dispatcher replied. "693c."

In the second squad car, Nathan followed Adam and Shane. They were senior officers in this arrest, but this was like the neighborhood Nathan grew up in on Albany's east side. This westside area had long ago seen its best days and showed no hope of rebound.

The farther they drove, the rougher the neighborhood. As the cruisers approached the house, two gang members sitting on a front porch next to the target house yelled, "5-0," then walked across the yard. Not for a fight, Adam hoped as he and Shane pulled up and stepped out of the car. He studied their faces. They didn't match the mug shots accompanying the warrant.

Nathan and David passed the house and turned on the next street, pulling around to the back.

"You want the door, Rookie?" Nathan asked.

"I got it. And I'm not a rookie anymore." David stationed himself on the grass at the base of the back door stairs. Nathan tipped up his sunglasses and positioned himself where he could see both the side of the house and David. Hands on his hips, Nathan had the steady eyes of a Secret Service agent. David practiced reaching for his Glock 23.

Nathan rolled his eyes. *Not a rookie anymore?*

In the front yard, Adam and Shane approached the porch. Shane talked into his shoulder mic, letting the other team know what was happening in front. The window blinds fluttered.

"I got a feeling about this one," Adam said to Shane, trying to watch the house and the gangsters on the lawn next door at the same time.

"I'm feeling it too."

Adam checked his radio. "3d, you got the back?"

"10-4," he heard Nathan say.

They walked up the steps cautiously. Adam hoped he appeared more confident than he felt. *After seventeen years, why aren't these kinds of moments getting easier?* He remembered something Jeff Henderson had said: "Confidence is what you feel when you don't understand the situation."

Adam knocked. A woman opened the door. She could have been twenty or forty. Crack did that—doubled a person's age.

"Yeah?"

"Hello, ma'am, we're from the Dougherty County Sheriff's Department. We have a warrant for the arrests of Clyde and Jamar Holloman."

The woman quickly exited, throwing her hands up. "I ain't gettin' in the middle of this. I ain't even supposed to be here."

Smart lady, Adam thought. *She's done this drill before.*

Adam and Shane stepped slowly into the dark house, each holding a flashlight in one hand, free hands on their guns.

The house was a mess, clothes and food wrappers everywhere. Next to the couch Adam saw a crack pipe and a smashed Coke can.

"They use the same interior decorator you do, Shane."

"Just watch my back, Mitchell."

Adam turned off the television. If the Hollomans were hiding in the house, he needed to hear them, not a mattress commercial.

Without the TV's interference, Adam could hear the ceiling creak. He pointed his flashlight upward and made his way to the hall. Shane backed in behind him, keeping his eyes on the front door.

Adam noticed a string hanging from a pull-down attic staircase. It swung gently.

"Shane," he said, pointing. Adam walked to the other end of the hall so both sides were covered.

He tapped the ceiling with his flashlight.

"Clyde and Jamar Holloman, we have a warrant for your

arrest. We can do this the easy way or the hard way. I suggest you come on down."

The creaking continued. Adam nodded at Shane. They both drew their guns, trigger fingers on the frames.

Adam took the string in his left hand and mouthed, "One, two, three." On three, he pulled the cord.

The stairs unfolded. Shane aimed both gun and flashlight into the attic. He saw nothing.

"This is your last chance," Shane said. "Don't make this harder than it needs to be!"

The creaking continued. In the ten seconds or so he had to think it through, Adam wondered if they should call for K9 backup. If they sent Sawyer the patrol dog into the attic, they'd run no risk to a human officer. But it might be a thirty-minute wait.

If Shane got blown away when he stuck his head up in the attic, Adam would always regret it. But it was his job to make the call.

The same line of thinking ran through Shane's mind, so when Adam gave the signal, he swallowed hard, then with gun ready, took a few steps up the ladder and popped his head through the attic opening.

Daylight shone through the gable vents of the attic. Something moved. Instinctively Shane's finger jumped to the trigger. Three feet from him stood a black boy maybe eleven years old.

"Oh, man." Shane lowered the gun, thinking about what would have happened if he'd squeezed that trigger. "What are you doing up here, kid?"

"Uncle Clyde told me to walk around."

Adam called up from below, "Where is your uncle Cly—?"

A downstairs closet door flew open, and two young men leaped out.

"Back door!" Adam yelled.

David heard the call from inside and stepped closer to the door just as it flew open. One of the two-legged freight trains ran him down. Both the Holloman brothers charged toward a neighbor's yard at full speed.

Nathan took off on foot to chase them as David pulled himself to his feet.

"Get the car!" Nathan screamed.

Adam bolted out the back door and joined Nathan in the foot chase. Clyde and Jamar jumped the same fence, then split up. Nathan and Adam cleared the fence and continued the chase separately.

Shane pulled out in the squad car, listening to Adam bark off street names.

Clyde Holloman ran between houses like a scalded dog, Nathan close behind and gaining a little ground. Cutting through a cluttered backyard, Clyde pushed over anything he could, hoping to trip up Nathan, who dodged a bucket, a lawn chair, and a garbage can.

Meanwhile Jamar sprinted across a neighborhood street and into other yards. He ran on one side of trees while Adam ran on the other, trying to close the gap. As Jamar glanced behind to see if Adam was there, he slowed a little. When they both cleared the length of the trees, Adam, a couple of feet behind him, reached out and nearly grabbed him.

Just a little faster and I'd have had him!

"Shane! 700 block, Sheffield! North! North!"

Shane turned the car sharply, caught sight of Adam in pursuit, and grabbed the radio. "Units in pursuit of a black male wearing black do-rag, brown sleeveless tee, gray cargo shorts . . . heading northwest on the 700 block of Sheffield."

In the other cruiser, David raced down a neighborhood road,

searching for Nathan, when he heard his partner yell over the radio, "Thomson! 400 block of Hartford! David, help me out!"

David, alone in the car, was bewildered. "Hartford . . . where's Hartford?"

Adam followed Jamar into another backyard. Jamar ran through an open carport, overturning trash cans and bicycles as he passed. Adam jumped over and around them, out of breath.

As Jamar came to the next street, Shane skidded, nearly hitting him. Jamar changed directions toward another yard. Shane leaped out of the car. "Switch!"

Adam jumped in the driver's seat and took off, breathing heavily. "I didn't sign up for hurdles."

Nathan chased Clyde Holloman down a side street and up to a tall fence. Clyde hoisted himself over. Nathan climbed the fence carefully to see what awaited him on the other side and saw Clyde sprint off again.

Nathan paused to breathe, then grabbed his radio. "Officer in foot pursuit on 300 block of Oakview northbound. Deputy Thomson, where are you?"

David turned down another road, studying signs. "Oakview?" David spoke aloud. "I haven't even found Hartford!"

Jamar still sprinted, but his tank was running low. He didn't see Shane in pursuit. Hoping he had left the cops in the dust, he spotted a small shed and ran behind it. He squatted down and peered around the corner, trying to catch his breath. From his waistband he pulled a baggie of crack and stuffed it under some bricks at the base of the shed.

Without warning, Jamar felt two darts pierce him, one between the shoulder blades, the other at the low center of his back. He convulsed and screamed, face on the ground, eating dirt. He felt like he was strapped to the electric chair and someone had thrown the switch.

Shane rolled Jamar over and handcuffed him. "Always has to be the hard way, doesn't it?"

Shane noticed the plastic drug bag. "Diggin' a deeper hole for yourself, aren't you?" He grabbed his radio. "I've got the suspect 10-95. Adam, help Nathan if you can."

"10-4. Good job, Shane!"

Adam turned onto Oakview, the last location he'd heard Nathan call. Adam spotted Nathan jogging along the street ahead of him, turning his head like a searchlight. He knew it meant Nathan had lost Clyde somewhere. Adam pulled up alongside Nathan, who slowed and jumped in the car.

"Where is he?"

Nathan took a deep breath. "Next street over, maybe? I think he's circling back toward Sheffield."

They drove down the side street and turned back on Sheffield, then spotted Clyde running perpendicular to them toward an intersection ahead.

Adam floored it and called, "Slingshot?"

"Do it!" Nathan positioned his hand on the door handle.

As Adam drew near, Clyde turned and saw the patrol car, then changed direction. Adam got within thirty feet of Clyde and hit the brakes while turning the wheel left. The car slid to the side. Nathan jumped out, hitting the ground in a sprint.

He used the speed from the car's momentum to catch Clyde in four seconds, tackle him, and slam him to the ground. Clyde lay motionless except for his heaving chest. Nathan drew Clyde's wrists behind him and locked the handcuffs.

"How far you have to make me chase you, man? You're killin' me."

Clyde still gulped air while Nathan pulled him up. "Come on; let's go. Got a reservation for you at the Cinder Block Hotel. They're keepin' the lights on for you."

Nathan walked him toward Adam's car. As Adam opened the back door, he nodded at Nathan. "Nice wheels."

"Thanks. They got a workout, that's for sure. My bad toes are killin' me."

David drove up with Shane in the passenger seat and Jamar in the back.

"Welcome to the party," Adam said. "What'd you do, David, go out for a burger?"

"Traffic ticket," Shane said. "They pulled him over for drivin' too slow."

David's face was cherry red. "Sorry, guys. My bad. I got turned around."

Shane walked to Adam's car, passing Nathan and flashing him a look that said, *I like my partner better than yours.*

Nathan walked over to David, locking his eyes on him. "Man, you gotta learn the streets. I needed you."

"Yeah. I know the other parts of town. I'm just not as familiar with this . . . area."

"Well, I grew up in an area like this, but the difference is, I know that one and this one and the other parts too. And if I didn't, I'd be studying it every night."

"Look, I said I was sorry. It won't happen again."

As the four men got into their cars, a broad-shouldered man with the body of an NFL linebacker watched at a distance. Sitting by himself in the driver's seat of his dark-green Cadillac DeVille, TJ watched the two officers in the first car get in, in front of his man Clyde. Then he saw the other two talking, ready to haul off Jamar. TJ recognized the black cop hangin' with the crackers. He was the one who'd messed up his 211 when he'd claimed that sleek whip at the gas station.

"Think you all that, don't you, little man? You all up in my grill now."

TJ made a gesture with his left hand as if he were shooting the deputies. "187," he whispered to himself, hood lingo for murder.

He popped his 'lac into gear, then stopped to inventory his arsenal, each weapon hidden in its own place under the seat. He reached over and pulled out his old deuce-five auto, which he'd used to kill a crack competitor last spring. He knew he should get rid of the gun, but it had sentimental value, a gift from his older brother Vince, now serving life at Metro State Prison in Atlanta.

Next TJ pulled from under his right leg the Smith & Wesson that he'd used to rob a convenience store two years ago, after he'd been on the outs from Lee State Prison three days. He reached under the seat beneath his left leg and grabbed his .357.

TJ was the son of no man and the father of a gang of men. He could do whatever he wanted. With these cops stepping on his territory, maybe he'd give them something to remember him by.

CHAPTER FIVE

ADAM SAT in the driver's seat, ignoring the perp. Once he got the outlaws to lockup, they were no longer his responsibility. Good riddance . . . until he saw them on the street again way too soon because of overcrowded jails and merry-go-round justice.

As if reading his mind, Shane said, "These guys aren't scared of jail. Why should they be? Three hots and a cot. This is Rome, and the barbarians are winning."

Adam sighed. "They say the repeat rate for juvenile offenders in Dougherty County is 80 percent. Can you believe that?"

"Sure. They can be in and out of the detention centers within a month. They learn new crime skills while they're there. Thirty days later they're back on the streets practicing their newly acquired expertise."

Adam glanced in the rearview mirror, studying the boy in the backseat. "How old are you, Clyde? Eighteen?"

Clyde shot him a two-barreled scowl. "Nineteen."

"Who do you live with?"

"My auntie. Gonna arrest her too?"

"Where's your daddy?"

Clyde stared at him like he was crazy. "Ain't got no daddy."
Shane turned to Adam. "Why'd you even ask?"

Adam thought for a while but remained silent.

★ ★ ★

An hour later Nathan drove the patrol car with David beside him. "Something bothering you?"

"Nah."

"Well, quiet is okay. But if something's bugging you and you want to talk about it, feel free."

"I'm good."

Fifteen minutes passed while David remained mute despite Nathan's small talk. On the outside, David Thomson was finally making something of his life. Inside it was all loose ends, without anything to tie them together. David's guilt followed him everywhere, gnawing on his mind like a dog on a bone.

Nathan turned to David. "Ever been to Aunt Bea's Diner?"

"No."

"Hope it's still there."

The building was an urban planning nightmare, unmolested by the wheels of progress.

"Welcome to the diner time forgot," Nathan said as they strode through the door.

David looked at a table and imagined it would take a crowbar to remove the syrup bottles from the lazy Susan. He walked back to where he could see the grill, wondering if the kitchen harbored an Ebola culture. He was relieved that, though ancient, Aunt Bea's seemed clean.

They ordered from a menu that appeared to have been produced by a Remington typewriter in the seventies.

Meanwhile, David seemed determined to remain skeptical.

But by the time he was three bites into the cheeseburger, his attitude had been realigned.

Some guy who looked like he'd never left Woodstock, inhaling through the sixties and never exhaling till the seventies, popped a quarter into the Rock-Ola. On came "Mr. Tambourine Man."

"Tell me about your former partner," Nathan said.

"Why?"

"If you were taking someone's place at a job, wouldn't you want to know about him?"

David put on the plate what had nearly been his last bite of cheeseburger. He begrudgingly wiped his fingers with a napkin. "His name was Jack Bryant."

Nathan waited. Nothing came.

"And?"

"What more do you want to know?"

"Why is this so difficult? Ask me about my last partner and I'll tell you all about him. Seymour James. Fifty-three years old. Wife and three kids, like me. Smart guy and funny. Coaches Little League. Orders his cheeseburgers rare. Seattle Seahawks fan, but the Falcons are gradually winning him over."

"Bryant and I didn't always . . . get along very well."

"Why?"

"I was a rookie; that's why!" David raised his voice a few decibels too loud. Four people turned and stared.

"Okay," Nathan said. "I get it. Why did he transfer?"

"He and his wife split up. So he moved back to Chicago to go into business with a friend."

"No longer a cop?"

"It's some kind of security business."

"No kids?"

"Two."

"And he moved to Chicago?"

"Yeah."

"So now he doesn't see his kids?"

"I think he took them for a week this summer."

"Well, good for him," Nathan said with a frown.

"Hey, he's an okay guy."

"I would think an okay guy would either stay at his job or find one where he could stay near his kids."

"Why are you judging him like that? You don't even know him."

"No, I don't. He was probably a good cop, and I'll bet he's a great security guy. All I know is, those things aren't as important as being a good husband and a father."

"His wife left him."

"Was that because he was such a great husband?"

"Look, man, what's it to you?"

"I'm talking about a guy being there for his wife, making it work. And if you're separated, being there for your kids so they can still see you several times a week. At least they don't have to say, 'My dad left me.'"

Both men were adrift in thought. When the huckleberry pie with French vanilla ice cream appeared, it brought them back to dry land.

Nathan took a deep breath. "David, you're right. I didn't know your partner. And I shouldn't judge him. I'm sorry. It's a sore spot; my mom never had a decent husband, and I never had a dad."

David restricted his eye contact to his steadily disappearing huckleberry pie. The conversation was over.

In the Mitchells' backyard, Emily threw a tennis ball to Maggie, her year-old golden retriever.

"Can't I let her in, Mama? She won't make a mess."

"We've been over this, Emily. Your father let you get Maggie on the condition that she can't be a house dog."

"Couldn't she just *visit* the house and sleep in the backyard?"

"No dogs in the house. That's your father's rule. And his father's rule before him."

Adam stepped out on the porch. "Come inside, Emily."

"I want to play with Maggie." She gazed at her mother, then at her father. "Does it say in the Bible that you can't let dogs in the house?"

"Well, no. I don't think so . . ."

Emily smiled broadly. "Then can she sleep in my room?"

"No. I told you; we can't have an indoor dog."

Maggie drew up close to Adam's feet, nuzzling him. Emily scratched her under the ear while the dog emitted groans of ecstasy. There was nothing Maggie loved more than snuggling close to Emily. Victoria had earned Maggie's affection by grooming her with a stainless steel brush. An occasional pizza-flavored toy hadn't hurt Maggie's feelings, either. And though he did nothing to encourage her, the golden hadn't given up on Adam.

Emily buried her face in the fur on Maggie's neck.

Adam thought this was all too much fuss over a dog. But he did enjoy his little girl's smile and her contagious giggle.

Javier Martinez was thirty, short and stocky, strong and boyishly charming. He was working happily at a construction site— double-checking a blueprint—when he was approached by the foreman's assistant, a friendly giant named Mark Kost. "Hey, Javy," Mark said, slapping him on the back. "Boss wants to see you."

Javier took off his white hard hat and wiped the sweat from his forehead with the sleeve of his old brown T-shirt when he entered the foreman's office.

The foreman sat behind a desk in a small trailer lined with wood paneling fresh from 1972.

"Mr. Simms, you wanted to see me?"

"Yeah, Martinez, have a seat."

Simms, eyes down, shuffled some papers. Finally he stopped, adjusted his glasses, and glanced up. "Look, Javier, the past two weeks you've done great work."

"Thank you, sir."

"But this project is over budget, and I have to let a few guys go."

"I don't understand. Did I do something wrong?"

"It has nothing to do with your performance. It's just . . . you were one of the last guys I hired, so you gotta be the first I let go. Sorry. Don't take it personally."

Javier didn't know how else to take it. "Sir, please. I have a wife and kids. It's very hard for me to find work."

"I really am sorry." Simms handed him an envelope. "I added a few extra dollars."

Javier held the envelope, stunned, then slowly got up. He walked to the door, fighting the desire to plead for his job. He dreaded facing his sweet wife with the discouraging news of her husband's unemployment . . . again.

He walked four miles to a small, low-income house. A steel-blue Continental manufactured during the Carter administration sat in the driveway.

Inside the house, Carmen Martinez attempted to clean while Isabel, five, and Marcos, three, chased each other through the kitchen.

"I'm going to get you, Marcos!"

"No, you're not!"

"Isabel! Marcos! *Dejen de correr!* Stop running and clean up your toys! I need to start lunch."

She turned to see Javier standing quietly in the doorway. "Javy! What are you doing home? Why aren't you at work?"

"They let me go."

"What? Why?"

"I was the last one hired. They went over budget."

"Why didn't you call me? I would have talked to them not to do this. We have two children to feed, and . . ."

"I tried to tell that to Mr. Simms. It made no difference."

"Javy, we owe four hundred dollars in a week. All we have is leftover rice and beans. Marcos needs shoes."

"I tried to tell him, Carmen! I tried." Javy handed her the envelope. "Here's three hundred dollars. Get what you need for the children. I'm going back out to look for work."

Javier moved toward the door. As he walked away, he felt Carmen's hand on his arm.

"Javy, wait. I'm so sorry. I didn't mean to react that way. Why don't you take the car? We'll walk to the store."

"I cannot drive while my family walks. I will do the walking. Carmen, God will find me work."

Javier paused. "Do you have anything I could take with me to eat?"

Carmen surveyed the meager options. "A tortilla?"

Javier smiled weakly, took the tortilla, and walked out. He didn't have to see Carmen's tears after he left their home. He'd seen them before.

CHAPTER SIX

ADAM HAD WATCHED the late-night comedians, and morning came too early. He groused to himself about having to get up at 6:00 a.m. for the Responder Life breakfast. The chief coffee maker—Victoria—wasn't up yet. He'd have to survive somehow.

Whose idea was a 6:30 breakfast?

Adam showered, stumbled in the dark to dress, then hurried through the living room and out the door without even seeing Steve Bartkowski.

He entered the rec center ten minutes late. *Sure hope the coffee's good.* Grateful it was a legal drug, and in this case a free one, he sipped coffee to pull himself back into the world he'd checked out of only five hours earlier.

Breakfast was decent, though no threat to Pearly's, Adam's favorite restaurant. He focused on the Denver omelets and Danish, while Nathan, sitting across from him, met people right and left.

After the meal, Chris Williams, Albany's assistant chief of police, introduced the speaker, Caleb Holt, fire captain at Albany District. Adam had seen Caleb around town and at a couple of crime scenes where there was rescue assistance. Caleb was a local hero for his dramatic rescue of a little girl. He talked about how God saved his soul and saved his marriage and saved him from pornography.

It sounded to Adam like a little too much saving. He was grateful to be a Christian and be saved from hell. But he'd always been wary of those who tried to make him feel guilty because he wasn't doing more. He was comfortable with his decent, churchgoing life.

If it ain't broke, don't fix it.

After the breakfast wound down, the deputies headed to the sheriff's office and sat through a routine muster. Before dismissing the troops, Sergeant Murphy said, "Deputy Fuller, I need to talk with you."

When Shane and Adam came up together, Murphy said, "Deputy Mitchell, just do some paperwork until we're done, okay?"

Sergeant Murphy had called them both deputy. Official titles meant business—or trouble.

When Adam walked past Sergeant Murphy's open office door, he saw Diane Koos, the public information officer, inside. Koos was an attractive, quick-witted professional who had been a local news anchor before the sheriff had surprised everyone by offering her the PIO job. She'd surprised everyone by taking it. She was tough, no doubt about it, and meetings with the PIO were rarely good news.

It was 8:50 a.m. before Shane appeared at the desk where Adam read and signed a few reports.

"Let's get out of here," Shane said through clenched teeth.

"What happened?"

"We'll talk in the car."

The moment the doors closed, Shane practically yelled, "Jamar Holloman's attorney filed a complaint against me."

42

"Brutality? You didn't do anything but chase and handcuff him, did you? I mean, besides tasing him."

"That's it. But they claim I didn't warn him before I tased him."

"Is that true?"

"I won't lie to you, Adam. I did not say the words, 'I'm about to come around the corner of the shed and point a Taser at you and pull the trigger if you run.' But I'm there by myself, no partner to tackle the guy when he takes off. And that's exactly what he would have done. He ran halfway across Albany with us chasing him!"

"I ran the first leg of that relay, remember?"

"I'm thinking, obviously the Tasers have cameras in them now; you *know* what I did, so *why are you asking?* But Sergeant Murphy gives me a perfect opportunity. He says, 'The camera comes on just before you tase him. So it's possible you warned him before it was recording.' You should have seen the PIO scowl at Sarge."

Shane raked his fingers through his already-tussled hair. "So Koos wants to know if I'm aware of how far a Taser will fire. I say, 'Twenty-one feet.' She asks how fast can a guy go from a dead stop and reach twenty-one feet, and wasn't I capable of uttering a warning in that amount of time. Of course she's got a folder of information from books and procedure manuals. She doesn't know any of this stuff without researching it."

"What happened next?"

"Stiff as a corpse, but colder, Koos asks me if I'm 'guilty as charged.' I say, if you mean, did I shorten the chase by tasing a guy who'd proven he's a runner and wasn't going to turn himself in, then 'yes, I'm guilty as charged.'"

"Shouldn't running from his house, where we came with a warrant, and knocking down a deputy qualify as a clear intent to evade arrest? And shouldn't the fact that you and I chased him for a mile or more serve as a clear warning that we will do what is necessary to apprehend him?"

Shane's neck was splotchy red. Adam had seldom seen him so upset. "Sure wish you'd been there with Sarge and Koos. I could have used you. I had my hand slapped for doing my job! Never mind the risk I took sticking my head up in an attic where two armed felons might have been waiting to blow me away. Never mind the fact that there wouldn't have been a chase if he hadn't run and that we confiscated the drugs he was carrying."

"Are you getting a reprimand?"

"Yep. An official written reprimand. Goes in my file. If that file gets thick enough, someday they can dismiss me. That's great for morale, isn't it?"

As they pulled up to a stop sign, Adam said, "You know, Murphy gave you the opportunity. You could have claimed you warned him. It would have been your word against Jamar's."

Shane shrugged. "Well, sometimes the truth hurts; in this case it hurts my record. No good deed goes unpunished, huh?"

Adam clenched the steering wheel tightly as he drove. "Just because Jamar ran doesn't mean he couldn't have been armed. I mean, as you warned him about using nonlethal force, what would have kept him from taking you down with lethal force?"

"I *definitely* needed you in that room. The PIO is hopeless. Sergeant Murphy just sits there because Koos answers directly to the sheriff, and I end up being the bad guy. It's not as fun being a cop as it used to be. It's not only that the streets are more dangerous. Nowadays, we have to be so worried about what the public thinks. And the criminals and their attorneys. And the PIO. Seems like nobody's on the side of the guys patrolling the streets."

"You're preachin' to the choir."

"And I wonder if one day me having to think twice before I use reasonable means to subdue someone will give him just enough time to kill me." He turned to Adam. "Or you."

CHAPTER SEVEN

AFTER A LONG DAY, Nathan savored the welcome aroma of lasagna and garlic sourdough bread enveloping him as he opened his front door.

Nathan rounded the corner to the kitchen and saw Kayla, wearing her favorite yellow V-necked tee with black slacks. He grabbed her from behind, one hand on each side of her waist.

"Nathan Hayes! What's wrong with you? You're lucky I didn't have a meat cleaver." She turned and embraced him.

Life hadn't been easy the last few years, but at least their marriage was doing well. Even though he hadn't grown up in a house with a great marriage, or any marriage at all, he was determined that he would have one and that his children would experience the benefits.

Though they'd been in town only three weeks, Kayla made the house more like a home every day. Pictures were already hung on the walls as if they'd been there for years. She was already engaged with church, at the kids' schools, even volunteering at the Pregnancy Resource Center, where she counseled girls in crisis. Every day was an adventure for five-year-old Jordan, who loved the new house. Baby Jackson seemed unaffected by his carjacking adventure. Every family member seemed content.

Except one.

Jade, age fifteen, was the exception. And Nathan didn't know how to help her make the adjustment.

About 8 p.m., after dinner, Jade stepped into the hallway in jeans and layered gray and pink tank tops. What registered with Nathan simply as "teen music" pushed its way out of her room to the far reaches of the house. Jade's iPod had slid to a watery demise in the bathtub, and now the whole family was being subjected to her musical tastes.

"Turn that down," Kayla called from the kitchen, where she was clipping Jackson into his high chair.

Jade returned to her bedroom and lowered the volume approximately one half decibel.

"I think your mother meant for you to really turn it down," Nathan said, reaching to the CD player's dial and lowering it to half volume.

As he walked out of the room and turned toward the kitchen, Jade gave Nathan her default expression—half-frustrated, half-indignant. For Nathan it was a sad change from how she'd responded to him as a little girl, celebrating his arrival with shouts of "Daddy's home!" and hugging him long and hard. Nathan had never expected Jade to become so distant. She'd been angry about the move to Albany. She knew her friends in Atlanta had been heading down the wrong roads, but still she resented this "fresh start."

Nathan opened the refrigerator and grabbed a cup of yogurt, thinking more about Jade than what he was doing. Sometimes he wondered if he was losing his daughter.

A minute later, the sounds in the hallway said a fight was brewing. Jade's voice was shrill: "Mom, tell Jordan to leave me alone! He won't stay out of my room!"

Nathan heard Jordan's high-pitched five-year-old voice. "I'm not bothering her!"

"Yes, you are!"

Kayla marched down the hallway, holding a jar of baby food and a spoon. "Jordan, I told you five minutes ago to go brush your teeth and get your pj's on. Do I need to get Mr. Pow-Pow?"

"No, ma'am."

"Then let me see you moving in that direction."

Jordan ran across the hallway to the bathroom, stuffed T rex in hand.

"And, Jade, don't stay up all night texting that boy. We need to know more about him before you even *think* about developing feelings for him."

"What boy are we talking about?" Nathan asked, stepping down the hallway, eating the last spoonful of yogurt.

Kayla answered as she opened the baby food jar, "Another saggy pants boy is interested in Jade, but this time he's seventeen."

"Mom! He's *not* a sagger. And it's no big deal!"

"It is when you're fifteen." Turning to Nathan, Kayla took his empty yogurt cup and tucked the jar into his hand. "Hold this; I gotta change Jackson's diaper."

Nathan assumed Kayla's place outside Jade's room. "Did you meet him at school?"

Jade stepped into the hallway and stood across from Nathan. "Yes. He's nice. His grandmother goes to Mt. Zion."

"Good for his grandmother. Does *he* go to Mt. Zion?"

"I think so, maybe, when she takes him."

Nathan heard the implicit *if you really must know.*

I really must, he thought. "It's not his grandmother who's texting you, and I don't expect her to think of taking you out."

The phone rang. Nathan absentmindedly stirred his spoon in the baby food.

COURAGEOUS

"He's an honor student. He's the only one in the class who got a higher score than I did on the econ test."

"He's two years older and you're in the same economics class? Okay, that doesn't matter. Here's what matters: Is he a Christian?"

"I don't know him that well."

"That should come up early. If it hasn't, it's not a good sign."

"He's a nice boy."

"Does this nice boy have a name?"

"Derrick Freeman."

Jordan ran back into Jade's room wearing mismatched pajamas.

"Has Derrick Freeman asked you out?"

"Uh . . . yes."

Nathan sighed and gazed into her eyes. "Jade, baby, we already talked about this. You can't go on a date with anyone until they come talk to me. And they have no business talking to me until you're seventeen. Haven't I been clear about that?"

"But it's not a real date. We're just talking about going to the mall."

"If a boy asks you to go anywhere with him, it's a date. To the library to study? Date. To the park to play Frisbee? Date."

Jade folded her arms and pouted. Nathan, without thinking, ate a spoonful from the jar he was holding. Suddenly realizing it wasn't yogurt, he gagged and spit the baby food in the trash.

Kayla came up the hall with a diaper in one hand and a phone in the other.

"Kayla, what are we feeding him? That stuff is nasty!"

"That's broccoli and carrots, and it's his favorite. Just 'cuz you saved him from a gangbanger doesn't mean you can steal his food." She held out the phone. "It's Adam Mitchell."

48

"You wash your hands?"

"You're lucky it's not my left hand," Kayla said, pushing the diaper toward his face. He retreated, then took the phone.

"Sounds like it's not a good time to talk," Adam said.

"No, it's fine," Nathan said, disappearing into his bedroom. "You rescued me from the Hayes family circus. Performances nightly."

"Just wanted to invite you to join us for a barbecue Saturday at my place. I'm grilling, and Shane and David are coming. Wife and kids are welcome. You in?"

"I'll check with Kayla, but I'm 90 percent sure. Sounds like fun."

In the hallway, Kayla had picked up where her husband left off in the conversation with Jade. It was a conversation that would probably go on another three years. She didn't look forward to it.

Nathan rejoined the discussion just as he heard Jade raise her voice. "It's not fair!"

Her mother told her, "Jade, we have your best interests in mind. You've got to trust us."

"Sweetheart," Nathan said to his daughter, "don't let yourself get worked up."

Jade tried to be calm with her dad, which he interpreted as an attempt to send the message that her mother was overreacting. "I'm not getting worked up. I just wish you wouldn't judge people you don't know."

"That's the point," Nathan said. "We don't know him. If I got to know him, maybe I'd judge him to be a fine young Christian man who will guard his purity and yours, a boy who knows he answers to God and to me as your father. If that's the case, we're gonna get along great!"

"Nobody's like that, Daddy."

"Don't set your sights low, baby, or you'll end up with dirt."

Jade sighed. "When will you believe I'm mature enough to spend time with a boy?"

Suddenly Jordan ran by with her phone, and Jade shouted, "Jordan Hayes! That's *mine*! Give it back!" She ran over and yanked it out of his hand, then went to her room and slammed the door.

Jordan's head hung low.

"Son," Nathan said, "you know you can't play with your sister's things without her permission."

Kayla squatted down to his level. "You wore these pajamas every day last week. I put them in the dirty clothes basket for a reason. Go put on a clean pair."

"Yes, ma'am." Jordan ran into his room.

Kayla cracked open Jade's door. "Jade, I'm sorry, but I need to feed Jackson. I'm at the pregnancy center in the morning, and I've got to get him down."

"I'll put Jordan down," Nathan said.

"Thanks, babe," Kayla called.

Nathan picked up his son, who giggled all the way to bed. "All right, buddy," Nathan told him. "Let me say a prayer; then you need to get to sleep."

"Daddy?"

"Yes?"

"Do the bad guys ever shoot at you?"

"Well, almost never. But if I think they might, I have a special vest that can stop a bullet."

"Do you wear it every day?"

"I did in Atlanta. But I don't have to here. It's safer. And on hot days I sweat like crazy." He smiled. "So I don't normally wear it. But don't worry; I'll wear it when I need to."

"But, Daddy, how will you know when you need to?"

★ ★ ★

Adam's phone rang at 3:50 a.m., too early to qualify as morning. He knew it couldn't be good news.

"Hello?" Why was he trying to sound like he'd been up for hours?

"Adam, it's Sam Murphy. Sorry to wake you."

Sam? Sergeant *Murphy?*

"I'm afraid I have some bad news."

"Who?" Adam realized he hadn't asked *what*, but at this hour the two questions were the same.

"It's Jeff Henderson."

Adam could sense Sarge's hesitation.

"A neighbor found him dead."

"Jeff? Dead?"

Victoria sat up and turned on her reading light. Her face looked like Adam felt.

"I'm sorry. I know you used to be partners."

"How did he die?"

"Gunshot."

"A break-in? Do they know who?"

"Detectives are at the scene. We should know more by the time the shift begins. I'm really sorry."

Adam put down the phone.

Victoria's voice shook. "Jeff Henderson?"

"Yeah."

"How?"

"Shot. They don't know the details."

"Emma and the kids are in California, aren't they?"

"Last I knew."

"Has someone called her?"

"I'm sure they will. Maybe they'll wait until they know more."

"They shouldn't wait. Wives need to know right away."
Victoria put her hands over her face and cried.

Adam put a hand on her arm. He knew her tears weren't
only for Jeff and Emma and the kids. When a cop dies, every
other cop's wife cries for herself and her children too.

★ ★ ★

Adam arrived at the station two hours early and went to
Sergeant Murphy's office. Murphy was on the phone. His eyes
were vacant.

"I'm so sorry, Emma. So sorry."

Adam sat by his desk, listening. Murphy stared at the phone.
Apparently Emma had hung up.

"You're early, Adam."

"Couldn't stay home after your call."

"Sorry about that. It's three hours earlier for Emma on the
West Coast. I debated about waiting. But my wife insisted I
call."

"Obviously Emma's devastated. What did she say?"

"She kept saying there must be a mistake. It wasn't possible."

"Was it a single shooter?"

"Yeah," Murphy said.

"We have a name?"

"I'm afraid so."

"What do you mean, Sarge? It's good we know who did it,
right?"

"It was Jeff Henderson."

"I know who died. I'm asking who killed him."

Sergeant Murphy put his head down, his thumb and index
finger rubbing his closed eyes. "He killed himself."

CHAPTER EIGHT

FRIDAY WAS ONE of the worst days of Adam's life.

Adam was asked to say a few words at Jeff's funeral. He declined. He wasn't going to stand in front of a large group. He'd say the wrong words and embarrass himself.

So Adam wrote a note about Jeff, about how kind and patient and understanding he'd been and how much help he gave during Adam's first four years on the force. As the sheriff read his words, Adam caught Emma's eye. She sat across the aisle in the front row, puffy eyed, appearing older than her fifty-seven years. He wondered if Emma wished Jeff had been as kind, patient, and understanding with her and the children as he'd been with Adam.

Jeff's younger children, nineteen and twenty-four, sat with their mother. Brent, the youngest, had his dad's square jaw and blue eyes. Jeff's oldest son and his wife hadn't bothered to make the trip from California. Neither had his daughter's husband, nor any of the grandchildren. Was it anger or overwhelming grief because Jeff had taken his life? Or was it because they thought he'd been a rotten husband and father?

Adam pondered how unfair it was to judge a cop; they

couldn't understand what it was like. Then he chided himself. *At least I could have taken him to Pearly's and bought him link-sausage biscuits like the old days.* He'd seen sadness in his old friend's eyes during their conversation. Why hadn't he taken the initiative?

Adam felt a sudden wave of anger. Why hadn't Jeff reached out for help? Why hadn't he called someone? Why had he trusted his own judgment, put that old Sig Sauer in his mouth, and pulled the trigger?

But what Adam felt wasn't just grief and anger. It was fear. In a special meeting at the sheriff's office two days earlier, they'd brought in the police psychologist who explained what they'd all heard before—that the suicide rate among cops was higher than the general population. The psychologist said three times as many police officers had taken their own lives than had died in the line of duty. In one eight-month period, eight different California Highway Patrol officers had committed suicide. How this was supposed to be helpful, Adam wasn't sure. Should they feel better that Jeff's suicide wasn't that unusual?

Adam knew Jeff not only because of their old partnership, but because he knew himself and the police culture. Most cops thought asking for help was a sign of weakness. Cops were supposed to *solve* problems, not *be* the problem. He was taught to suppress his emotions in the middle of crises and soldier forward. Later on you could be emotional, they'd said. But when is later on? There's no later on because you're still a cop. Even when you don't wear the uniform, you're always a cop.

So Adam sat in his own private world, jerked back to reality only when he felt Victoria squeeze his hand.

Nearly two hundred uniformed officers were there. They represented the Dougherty County Sheriff's Department, the Albany Police, and at least a half-dozen surrounding agencies.

Had Jeff died in the line of duty, there might have been six hundred or more uniformed officers from all over south Georgia. The governor might have attended. They would have had an honor guard that folded the flag, presented it to Sheriff Gentry, who would have presented it, in turn, to Emma. At the funeral they would have had a twenty-one gun salute, and taps would have been played.

When a minister stood up and said Jeff was in a better place, Adam tried in vain to remember what Jeff had told him about his spiritual beliefs. His thoughts wandered through what could have, should have, or might have been.

An hour later Adam stood at the graveside.

Nathan hung behind as people began drifting away. He approached Adam from behind and laid a hand on his shoulder. "I know you were close. I'm sorry, Adam. Where was he at spiritually? Did he know Jesus?"

"I don't know."

"Did he go to church somewhere?"

"I'm not sure."

Nathan saw Adam's face and knew he shouldn't ask any more.

But Adam was asking himself those same questions. He had known Jeff Henderson for seventeen years. He'd spent about a third of every week with him over a four-year period and had been to dozens of ball games and on three vacations with him and his family. And still, he didn't know the answers.

★ ★ ★

Later that afternoon, after his shift was over, Adam Mitchell finished his shower and was nearly dressed when his peripheral vision caught a sumo wrestler lumbering his direction.

"Hey, Mitchell." Brad Bronson bulled his way across the

locker room. Adam examined Bronson's T-shirt, an XL, but the shirt didn't make it down to his belly button. If one size fits all, his shirt was not that size.

Adam focused on Bronson's unibrow for fear of looking elsewhere. "What's up, Sarge?"

"That rain was somethin', wasn't it? My front walk's *kivvered* with mud. I slipped this morning and liketa broke my neck."

"Uh-huh." Adam had never met the folksy side of Brad Bronson. It unnerved him.

Bronson pushed hard on his neck, which made an alarmingly loud cracking sound. "Too bad about Henderson."

"Yeah."

Bronson's thoughts jumped like a rock skipping across choppy water. He'd never met a transitional sentence he liked. "You ever have to deal with that Koos woman?"

The swift switch of topics startled Adam. "Diane Koos? The PIO?"

"Why did they put a civilian over sworn-in cops? Makes no sense."

"She's not really over us. She was hired by the sheriff to help us with some of our PR problems. He decided to hire outside the department for a change to send the message we aren't covering anything up."

Bronson stared at him. "You think I don't know that?"

"Well, you—"

"That Koos woman worked ten years for television news!" He said it like she'd spent her life selling crack to preschoolers. Bronson revved his cement mixer, then spit on the locker room floor. Adam's eyes didn't follow. He didn't need a memory of any fluid that came out of Bronson's body.

"I know," Adam said. "She lobbied for Shane's reprimand for failing to warn a runaway perp before tasing him."

"And he got the reprimand, which means she *is* over us—or may as well be. She knows jack about being a cop. And she has the sheriff's ear. Walks around in spiky shoes that hurt her feet, then takes it out on us. She was out to get me when she was a journalist, and she's still putting the heat on me."

"Something you said?" Adam suggested. "Or does this have anything to do with the guy at the Albany mall you head-butted into unconsciousness?"

"That's just an excuse," Bronson said.

"You have to admit it's a pretty *good* excuse."

"The perp was a power lifter. On steroids and crack. They act like he was a one-legged pacifist grandma with the flu."

"Well, what can you do about it? I mean, other than not head-butt people at the mall."

"The Koos keeps it up and I'm gonna break her broom in half."

★ ★ ★

Derrick Freeman entered his grandmother's tiny apartment after midnight. When he opened the door, a light turned on. A frail white-haired woman stood waiting in the tiny living room. The deep lines in her face showed worry and fear.

"You been drinkin', Derrick."

"No, Gramma."

"Don't lie to me, boy. I smell the alcohol from here. And I saw the boys you were with. I've seen 'em before. You know how I feel about the gangs!"

"Yeah, I know."

"You're a smart boy, one of the smartest at your school. I work two jobs so you'll be able to go to college. I don't work so that you can flush it all down the toilet."

"You don't know what you're talkin' about."

"*I* don't know what I'm talkin' about? I've been alive four times longer than you have, boy. I know all about gangs. I saw them take down your daddy before you even got to know him. Your brother was next. You think it doesn't break my heart every day for Keishon to be doin' time? It started like this, hangin' around with the gangsters; then he got beat in. Then they owned him and took him down."

"That's not what happened, Gramma. And he's not dead; he's in Georgia State Prison. He'll be out in a few years."

"You were what, fourteen, so you know how it went down? And you think everything will be fine when he gets out? Those boys are Gangster Nation, aren't they? They makin' you feel important? They just wanna suck you in. They get you to do drugs, then push drugs, make dirty money, hurt innocent people. You steal for them, you belong to them. God didn't make you to be nobody's slave, boy. White man's or black's."

"That's not how it is. They're my friends, my brothers."

"You'll find out what they are when it's too late. They go after kids who are dumb and desperate. That's why I've made sure you did your studies and stayed away from the gangs. But I can't make you anymore. You gotta decide for yourself."

"You got that right. That's what I'm gonna do. Decide for myself."

"Derrick, please." His grandmother reached to touch his shoulders. "Your mama was shanked by a boy in the gang. For what? She had ten dollars on her. He wanted crack. You become part of the GN, and you're spittin' on your mother's grave."

"My mama has nothin' to do with this. I barely even knew her."

"You barely knew her because the gang took her from you and me and Keishon! You don't understand what kind of life you're playin' with. Gangbangers become targets; their families become targets. You want me to be a target? You have a girl-friend, she'll be a target."

"They don't care about you, Gramma."

"You're right about that. The question is, do you care, Derrick? They might kill you. They might even kill for you. But I would die for you. That's what I *been* doin'. Except for your uncle Reggie, I'm the only family you've got now. You still have a chance, son. A good education will get you a good job; it'll give you options. Just finish high school and get away to college. There's no life for you here, Derrick."

"They're my friends, Gramma. I can finish high school with-out even tryin'. I can still go to college if I want to."

"They're gonna smoke you like a cigarette and throw you on the street and grind you into the ground. That's what the gangs do."

He turned away and walked toward his room.

Derrick's gramma wasn't finished. "Maybe you'd listen if I was a man. God knows, I wish you had a man in this house to tell you what it's really like. Maybe you don't think I'm much. I've had to be a mother and a father to you, but I just can't be what I'm not."

"I'm goin' to bed."

She stepped toward him and put her hand on his shirt. "Don't let 'em beat you in, Derrick. I'm losin' you like I lost your mother and your brother. They gonna take you from me. I see it in your eyes. Please, don't let them do it."

She clutched his sleeve, and he pushed her away hard. Her head hit the wall with a loud thud. She slumped to the floor, a low moan spilling from her lips.

He walked into his bedroom and slammed the door. He was sick and tired of his gramma, tired of her warnings and her constant yammer.

She's an old-head; she don't know nuthin'.

CHAPTER NINE

ON SATURDAY MORNING, Adam drove to Shane's house. Emily was singing in the backseat as her father pulled his sterling-gray Ford pickup into the driveway.

Shane held a plastic Walmart bag.

"What's in the bag?" Adam asked as Shane got in the truck.

"It's a couple Bulldogs T-shirts for Tyler," Shane said.

"Let's see them."

"Nah, they're wrapped. How's my little girl?"

"I'm fine, Mr. Shane!" Emily answered.

The radio was on as they rolled down Westover toward the bank.

"I beat Daddy in Yahtzee last night," Emily said.

"I'll bet you did."

"You were *ahead* in Yahtzee," Adam said. "We weren't able to finish, remember?"

"You got a phone call. But I *was* going to beat you!"

Shane smiled. "I appreciate you driving me around on a few errands. My car should be ready in a couple days."

"Not a problem," Adam said. "Now your shirt, *that's* a problem."

It was a banana-colored Tommy Bahama knockoff littered with white hibiscus.

"You don't like my shirt?"

"Well, 1985 called. It wants its shirt back."

Shane turned around. "Emily, what do you think of my shirt?"

"I love it!"

"Your daughter likes my shirt."

"My daughter's nine years old."

"Your daughter got half her genes from her mother. That's her only hope. Tyler thought this shirt was cool, so I got it."

"So your twelve-year-old son gives you fashion advice?"

"I see no one gives you fashion advice. Unless it's Waldo. Where is he, anyway?"

Emily giggled.

Adam couldn't win. "Hey, how *is* Tyler?"

"I only get him every other weekend, and it's only after Mia has filled his head with toxic opinions of me. You know, a third of my paycheck goes to alimony."

Adam gazed at Emily in the mirror. "Shane, let's talk about this later, okay?"

"What's alimony?"

"It's just a bad condition Mr. Shane has—makes him wear ugly clothes."

Emily laughed. Shane surveyed Adam. "You know what I like about you?"

"What?"

Shane pretended he was trying to remember. "Never mind. I was thinking about somebody else."

Shane chuckled. Adam did his best not to.

Adam parked his F-150 alongside the curb at the far end of the Flint Community Bank parking lot. Shane got out.

"All right, you got five minutes, cabana boy."

"Mr. Shane, can you bring me a lollipop?"

"Yes, I will, sweetheart." Shane pointed at Adam. "I'm not gettin' you one."

Just after Shane closed the door, a catchy song came on the radio.

I'd like to sail to lands afar
out on a boat that's built for two.

"Oh, Daddy, turn it up. I love this song!"

Adam raised the volume. "I've heard this before."

Emily opened the back door and jumped out onto the grass.

"Hold on! What are you doing?"

Emily opened Adam's door and grabbed his arm. "Oh, Daddy! Come dance with me!"

"Wait, honey. We're right by the bank! This is not where people dance."

"Please, Daddy! Just for this song. Come dance with me."

Emily continued pulling on Adam's arm. He turned and placed his feet outside the car but stayed seated. "Emily, people can see us."

"That's okay. They won't mind, Daddy. The song won't last forever. Please."

"Tell you what. You dance and I'll watch."

Emily peered at him and frowned, then began to dance on the grass. "Okay, Daddy," Emily said. "When you're ready to dance with me, this is what you do. First, you put your right hand around my waist like this, then hold your other hand out like this. Then we sway back and forth to the music." Face animated, she gestured gracefully while talking, lost in the moment.

Worries seem to fade away,
they become as distant memories
when we're together.

Adam watched his daughter with delight. The world was dark, but Emily was sunshine.

"And . . . we can spin."

Adam smiled as he watched, enjoying the music and the way Emily made it come alive. Her blue sundress flowed around her as she spun. She looked like a princess. For the moment Adam didn't think of suicides, drug dealers, or fights with Victoria or Dylan. All he thought of was the magical beauty he beheld in his daughter.

"Are you sure you don't wanna dance with me?" Emily pleaded.

He glanced toward the parking lot, then back at Emily. "I'm dancing with you in my heart."

As the enchanting song continued, Emily twirled and dipped and held her hands out as if dancing with a partner. Just before the song ended, Shane approached the truck. "Emily, are you trying to teach your dad how to dance?"

"He won't dance with me."

"That's because he's an old fuddy-duddy."

"Okay, everybody in. Mr. Fuddy-duddy is leaving."

As the doors shut, Emily asked, "What's a fuddy-duddy?"

"A fuddy-duddy," Adam said, directing his gaze at Shane, "is anyone who still uses the term *fuddy-duddy.*"

Adam pulled out of the parking area and onto the road.

"Who taught you how to dance, Emily? I know it wasn't your dad."

"Hey, I dance at home with my wife." Adam cringed as he

said it since he probably had done it twice, the last time before Emily was born.

"I've never seen you dance with Mommy."

"The truth comes out," Shane said.

"You know, you could be walking right now . . ."

"But I'm not!" Shane grinned.

"So I'm supposed to drop you off to meet Tyler?"

"Yep. We're going to hang out for a couple of hours."

"You got a ride to the barbecue?"

"No problem."

"Bring Tyler."

"Nah. Mia's got plans for him later."

Five miles from the bank, two men leaned against a railing at Albany's All American Fun Park.

"Isn't this kinda weird," the skinny, windblown one said, "two grown men meeting here?"

The slick operator wearing stylish sunglasses said, "Nope. Everybody assumes we brought kids. We're just two strangers making small talk while the kids have fun. Smile and wave once in a while, to no one in particular."

The speaker smiled and waved to fifteen kids playing video games. Then, just as a loud bell rang and everyone turned toward the Fascination tables, he reached in his bag, took out a bulging sack, and dropped it into the other man's open backpack.

The second man reached down and zipped up his bag. "Will there be more, or is this it?"

"I'll contact you. Don't try getting in touch with me. That keeps us at a distance. It's better this way."

"For you, maybe. What about me?"

"Hey, it's easy money. I could find someone else to deal with if you're getting cold feet. Give it back and I will."

"No. I'll do it. You want the money now?"

"You wrapped it in foil and put it in a brown paper bag like I told you?"

The skinny man nodded and waved at some middle schoolers on a ride.

"Good. When you see me by that foosball machine, leave the money here at the base of this post and walk away. I'll just stroll on over and pick it up. No one sees us together again."

Nathan, Shane, and David gathered in Adam Mitchell's backyard, on a flat lawn with a scattering of pine trees on the perimeter. Outside Adam's ranch-style brick house edged with variegated willows, they sat at a dark-gray cast aluminum table with matching chairs. Adam's gas grill was black and stainless steel with a side table on the left and a spare burner perfect for keeping the baked beans warm.

Shane was still in the same loud yellow shirt Adam had razzed him about. The other guys weighed in on it mercilessly. Everyone had enjoyed the feast—chicken, steak, burgers, and Victoria's killer potato salad. Now the wives and kids were gathered inside, leaving the men to themselves.

While the guys picked at the last of their meals, Adam gathered his tray of secret ingredients and started toward the house.

Nathan finished off his bottle of water and launched it. The bottle hit the far rim of the trash can and fell in.

"Bet you can't do that again," Shane said.

Nathan reached for Shane's Coke can.

"Hey, I'm not done!" Shane grabbed it from him.

"Okay, when you're finished, I'm gonna do it again."

Adam walked back to the table after being interrogated inside by Victoria and Kayla. "They're in there with the kids dying to know what we're talking about. I told them we're debating the Falcons' roster for this fall."

"Speaking of which," Nathan said, "I saw Bartkowski's photo on your wall. I'm a few years younger than you, but he was still playing when I was in middle school."

"Well, he's got a special place in my heart," Adam said. "Watching the Falcons was one of the few things I ever did with my dad. When he was home, I mean. He was an Army colonel, and he had important friends with contacts in the Falcons' front office. That's how he managed to wrangle that photo for me. He missed my high school graduation, so that was his makeup gift."

"That's a pretty good makeup gift!" Shane said.

Adam said nothing. But he thought how nice it would have been for his dad to have come to his graduation *and* given him the signed photo.

"Well, this barbecue was great," David said. "It reminded me of my dad. He used to grill all the time."

"Mine too," Adam said. "Speaking of dads . . . that e-mail the sheriff read the other day? You think it was accurate?"

"The one about fathers?" Nathan asked. "And fatherlessness?"

Adam nodded.

"I agree with it. I grew up seeing that kind of stuff all the time. You know how many of my childhood friends went to jail or died before they turned twenty? And how many are still crack addicts? And no, it's not about being black; it's about being poor and hopeless. I wondered where all the good fathers went to."

"Ain't that the truth," Shane said.

"What?" Adam said. "I remember you talking about your dad, Shane. Wasn't he an usher or something at your church?"

"Yeah, that doesn't mean anything. Soon as the church

service began, he'd step out back for a smoke. The problem wasn't the smoking—but why even go to church if you're going to just stand outside? One time he says, 'I'd better not catch you drinkin'.' He had a beer in his hand when he said it!"

The guys shared knowing glances.

"My mom used to nag him . . . until they got divorced. Look, it's not like I don't love the guy, but it's kind of hard to respect a hypocrite."

"What about you, David?" Adam asked.

David took a while to answer. "I had a good dad, I guess. I mean, nobody's perfect. My parents split after he had an affair. I think he regretted it."

"Did he tell you that?" Adam asked.

"Not in so many words, but I got that impression. I struggled with it for a while. But divorce comes with the territory now."

"I disagree, man," Nathan said. "Divorce happens because you make it an option."

"But you can't always work stuff out," David said. "Sometimes you need to part ways."

"I think I agree with Nathan," Adam said. "Calling it quits has become too easy. People don't fight for their marriages anymore."

"When you get married and have kids," Nathan said to David, "you're gonna figure out real quick how much you don't know. Man, if it wasn't for my faith in God, I'd be in a tailspin right now."

"Yeah, me too," Adam said.

"Guys . . . not everybody believes in that stuff," David said. "You're all religious, and that's fine. But you can't think religion is the only way to live your life. I mean, didn't your parents get a divorce, Nathan?"

"That's the problem. They were never married."

The other guys appeared surprised.

"Listen, my dad never professed to be a Christian. He had six children from three women. I was the fifth. By the time I was born, he'd already left. I'll tell you what, man. I'm thirty-seven years old, and I have never met my biological father."

"No kidding?" Adam said. "That's rough."

"If I have five siblings I know of, from three different women, who's to say I don't have more? And statistically, some of them would probably have been killed."

"Killed?" David asked.

"You know—what they do with unwanted kids before they're born. One half of all black babies are aborted."

"I never knew that," Adam said.

"Some people think that's better than to grow up unwanted," Shane said. "I mean, look at the problem on the streets."

Nathan weighed his words. "But does it occur to you that abortion isn't just a symptom; it's also an underlying problem? Black men, all men really, have been told abortion is between a woman and her doctor. Well, if I have no say over whether the child even lives, if that's entirely the mother's call, then why should I have anything to do with raising the child? The man is either the father of the child or he isn't—you can't have it both ways."

"I've never thought about it like that," Adam said.

David looked at Nathan. "Looks like you turned out all right."

Nathan leaned back and smoothed his hands over his shaved head. "That's because of a man in my neighborhood named William Barrett. When I was a teenager, just about to be swallowed up by a gang, he grabbed hold of me and wouldn't let go. He mentored me and changed my life. Taught me about God. We still stay in contact, and he's one of the reasons I wanted to move back to Albany. I want my kids to know him. Every Father's Day, he's the one I call."

"Did he make up for you not having a dad?" Shane asked.

"Nothing makes up for that. I'm telling you, not having a father has scarred me in more ways than I can count. Not having a dad to watch me play ball, my mom working two jobs, so she couldn't be there either. At times I was just sad. Other times I got real angry."

David squirmed.

"Ever try to track him down?" Adam asked.

"I tried a few times. Then stopped. His name is Clinton Brown, but he uses aliases, so I always hit a dead end. I could have tried harder."

"Why didn't you?" Adam asked.

"Afraid of what I would say."

After a long pause, Shane shifted uncomfortably, stood, and said, "Look, guys, I've enjoyed our little heart-to-heart, but I need to go pay some bills while there's still something left of my paycheck."

Shane turned to Adam. "Speaking of paychecks, I talked to my man, Javier, about your shed. That guy did a phenomenal job on my deck, and he's available next week, but he wants $150 a day."

"Ouch. Well, I've got to have somebody who knows what they're doing. I'm taking vacation time—got to get it done. If he could be here 8:00 a.m. Monday . . . that would be great."

"Okay, I'll call him. See you in church tomorrow."

"You got it."

As Shane stood to leave, Nathan grabbed his Coke can and shot it from the other side of the table. It landed in the trash can.

Nathan smiled. "Told ya."

CHAPTER TEN

THE REST of the household lay calm, but Javier Martinez, dressed in old jeans and a dark-red T-shirt, was animated as he spoke on the phone at 7:30 a.m. "Great! Thank you. I'll be there as soon as I can. Good-bye."

Javier's wife, Carmen, walked into the kitchen wearing a robe. Hair frizzy, and with no makeup, she was groggy, having awakened minutes earlier. "Who were you talking to?"

Javier was putting on his construction boots. "I got the job! But I need to leave right now. They're building a new office on Westover, and they need more men."

"Thank God, Javy! The rent is due Friday. I would tell you to take the car, but the tank is empty."

"I don't mind walking when I have good news!"

Javier stood and put his hands on her shoulders, then gazed straight into Carmen's eyes. "I told you God would give me a job." He kissed her on the forehead. "I would give you a big kiss on the mouth," he said playfully, "but your breath is very bad this morning."

Javier left with a smile.

"I love you too," Carmen said, only slightly sarcastically. She blew into her hand and inhaled, scowling. Her husband could be annoying, but he was a truthful man. She went to brush her teeth.

It took Javier nearly thirty minutes to reach the construction site. It was just after 8:00 a.m. when he walked briskly up to the foreman, who gave instructions to three men and sent them off to do their jobs.

"Hello, sir," Javier said. "Are you Richard?"

"Yeah."

"My name is Javier Martinez. I was told to come see you for work."

"I just hired the last three guys we needed. Sorry, man; we're good to go." He walked toward the office.

Javier followed, pleading. "I can do most anything, sir . . . woodwork, brickwork, even drywall."

"Look, I said I got what I need, all right?" The foreman turned and walked away. Javier stood there dismayed. He watched the other workers, waiting for someone to realize a mistake had been made. No one needed work more than he did. It was as if he were invisible. Nobody noticed.

After a few moments, reality sank in. His shoulders sagged, and he turned to go.

Javier wandered down a side street off Westover, face downcast. If only the car hadn't been low on gas. If only the other men hadn't gotten there first. If only they needed just one more guy.

As he walked aimlessly, Javier stepped off the street into an alley between houses. He began to pray aloud, facing the sky and gesturing.

"*Señor, no comprendo.* I am trying to provide for my family. I need Your help. *Por qué no me ayudes?* Have I done something to displease You?"

Javy walked on, his emotions turbulent, wishing for a rock to kick.

"*Dije a la familia que nos ayudaría.* I told my family You would help us, Lord. What can I tell them now? Are we going to lose our home?"

He stopped in the middle of the alley. Overwhelmed, he put his hands on his face, then stretched out his hands and cried, "What do You want me to do? *Dios,* por favor, *que debo hacer?* God, *please* show me what to do!"

Why did God seem so silent?

If Javier's own children ever asked him for help finding work, he wouldn't dream of refusing them. Then why was God refusing Javy? *Por qué?*

"Hey, Javier!"

Javier blinked. Had he heard right? He turned and saw someone he didn't know standing in a driveway sixty feet away, holding a tape measure.

"What are you doing?" the man asked him. Javier glanced over his shoulder to make sure the stranger wasn't talking to someone else. But the man had called him by name.

"I'm not paying you $150 to just stand there! Let's go!"

In the Mitchell yard, Adam snapped the tape measure shut and clipped it to his belt, then noticed the stunned expression on Javier's face as he tentatively walked toward the yard. *Did I scare him? Maybe he doesn't understand English.*

"Adam, be nice!" Victoria approached Adam from the house, a water bottle in her hand.

"He's late. He was just standing in the middle of the alley. I'm paying him by the day, and he's not cheap!"

"You need his help, so you'd better start off on the right foot! Don't go cop on him, okay?"

Adam sighed, then turned to Javier as he cautiously walked up the driveway.

Adam extended his hand. "You *are* Javier, right?"

Javier, wearing a bewildered expression, shook his hand. "Yes. I am Javier."

"Adam Mitchell. I didn't mean to yell at you." He glanced at Victoria. "I should have come out and talked to you. This is my wife, Victoria."

Victoria reached out her hand. "Hey, Javier, nice to meet you. I'll go get you a water bottle."

Adam pointed at the table. "Okay, I've got the plans for the shed right here. My old one's falling apart. I figure it should take both of us a week or so. Wait. You didn't bring any tools?"

"Uh, no."

"All right, we'll just have to share. Have you ever built a shed before?"

Javier gazed at the plans. "Yes."

"Sorry. I don't mean to put you on the spot, but do you have a work permit?"

"Yes, I do."

"Good. Let me show you what we're doing. But first, so there's no misunderstanding, I want a solid eight hours of work, not counting breaks for water or looking up at the sky or talking to yourself. You're good with $150 a day, right? Because if you're looking for more, I need to know right now."

"$150 a day . . . would be very good!"

"Okay. Good. Let's get going!"

Adam and Javier leveled the ground and set concrete blocks for the foundation. After four hours of nonstop work, they had the rim joists leveled and the floor joists nailed to the hangers. Adam sat down to eat the lunch that Victoria brought for them. His shoulders ached. Javier walked over, put an apple in his mouth, and went back to work. Adam rolled his eyes. *This is the guy who was goofing off in the alley this morning?*

Taking a big bite of his apple, Adam got up to join Javier.

★ ★ ★

Javier insisted on finishing the studs after Adam went in to get cleaned up. So at 6:30 that evening, when Javy was finally ready to go, Adam wrote him a check for $150.

Javier sang during most of his thirty-minute walk home. Hardly able to contain himself, he opened the door softly and peered in to see Carmen sitting with Isabel and Marcos, reading a book.

"Javy, is that you?"

Isabel and Marcos got up and ran to him. *"Papi! Papi!"*

His children hugged his legs. He knelt and embraced them, unmindful of his sweat-drenched shirt.

"Cómo están mis niños preciosos? Have you been good for your mother?"

"Sí, Papá!" Isabel said. "Come tell us a story!"

"I will, Isabel. Let me get cleaned up and eat. I have a special story to tell you. A true story that happened to your *papá. Hoy mismo!"*

"All right, get ready for bed and give Daddy a chance to eat."

Isabel and Marcos ran down the hall toward their room. Javier sat at the kitchen table as Carmen opened the refrigerator and pulled out his dinner.

"How did the job go?"

"Terrible . . . then *wonderful!"*

"What is that supposed to mean?"

"I went to that job this morning, and they said they did not need me."

75

Carmen stopped, plate in her hand. "You didn't get the job? Where have you been all day?"

"That's the thing. I was walking home asking God what He wanted me to do. I was hurt and confused. I didn't understand why God didn't help me when I try so hard to provide for my family. I asked Him to show Himself. Then, out of nowhere, this guy I had never seen before calls me by name and asks me to help him build a shed."

"How could a stranger call you by name?" Carmen asked.

Instead of answering, Javier reached in his pocket and pulled out a check, then placed it on the table.

"You made *$150* today?"

"Yes!"

"I don't understand. How did he know you? Why would he hire you off the street?"

"I have no idea."

"Why didn't you ask him?"

"I was scared. At first I thought he might be an angel, but he got angry when he hit his finger with his hammer. Plus, he is married and has children. I think this is not like angels."

"Are you going back tomorrow?"

"Eight o'clock. He says he wants me to work all week. But I think we can finish in four days."

"Four days at $150 a day? Javy, $600?"

Javier sat quietly, moisture gathering in his eyes. "Carmen, there have only been a few times in my life when I felt like God was helping my faith . . . and today was one of them. It felt so good to work hard, knowing He had answered my prayer."

Carmen reached over and took his hand. "I think it is a miracle. But I know God loves you, Javy. He listens to you because you honor Him."

Javier bowed his head.

"And all I want to do right now," Carmen said, "is to hug you and to kiss you."

Javier smiled and moved toward her, but she put up her hand. "But you smell so bad that I can't bring myself to do it."

Javier grinned at Carmen's revenge for his comment about her breath. He wagged his finger and jumped up. "Give me fifteen minutes! Then I will tell the children my story, and I will see *you* when I am finished!"

"I will heat up your dinner, *mi amor!*"

The Mitchell family sat at a Mexican restaurant two miles away. Adam, tired and sore, praised Javier's work. "Javy's a machine."

Victoria smiled. "I can't believe how much you got done."

"The teacher liked my artwork, Daddy," Emily said, unfolding a piece of paper. "I drew a picture of you and Mommy and Dylan and me and Maggie."

Victoria reached for the drawing to get a closer look. Dylan's eyes never left his plate of nachos.

"Good for you, Emily," Adam said. He noticed that in the picture, Maggie was on the couch. His daughter's campaign to gain Maggie's entrance to the house was relentless!

Emily spoke, but Victoria had to lean forward to hear her as the wandering mariachi band drew nearer, complete with trumpet, violin, guitar, bass guitar, and accordion.

"Can we choose a song for them to sing?" Emily repeated.

Victoria nodded. "Sure."

They performed something called "El Rey," and Emily said, "Sing another one!" She added the fateful words: "Last week was Daddy's birthday."

"His *fortieth* birthday," Victoria said.

Now they put the birthday sombrero on his head. He

pictured himself pulling his Glock 23 from his shorts pocket. That would make them stand down. But it might spoil the festive mood.

While they sang "Happy Birthday" in Spanish, the lead vocalist placed a hand on Emily's shoulder. Adam bristled, nearly coming up out of his chair. He felt a sharp kick to his ankle. Victoria glared at him.

Adam restrained himself as the man's hand went back to his guitar. But he kept his eye on the man and on Emily.

Before the song ended, Adam removed the sombrero and gave it to the band. Victoria tipped them.

After the fourth bite of his meal, Adam got a call from Sergeant Murphy. He stepped away for three minutes, then returned. Five minutes later the phone rang again; this time it was Shane.

Victoria shook her head at Adam the moment the phone rang. *Just turn it off,* her eyes pleaded.

"It could be important," he said as he stepped away. Shane had a possible breakthrough in an arrest they'd made two weeks earlier. Fifteen minutes later—though Adam imagined it was five—he returned to a table where all the plates but his had been cleared. Victoria's gaze was colder than Adam's chicken burrito.

"Where's Dylan?" Adam asked.

"Jeremy, one of the boys on the track team, saw him, and they went to Best Buy. Jeremy's taking him home."

"He couldn't finish dinner with his family?"

"He *did* finish dinner with his family. We all did. I mean, three of us did. The fourth was doing something more important."

The drive was silent. At home, while Emily took her bath, Adam approached Victoria in the bedroom. "Did you have to scold me in front of Emily?"

"Which do you think hurt our daughter, you choosing your cop friends over your family and then blaming your son, or me simply pointing out to you what Emily already knew?"

"It's not that big of a deal. Emily got over it by the time we left the parking lot."

"She's quick to forgive, but the time is still lost. I'm so glad you love your little girl, Adam. But remember, she has a brother, who happens to be your son."

"Think it's too late for us to place him for adoption?"

"That's not funny, Adam!" Her eyes went from ice to fire in an instant.

"It's just that Emily is so low maintenance."

"Is that what makes you love someone? That they're low maintenance?"

"It sure doesn't hurt."

"Emily doesn't demand much from you. Maybe that's because I'm the one who's raising her."

Why did she have to twist the knife? Nobody understands cops. Not even their families.

Victoria put up her hands. "You know those fatherless boys you talk about, the ones causing all the problems? Maybe you'd better do something to keep your son from becoming one of them!"

★ ★ ★

Adam sat in his black leather recliner. Feeling guilty, angry, misunderstood, disrespected, and just plain exhausted, he began his evening ritual of flipping through channels. Here Adam Mitchell could be in control.

After Victoria helped Emily with her homework, the two sat together on the back porch, next to Maggie. The beautiful golden retriever licked Emily's face gratefully.

Maggie's despondent expression as they shut the door made her seem almost human. Victoria told Emily to wash her hands, then took a lint brush to her daughter to get off Maggie's hairs. Adam wasn't a fan of dog hair. Still, Victoria didn't like feeling that she was hiding evidence from a cop.

Emily, in her pajamas, walked down the hall toward her father. She crawled onto Adam's lap and lay against his shoulder. He enjoyed having her nearby but wasn't in the mood for chatter, so he continued to watch the news. It didn't occur to him that some of the subject matter wouldn't make sense to a nine-year-old and some of it might scare her.

A few minutes later, Dylan walked in the front door in his running gear, sweating from another humid Georgia evening. He stepped quietly behind his dad.

Barely turning his head, Adam called to him, "Dylan, you need to run earlier. Ten thirty is too late to be out."

Dylan stared at his sister, snuggled up with her dad, and set his jaw. He walked to the kitchen, grabbed a couple of granola bars and a glass of milk, then disappeared into his room.

Once in his room, Dylan picked up his newest Batman graphic novel. He lost himself in a world where good was good and bad was bad. Where men of courage, and in Robin's case, a boy of courage, stood up and made a difference. After reading for fifteen minutes, he deliberated for ten seconds whether to do homework or play video games. It was an easy choice.

In the living room, Victoria saw the clock and realized how late it was. "Emily, sweetie, come on. Let's go to bed."

Emily crawled off Adam's lap, watched his eyes remain locked on the television, and walked down the hallway. The bounce in her step was gone. She walked through her doorway, then looked one last time down the hallway. She saw only the back of the recliner . . . and the back of her father's head.

CHAPTER ELEVEN

"PROMISE NOT TO TELL on me?" Nathan asked.

Kayla eyed him. "Depends on what you did."

"I ran a background check on Derrick."

"You're not supposed to do that, are you?"

"Well, not usually."

"Then you were a bad boy," Kayla said, sitting on the bed. "Now I want you to tell me everything you found out."

"No police record."

"That's great news!"

"I called the school and talked to a cooperative vice principal. Derrick doesn't dress like a gangbanger or wannabe. He's a very good student."

"I'm impressed."

"Yeah, it's good he's not a convicted felon. But it doesn't change the fact Jade's not old enough to date. I won't let her go with him in a car. I want to make sure you and I are still on the same page."

"After all your detective work, you don't trust him?"

"At night? In a car? With a teenage girl? Why should I trust him?"

"Come on, Nathan. I came down hard on Jade about Derrick too. But let's not be overprotective. At some point we'll have to trust our children."

"I trust Jade to be a fifteen-year-old girl. I do not trust her to use a shotgun or pilot the space shuttle. And I don't trust her to know what to do when—notice I said when, not if—this two-legged mixture of oozing hormones makes the move on her."

"Like you made the move on me?"

"My point exactly! I shouldn't have made that move, and you were right to stop me. But I don't want it all to fall on Jade's shoulders. You were eighteen; she's fifteen. You and I both made mistakes before we met each other. My mother and your parents could have done a lot to help prevent them. Isn't that what we've said?"

"The kid's an honor student. Isn't he the kind of young man we want our daughter to be attracted to?"

"We don't want her to be attracted to *any* guy . . . yet. Seen the T-shirt that says D.A.D.D. Dads Against Daughters Dating? I think I'll get one. Anyway, a guy can be both an honor student and a jerk! We don't know anything about his spiritual life."

"I know, but there aren't many boys at church. And Jade says most of them are nerds."

"Hey, if she has to be interested in a boy . . . a nerd would have advantages."

"You're being unreasonable."

Nathan stopped the conversation there because he needed to think. Something inside him said that as wonderful as his wife was, and as important as her opinion was, and even though in many areas she was smarter than he was . . . weren't husbands and fathers supposed to lead? Wasn't that what the Bible said?

He realized Kayla might understand Jade better than he did. But he knew he understood young men in a way his wife and daughter couldn't. Nathan believed, deep inside, that he needed to step up to the plate. But starting that uphill climb seemed a daunting proposition his life hadn't prepared him to handle. Maybe he should just settle for being a better-than-average dad and hope for the best with his daughter.

★ ★ ★

Nathan and David were sent to a domestic disturbance where a husband had slapped his wife around, but she refused to press charges. The children were still crying when they left. Nathan's insides churned. They were overdue for a break on their way back to the sheriff's office to file paperwork.

"Do you think about your dad?" David asked Nathan.

"Why?"

"Just wondered. Sometimes I think about mine."

"Your parents split, you said. Well, at least until then you had a dad."

"Sort of."

"What do you mean?"

David stared out the window. "Where we going for break?"

"Wherever you want. How about Elements Coffee Company? Or we can stop at a 7-Eleven for a cheappuccino."

David paused and thought about his dwindling checking account. "7-Eleven sounds good."

"I'll buy."

"Okay, Elements."

Ten minutes later they sat in the progressive coffee shop.

David stared into his coffee as if searching for himself in it. Nathan was determined to wait for him to talk when he was ready.

David didn't know how else to put it. He set down the cup. "You know what artificial insemination is?"

"Um . . . yeah, I think so."

"That's where I came from. I didn't know until I was ten, and even then I didn't understand it. But my big sister knew, and she told somebody; then it spread. I was in seventh grade by then, but kids teased me about it."

"Was your sister . . . ?"

"They adopted her. But then my mother wanted a biological child, and my father, or whatever I should call him, had dead sperm."

"He was infertile?"

"Whatever. Anyway, I thought he was my real dad. Then when I had stomach problems, my mom pulled out some medical records from the safe. I read them. I saw the name of my real father."

"You did?"

"Yeah, his first and last name: 'Anonymous Donor.'"

"That was all?"

"Kind of funny, isn't it? I read up on it. It got started in the seventies, and by the eighties they had sperm banks all over the country. I'm one of the products. Lots of TLC goes into that, huh?"

"Have you searched for your biological father?"

"No. It just seems too . . . weird. It's one thing to search for a woman who gave birth to you. But hunting for a sperm donor?"

Nathan turned up his hands. "I don't know much about this, man. Sorry."

"I wouldn't either if it wasn't who I am."

"It's not who you are, David. A person is a person, regardless."

"Yeah, I've read *Horton Hears a Who!* It's easy to tell myself it doesn't matter. But the fact is, it does."

"But you still had a dad, a steak-grillin' dad. You said that."

"My mom had a husband, and yeah, I usually call him Dad to fit in. But that's not how I think of him anymore. When my parents split, my sister's the one my father asked custody for! Maybe I was just a reminder that some anonymous donor gave my mom something he couldn't."

"Have you kept in touch with him?"

"Nope. He said he was sorry he left for the other woman, but it's not like he came back. He married her. Then I found out there'd been others. My mom says there have been others since then, too, so his second wife is 'getting some payback,' as Mom puts it."

"Has he made contact with you?"

"He got custody of my sister, who had major issues with Mom. I've only seen him once and Wendy twice since then. No reason to get together. My family's split right down the middle."

Nathan sighed. "I guess my dad wasn't much more than a sperm donor himself. I know his name, and that's about it."

David's eyes twitched. "Look, Nathan, I really don't want the other guys to find out what I told you. I'm not up to the 'your daddy was a sperm donor' jokes. They already beat up on me for being a rookie. Nobody takes me seriously."

"That's not how it is, David."

"Please don't tell anyone."

"They won't hear it from me. We're partners. You have to be able to trust your partner. Right?"

"Right."

Nathan glanced out the window a moment, then met David's eyes. "For what it's worth, even though I don't have a father on earth, the Bible says I do have a Father in heaven. God created us. He searches for us when we're lost, and He forgives us. And it says the way to know the Father is through His Son Jesus."

David listened.

"I want to tell you just two verses I've memorized, okay? First, Psalm 68:5. It says God is 'a father to the fatherless, a defender of widows.' Your mother and mine weren't widows in the way we normally think because our dads didn't die. But they're like widows because they were abandoned and husband-less, just like we're fatherless. Does that make sense?"

David nodded.

"The other verse is Psalm 27:10. It says, 'Though my father and mother forsake me, the Lord will receive me.' When I came to faith in Christ, God became my Father."

David looked doubtful.

"This isn't pretend, David. It really happened and it changed my life. When William Barrett showed me what a dad could be like, it made me open my heart to God as a Father. The search for *a* father is a search for *the* Father. God is all-powerful and proved His love by going to the cross for me. In my life, that has made all the difference."

Nathan stood, smiled, and put his hand on his young part-ner's shoulder. "Next time we get the cheappuccino. And it's on you."

TJ and his Gangster Nation gathered in a vacant building to jump in their new recruit, who would join the family with his blood.

Several young boys gathered outside to watch the initiation through a window. Someday, they hoped, they would join the gang too. The women's world of home and church wasn't for them. What they couldn't find there, they would find someday in a street family where the leaders were men, untamed and unfeminized.

TJ circled the boy, watching to measure his fear. "You ready to become a man, baby G?"

Derrick Freeman, dressed in his school clothes, swallowed hard, then nodded. TJ slapped him to the ground. Ten other gang members hit and kicked him. After thirty seconds, blood flowed. TJ yelled, "Fight back, tiny!"

Derrick fought, swinging his long arms. He got in a few good hits. Some hit him harder while others gave him a wider berth.

"That's it," TJ yelled after two minutes that felt like two hours to Derrick. "I said, that's it!"

Everyone backed off.

Though bleeding badly, Derrick had drawn blood on a couple of them too.

Derrick held his stomach and breathed hard. His golf shirt was dirty and ripped, his face bruised and scratched.

TJ sat in front of Derrick on a makeshift throne. His head was wrapped in a black bandanna. His gold chain with the crown pendant stood out against a black tank top.

"You done good, little G," TJ said. "Tore up your preppy outfit, didn't they? Don't go high sidin' us, honor student, thinkin' you're better than us. Got that?"

Derrick nodded, wondering what he dared not say aloud— *If this is family, why'd you have me beat up so bad?*

TJ leaned forward and stared Derrick down. He spoke not only to him but to every member of the gang. "You said you wanted in. This is how we do this thing. And the pain you feelin' now ain't nothin' compared to what we'll do if you ever try to leave or turn on one of us."

"So I'm in?" Derrick said.

"Yeah, you in. You ain't just a hood rat now. You family. Once you in, we take care of our own, dawg. You belong to *us* now. Get him up, 'Toine."

The big man pulled Derrick to his feet. A voice deep inside

Derrick, which he feared was his grandmother's, said, *"Why would you* want *to be* in? *What you need is to be* out. *"* But that voice was overpowered by another that said, *"You're legit now. You belong. You got a real family of men, not just a gramma. "*

TJ stood up and stepped toward Derrick. "Now that I ain't got Clyde and Jamar no more, thanks to them county brownies, I'm gonna need someone makin' those runs for me."

Derrick wasn't excited about selling drugs, but cash was king.

TJ beckoned to Antoine. "Get me a deuce-deuce."

Antoine tossed the little gun to TJ, who handed it to Derrick. "This your first piece?"

Derrick nodded, taking the .22.

"You show what you can do with it; then Daddy get you somethin' bigger than this peashooter."

TJ put his arms around Derrick, hugging him.

It felt like the hug of a father. At least Derrick imagined it did.

Since he had never experienced a father's hug, how was he to know the difference?

CHAPTER TWELVE

ADAM TRIED to wait it out, but Javy never stopped. Finally Adam said, "I'm meeting some buddies for lunch. Take a break!"

Javier waved and went right on working. Day before yesterday Adam had been worried the guy wouldn't be a hard worker; now he was bugged that Javy worked harder than he did. He could barely keep up.

Adam turned down Westover toward Old Dawson, then to Meredyth Drive, his mouth watering for the beef brisket at Austin's Barbeque & Oyster Bar. As he pulled into the parking lot, he deliberated about which two of the six sauces to combine on his brisket. Manual labor gave him a king-size appetite.

He entered wearing a sweaty gray T-shirt, jeans, a navy-blue DCSD ball cap, and work boots. Nathan, David, and Shane were wearing their uniforms and were halfway through their meal. As he approached the table, Adam noticed the remains of fried dill pickle chips and cheese grits.

"Okay, guys, I'm seriously hungry. While you drive around town on your backsides, I've been doing honest work." Adam gripped the menu tighter as if trying to wrest from it something it was holding back. "Well, brisket sounds good. Or a side of oysters. Maybe pork chops. Or some wings. Fried shrimp might hit the spot. What's the Wednesday special?"

A tall, cute brunette approached the table. "My name's Julianna, and I'll take your order. Have you decided?"

Shane said to her, "This will go faster if he just tells you what he doesn't want."

"Okay, okay. I'll have the brisket. And . . . a half side of ribs. And mashed potatoes. And mac 'n' cheese. And green beans to make it healthy."

The server stared at Adam. "Are you expecting someone else, sir?"

"No. If anything's left, I'll take it home in a doggie bag."

"How big is your dog?" Julianna asked. The other guys grinned.

"For the sauce I want . . . chipotle and . . . honey spiced. Or . . . the pepper and mustard's good, isn't it? Remind me of the others; does one of them have bacon?"

After the usual ribbing, Nathan turned to Adam. "Hope you're enjoying your vacation 'cause you missed a nasty fight on Ninth Avenue this morning."

"Vacation? I've spent the last three days building a shed, and it's kickin' my tail."

Shane winced. "Hey, I really am sorry about Javier not show-ing up. I meant to tell you that he called me Sunday night from the hospital. He has some serious kidney stones."

"What are you talking about? He's been helping me with my shed for the last three days."

"No, I'm talking about my friend Javier."

"That's who I'm talking about. He showed up Monday morning, and he's been working like a machine."

"Impossible. The guy's in the hospital."

Adam put down the menu. "Shane, he's at my house right now."

"You're outta your mind."

"What does Javier look like?" Adam asked.

"He's six-two, thin as a rail. Has a goatee."

"I'd say no taller than five-nine, probably 240 pounds. Clean shaven."

Nathan said, "I'm no genius, but you guys aren't talkin' about the same dude."

Shane smiled broadly and laughed. "I don't know who's at your house, Adam, but it ain't Javier!"

Adam jumped to his feet. "I'll talk to you guys later."

There was a stranger on his property. Brisket would have to wait.

★ ★ ★

Adam exceeded the speed limit and pulled into his driveway four minutes later. He was relieved to see Javier exactly where he'd left him, nailing boards into the shed frame—as opposed to chasing Victoria with a nail gun. Adam jumped out with a cold-cop expression.

"Hey!"

"Back from lunch already?"

"Javier, what's your name?"

Javier eyed Adam. "Javier?"

"No, what's your full name?"

"Javier Eduardo Martinez. What's *your* full name?"

"Adam Thomas Mitchell." *What's that got to do with . . . ?* "You know Shane Fuller?"

"Shane Fuller? No. What's his full name?"

"It's Shane . . . no, no. Who told you I was building a shed?"

"You did."

"Who told you I'd pay you $150 a day?"

"You did."

"What? You're not the guy I thought I was hiring!"

"Then how did you know to call me Javier?"

"I thought your name was Javier."

"It is."

Adam scanned his brain cells. They were already in jeopardy from not having had one bite of brisket or mashed potatoes.

"Why were you standing in my alley Monday morning?"

"I needed a job. Why did you ask me to help you?"

"Because I thought you were a guy named Javier."

"I am."

"No, I mean . . . you don't have kidney problems, do you?"

"No." Javier paused. "Do you?"

"*No.*" Adam stood still, hoping for a burst of clarity that didn't arrive.

"I can tell you this," Javier said. "By you giving me this job, it has been an answer to my family's prayers."

"Well, you're doing good work. Uh . . . you sure I can't get you anything to eat?"

"No thanks. My wife's lunch was big enough."

Adam walked away, wondering whether he should go check the fridge, hurry back to Austin's Barbeque, or just find an animal on the street, shoot it, and throw it on the grill.

He said to Javier, "I'm going to go get some lunch."

"You are hungry again? *Already?*"

That evening the Hayes family was preparing for dinner when a tricked-out Dodge rolled down their street and stopped in front of their house. The driver stepped out with a newfound swagger and rang the doorbell.

When Jade opened the door, her eyes opened wide. She smiled, stepped outside, and closed the door behind her.

"Hey, how are you doing?" she asked.

Derrick wore a yellow- and white-striped golf shirt, untucked, with baggy jeans and new Nike Air Force 1s. He had a Band-Aid on his face and an obvious bruise on his jaw.

"Whassup?"

"What happened to your face?"

"Nothin'. Was just playin' around with some friends. Check out my ride." Derrick pointed to the freshly waxed inferno-red Magnum with nineteen-inch custom chrome wheels.

"Is that your car?"

"Nah, it's a friend's, but I can drive it whenever. I really came to see if you want to get something to eat with me."

"Ummm . . ." Jade searched for words. "I'd have to ask my dad. . . ."

The door opened, and Nathan stood there a moment wiping his hands on a kitchen towel. He saw Derrick, then the car, and stepped out on the porch. Jade winced.

"Jade, dinner's almost ready."

Nathan turned and looked Derrick straight in the eyes. He wished he were still in uniform, carrying his sidearm, so Derrick could make a permanent association between him and lethal force.

A boy coming to see his daughter. Strike one. Nevertheless, Nathan determined to be friendly and reasonable.

"Hello, how are you?" He extended his hand. Derrick gave him a weak handshake. Strike two.

"I'm good. You must be Jade's dad?"

"I am. And you are?"

Jade nervously spoke up. "Daddy, this is my friend Derrick."

"Nice to meet you, Derrick. You just in the neighborhood?"

"I came to see if Jade wanted to get something to eat with me. I'll bring her back later."

Strike three.

"Jade, why don't you go inside?" Nathan said. "I'll be there in a few minutes."

Jade glanced helplessly at Derrick as she closed the door.

"Derrick, I appreciate your interest in my daughter. But until she's older, we won't allow her to date."

"This ain't really a date. We just tryin' to hang out."

"Well, it's important to us that she be older. And for us to know who she's with."

"What? You got a problem with me?" Derrick felt certain he could take down this old guy easy. But it wouldn't score points with Jade.

Her father had more to say. "We just don't know you, that's all. Even when she's older, any young man who wants to spend time with her will have to explain the purpose of the relationship."

"The *purpose*?" Derrick said the word as if he had never heard it before, which struck Nathan as strange coming from an honor student. "It ain't like I'm gonna take advantage of a fifteen-year-old girl."

"Oh, I agree! You've got that right!" Nathan took a deep breath before continuing. "Look, Derrick, if you'd like to get to know us better, you're welcome to join us for lunch on Sunday. We'd be happy to have you."

Derrick acted like Nathan had invited him to dive off an oceanside cliff at low tide.

"How did you get that bruise on your face?" Nathan asked.

"That's none of your business."

"The moment you showed interest in my daughter, every-thing about you became my business."

Derrick turned toward his car. He called over his shoulder, "You should let Jade make her own decisions!"

Nathan knew how to deal with difficult people in a calm and measured way. But this time, given what was at stake, he felt different. Part of him wanted to go after this smart-mouthed punk. He could take him down without breaking a sweat. But it wouldn't score points with Jade.

And it wouldn't be right.

Nathan watched Derrick drive away. Only after the car had turned off his street did he walk back in the house, telling himself to be calm, figuring someone in the family would need to be.

As Nathan closed the door, he saw Kayla still peeking through the blinds.

"I do *not* like that boy," Kayla said. "He's very disrespectful."

Jade sat at the far end of the couch hugging a pillow, fighting tears. "How can he be respectful when Daddy runs him off like that?"

Nathan paused, preparing himself to speak more calmly than he felt. "Jade, if he shows no respect for us, then he won't respect you either, sweetie."

"Baby," Kayla pleaded, "you've got to trust us. That boy has a lot of growing up to do."

While a torrent of words ricocheted off the insides of all three heads, silence prevailed.

Kayla said, "We'd better go eat while it's still hot."

"Come on, Jade," Nathan said.

"I'm not hungry!"

"I'd still like you to sit with us."

Jade, feeling like a prisoner without options, said, "I need to use the bathroom." She went in, locked the door, and texted Derrick: **IMS my dad was so rude. TTYL.**

Fifteen seconds later she was at the dinner table.

After five days of steady work, and nearly finished with the shed, Adam and Javy placed the last few roof panels. As they went, they double-checked the position of each board. Few things seemed as sweet to both men as finishing a job that qualified for a big "Well done."

Adam said to Javy, "Let me be sure I got it. Carmen's your wife, and your children are Isabel and Marcos?"

"Yes. Carmen teaches them at home."

Adam thought he heard a faint sound and glanced around. He couldn't pinpoint it.

Javy said, "And you have two kids?"

Adam nodded. "Emily, whom you met, is my sweet nine-year-old. Dylan's my stubborn fifteen-year-old."

Javier smiled.

"I think he's just going through a stage. No track practice today, so you can meet him in a minute when he comes home. I think Emily's at a birthday party."

Twenty feet away, on the workbench, Adam's cell phone vibrated.

Adam said, "You know that thread factory on Clark?"

"Yes, I've seen it."

"I know the guys who run it. I could talk to them about a job."

Javier froze. "You mean a full-time job?"

"Why not? I'd recommend you."

Javier smiled. "I would be very grateful."

Both men heard a siren and turned toward the street. A sheriff's patrol car stopped in front of Adam's driveway. Shane Fuller jumped out, panic on his face. "Adam, I need you to come with me right now."

"What's wrong?"

Shane struggled for breath. "Emily."

"What?"

"She's been in a wreck."

Javier watched as Adam ran to the car with Shane and jumped in the passenger side. The car sped away, lights flashing, siren blaring. Javy could think of just one thing to pray. *"Dios, vaya con ellos."*

As the cruiser rounded the corner onto Westover Boulevard, Adam caught enough breath to speak. "Talk to me, Shane!"

"The Martins picked Emily up after school."

"Yeah, the party. What happened?"

"Their SUV was hit by a drunk driver at a four-way stop. On Emily's side."

Adam stared vacantly at Shane and removed his sweaty cap.

"Nathan went to get Victoria. It doesn't look good, Adam."

Adam put his hands over his face and leaned forward. "Oh, God, help my daughter. Please, Lord! Please help my little girl!"

The patrol car pulled up to Phoebe Putney Memorial Hospital's emergency room entrance.

Adam ran in the door. He heard voices to his right and saw Victoria, two nurses and a doctor standing by her. One nurse had her arm around Victoria. Adam dashed down the hallway. When she saw him, she collapsed against his chest.

Two others stood nearby, heads bowed—Captain Caleb Holt and another fireman. Holt's white shirt was bloodstained.

Adam held Victoria. Beyond the hospital staff he saw Nathan and David, now joined by Shane.

No one looked Adam in the eye; no one offered words of hope.

Their body language screamed a message he couldn't bear to receive.

"I want to see her," Adam said.

They led him toward a room with medical equipment scattered in frantic disarray. He saw what seemed to be a mannequin from a children's clothing store.

The sheet had a few red spots on it. Adam hoped it was someone else's blood, someone else's little girl. Then he saw, carelessly thrown on the floor, a sheared, bloodstained, blue polka-dot sundress—the same one she'd worn five days ago when she'd asked him to dance. A sheet partly covered the body.

Other girls must own the same dress. It doesn't have to be Emily.

Victoria wept as she leaned over what was left of her daughter. Adam, still denying it, finally saw the little girl's face. In that moment the weight of the world fell on him.

The doctors *had* to be wrong. Adam reached to feel her pulse. He waited for just one heartbeat, a single twinge of movement, a blip on that vacant screen, any hint of life. But though he pressed his fingers harder and harder on her wrist, he got nothing back.

No. No. No.

Every bone in Adam Mitchell's body melted. He began sobbing.

His little girl was gone.

CHAPTER THIRTEEN

ADAM MITCHELL would wake up from this nightmare.

He had to.

Pictures of Emily and dozens of colorful bouquets surrounded a small white casket. Every seat in the church was filled with uniformed officers, friends, and family—all wishing for some way to dull the Mitchells' grief.

Part of Adam appreciated the church folk. Part of him didn't want to appreciate anything related to church because church was God's thing and God had taken his daughter.

Three days had passed, and Adam Mitchell had heard countless words of comfort. So many that he was numb to them. He'd heard Romans 8:28 spoken by well-meaning people, but he was not about to accept that God was going to work his daughter's death for good. No statement provoked more anger than that one.

Adam, Victoria, and Dylan sat in the front row of the church auditorium. He looked around to see familiar faces, including Sheriff Gentry and his wife, Alison, and Caleb Holt with his wife. Holt had been the first to reach the scene and administer first aid to Emily.

Adam stared at the coffin. *Coffins are for people I didn't know or old people ready to die.* Jeff Henderson had been an exception. But Jeff had made his choice. Emily hadn't. Nine-year-olds shouldn't die. Period.

Victoria focused straight ahead, eyes wet. Dylan leaned forward with his elbows on his legs, hands clasped in front of his chin, head down. Adam had tried once at home to talk with him, but they were too out of practice.

The room was packed with people at various degrees of grief. Some had experienced the bottomless depth of this kind of a loss. Others could only imagine. None could ease the pain of the Mitchell family's shattered hearts. Relatives sat behind them, but not even their presence seemed to comfort. They might as well have been strangers.

Adam's thoughts wandered as the room darkened abruptly. Images, accompanied by soft music, appeared on the huge screen. Victoria had assembled photos of Emily as a newborn at the hospital. Of six-year-old Dylan holding her carefully, afraid she might break. *And now she has.*

Sweet, wonderful, unbearable images of Adam walking with her on the beach, of him holding her up in a tree, carrying her on his shoulders. Photos he had taken of Emily with Victoria, planting tomatoes in the backyard, and playing with Dylan on the swing Adam had built.

Suddenly Adam became aware of the lyrics. The daughter was asking her father to help her practice dancing. "So I will dance with Cinderella while she is here in my arms . . . I don't want to miss even one song 'cause all too soon the clock will strike midnight and she'll be gone."

He heard Emily's voice: "Oh, please, Daddy, please!" *I missed the song. I missed my chance to dance with her.*

Still beating himself up, Adam looked back at the screen to

see Emily at birthday parties and by the Christmas tree, with new dolls and playhouses, where she'd pretend she was a mom and had babies. And now she never would. And playing soccer at the Legacy Sports park and taking ballet lessons and at a piano recital. Adam felt captivated by her smile with its otherworldly innocence.

She'd asked him, just a few months ago, what heaven was like. His response was "I don't know. The Bible says it's a good place; I know that." What a lame answer. He'd never even bothered to learn. Now she knew. But he still didn't.

What was that photo on the screen? When was it taken? Her graduation from kindergarten? Wait, of course, he'd intended to come, but there was a shoplifter at Walmart. He had to go. No. He didn't *have* to go. He'd chosen a bleary-eyed teenager on crack over his own daughter.

There were more events he didn't remember—photos of parties or dinners he'd been late for. Each of them stung like a hot poker. There was the family of four on vacations, at sporting events, on the back lawn. The slides ended with a picture of the whole family in which Emily's smile stole the show. Then a Bible verse: "Jesus called them to him, saying, 'Let the children come to me, and do not hinder them, for to such belongs the kingdom of God'" (Luke 18:16).

Nice words. But, God, why would You let this happen? Why not stop that miserable drunk? Why not let him come through that intersection ten seconds earlier or ten seconds later? How am I supposed to believe You care?

Pastor Jonathan Rogers got up behind the pulpit, eyes puffy. "I won't pretend this is easy. The Mitchell family has been part of our church for many years. And Emily . . . was a delight. She *is* a delight.

"At a moment like this, silence seems to be the only expression that fits. What can we, as mere men, say to a grieving and shattered heart? We speak today because we have a living hope.

"Death is life's greatest certainty. Of those who are born, 100 percent die. But death is not an end. It's a transition. Death dissolves the bond between spirit and body. Ecclesiastes 12:7 says, 'The dust returns to the ground it came from, and the spirit returns to God who gave it.' But I stand before you today to declare that we have a living hope and that causes us to rejoice greatly. Death is simply a doorway to another world.

"Death will come whether or not you're prepared for it. Talking about death won't hasten it. Denying death won't delay it.

"Death brings us face-to-face with our Creator. There is a God, and all of us will stand before Him. Hebrews 9:27 says, 'Man is destined to die once, and after that to face judgment.' The question we each must answer is, are we ready for death? Little Emily was ready."

Adam agreed with the words. But he felt he should be able to stand on them. He couldn't. The ground had caved in beneath him.

The pastor said, "The greatest memory I have of Emily is when I sat at home with her mother and father and watched her dad get on his knees with her and help her invite Jesus into her heart."

Adam remembered that day praying with Emily, and he clung to it. Yes. He'd done something *right* as a father.

"You see, our hope today is founded on the fact that Jesus is no longer entombed. He lives. And because He lives, Emily lives. And because He lives, the grieving, broken heart has hope and reason to rejoice. Little Emily loved Jesus. I don't have the slightest doubt that she's with Him."

A half hour after the service, Victoria had received and given comfort from more people than she thought she knew. When she was hugged by someone she was certain she'd never seen before, she gripped Adam's arm and said, "I have to get out of here."

Adam searched for Dylan. A friend's parent told him their son had left with him. Adam got Victoria out to the car, and they both sat there. Adam laid his head on the steering wheel.

"Will we get the stuff on the tables back?" he asked. "All the pictures and Emily's notebooks and soccer trophies?"

Victoria didn't seem to understand the question. Adam felt childish. He didn't know why he had asked her. She needed his help. But he had nothing to offer her.

He felt like he was floating in an unreal world, disconnected. He felt everything—but knew nothing.

Adam had seen many people die, children included. But this wasn't someone else's daughter. It was his. Adam wasn't watching the news. He and his family *were* the news.

The afternoon of Emily's funeral lasted a month, a month in which he'd aged three years. He felt hungry, but not for food. The emptiness was one he couldn't fill.

Did he want to go on living in a world without Emily? No. Would he ever want to? He couldn't imagine it.

Adam Mitchell had some things he wanted to say to the Almighty.

We go to church; we put money in the offering plate. We try to live decent lives. Is this how You repay people who believe in You? She was my little girl. You had no right to take her from me!

The next day was a blur. People kept bringing food, flowers, cards.

When the last visitor left, he withdrew to Emily's room—all little girl, with its purple feather boa on the footboard and its pink and purple patchwork bedspread. He saw the sign above her bed as if for the first time, and fresh waves of grief washed over him: *My prince did come. . . . His name is Daddy.*

Where was your prince when you really needed him? And where was God?

Victoria shuffled into the doorway and found Adam leaning against the bed, holding a picture of Emily. She walked in and sat down, crossing her legs like she used to as a teenager. But the lines etched in her face over the last four days made her look older than thirty-eight.

After a long, empty silence, she said, "Make sense of this for me."

Adam didn't know what to say.

Victoria cried. "I feel like I'm in a fog or some type of black hole, and I really want to get out."

Adam's vacant eyes finally showed empathy.

Victoria was distraught. "Were we wrong to let her go to that party? If I had said no, she would still be here."

Adam shook his head. "Victoria, how could we have known?"

"Why was she the one who had to get killed? Why is that drunk still alive?"

Adam stared at Emily's picture. Finally his thoughts found their way to his voice. "There are so many things I didn't say. I should have been a better father."

Victoria turned weary eyes toward him. He half expected her to reassure him, saying, "No, you were a good father." Instead she said something else, something startling: "Adam, you're *still* a father."

He felt the stab. But he realized its truth. He had one child left. Only one.

Instead of holding the picture of his daughter who wasn't here, why wasn't he holding his son who was?

Adam got up and walked down the hallway to Dylan's room.

He tried to turn the doorknob, but it was locked. He knocked three times. No response.

He turned to the doorframe across the hall, reached up, and felt a small, straight key. He stuck it in Dylan's doorknob and popped the lock open.

Dylan was on the floor, headphones on, playing a video game.

In a mirror on the wall, Adam saw the reflected face of his son. A stoic face as empty as Adam felt. He entered the room and sat down next to him.

Dylan turned, paused the game, and removed his headphones. "How did you get in here?"

"I know where the key is."

"Were you calling me?"

"I just wanted to see how you were doing. Are you okay?"

"Is anybody okay around here?"

Adam sat quietly, trying to choose the right words. "Is there anything you want to talk about?"

"Why do you want to talk? Everybody who comes into this house just keeps saying the same things over and over."

"They're just trying to help, Son."

"Well, they're not."

Adam felt not only his boy's grief, but his hardness. *No one teaches you how to grieve until you need to, and by then, you don't want any lessons.*

"Dylan, we're all hurting. We need each other."

Dylan stared at the frozen image of his video game. "You don't need me."

Did my son just say that?

Adam stared into nothingness.

"Can I play my game now?"

Adam felt a wave of hopelessness. Finally, not knowing what else to say, he said, "Yes."

I've lost my daughter and *my son.*

He got up and walked out the door. Behind him, Dylan put his headphones on and went back to a world where he was in control. A world where good defeated evil, and nobody's sister died.

Adam gazed into Emily's room and saw Victoria lying on the bed, holding Emily's stuffed dog.

He stood alone in the hallway, leaning against the cold wall.

He felt like he should hold someone.

But he needed someone to hold him.

CHAPTER FOURTEEN

THE GANGSTER NATION assembled on the fringes of Gillespie Park with Rollin' Crips on their mind. One of their gangstas, Ice Man, had been put away by a Crip. TJ took it personally.

He convened the gang here to plan moves, tactics, and strategies for kicking a rival gang. Thirty homeboys showed, not his full set, but TJ couldn't afford to take his dealers off the streets tonight. Junkies would get their stuff, and he didn't want them getting it from his competition.

Derrick studied the fashions, which baseball caps were worn, whether they were backward or tipped to one side, and if so at what angle. He saw a variety of do-rags, an old-timer with a hairnet—dude looked like he was thirty-five, ancient for a gangbanger. Some had long hair combed straight back into a tail or braided at the neckline.

Derrick saw many tattoos, variations of Gangster Nation tracks. Some serious soldiers dressed in combat black to blend into the night. Though it was almost dark, most of them wore shades.

The girls, outnumbered two to one, wore variations on the

guys' clothes, mostly darker colors. They wore heavy makeup with excessive dark eye shadow.

Someone blasted music celebrating sex and violence and cop killin'.

TJ's father had been part of the Gangster Nation twenty years earlier, but his son never knew him. He'd learned of his daddy's rep from his mother. TJ's father never married her. They sent him to Lee State Prison at age twenty-two. Released after three years, he died in a street fight six weeks later.

TJ, at twenty-eight, was a survivor, a veteran with charismatic charm, an entrepreneur with a thriving drug business that centered on crack cocaine but had expanded to everything from weed to the lucrative prescription drug market.

A Turkish rope of heavy gold hung around TJ's neck; its crown pendant with tiny diamond studs shimmered even in the gloom, a match for his huge gold belt buckle.

Diablo stood behind him next to Antoine, TJ's minister of defense. They wore gray work gloves for handling weapons and doin' work—which tonight meant taking people down.

"Soldiers watchin' for 5-0?" TJ asked. "We got to do some discipline."

Antoine grabbed a boy younger than Derrick, maybe sixteen.

"Somebody say you snitchin' on us, boy," TJ said to Pete.

"No way, man," Pete said, voice trembling.

"Cops been talkin' to you?"

"They talkin', but I ain't listenin'."

"Well, maybe you talkin' and maybe you ain't. So we gonna give you a reminder of what happens if you do."

Derrick watched in fascinated horror as they beat and kicked the boy until he was almost unconscious. It didn't seem right if they weren't sure he'd been snitchin'. But Derrick stepped forward and got in a few licks, just to make sure everyone knew he was part of the family. Being jumped in meant taking any treatment the gang leaders chose to dish out.

TJ greeted Derrick, flashed the gang sign, and watched Derrick's return. He nodded his approval.

"You long way from OG. You still just a baby gangsta, a tiny. You gotta promote the set, recruit for it, buy and sell for it, be willin' to die for it. You down?"

"Yeah," Derrick said, filled with pride and terror.

"You strapped, little homey?"

Derrick nodded.

"You been practicin' with that deuce-deuce?" TJ asked.

Derrick nodded again. Truth was he'd only shot it four times when his gramma was at work. He'd fired it into some phone books in the basement before it jammed. Seeing all the weapons tonight had frightened him. But he knew he didn't dare let on.

TJ showed him his sawed-off shotgun. "Boomstick's easy to carry and sprays fast, so you don't have to be too accurate. Problem is, if you has to shoot more than fifteen feet, you not gonna get a funeral out of it. But you can still do some damage, man. Maybe next time you shoot the boomstick. You wit' me?"

"Righteous, man. I wit' you." Derrick's voice cracked.

The riding party filled six cars and took off. Derrick trembled as he sat next to Antoine. Lights off, they cruised to a house where the Crips were hangin' and slangin', a dozen on the outside, as many inside. All celebrating the GN's funeral.

TJ jumped out of a car. Taking quick aim, he shot out two streetlamps with his gauge. Glass fragments rained all over TJ, exhilarating him.

Shadowy forms ran in confusion in the front yard. One gangster let loose with what sounded like a cannon. *Boom! Boom! Boom!* Someone yelled, "Nation!"

The big bass of a .45 reverberated. Derrick heard another shotgun. The enemy scattered like starlings. Terrified, he fired his .22 in the general direction of Crips without aiming. Then he retreated and hid behind TJ's car.

TJ fired the shotgun again, and the buckshot hit two Rollin' Crips, both with their backs turned. One fell; the other kept running but pulled up limp.

"Move in," Antoine said.

While the others moved forward, Derrick stooped down and got in the back door, then slumped low in the seat. After a few minutes of gunfire and shouting, all four doors were yanked open, and the car filled. In the rush everyone assumed Derrick had ducked in the car from the other side. Tires screeched as cars pulled away.

Antoine still stood by a telephone pole, his 9mm pointed at the house.

The Rollin' Crips, thinking the Nation gone, moved outside the house. Two Crips got up just in time to be targeted by Antoine. He shot three times and knocked them both down.

When the GN got back to their turf, less than two miles away, the set retreated into an abandoned church to tell war stories, which got grander as time went on. Derrick ran to the back of the room and threw up on the floor. Some of the boys laughed at him.

"You hurled, honor student, but at least you didn't bail!"

It was TJ. He slapped Derrick on the shoulder.

"Let's drink some forties and get chewed! Time for chillaxin'!"

After the crowd dispersed, TJ took Derrick aside.

"Bend the corner here, cuz." He seemed almost tender. "Bangin' ain't no part-time thing. It yo life now, hear me? Homeboys is yo family. We yo daddy and yo brothers. Gangster

Nation women yo mama and sisters, and they more than that too. Know what I'm sayin'?"

Derrick nodded, though for the most part he didn't.

Derrick went to TJ's crib to clean up and spend the night. He'd told his gramma he would spend the night at Robert's, studying for a math test.

It was almost three o'clock before TJ stopped talking, nearly four before Derrick fell asleep on a spare mattress. He really did have a math test. This time he'd wing it. That was okay. Being an honor student wasn't important to him anymore.

This was Derrick's family now. Why should he even show up at school? His gramma had it all wrong. Why should he want *out* of his life here now that he had such a great opportunity to be *in*?

Images flashed through Derrick's mind as he slept, feeding his dreams. Flashes of light, tumultuous sounds, and grotesque body shapes rolled past.

He trembled uncontrollably, trying in vain to stop. His mind replayed those Crips who'd fallen, one boy in particular who had looked about fourteen. Derrick hoped he wasn't dead. He knew as Gangster Nation he was supposed to hope he was. But weren't they just other kids like Derrick? Had Derrick grown up in their neighborhood, wouldn't he be a Rollin' Crip too?

Derrick Freeman felt a lump in his throat. He lay there feeling proud, exhilarated, ashamed, and terrified.

CHAPTER FIFTEEN

EMILY MITCHELL, wearing a white dress, ran toward her father. She looked up at him and extended her arms. Adam lifted her up into a warm embrace. She hugged him tightly, then let go and beamed. Adam lowered her to the floor, and she began spinning and dancing.

Suddenly the little girl disappeared, and Adam found himself looking at Emily, age twenty-two, wearing a wedding dress. Her bridesmaids surrounded her, arranging her dress, her hair, her veil.

Adam wore a tuxedo. Emily looked up, smiled, and reached out her hand. He stepped forward to take it, but his hand passed through her as if she weren't there.

Adam's eyes popped open. It was the black of night. His T-shirt was drenched in sweat. Tears streamed down his face. He sat up in bed, then swung his feet to the side, trying to silence his sobs.

"Adam?"

"We'll never get to see her graduate. I'll never get to walk her down the aisle. How am I supposed to let her go?"

Victoria sat up and rubbed his back.

"I should have danced with her. Why didn't I dance with her?"

He went to the medicine cabinet and took a couple sleeping pills.

Unable to bear more sadness, his heart turned to anger. For the next hour he lay in the darkness, imagining scenarios in which he confronted his daughter's killer. Face-to-face, he would invite the drunk to take one swing at him; then he would beat him into the ground and make him pay for what he'd done.

Of course, how would it help Victoria and Dylan if he went to prison? Adam believed he would never actually hurt the man. But apart from the misery it would bring his family, right now he couldn't think of a compelling reason not to.

He felt the sleeping pills trying to take effect, but his eyes resisted, remaining wide open.

Adam walked alone through Riverside Cemetery. Victoria wouldn't come. She couldn't bear to think of Emily in the cold, dark ground.

A hard wind the night before had strewn new leaves, half-opened blossoms, and small twigs across the lawn. The huge moss-covered oaks, with their long, reaching arms, had governed these grounds for centuries.

He walked past the hundred or so numbered graves, unidentified. Caskets had been washed out, separated from their tombstones, in the Albany flood of 1994.

What would it be like to not know where your loved one was buried? Yet was it really any better to think of Emily in the grave that bore her name?

Adam walked to the graveyard's edge.

Some areas were ordered and symmetrical, like a military

cemetery. But this particular section seemed to have no rhyme or reason, with tombstones as varied, random, and tilted as life itself.

Adam noted the loveliness of the graveside flowers. Stooping over a purple chrysanthemum, he saw a droplet of water reflect the last gleam of sunlight, turning it into a miniature rainbow.

How could death and life exist in such close proximity? Why did such a living, vibrant world languish under the sentence of death? *It's all wrong. This is not the way the world is supposed to be.*

Adam pondered that if the gospel he'd long believed was true, if the Bible wasn't lying, if Jesus was right, then God had not made the world like this. In the beginning, He had made a perfect world.

Adam thought about the novels he'd read, the movies he'd watched. Beginnings were often positive, endings triumphant, but in the middle of the greatest stories came death and loss and despair, followed by redemption. Was he living in the middle of the story? If so, he longed for the ending.

God, You don't know what it's like to have Your child die.

Ten seconds later the truth dawned on him. The center of the faith he professed to believe was that God's Son had indeed died. And that He had chosen to do so.

Then if You know how much it hurts, why did You take Emily away?

Adam walked to Emily's section of the graveyard. He looked down at a small marker along the way.

Eleanor Marie Davidson
Born April 3, 1873, died June 12, 1876
Like Enoch, taken before his time, our daughter
is now in the Redeemer's hands.

Jesus said unto her, "I am the resurrection, and
the life: he that believeth in me, though he were
dead, yet shall he live."

Adam wondered what his own tombstone would say.
Victoria would be kind. But what if she were honest? Would
she write, "Adam Mitchell, he was a decent cop but not much
of a husband"? What if Dylan were forced to write something?
"Adam Mitchell, my father who loved his daughter and his job
more than he loved me"?

Finally Adam arrived at Emily's grave. He had come intend-
ing to visit her. But as he stood, he became profoundly aware
that Emily wasn't here. It was a memorial *to* her, not a resting
place *for* her. If his faith were false, she had ceased to exist. If it
were true, she'd gone to live in another place. Either way, she
was not here.

He had never felt it more important to believe that the
Christian faith was true. But other than attending church,
something he could do in his sleep and sometimes had, he'd
invested little time and energy to cultivate the faith he now
tried to draw strength from. He'd always been surrounded by
the Christian faith but never immersed in it, never filled with it.

Perhaps that was why he felt unable to find more comfort
in it now.

Adam often cleaned his gun in the bedroom, away from family.
Today, as he ran a cloth over it, he thought about how much
better off Victoria and Dylan would be without him. How
much better off *he* would be without him. He could make it
look like an accident.

"He was cleaning his gun, and it went off."

Do it now, a voice seemed to say. *The pain will be gone.*

He decided to load the gun with a round. Just one.

In his mind's eye, he saw himself raise it to his head. He seemed to actually feel the muzzle against his right temple.

"Adam! What are you doing?"

Startled, he looked up at Victoria. He hadn't actually pointed the Glock at himself, but somehow she sensed his thoughts.

"Just cleaning my gun."

"Are you all right?"

"No."

Victoria didn't leave the room until she watched him put away the gun, packing it high in the closet.

That voice in his head troubled him. He'd never had such thoughts before. But then, his daughter had never died before.

He thought about his old partner Jeff with more empathy now.

Adam wandered into the living room, tried the TV, found nothing, then aimlessly flipped through hunting magazines. Maggie whined and scratched on the door.

"Could somebody shut that dog up?" he said, louder than intended.

Victoria called, "I've tried."

Maggie was inconsolable. She'd hardly eaten anything. Now she whined incessantly. Sometimes she'd let out a mournful howl, as she did that very moment.

Adam strode heavily to the back door and opened it. "Shut up!"

Maggie squealed as if in pain.

Adam saw in her eyes what he felt in his heart: *Where is Emily?* The poor creature didn't understand.

Welcome to the club.

Adam sat on the back porch steps. Immediately Maggie buried her face in his shoulder.

"No, get down, Maggie! Get down."

She backed away, cringing.

"Sorry, Maggie. It's okay." This time he let her come. She pressed her nose into his ear and licked the side of his face.

Soon Adam was lost in reflection, Maggie a safe conduit of his thoughts. Finally he got up to go inside.

He turned and watched Maggie's eyes as he closed the door. Silence lingered for only a moment before the dog let out a small whimper. Adam looked around; not seeing Victoria, he opened the door. Maggie dashed in before he could change his mind. She ran down the hallway to Emily's room and turned quickly into it, bumping off the doorjamb like a billiard ball.

Victoria heard the commotion and strode quickly into the hallway. "Maggie . . . outside!"

"No, it's all right," Adam said. By the time he arrived, Maggie lay on Emily's bed, her head on the bedspread covering the pillow. Adam sat down by Emily's bed, as he'd often done since the accident. Maggie settled in close to him. The first time she licked his face, he fought it. Then he tolerated it. Then he enjoyed it.

Her rhythmic breathing and occasional contented sigh soothed him. She looked at him with soulful eyes. It occurred to Adam that she didn't just want him to console her. She wanted to console him.

Victoria came to the door and saw Adam with Maggie's head resting on top of his, both of them looking more at peace than Victoria could remember in this hellish string of days.

"It's okay, Maggie," Victoria heard Adam say. "It's okay, little girl."

CHAPTER SIXTEEN

"EVERYBODY KNOWS this isn't a date! All we're doin' is sittin' in the school parking lot, listenin' to music on this fine stereo, eatin' Taco Bell. I drove to get it; you didn't even leave the school! All you did is walk to the parking lot. If that's a date, then I'm LeBron James!"

Jade laughed. Derrick was in a better mood today, not so preoccupied and stressed out. She pushed away her guilty feelings. *What's wrong with listening to music in broad daylight on a beautiful spring day?*

Derrick stared at her, wanting a response.

"I just want to be able to tell my parents I'm not dating. I'm glad you're not mad about that."

"I'm not mad. I'm just sayin', you respect your parents' right to live their lives, they oughta respect your right to live yours."

Jade finished her chicken chalupa and looked at her watch.

"We got twenty minutes," Derrick said. "What you wanna do?"

"We can study for the economics test."

"I don't care about tests."

"But you're the one who beat me on that first econ test!

119

Then you got a C on your last test, and you didn't even turn in your paper."

"That was then. This is now. I'm into some new things now, important things."

"What things?"

"We can talk about that later. Right now, let's mellow, huh?"

He asked her questions about Atlanta, why she'd moved, who her friends were there. She vented about having to leave them behind. It didn't seem fair for her parents to drag her away. Derrick asked about Atlanta gangs, which she knew little about. She wondered why he asked.

As they talked, Derrick reached over and held her hand. She seemed tentative at first but adjusted. He squeezed and she squeezed back. Nice. He leaned over and kissed her on the cheek.

"Derrick!" she said, but she could have turned away. And she wasn't mad.

"Now that wasn't so bad, was it?"

She glanced down. "I guess not."

"You *guess* not? Come on, give this guy a little respect, huh?"

Jade looked at him. "No, it wasn't bad." She opened her door.

He opened his, and they headed to their classes.

As they walked, he put his arm around her briefly. When they came to the hallway where they had to part, she waved good-bye. He glanced over his shoulder, and she was still looking at him.

Now we're cookin'.

David spent ninety minutes on his computer on Google Earth, seeing the overhead view, then looking at the drive-by photos of the less-familiar parts of Albany, street by street. He did this most days, determined not to humiliate himself again by failing his partner.

As the evening went on, David felt increasingly lonely. All lights were off. As his grandfather would have said, it was dark as the inside of a cow. David lay back in his beanbag chair, self-medicating with a bottle of cheap wine. At first he enjoyed the taste, but he finished numb. His baseline unhappiness persisted, as it always did. The wine never kept its promises.

A vague dread haunted David Thomson. He told himself he had nothing to fear, but when he looked out at the world and in at himself, he knew otherwise. Subconsciously, he realized that facing life would mean facing his failures. So he spent his days at a job that would make up for his failures and his nights perpetuating them.

Drinking didn't make him happy; it just helped him momentarily forget his unhappiness. Then, when he was sober, it gave him one more thing to be unhappy about and one more reason to drink again.

At Valdosta State he'd lived in the dorm—there was always something to do and someone to do it with. Playing college football, he had his teammates, even in the off-season, and lots of girls who hung around the players. But here he didn't know many people. And he wasn't the type to get to know them.

Instead of going to bed, he decided to throw cold water on his face, gargle, and catch a movie at Carmike Cinemas on Nottingham Way. With sixteen theaters and a full parking lot, he figured there must be something interesting. There wasn't. But that didn't stop him from watching another forgettable movie. So forgettable that when the big, bald guy waddled in ten minutes late and sat in front of him blocking his view, David hadn't budged.

Near midnight, David meandered out of the theater toward his beat-up old Chevy Cavalier parked by itself, a hundred feet away, by the dumpster of an adjoining business.

When he got five feet from his car, he heard a deep voice from behind the dumpster.

"Hey, little 5-0. Whassup?"

The voice came out of the darkness, and David reached into the front right pocket of his cargo pants.

TJ never flinched. This cracker thought he could pull a piece on the Gangster Nation? Before the cop could touch his gun, Antoine grabbed his wrist from behind and pulled the gun out of his pocket.

"Nice. Looks like we got a 19C. The 5-0 love their Glocks."

David couldn't recall any off-duty ambush in the safe part of town being addressed at the academy.

The gangbangers wore black bandannas covering their noses and mouths.

"You think you somethin', doncha, college boy?"

While Antoine held him still, TJ was mad doggin', looking the guy over from head to toe, assaulting him with his eyes.

"Me and my road dog here, we gonna bust yo grill, Wonder bread!" TJ pushed David. "We gonna open up a can on you; whatchu think about that?" He pushed him again, harder. With the third push, David fell back. His head hit the dumpster with a dull thud. While he was down, TJ kicked him twice in the stomach.

TJ pulled David to his feet, looked him in the eyes. "Might let you live so you can deliver this message to yo black sell-out partner who messed with my 211. You took my homeboys Clyde and Jamar from me, so maybe I take the two of you from the sheriff. Might use yo 19C, huh? Or maybe I just start off warmin' up my fists and my feet."

He let loose with a left jab that jarred David's teeth. David hit the ground again, dazed and in pain.

"Clocked that dude," TJ boasted.

"You don't need me," Antoine said, looking around. "Let's get outta here before somebody notices."

"Get the car while I finish this."

Antoine ran across the alley into the adjoining parking lot while TJ stood over David.

He hit David again like two bursts of a jackhammer. David scuttled on the pavement, crablike, trying desperately to find his footing. Finally he fell back, helpless, legs splayed, barely conscious.

"You ain't nothin', boy. You know that? I got yo life in my hand right now. I decide if you live or die."

David had never felt such fear. It ran through his body like freezing water, almost paralyzing him. The blood in his mouth tasted like death.

Suddenly a magnetic-gray Toyota Tundra truck with a front winch and oversize tires screeched to a stop six feet away. Through the blinding headlights, David saw something enormous leap out.

David's assailants were normally the biggest boats in the dock; not this time. The new arrival charged onto the scene like a rhinoceros on meth. He squared off with TJ and tackled him. But the gangster sprang off the ground as if launched by a broken coil. TJ screamed and cursed as he pummeled his opponent's huge solar plexus. The large man first moved backward, then suddenly, in a moment between punches, leaned forward on his toes and grabbed TJ's ears. He projected his forehead into TJ's, knocking him off his feet.

Stunned, TJ pulled himself up just as Antoine arrived with the car.

A shrill sound pierced the air. An Albany city police car rushed in with lights flashing and siren blaring. TJ sprinted toward the Caddy and jumped in; Antoine peeled out.

The big man turned to the cops. "Call an ambulance! This kid needs help." Then he turned in the direction the thugs had driven off and hollered, "You wanna fight me again, big boy, you better pack a lunch . . . and bring a flashlight! You want my home address? I'll be waitin' for ya, punk. I'm meaner than a junkyard dog!"

He approached the officers while wiping blood from the corner of his mouth. "We're sheriff's deputies, Dougherty County."

The Albany police officer asked, "Your name's Bronson, right?"

"How'd you know?"

"Word gets around."

The city officer turned to his partner. "Radio it in. Tell dispatch they're headed south on Nottingham Way. And send an ambulance here. We've got injuries." He looked at David, flat on his back.

David kept still as he struggled to gather his composure. He had taken a beating, and his heart was still racing ninety miles an hour.

Bronson looked down at David, who pulled himself up to a seated position. "You look like somethin' the hound's been hidin' under the porch."

David looked at Bronson. "Where did you come from?"

"I watched the same lousy movie you did. When I got to my car, I saw the guys come after you."

"You called it in, right?" one of the officers asked. "How come no county cops have shown?"

"We're off duty. Didn't need backup."

"I'd say you were lucky we happened to drive by to witness it. Anything you want to tell us about the suspects?"

"Yeah," Bronson said. "The guy I *suspect* was beatin' the crud out of Thomson here was on crack. I *suspect* his central nervous system was firing on all cylinders."

"Anything else?"

"Well, I *suspect* he shouldn't have messed with me. But you can't fix stupid."

David's face felt like raw hamburger, but nothing seemed broken. He stood now and brushed himself off even though the officers told him to take it easy until the ambulance arrived.

"You really surprised him with that head-butt, Sarge. Thanks."

Bronson smirked, using his sleeve to wipe a trickle of blood from his forehead. "Like my old partner Ollie used to say, 'Messin' with me's like wearin' cheese underwear down rat alley.'"

CHAPTER SEVENTEEN

"THERE'S NO REASON for me to be in this hospital," David said to Nathan early the next morning.

"They were concerned about a concussion. They'll let you go in a couple of hours. You were fortunate, David. When gang members go after a cop, they mean business. They'll treat him like a rival gangbanger. You ever seen two gangs take each other on?"

"I've seen the Bulldogs play the Yellow Jackets."

Nathan laughed. "Put lethal weapons in their hands late in the fourth quarter, and you've got the idea."

"Bronson caught the dude by surprise with that head-butt. That was a major *thunk*!"

David peeked over the side of the bed to look at the little duffel bag next to Nathan's chair. "Something smells good and it's not hospital food."

Nathan looked both ways and then pulled out a sack. "Not sure I'm supposed to do this."

He opened the sack. Based on scent alone, David said, "Pearly's? Link-sausage biscuit?"

Nathan stepped to the door. "I'll stand guard while you take care of business."

For the next ten minutes David visited a better world.

"Thanks, Nathan. That was almost worth gettin' beat up for."

After more small talk, David looked at Nathan and cleared his throat. "Can I ask a question? When you were dragged alongside your truck, were you scared?"

Nathan laughed. "Of course I was scared!"

"So you're afraid of dying?"

"Well, yes and no. A certain fear of death is healthy. But I believe that when I die, I'll be in heaven with Jesus. So I can be scared of dying but not be scared about where death will put me. Does that make sense?"

"Not really."

"Why'd you ask?"

"Because last night I thought I was a goner. You know how people say your life flashes in front of you?"

Nathan nodded.

"It's like that was happening. I didn't feel like I was ready to leave this world. I have some things I need to straighten out first."

"That feeling comes from God, David."

"I was afraid you'd say that."

"In the Bible, Solomon talked about how wealth doesn't make you happy, status doesn't make you happy. There's an emptiness inside you. He says in a book called Ecclesiastes that God has put eternity in our hearts."

"What does that mean?"

"That there's more to life than what we can see, and life outlasts this world and will continue in another one."

"I'm not sure I believe that."

"I think you do, David. You just don't know it yet." Nathan paused to think. "Sometimes we have to go down a bunch of dead-end streets before we're ready to take the one road that leads to God. Jesus meant it when He said, 'I am the way and the truth and the life. No one comes to the Father except through me.'"

"That's a little arrogant, isn't it?"

"Yeah, it would be. Unless it's true. In which case, I'm glad Jesus let us know."

"That's one way to look at it."

"Yeah, it is. How do you see it?"

"I haven't given it much thought."

"It's worth thinking about. It's the most important question in the world."

"What is?"

"The question of who He is. If you get it right about Jesus, you can afford to get some things wrong. But if you get it wrong about Jesus, in the end it won't matter what else you got right."

"You seem pretty sure of yourself."

"Myself? No." Nathan laughed. "The only one I'm sure of is Jesus. Last night was a reminder, David—our lives hang by a thread. I mean, think about Adam Mitchell's daughter. One day it'll be me and you. We'll be yanked out of this world. If it turns out Jesus was right and you've ignored Him, you'll be sorry."

"You mean hell?"

Nathan nodded.

"You really believe that stuff?"

"Yeah, I do. Jesus had a lot to say about hell; He talked about it like it was a real place. And I believe He knew what He was talking about."

"You make it sound like Jesus is real, like He's alive."

"Exactly. He took care of all the ways we've messed up— wiped our slates clean when He died on the cross; then He rose from the dead, and He's alive today in heaven. He promises

He'll be back to set up His Kingdom. He loves us, David—He has scars to prove it. He's earned my trust."

David felt his mind spinning. He wasn't sure what he believed. But after this fight with death, maybe it was time to figure it out before the rematch.

★ ★ ★

At 9:00 a.m. Adam, dressed in dark khakis and a green shirt, sat in an office chair. Pastor Jonathan Rogers, wearing a muted-blue button-down, gray vest, and slacks, sat across from him in a room lined with dark wood shelves filled with books and pictures.

After Adam called him "pastor" twice, he said, "Please, call me Jon."

Adam opened his hands. "A man shouldn't have to outlive his child."

"It's got to be terribly hard," Jon said. "My children are grown now, and I've got grandchildren; I can't imagine anything worse than what you're going through, Adam. I'm truly sorry."

"It's so senseless. She was my little girl. God had no right to take her from me."

Jon considered his response. "True, it's senseless to *us*. But we know God had a reason for His own Son's death. Do you think it's possible He had a reason for your daughter's?" He paused before continuing. "But you're wrong about something. Emily did *not* belong to you."

Adam looked up sharply. "What do you mean? She was my daughter."

"Yes, and she'll always be your daughter. But we don't own our children. God owns them. We're entrusted with their care."

"But she was only nine!" He heard the anger in his own voice and thought about how Victoria would react if she heard him talk like this to a pastor. He put his face in his hands.

"Adam . . . have you thought about taking your life?"

He startled. "Did Victoria say something?"

"No. I just wondered."

Silenced prevailed for a minute. "When my old partner, Jeff Henderson, killed himself, I scorned him for taking the coward's way out. But for the first time, I understand why people do that."

Jon leaned forward. "Your job isn't over until your life is, and it's not up to you to decide when that is. That's playing God."

"Pastor—Jon—I'm not going to take my life, okay? But . . . yes, the thought crossed my mind one evening."

"Obviously I'm concerned about that, Adam. But it's not just suicide. Many people give up. They keep breathing but stop living."

Adam understood.

"There needs to be a grieving process. When my wife died, I didn't know what to do. And the only thing I could think was 'How do I get over this?' But I learned you don't get over it; you get through it. The Lord is the one who carries you through."

"How are you supposed to heal when you lose someone you love?"

"I've heard it said it's like learning to live with an amputation. You do heal, but you're never the same. But those who go through this and trust the Lord find comfort and intimacy with God that others never experience. Now, you've got to give yourself time to grieve. But you also need to make efforts to move forward with your life."

"I can't stop thinking about her."

"You don't need to. Because of what God did for her on the cross, she's with Him now. I have a question for you. If you had the power to bring her back here, would you do it?"

"In a heartbeat."

"If you understood how happy she is with Jesus, would you really call her back from a world without sin and death? Back to a place where one day she'd have to die again?"

Adam thought but didn't respond.

"I don't believe you would, Adam. It would be selfish. Once someone meets Jesus on the other side, I think the last thing they'd want to do is come back here."

"You know I'm a cop, right?"

Jon laughed. "Five years ago you pulled me over for speeding. Remember?"

"Yeah, I hoped *you* didn't. Anyway, I see more than my share of death. It's always been somebody else's family. This time it wasn't somebody else's child. . . . It was mine. But now I've got a knot in my stomach that won't go away. I don't know what to do."

Jon Rogers leaned forward and listened.

"I can't make sense of anything, you know? I feel like I'm in the dark. But it's more than that. I'm angry. I think about that drunk—about wanting to go after him."

"That drunk has a name."

Adam sat back.

"His name is Mike Hollis," Jon said. "You know him, don't you?"

"I used to buy heating oil from him. He's been unemployed awhile, I think."

"That's right. He's a real guy who's had hard times. Some people turn to the bottle. It's wrong, but with the pain you're in, you should understand how desperate people get when they can't make it go away."

"You're going to tell me to forgive him, aren't you?"

"Doesn't matter what I tell you. It only matters what God tells you. And, yes, He does tell us to forgive. Mike Hollis hitting the bottle is understandable. So is your anger against God. But that doesn't make it right."

"Who said I was angry against God?"

"No one. I heard it in your voice."

"Doesn't He want me to be honest?"

"God knows how you feel, so there's no sense in pretending. Just don't think that *feeling* angry means you have a right to *be* angry. By all means feel bad, Adam. Weep. Jesus wept when His friend died. But that's not the same as blaming God. We don't have a right to blame someone who cannot do wrong. Someone who loves us so much He paid the price for our wrongs."

Adam shifted in his chair. Part of him rebelled against the straightforward talk from the pastor. But part of him welcomed it. Cops shoot straight with each other, but not a lot of people shoot straight with cops. He liked that Jon Rogers wasn't afraid to tell him the truth.

"I want to be there for Victoria, but my emotions are all over the place. And Dylan's closed me out. I don't know what to do." Adam shut his eyes tightly, trying to stop the leak.

Pastor Rogers thought for a moment. "A crisis like this doesn't cause our relationships to go bad, but it does have a way of showing where they're weak. Many marriages don't survive the loss of a child. You need to reach out to your family and grieve along with them."

Rogers paused. "Do you know how my wife was killed?"

"Yeah, I remember. I wasn't at the scene, but a buddy was. To be honest, Jon, that's why I agreed to talk to you when Victoria suggested it. I didn't want to be preached at by somebody who doesn't understand."

"Losing Abby was terrible, the worst thing that ever happened to me. I won't say it was easy to forgive that teenager,

Ryan, for smoking pot and fiddling with his CD player when he ran her down at the crosswalk."

"How did you make it through?"

"Time helps, if you use the time well and focus on what brings healing. It's still tough sometimes. I won't be completely over it until I get to the world where God says He'll wipe away the tears from every eye."

"What helped you?"

"God's Word. The same Bible I'd taught to others became more real to me. And the church helped me, just like they'll help you, if you let them."

"Well, if food quantity indicates love, we're loved."

"Got some lasagna?"

"How did you know?"

"If I looked deep enough in my freezer, bet I could *still* find some."

Adam smiled. "Victoria will enjoy hearing that."

"I know this will be hard to hear, but the Lord loves Emily more than you do. The hard choice for you is whether to be angry about the time you didn't have with her or to be grateful for the time you did have."

"I do want to be grateful. I *am* grateful."

"How would you like me to help you, Adam? Tell me what's most on your mind."

"Well, I want to know what God expects of me as a father. And I want to know how to help my wife and my son."

"I can tell you how to find some answers. But it's going to take time and energy. If you follow through, you'll become a better father and husband . . . and even a better son to God your Father. I've got two suggestions. First, there are a few books and a software program I want to give you. If you're serious

~about getting help and finding perspective, you'd better become a student of God's Word."

"What's the second suggestion?"

"There's someone I want you to visit."

CHAPTER EIGHTEEN

SOME JOBS A PERSON could return to without full focus. Sheriff's deputy wasn't one of them. They called it "fitness for duty." Adam's superiors asked him to take all his accrued vacation time as a leave of absence. He only had twelve days, so the department invited officers to transfer time from their banks to his. They came up with an extra thirty days of paid leave. When he heard this, he cried for an hour. Yeah, being a cop was hard on the family. But cops would bend over backward to help a fellow cop in a family crisis.

Adam spent the first few days of his leave in decompression mode. But he took seriously Jon Rogers's recommendation that he study Scripture to discover what it said about being a dad and a man. And once he started digging in, he found himself drawn further and further into the truth of Scripture.

Now, six weeks later, his leave had ended, but Adam hadn't stopped studying. He sat at the kitchen table and typed on his laptop next to an open Bible and a stack of books.

Victoria walked in and looked over his shoulder. "You'd think you were going for a doctorate."

"I feel like it. This Bible software the pastor gave me is

incredible. I've been everywhere in Scripture, finding all these passages about fathers and sons."

She slipped on her shoes and picked up her keys.

Adam looked at her. "Where's Dylan?"

"In the shower. He just ran five miles. Says he needs new running shoes. I need to go to the store for a few things, okay?"

Adam leaned back in his chair and stretched. "I don't think I could run five miles."

"Who says you have to?"

"I've been thinking about running with him."

Adam didn't remember ever seeing Victoria's jaw drop like it did then.

"Really?"

"I'm realizing that I have to learn to do the hard things. I've never enjoyed running. But it may be the best way to spend time with Dylan."

Victoria came back and looked at the computer screen. "How *is* your research going?"

"Sobering. I've been doing about half of what I should have been doing as a dad. There is so much in Scripture about being a father. I never took time to look it up."

"Like what?"

"Well, here's what I just read." He flipped the pages of his Bible. "The last verse of the Old Testament, Malachi 4:6. It's quoted in Luke 1 about the Messiah: 'And he will turn the hearts of fathers to their children and the hearts of children to their fathers, lest I come and strike the land with a decree of utter destruction.'"

"That's solemn stuff."

"You're telling me. Either God turns the hearts of fathers and children toward each other, or our culture will be destroyed! Politicians can't change hearts. It all starts in the family."

Adam's cell phone rang. He looked at the caller ID. "It's the sheriff. Hello, sir. Yes, sir, it's good to be back. Will do. Thank you, sir."

Victoria kissed Adam on the head on her way out, whispering, "Love you."

Adam turned. The phone still pressed to his ear, he said to Victoria, "Love you. Bye."

He spoke into the phone. "Sir . . . Hello? Are you there?"

Once again, Adam Mitchell had told the sheriff he loved him. He hit the table with his fist. "Adam!"

Adam knocked on Dylan's door. "Can I come in?"

"Yeah."

Dylan sat on his bed, hair wet. He wore a T-shirt and blue jeans, homework on his lap, game controller nearby.

Adam moved some clothes off a chair and sat down. "Got a lot of homework?"

"Not a lot."

"Got your learner's permit?"

Dylan eyed his wallet on the dresser. "Why?"

"'Cause I need you to drive me to the mall to get you some new running shoes. I may get a pair for myself."

Now Dylan's jaw dropped, and Adam noticed how much he looked like his mother. *I seem to be taking everyone by surprise today.*

"Are you serious?"

Adam held out the keys. Dylan grabbed them as he vaulted off the bed.

Ninety minutes later, when they returned home, Victoria stood in the living room, hands on her hips. "Where have my men been and why didn't they answer their cells?"

"Oops," Adam said. "Guess mine was muted."

"You never mute it!"

"I left mine home," Dylan said.

Victoria stared at them.

"Well, Dad asked me to go with him to get running shoes. Guess I wasn't thinking. Then we stopped at Starbucks."

Victoria grabbed the bag and opened a shoe box.

Adam said, "They fit great. We're going out for a run."

"A run?" Victoria looked at Dylan. "You already ran this afternoon!"

"No problem. This isn't going to wear me out."

"We'll see about that," Adam said. "I'll find some shorts."

"Look deep in the bottom drawer," Victoria called. "I think there's a pair with an expandable waistband."

★　★　★

The next day, after their morning patrol rounds, Adam and Shane arrived at the Coats & Clark factory, where Javier waited outside.

"Hey, Javy!" Adam called out. Javy climbed in, and they headed east on Clark.

Javy examined the backseat. "I've never been in the back of a police car."

Shane smirked. "Yeah, that's what they all say."

"We'll have you back in an hour," Adam said. "So what do you want for lunch?"

"I'm thinkin' Moe's, partner," Shane said. "You know what they say, 'Seven days without a chicken burrito makes Juan weak.'"

"Stick with the donut jokes," Javy said.

The dispatcher's voice boomed over the radio: "SO to 693c."

"693c, go ahead."

"Deputies need assistance in reference to a 10-95 at the intersection of Plantation and Foxfire."

"10-4," Shane responded. He turned to Adam. "That's gonna be gang related."

"Javy, we'll do lunch after this. If I tell you to get down, then get down, all right?" Adam turned the car around sharply and stepped on it, flipping on the lights without turning on the siren.

"What kind of gang?" Javier asked.

Shane shrugged. "Not much difference. They're all just jail prep programs."

"I started a gang once," Javy said.

"What? You were in a gang?"

"We were the Snake Kings."

"The Snake Kings?"

"Yeah, we had lots of snakes in our neighborhood, so we would throw rocks and try to kill them." They laughed.

"How many were in your gang?" Adam asked.

"Three. My brothers and I."

"So you killed a lot of snakes?"

"Just one. But it was a big one. We thought we were heroes."

Within two minutes they pulled up to the curb behind another squad car, where two officers escorted three guys in handcuffs out of the house.

"Javy," Adam said, "I need you to stay in the car. Back in a minute."

Adam and Shane walked to the other officers.

"Whaddya got?"

"Three. Possession with intent to distribute. Possession. Possession," Deputy Craig Dodson said, pointing to each suspect in turn. "We need y'all to go 10-95 to jail with one of them. Got to separate 'em. Can you swing it?"

Shane looked at Adam and whispered, "Not with Javy in the back."

"Wait here; I've got an idea."

Adam walked to the car and opened the back door. "Javy, I need a favor."

They talked quietly; then Adam returned to Shane, and the two of them brought the 'banger to the car.

Lamont was taller than Adam and wore a blue plaid cap cocked to one side. He tried hard to look like none of this bothered him.

Adam turned to him before opening the patrol car door. "You heard of the Snake Kings?"

"The who?"

"The Snake Kings. You ever crossed them?"

"I ain't heard of no Snake Kings," Lamont said with a tone that suggested, *And if I ain't heard of them, they ain't nuthin'.*

"Well, we got the leader in the back. If he tries to go for your throat, you yell and I'll stop the car."

"Wait. Hold on. I ain't gettin' in the back with no killer."

"Just stay on your side. Don't look at him. Don't talk to him and you'll be fine."

Adam opened the door and looked at Javy, who had his hands behind his back as if handcuffed. His hard and distant face surprised Adam. This hombre took his job seriously.

"Martinez, you hurt this guy, I'll put you under the jail. You got it? Don't touch him! All right, get in."

"Hold on, man. I ain't gettin' in the car with no Snake King."

"Get in the car. Stay on your side. You'll be fine," Shane announced.

Adam pushed Lamont down and shut the door. The perp peered at Javy, who gave him a cold, menacing look. Lamont fixed his eyes straight ahead, swallowing hard.

Adam and Shane got in the front seat, barely maintaining their composure. As Adam started the engine, Shane got on the radio. "Dispatch, this is 693c. We're 10-95 en route to the jail. ETA ten to twelve minutes."

"10-4, 693c."

Javy turned toward Lamont and began to snarl in Spanish. *"Vamos a almorzar."*

Adam's high school Spanish was rusty, but he recognized the word *lunch*. Lamont clearly didn't understand a word because he just trembled.

Javy made each innocuous syllable sound as menacing as he could. *"Voy a comprar un bocadillo de pollo . . . y una limonada."*

Adam smiled. *I am getting a chicken sandwich and a lemonade!*

Lamont squirmed. "Hey, man, what's he saying?"

"Don't talk to him!" Adam said. "Just stay on your side."

Javy shot Lamont an intense look. *"Quizás papas fritas . . . y un batido!"*

Fries and a shake? Javy, you are too much!

"He's threatening me! I think he wants to kill me. I can see it in his eyes!"

"Calm down!" Shane said. "If he wanted to kill you, you'd be dead by now!"

Javy quieted a moment, then looked at Lamont. Javy acted like he was pulling at his cuffs, then suddenly exposed his left hand, holding it up threateningly and hissing the words "Snake Kings!"

Lamont twisted frantically. "He's free! He's free! He's gonna kill me! Stop the car!"

It was all Adam and Shane could do to keep themselves from busting up. But they had to keep the facade up for Lamont, who couldn't get to jail fast enough.

CHAPTER NINETEEN

THAT EVENING, Adam, Victoria, and Dylan sat around the dinner table. Adam told them Javy's story. "It was the funniest thing I've ever seen. But it gets better. Javier pulls one hand out from behind as if he got out of the cuffs, and I thought Lamont was gonna wet his pants. He says, 'He's gonna kill me!'"

Adam laughed so hard he had to hold his stomach. Each person's laughter was contagious, every outburst leading to another. Slowly they quieted down. Adam wiped his eyes.

"Lamont keeps begging me to stop the car. So I say, 'Give me some names of who's been supplying the drugs, and I'll stop the car.' So he rattles off three names, and Shane writes them down."

"Did you stop the car?"

"Yeah, thirty seconds later when we arrived at the station!"

"Did he figure out it was staged?" Dylan asked.

"No way. He's probably telling guys in jail about the Snake Kings right now. I only asked Javy to pretend he was a gang leader. The rest was his idea." Adam smiled broadly. "I've never seen anybody so anxious to get to jail!"

"Javy's got a crazy side," Victoria said. "Once he gets comfortable around you."

Adam paused. "The guys like Javy. We've kind of adopted him into our group. And that's good for cops. I mean to have a noncop in the mix."

Victoria toyed with her dinner. "I still can't believe Carmen brought us those three meals after the funeral. That was so sweet."

Adam looked at Victoria and set down his fork. "You know, I just realized something. I had a good day today."

Victoria studied his face. She realized her day hadn't been bad, and it had just gotten better.

"We're gonna be okay, aren't we?" Adam went on. "I mean, this family's going to be all right."

Adam turned to Dylan. "You doin' all right, buddy?"

Dylan stared, then nodded. He pushed his food around the plate. His face reddened. Finally, as if out of nowhere, he said, "I wish I'd been a better brother."

Suddenly the dam broke; tears fell from Dylan's eyes. Adam and Victoria found themselves crying too. Adam got up, moved around behind Dylan, then embraced him with a strong right arm. Victoria joined them.

Adam held Dylan and talked into his ear, feeling a closeness and commitment to his son stronger than anything in recent years. "I love you, buddy. You are my son and I'm proud of you. Don't you ever forget that, okay? Don't you ever forget that."

Adam looked up. "What's wrong with us? We're laughing our heads off one second and bawling the next. Are we all basket cases?"

Victoria said, "As long as we're in the basket together, I don't care."

Adam looked at his wife and son, feeling a surge of fresh

hope. He hadn't recognized each milestone of his life as it came. But this one seemed unmistakable. When he wasn't looking, the healing had begun.

★ ★ ★

After work Adam entered the Whispering Pines Retirement Center, still in uniform. Many places he preferred civilian dress, but elderly folk respected the badge. *Why do the very young and the very old love cops, while the people in between often can't stand us?*

No sooner did he walk in the door than he heard a voice call, "Adam, over here!" It was Tom Lyman. Tom was stationed in his wheelchair, enjoying the sunshine in the atrium, surrounded by plants and flowers.

Adam shook Tom's hand and gave him a gentle hug. This was the sixth time they'd met. He'd come almost every week since Pastor Rogers introduced them. At first, Adam thought the pastor had just wanted to keep him busy serving others so he'd forget his own pain. At eighty-one years old, Tom could use some encouragement. But Adam had no clue then how the tables would turn.

"You look good, today, Adam!"

"Thanks, Tom. You too."

The man's ruddy complexion radiated life. A smile was his mouth's default position. "Ready to tell me what you've learned?"

"I printed out some of my notes." Adam handed a half-dozen typed pages to Tom.

"Lots of Scripture, I see," Tom said, adjusting his glasses. "Could you grab us some coffee while I start reading?"

Adam walked around the corner, smiling at several of the workers, and helped himself to the coffee. Black for him, lots of cream for Tom. He felt like he'd known Tom twenty years and wished he had. Tom had introduced him to World War II veterans, men who told him stories about another time. They were old as bronze statues, part of history. Often they'd talk about whatever they happened to remember. Yanked out of the present, Adam discovered the richness of the past in people's stories. One man in his nineties told him about the "old sheriff," by which he meant Albany's sheriff in the 1930s.

Adam took his time, visiting with a few residents, because Tom liked to read Adam's reflections before they talked.

He returned with coffee just as Tom finished the last page.

"Thank you, Adam." Tom sipped it and smiled. "Just how I like it."

"I've read a couple of those books you gave me." Adam pulled out a battered volume that he'd borrowed from Tom. "*The Knowledge of the Holy* is really something: 'What comes into our minds when we think about God is the most important thing about us.'"

"Very good. You see how it feeds your mind and heart in ways the newspaper and television never will?"

Adam nodded. "But I'm no theologian."

"We're all theologians, Adam. Either good ones or bad ones. I'd rather be a good one, wouldn't you?"

"Do you know how long it took me to memorize that one line from *Knowledge of the Holy*, just so I could impress you? I've tried memorizing Scripture, but I don't think I'll ever be good at it. I don't have the kind of mind that memorizes."

"Name the starting defensive line for the Falcons last year."

Adam rattled off names, position by position, including two guys who replaced injured starters.

"How many home runs did Hank Aaron hit?"

"755."

"Sing me the words to *Gilligan's Island*."

"*What?*"

"I'm serious."

After Adam made sure his shoulder mic was off, he sang all the words, and Tom joined for the last verse. They both laughed.

"See? Your brain can remember far more than you realize. The point is, you're not used to memorizing Scripture, but the more you do it, the easier it will be."

Tom leaned over and placed a hand on Adam's arm. "Adam, I think you and Victoria should consider taking a grief class. I went through one three months after Marianne died. I was skeptical. At first, I did it for my daughter's sake. But she was right. I needed it. Talk to Pastor Rogers."

"He mentioned one, but I didn't think it was right for us."

"It could be a big help. One couple from that class still comes and visits me, and they bring their children. One of them, Kyle, is in high school now. He and I have a weekly Bible study."

"You study with a high school boy?"

"Absolutely. We memorize Scripture."

"So I'm not the only one you keep busy!"

Tom chuckled. "I don't view this retirement center as a place to watch TV and play bingo until I die. I view it as a center of operation from which I can touch the world for eternity through my prayers and conversations. My role model is Caleb in Joshua 14. At age eighty-five he asked God to give him the hill country in the Promised Land, and he would drive out the giants who lived there. Well, he was four years older than I am! If he was fighting giants, I can sure meet with you. And Kyle, my high school friend. And George, Bruce, Benny, Nick. And Javier."

"Javier? What's he look like?"

"Average height and weight. He's seventeen. Why do you ask?"

"Never mind. Listen, Tom, I've got to get to Dylan's track meet. But remember, next Thursday I'll pick you up to meet Victoria and Dylan."

"Looking forward to it. It'll beat the dickens out of bingo!" He laughed. Adam put his arm around Tom's shoulder, smelling Old Spice and feeling the frail body that surrounded that big heart.

When Adam walked out the door, his steps were lighter than when he'd arrived.

Tom Lyman, eighty-one and confined to a wheelchair, was genuinely happy and content. And he was one of the most intentional people Adam had ever met. Tom did far more of consequence in this rest home than 95 percent of men did outside it. And at least until recently, Adam had been part of that 95 percent.

Adam Mitchell supposed he might be halfway through his life in this world. He wanted the remaining half to look more like Tom Lyman's.

CHAPTER TWENTY

ADAM AND SHANE drove the forty miles on Route 82 east from Albany to the Georgia Public Safety Training Center in Tifton. The larger-than-life persona sat behind them, overfilling the backseat.

The passenger wasn't a criminal. He was far scarier. And there under duress. A lingering smell of cigar smoke kept Adam looking to see if he'd lit up.

"What a waste of my time." Sergeant Brad Bronson's jowls wobbled like folded pie dough.

"When you were in training," Adam said, "didn't you want to hear from experienced cops?"

"I got better things to do than be a nursemaid to a pack of wet-diapered wannabes."

"It's just Q & A. You'll be great." Shane winked at Adam, daring his partner to be playful in the face of Bronson's rank and imposing presence.

"Don't tell me what I'll be, Deputy." Sharing a car with Bronson was like occupying a small stall with a big bull.

Adam made his sixth try at conversation. "Sarge, I know you like to drive your own car. Alone. But they stuck you with us today. Did they tell you why?"

"Are we being punished?" Shane said under his breath.

"No, you chucklehead, *I'm* being punished. They tell me they don't want me to be a loner. If I don't stop bending the rules, they're gonna force a partner on me. Never mind that I've put away more lowlifes than the two of you and any three kiss-up-and-toe-the-line deputies combined."

"You're not the only one that would be tough on," Shane said, grinning.

"Fuller, I have one nerve left, and you're getting on it." Bronson waved his meaty hands, soft everywhere except on the palms, where they were nothing but calluses. "You're exactly why I don't want some half-wit riding shotgun with me."

Adam studied Bronson, an alarmingly small percentage of him, in his rearview mirror. He was grateful it didn't say, *Objects are closer than they appear.*

Adam said, "Ever since I've been on the force, they've let sergeants ride without a partner."

The bull pawed the dirt, ready to charge. "Yeah, I remind them that's policy. Then they say, 'We make the rules and we can change them.' They're a bunch of sniveling bureaucrats listening to some anticop civilian feminazi."

"Sheriff Gentry is a sniveling bureaucrat?"

"I call it like I see it."

After twenty more minutes of this, they walked through the front door of the academy. They showed their credentials at the front desk, and a young freckle-faced blonde ushered them through inner doors.

Captain Claudio Grandjean, director of academy training, was fit, with a shaved head and rugged features. "Thanks for joining us, gentlemen. We've got a class of recruits ready to hear from our experts."

"Makes us sound important," Shane said.

"Well, since you actually do what we're training them to do, you *are* important to these students. If you've got a few minutes after the class, you can watch them go through some training exercises."

"Whoopee," Bronson muttered.

"Sorry we caught you in a bad mood, Sergeant."

Adam and Shane looked at the captain, and both shook their heads.

"He's actually sunnier today than usual," Shane said.

The deputies-in-training, 80 percent male, were shockingly fresh-faced. Adam reminded himself that some were only four years older than Dylan.

Captain Grandjean stood in front of the class. "Cadets, let me introduce you to three officers working in Albany with the Dougherty County Sheriff's Department. Deputy Fuller, Corporal Mitchell, and Sergeant Bronson."

Shane smiled. Adam nodded. Bronson glared.

"The time is yours," Grandjean said to the class. "Any question's fair game."

Adam felt his stomach flip as he came to grips with what he'd tried to push out of his mind. He'd rather be abducted by aliens than stand in front of a group of people.

An athletic-looking cadet in his early twenties said, "I hear the starting wage for a deputy in Dougherty County is $26,000. So if you're married and have kids, does that mean most cops have to get a job on the side or something?"

Shane nodded. "That's a great question. One advantage to what you get paid as a Georgia cop is—you definitely can't afford a drug habit!"

They laughed . . . sort of.

"Nothin' funny about it," Bronson said. "Cops should be paid more than doctors. But it'll never happen, so why whine about it? Being a cop's the toughest job on the planet. If you're a weak cop, you'll fail your partner, maybe kill him. Your job is to keep him alive; I mean, only if that's important to you. If it isn't, you may as well just put your gun to his head and take him out—get it over with. If you can't hack it, just flunk out and sell vacuum cleaners."

The class stared silently.

Bronson had one more round in the chamber. "It's not a game out there. You hesitate and they'll kill you dead. Got that?"

Grandjean coughed uncomfortably. "Okay . . . next question?"

A wiry Hispanic youth asked, "It seems to me that cops need to take down the drug dealers. But you guys know who they are; you know a lot of them by name, right?"

"That's true," Adam said.

"Then why can't you just put them away?"

"It's complicated," Shane said. "The courts—"

Bronson waved him off. "The gutter slime you lock up tonight are out tomorrow. The justice system is a merry-go-round, minus the merry."

Shane attempted to resume. "Drug dealers—"

"They're a waste of protoplasm," Bronson said. "Selling drugs to kids should be a capital crime. Take down a murderer and you may save a half-dozen lives. Take down a drug dealer and you may save a hundred. Pushers should be shot, lethally injected, hung, then put on the electric chair for twenty years at a low setting."

A variety of questions followed about procedures, benefits, the increase in robberies and drugs. Dos and don'ts on foot chases. The Holloman chase provided some recent fodder for tale-telling. Adam was still nervous but was grateful he wasn't standing up there alone.

"I've heard every precinct has its own rules, and police and sheriff's offices can be very different. Does that get confusing?"

Shane nodded. "I have my own list of rules, and one of them is, 'Never do a shotgun search of a dark warehouse with a cop whose nickname is Boomer.'"

Everyone relaxed and smiled. Shane was good. Anyone who could put air back in a room after Bronson sucked it out was, in Adam's mind, a magician.

Shane rolled on. "It's good to think through your responses in advance to what people say when you pull them over. I like to say, 'Sure, we have a quota. Two more tickets and my girlfriend gets a toaster oven.' Or 'We used to have a quota, but now we can write as many tickets as we want.' Another one you'll use often is, 'Sir, just how big *were* those two beers?'"

"Okay," Captain Grandjean said, smiling. "Deputy Fuller could obviously go on. Any more questions?"

An early-twenties male said, "I'm getting married this summer."

"Congratulations," Adam said, mainly to keep Bronson from talking. "What's your question?"

"They talk about the high divorce rate among cops. Is that really true?"

Adam nodded. "Unfortunately, yes. Looking back, I'd say that of the guys I knew well in the academy and in my first assignment, three out of four are divorced."

"You're looking at one of the statistics. You can survive like Adam and his wife." Shane pointed to his partner. "But it's not easy."

"I've got a question," a big, strong-looking young man said.

Adam recognized him. He'd been a star at Shiloh Christian Academy in Albany, a small private school that won the state football championship. Adam still remembered how legendary coach Bobby Lee Duke nearly swallowed his trademark Tootsie Pop when Shiloh beat his Richland Giants. The kid had entered Albany folklore for doing a hundred-yard death crawl blindfolded, with a 160-pound player on his back.

"You're Brock Kelley, aren't you?" Shane asked.

Brock smiled. "Yes, sir. In my college classes, several professors taught that there are no moral absolutes. Most people I went to college with probably won't deal drugs. But a lot of them don't believe in ultimate right and wrong. Does that relate to all the junk you guys have to face?"

"I'm no college graduate," Bronson announced. No one in the room appeared surprised at this revelation. "I'm just a working stiff, trying to keep the next person from being mugged or raped or murdered by people who—guess what—don't believe in moral absolutes." He looked around. "Why would I be a cop if there wasn't right and wrong? On the street, steal somebody's stereo or girlfriend or gun, and suddenly they all believe in moral absolutes."

Someone asked, "So how do you balance following precinct policy and staying out of trouble with the media and the courts, with just staying alive?"

Shane said, "On the streets, cops have a saying: 'There's no justice. There's just us.'"

"What does that mean?"

"We can't control what the courts decide or what makes the media happy. We have a job to do, and nobody else has the guts or the know-how to get out there and actually do it."

Bronson said, "We're cops, not bleeding-heart social workers or two-faced politicians. I can't worry and second-guess myself. I tried to be nice once, as a young officer. I ended up with a broken nose. Didn't make that mistake again."

With five minutes left in the class, Brock Kelley said, "I have one other question. I'm a Christian. How hard is it for Christian cops to stay on track with their faith?"

Adam admired the kid's directness. "You see the worst out there. You get cynical. For a Christian, that negativity could skew how you view others and maybe get in the way of your faith."

Bronson cleared his throat, the cement mixer scraping everything off the sides. "Christians are soft, and soft cops aren't good cops. Some guy you're chasing turns around and reaches inside his jacket. A Christian wants to give him the benefit of the doubt. You hesitate and he shoots you or your partner, and one of you has no face. Give me an atheist partner. If the guy next to me wants to go to heaven, sorry, I'd rather stay here."

"I've always wanted to be a cop," Brock said. "And I don't apologize for being a Christian. I care about justice and I care about people, and I think that should make me a better cop, not a worse one." He glanced at Bronson, then focused on Adam and Shane. "I want to stick up for people who are weak. Police work seems like a good vocation for a Christian. Do you agree?"

"I'll tell you this, Brock," Shane said. "It's a tough job. As a cop, you seldom hear a crowd cheer. Instead you hear people boo. And it's tough to take. It's not just that you're underpaid. You're also underappreciated. If you can handle that, you'll be okay."

As Shane spoke, Adam eyed a slightly built young man in the back of the class. He looked down, avoiding eye contact. Adam sensed something was wrong with him.

Captain Grandjean looked at the wall clock. "Well, this has been all I hoped for. And quite a bit more."

He glanced at Bronson, not smiling, then addressed the class. "The job you signed up for isn't easy. It demands long hours, dedication, and sacrifice. You'll take an oath, and with that oath will come great responsibility. Resolve now never to abuse it."

After dismissing the cadets, Grandjean came and shook Adam's and Shane's hands. He turned to Bronson. "Next time, Sergeant, feel free to say whatever's on your mind." He didn't extend his hand. Neither did Bronson.

As they stepped into the hallway, they heard the click of high heels on linoleum. An immaculately dressed woman strode toward them, accompanied by a young male assistant whose loafers were trying to keep up.

"What's *she* doing here?" Bronson asked, too loudly.

She walked straight to Captain Grandjean. "What's *he* doing here?"

"I'll leave the two of you to work this out." Grandjean walked away.

Adam realized that left either him or Shane to be their referee, and he knew how Shane felt about her.

Dressed to the nines in an impeccably tailored navy business suit, Public Information Officer Diane Koos grinned at Bronson, but just with her teeth. "I'm here to speak to the recruits about the modern approach to police work, showing moderation, being the kind of cops who serve the community and are respected by the media, and the importance of following the rules." Her perfect updo gave the impression that her mahogany hair obeyed every one of those rules.

Bronson refrained from spitting on the floor. Barely. "Yeah, if anybody could give a fifty-cent answer to a nickel question, it would be a PIO. And a former media pretty face."

Shane smiled, earning him the evil eye from Koos. She looked at Adam like he was her one hope for empathy. "I work for the sheriff's office now. We're on the same team."

"That dawg won't hunt," Bronson said.

"What's that supposed to mean?"

"That we ustacould actually do our jobs, but now you wanna play Xena the warrior princess. You'll teach these recruits to be sniveling cowards who treat criminals like royalty while two-bit thugs rule the streets."

Hands on hips, freshly manicured fifty-caliber fingernails protruding, Koos barked, "You are *impossible*, Bronson."

"*Sergeant* Bronson. I'm a sworn officer. At the television station did they swear you in to risk your life to protect others? Or did they just slap makeup on your mug and teach you to throw stones at the cops who put their lives on the line?"

"You're a dinosaur, Bronson, and you're headed for extinction. The times have passed you by."

Bronson glanced at Adam and Shane and said, "She's never been the same since that house fell on her sister."

Koos put her hand on Bronson's shoulder, not lightly. "I ought to just . . ."

Though a free-for-all would have been entertaining, Adam stepped between them to ward off an eye gouge or head-butt.

Grandjean appeared again. "Break it up, you two, or take it outside. Ms. Koos, your classroom's down there, second one on the left. It starts in ten minutes. I'll be there in five and introduce you."

★ ★ ★

Adam thought the smile on Shane Fuller's face might become permanent. Ten minutes after Bronson's encounter with Diane Koos, his partner was still giddy.

An academy training lieutenant approached Adam and friends. "Observers need to go upwind for this one." Several instructors donned gas masks.

The drill instructor spoke through his megaphone. "All

right, recruits, yesterday you had three hours of classroom training on chemical agents. Hope you listened.

"You need to understand what people—perps or civilians—
go through when exposed to gas. First we'll spray pepper spray
and other chemical agents off Plexiglas, which will bounce into
your face, which is typically the way you'll be exposed to it. This
won't be pleasant, but you'll survive. Don't run or we'll tackle
you. Don't put a sleeve to your face; you'll just make it worse."

The next few minutes consisted of clouds of either OC or
DOC or CS gas, Adam wasn't sure which. The recruits choked
and walked slowly; some fared better than others. Some who
had said, "Bring it on" now gasped for air and looked as disoriented and miserable as they felt. They lined up by the water
spigots, washing their faces.

Adam noticed that the recruit who fared worst was that
skinny, troubled kid from the back of the classroom. He sat
exhausted and dejected by the water fountain farthest away
from traffic. Brock Kelley came over and slapped him on the
back, saying a few words.

After the recruits headed to the locker rooms, Adam asked
the lieutenant, "How's this class overall?"

"Off the record? It's just okay. Brock Kelley is the star."

"The Jesus freak?" Bronson loaded up his throat.

"I believe he called himself a Christian," Adam said.

The lieutenant said, "It's a small class and several of them are
on the bubble. In a year with lots of good candidates, several
of these kids would flunk. But to be honest, we'll have to pass
anyone who's even marginal."

"And make his partner pay the price?" Bronson asked.

"What's the alternative? Fewer cops on the streets? We can't
recruit people from other parts of the country to move away

from home so they can be paid half of what they'd get staying. And even if they came, we wouldn't get the best."

"Who's that kid over there?" Adam pointed at the skinny young man still sitting by the fountain.

"Bobby Shaw," the lieutenant said.

"Is he going to make it?"

"He's one I'm talking about. Bottom of the class. Likable enough. Dad died in combat, I heard. His mom raised him. She actually called me to check on him."

"I guess I have to agree with Sarge that we can't afford to have guys on the force unless they're ready. Our lives are on the line." Adam looked at Shane. "I mean, would you want to be his partner?"

"Nathan still carries David, and David's way beyond that kid. Soft, fatherless guys aren't my first choice to help us arrest hard, fatherless young men."

"So, Shane, don't go buy a fishing boat and retire early. Let's serve twenty-five more years together."

"Okay, maybe by then I'll have that boat," Shane said. He lifted his coffee cup, and Styrofoam against Styrofoam, two cops toasted their partnership.

As they exited to the parking lot, Bronson muttered, "These academy brats are more ignorant than ever."

"Sarge—" Adam turned to Bronson—"didn't you go to academy?"

Bronson sized him up. "Yeah. So what?"

"Were you ignorant then?"

"Yeah, I was. I wouldn't want anyone to have been stuck with me as a partner."

"A kid has to start somewhere."

"Not with me he doesn't."

"Did you ever have a partner who was as good as you?" Adam asked.

"Yeah. My first partner, thirty-five years ago. Ollie Chandler. Taught me how to put a guy down with a head-butt. We used to practice on each other."

Adam touched his forehead and winced.

"You stay in touch with Chandler?"

"Not much. Lives in Oregon. At Christmas we exchange pictures of his dog, Mulch, and my Marciano. Three of the best friends I've ever had were dogs. Chandler's the fourth."

For a moment Adam saw the human side of Brad Bronson.

"I tell you, these academy punks got no class."

It had been a short moment.

This guy wouldn't know class if he stepped in it.

"You gotta be impressed with Brock Kelley," Shane said.

"You think I want a high school football hero?" Bronson asked. "He'll imagine he's big stuff. Death crawl? Give me a break. He'll be the death of someone. Well, not me."

As Adam pulled out, Shane said, "Sarge, you and Diane Koos are like two goats in a pepper patch. You oughta ask her out for donuts."

Bronson muttered something unintelligible.

Shane turned his head. "Considering you thought it was a waste of time to come today, you sure had a lot of advice for those recruits."

"Won't make any difference," Bronson said. "Young is stupid."

Shane looked in his mirror. He smiled and whispered to Adam, lower than before, "In that case, the sergeant's definitely not stupid."

Five seconds passed before Bronson said, "Fuller, it would take you three promotions to make stupid."

CHAPTER TWENTY-ONE

ADAM, NATHAN, David, Shane, and Javier all sat on Adam's patio. Used paper plates and empty Coke cans littered the table.

"That was one juicy bird, Corporal Grillmaster," Nathan said to Adam. "What's the secret?"

"Oil the grill, keep the chicken uncovered, put it slightly off-center from the flame, and never put on the sauce till two minutes before you're done cooking."

"The burgers were great too," David added.

Shane nodded. "If you're going to be a real man, Rookie, you gotta get the best beef you can and watch them grind it. Not yesterday, not this morning, but while you wait."

"My son," Nathan said, "the key to steak is to salt it generously. Then, even if your meat isn't faultless, the salt will break it in and hold its taste."

David studied his elders and said, "You know, you guys are really something."

"Thanks," the three men said, almost in unison. David hadn't meant it as a compliment.

"One day this young man will have his own family," Nathan said. "And he'll tell tales of afternoons spent in Mitchell's yard, soaking in grilling wisdom. And when he takes his kids to a Falcons game, he'll teach them how to tailgate. There's no price you can put on that."

Shane laughed. "With our salaries, who can afford to go to a Falcons game?"

"All right," Adam said, trying to change the subject. "If everybody's stuffed, I want to tell you guys why I had you over today. I need to ask you a favor."

Adam gave each man a sheet of paper. Javier's curiosity perked up.

Shane knew Adam had an agenda today, but he was surprised at what he saw.

Nathan looked at the sheet in his hands. "A resolution?"

"Yeah. I struggle with what kind of father I was to Emily and what kind of dad I've been to Dylan."

"Don't be so hard on yourself," Shane said. "You've been a good enough father."

"I don't want to be a 'good enough' father. We have a few short years to influence our kids, and whatever patterns we set for them will likely pass on to their kids."

The guys wondered where Adam was headed.

"We have the responsibility to mold lives. I don't think that should be done casually. Half the fathers in this country are failing, probably way more. And with the time I've got left, I don't want to be one of them."

"Look," Shane said, "I'm all for spending more time with your kids, but don't you think you're taking this a little too far?"

"Shane, time with our kids should be a given. We need to act strategically. It's our job to help them become the people God wants them to be—set the standards they can aim for."

"What kind of standards?" David asked.

Adam paused. "Well, when did you first think of yourself as a man?"

Shane laughed. "I can't believe we're talkin' about this."

"No, guys, humor me a second. Think about it."

Javier listened intently while Nathan finished quietly reading Adam's resolution.

"Okay," David said. "It was probably when I was first living on my own. Or maybe when I turned twenty-one. Toward the end of college."

"So when you became legal. Okay, what about you, Shane?"

He sighed. "Maybe when I got my license or my first job. What does it matter?"

"Javy?"

Javier had known his answer instantly, the memory still vivid. "When my father told me I was."

They all looked at him.

"When I was seventeen, he had to leave for three months for a job. He told me that he thought of me as a man—he wanted me to take care of my family. He asked me if I was ready. When I hesitated, he told me he *knew* I was ready."

Adam said, "Look, guys, I've learned that God wants me to teach my son how to love Him and trust Him and that it's my responsibility to call out the man in my son. I can't be passive about that."

"How did you come up with these?" Nathan asked, still intent on the sheet.

"I got them all from studying Scripture. This is a resolution of what kind of father I want to be. Each of you has permission to keep me accountable. In fact, I *want* you to hold me accountable."

All the men joined Nathan in reading it.

Finally Javier said, "Could I sign this too?"

Shane said, "If you're gonna sign it, Adam, maybe we all should."

"No, no. I'm not asking you guys to sign anything. I'm doing this because I need it and my family needs it. If you think you should do this, at least take a couple of days to think about it."

The head-butt from that giant Pillsbury Doughboy had hurt TJ. But what hurt worse was being humiliated in front of his minister of defense. TJ was mad. The Dougherty County brownies were now higher on his enemy list than the Albany city police—right up there with the Rollin' Crips.

Antoine warned TJ, "You kill a cop, they put you away fo' the rest o' yo life."

Cops might look the other way when it came to drugs. They wouldn't look the other way when they knew the identity of someone hunting them.

But the commander in chief of the Gangster Nation had been dissed—one-upped one too many times.

That black cop had taken back the truck TJ stole and arrested his homeboy Clyde. He'd get him back some day. But the big white cop had knocked TJ flat on the ground, and that ate at his gut. And if he didn't get some get-back, Antoine and the Gangster Nation might disrespect him. And for a gang leader, disrespect was the first step toward death.

He had to do this. And he wanted to.

You goin' down, fat man.

After putting the kids to bed, Kayla leaned against the kitchen counter and perused the resolution. Nathan sat across from her, watching her expressions.

"Wow. You're sayin' you wanna do this too?"

"That's what I'm sayin'. I've always thought I was good enough because I'm doing better than my father. But so what? Not like he set the standard high. That resolution hit me right between the eyes."

Kayla smiled. "Baby, there are some days when I'm glad I married you. And there are other days when I'm really, really glad I married you. And this is one of those days."

"So it's a really glad day?"

"Uh-huh. And when I see you do what only a good man does, it makes me want to bless you." She reached out to her husband's shoulder.

"You wanna bless me?" Nathan smiled.

"Oh yeah. But I've got a question. What does this resolution you're going to sign look like?"

"What do you mean? You just read it."

"I know what's in it. But surely this isn't what you'll sign. This is computer paper. I mean they didn't write the Declaration or the Constitution on scratch paper to sign it, did they?"

"I guess not."

"I think this resolution is something a father should frame and post on the wall."

"I don't know if Adam thought that far ahead."

"And how are you signing it? In blue jeans and a T-shirt? They swear in a mayor or a cop in a ceremony, right? And they're not dressed in shorts, are they? Is committing to be the best husband and father any less important?"

"No."

"I see a group of well-dressed men with their wives and children making this official. This is one of those important days, like a wedding or baptism."

Nathan considered her words. Kayla leaned close to him; her

dark eyes looked straight into his. "Baby, if you're gonna do it, then do it right."

Adam and Dylan jogged together after Sunday dinner had settled. As they continued running, Dylan picked up the pace. He breathed normally while Adam just pretended to.

"So how's track?"

Adam asked this for two reasons. First, because a father should ask his son about what's important to him. Second, because if Dylan talked, maybe he would slow down.

"Still don't know what races Coach Kilian will let me run."

"Which ones do you want to run?"

"I like running long distance, but I also want to do the 400."

Dylan kept up his pace no problem, so Adam finally slowed to a walk.

Dylan checked his watch. "But we've only run three miles."

"What do you mean *only* three? It's going to take a while to catch up to you. Eventually my athletic genes will kick in. You'll see. But for now, I need your help getting in shape to run down the bad guys."

"Having a Taser helps, doesn't it?"

"Yeah, once you catch them."

"If you catch me, you can tase me."

"Yeah, right. Say that when I'm armed!"

"It wouldn't matter. There's no danger of you catching me." Dylan smiled the biggest smile Adam remembered seeing for years.

Adam looked at Dylan and wagged his finger, then ran and very quickly slowed back to a walk. The joy of running hadn't kicked in for Adam. Maybe it never would. But the joy of talking and laughing with his son far outweighed the pain.

★ ★ ★

Two days later Adam sat by a watercooler after his workout in the sheriff's office gym. His time with Dylan made him want to get into shape. He thought he smelled something smoldering; then the sun went into eclipse.

"What's up, Sarge?"

"I'm thinkin' of taking out the Koos woman."

"Well, I guess you're both eligible, Sarge, but I don't think a computer would match you up."

"I don't want to date her! I wanna *take her out*."

"What did she do this time?"

"I got memos, one from the sheriff and another from the Koos. Seems one of the drug dealers I arrested wasn't happy with my service."

"What'd you do?"

"Just tweaked his nose when he smarted off."

"Tweaked?"

"I do a pretty good tweak."

"I can imagine."

"So I'm told that if I get one more reprimand, I go on unpaid leave. Step one of firing me."

"Sorry to hear it."

"I've thought about just strangling the Koos, but one thing's saving her."

"What's that?"

"I'd have to touch her to do it."

"So you looked like you had something on your mind, Sarge. Was that it?"

"Got some news about Mike Hollis."

Adam stiffened. "Is his trial over?"

"Not yet. But the prosecutor found something we didn't know."

"What's that?"

"Turns out the blood tests showed not just alcohol but cocaine."

"He was on coke?"

"Yeah. With the smell of booze all over him at the scene, nobody thought about anything else. The cocaine showed up in the tests, but somehow nobody noticed. But the DA's office did. It'll mean more prison time."

"Alcohol is all it takes," Adam said. "As far as Emily was concerned, I guess it doesn't matter."

"Except if it had only been alcohol, maybe it wouldn't have happened. A drunk drives bad; a stoned drunk drives worse. I knew you'd hear about it. Might be tough to handle with other guys around."

Adam nodded. "Thanks, Sarge. That was . . . kind of you."

Bronson walked away uneasily. Adam wondered if anyone had ever accused him of being kind.

CHAPTER TWENTY-TWO

AT THE SHERIFF'S department firing range, Nathan Hayes ran through a drill, shooting at targets as part of a live-fire obstacle course, while the range captain yelled commands about what to do next. Nathan successfully hit the great majority of his targets on the first shot. When he finished, the onlooking officers cheered.

David ran the same drill, firing into targets. Not bad for a while, but everyone groaned when he hit the target that said sheriff.

"Good work," the captain told Nathan. "You're still in the top three in the department."

He turned to David and said, "Deputy Thomson, you need to focus, son. You shot the sheriff again." He pointed to a cutout with a badge on it. "That's gonna get you range detail, and I want it cleaned up. Come back for more practice. You've got to get it right."

"They put that badge on a different target every time," David complained to Nathan.

"That's the idea."

171

"Well, I know what the sheriff looks like, and I would *not* shoot him."

As the training sergeant took down targets, Nathan and David cleaned their guns. Nathan tended to his Glock 22, a .40 caliber holding fifteen rounds, while David worked on his Glock 23, also .40 caliber and just as powerful but slightly smaller.

Nathan sensed something was on David's mind. He decided to keep quiet and give David the opportunity to talk if and when he was ready.

Finally David spoke. "This resolution deal has gotten pretty big, huh?"

"We decided to make it official and memorable. Maybe it'll stick with us more."

David worked quietly, then asked Nathan, "Do you really feel like it messed up your childhood—not having a dad?"

"More than you know. A lot of your self-worth comes from what your father thinks of you. I struggled with who I was my whole childhood. Tried to prove myself. I almost got in a gang. If fathers did what they're supposed to do, half the junk we face on the street wouldn't exist."

After a long pause, Nathan said, "David, something's on your mind. What is it?"

David shrugged.

"Are you nervous about being a father one day?"

David hesitated. "I already am one."

Nathan stared at David. "You've got a kid?"

"A girl. She's four now."

"My partner has a daughter and I didn't know about it?"

"I hooked up with a cheerleader in college. She got pregnant. I told her to take care of it, but she wouldn't do it. I got mad and left her to deal with it herself. She lives just thirty minutes away, but all these years I couldn't bring myself to go see her."

"And the 'it' she didn't take care of was actually a 'her' that she's been taking care of for four years, right?"

David stared at his hands.

"What's her name? Your daughter."

"Olivia."

"What's her mother's name?"

"Amanda."

"Did she ever get married?"

"No."

"How do you know?"

"A friend who went to college with us. He checks up on her. On them."

Nathan decided to hold back the questions and see if David would resume talking. After a minute, the silence became more awkward than speech.

"I never loved her. But listening to you guys talk about how dads not being there messes kids up . . . I don't want to be one of those guys."

"David, part of being a man is taking responsibility. Any fool can father a child, but it takes courage to *be* a child's father. To be there for them."

"I used to think I was a good guy. I'm just tired of feeling guilty."

Nathan looked at him. "Let me break it to you: You are guilty."

David sighed.

"Listen, one day you, me, and everyone else will stand before God. And He's gonna do what good judges do."

"Then I hope my good outweighs the bad."

"That's not how it works." Nathan searched for an illustration. "Let me put it this way . . . Who's the person you're closest to?"

"Probably my mom."

"Okay, suppose she was brutally attacked and murdered. The guy's caught and put on trial. But he says, 'Hey, Judge, I committed this crime, but I've done a lot of good in my life.' Maybe he helped the homeless forty times, and he can prove it. Now, if the judge let him go free, would you say that's a good judge or a bad judge?"

"A bad one."

"That's right. The Bible says God is a good judge. And He will punish the guilty, not for what they did right, obviously, but for what they did wrong. We're all sinners, David. Part of being a sinner is not realizing how bad of a sinner you are."

"Okay, I'm a sinner. How does knowing that help?"

"You need to realize how desperate you really are. A man who doesn't think he's drowning won't reach for the life preserver when it's thrown to him. Why bother when you think you're fine?"

"Okay. So I don't think I'm fine."

"All right then, you've grasped the bad news. Now here's the *good* news. Because God loves us, He sent His Son, Jesus Christ, to take the punishment we deserve. That's why He died on the cross."

"You really believe that, don't you?"

"I'm absolutely convinced of it. He paid the price for our sin. But that only applies when you accept it. God offers you a gift, but it's not yours until you accept it."

David processed his partner's words.

"David, if we could be good enough to get to heaven on our own, Jesus wouldn't have had to take our punishment. You and I desperately need what only Jesus can give us."

"So what am I supposed to do? Go to church?"

"Church can't save you. Once you turn to Christ, it can help you, but it's Jesus you need. That's why I asked Him to forgive me and save me."

"But you're still not perfect!"

Nathan laughed. "Not even close. But Jesus is perfect, and it's His perfection that covers me, so now I'm righteous in God's sight. That means when I die, I'll go to heaven instead of hell. I'm a new man because of Christ. You understand what I'm tellin' you?"

"I think I do, actually. I know I'm tired of the guilt, tired of feeling like I'm a failure."

"Then what's holding you back?"

David thought for a long minute. Finally he said, "Nothing."

A rough-looking, leather-skinned black man, multiple scars on his face and neck, knocked on the door.

Derrick's gramma answered. "Come in. He's gettin' ready to go."

"Derrick!" he yelled. "Get out here."

Derrick appeared from the back room. It had been a year since he'd seen the unexpected visitor. "Uncle Reggie? What are you . . . ?"

"We're takin' a walk."

"No way, I got some friends expectin' me."

"Then they'll be disappointed." He pulled Derrick out the front door.

They walked briskly down the street; Reggie's grip felt like a vice on Derrick's arm. "You been messin' with drugs and hangin' with 'bangers."

"Gramma don't know nothin'."

"She's forgotten twice what you'll ever know, punk."

"Where we goin'?"

"A little tour. Gonna show you what gangs and drugs will do to you."

Three blocks away they came to a back alley Derrick had stayed away from. Three addicts lay on the ground against the wall. Reggie stopped. "Look."

Reluctantly Derrick complied. Half their teeth were missing. They appeared like zombies, the living dead.

The smell overwhelmed Derrick. He gagged. He'd walked past dudes like this but never this close. They sat scratching themselves, trying to get rid of whatever was crawling under their skin.

"You see the scars on them?"

Derrick said nothing.

Reggie pushed his shoulder hard. "I said, *see the scars?*"

"Yeah, I see 'em!"

"It's not just the drugs. They've been beaten up and robbed again and again. See their skin?"

"Yeah." It looked ashen and sickly. How could black men be so pale?

Reggie gestured at a man with vacant eyes and a face as expressionless as a mask. They walked farther to a pair of cocaine addicts, united by their drug of choice and their utter ruin. These two appeared to converse except neither could understand the other. They were oblivious to Reggie and Derrick. A couple of times they glanced Derrick's way but looked through him as if he existed on another plane.

"See those men, Derrick? What do they look, seventy? They're probably no more than forty. They're not old, just ruined.

"You doin' crack yet? That'll take you out. You'll be just like them—dead or wishin' you were. Maybe make somebody else dead. Is that what you want? Rot in prison? The livin' death?"

"Just want to hang with my homies. That's all."

Near the corner liquor store, one of a dozen in a two-mile

radius, two old men and a young one sat with hands extended, looking like beggars on the streets of Delhi.

"See these guys? They started by just hangin' with their homies too. Most of them don't have a life three blocks away from this liquor store. They were nickel-and-dime 'bangers and dealers and hustlers. Now they beg for money. They eat rock and breathe liquor; that's all they do. Take a good look, boy. That's what you're gonna be."

This guy thinks he knows me? He ain't even talked to me for a year. "Never gonna be that."

"That's what they thought. Some of them were honor students too."

Reggie stopped again and pointed. "That's Kenny. Doesn't know how old he is. He just hustles for chump change, begging off little old ladies. He's still trying to be hip, shirttails out, hat on backward. Permanent adolescence. Ugly, ain't it? Like a twelve-year-old still wearin' diapers. Anybody offer you so much as a toke, this is where they sending you. Remember that, boy."

Derrick stared at the concrete.

"Last week I asked Kenny what he thought of his life. Know what he told me? 'I may not be in hell yet, but I can see it and smell it.' That what you want, boy? Answer me now."

"No. But you don't know what I got with the Gangster Nation."

"I *don't know*?" He pulled up his sleeve to reveal a prominent Gangster Nation tattoo. He pushed Derrick against the wall. "I was GN on the street before you were born and for seven years in a federal pen. Feds don't mess around. I oughta bust you up for tellin' me what I don't know. Outta respect for yo mama, I won't knock your teeth out."

"You been outta the gang a long time. You don't know TJ."

"Don't have to know him. I was number two in Albany's biggest gang, and look where it got me." He grabbed Derrick by the shirt and yanked him into another alley. It smelled like a latrine.

"Take a good look, Derrick. Breathe deep and smell it. If this is the life you want, here it is. If you're lucky. Wake up, boy. Our ancestors were slaves. Their hands and feet were chained, but they learned to use their heads. Your hands and feet are free. God blessed you with a good mind, but you're makin' yo'self a slave."

"I ain't no slave."

"Drugs take you to jail. Gangs take you to jail. You don't know nothin' about that world; I do. Seven years in prison. Know what it's like? No privacy, always noisy, television and radio blasts till you just stick your fingers in your ears and wanna scream. Threats and fights and hits. Ain't no life. You got jumped in, didn't you?"

Derrick started to lie, but why should he hide it? He was proud to be Gangster Nation. "Yeah."

"Well, I told you I was number two, an OG. Had the rep. Then they send me out on a drug deal and a get-back. I go to jail and then what? You do the time alone; nobody there to help you. You think they yo friends, but they ghost on you."

"Not goin' to any jail."

"Listen to you. You tryin' to be the ultimate cool, but you the ultimate fool. I been down the road you're just startin' on, and I know where it leads. Only one way to make it back. I'll tell you if you wanna know. But as long as you keep lyin' to yo'self, the truth's wasted on you."

"It's my life."

"You got that right. Your life to waste, to throw away, or to turn around now. I'll tell you now—I ain't gonna tell you again: get out while you still can."

They turned and walked home another way, through another maze of broken lives.

They were quiet until they got back to Derrick's front door. "Your mother's gone, D. I was never a good brother to her. For a while I thought you was makin' yo mama proud. Not anymore, boy. But it's not too late."

Derrick looked at his uncle Reggie. His face reminded him of a picture of his mother. For a moment he felt a connection, like maybe the man knew what he was talking about. But Derrick's thoughts drifted back to what it meant to belong to the Gangster Nation.

Reggie saw the moment pass, saw in Derrick's eyes that nothing he'd said would make a difference. "I want better for you, son. With yo mama gone, somebody's got to hammer on you. But you don't wanna hear it from me; fine, I won't come back. Some people want help. Can't waste time on somebody choosin' to throw his life away."

Reggie looked like an attorney finishing a closing argument to a jury who'd already made up its mind.

"Your choice, D. If you run with the 'bangers, then only three things can happen: you end up burned-out on the street, wasted in prison, or lyin' in the chalk circle. No other options."

As always, the legendary Pearly's on Slappey Boulevard, the mother of all country-style kitchens, was crowded and loud. It was *the* place for breakfast. And lunch. Finicky food critics would never admit to eating at Pearly's; they just came here undercover whenever they wanted real food.

Pearly's had the market-tested efficiency of a New York stand-up counter that maximized every square foot, combined with the down-home collegial feel of an old South barbershop.

179

COURAGEOUS

The master menu hung on the wall, and Adam looked at it the way a marksman eyes a target. With the long lines at Pearly's, Adam intuitively expected a lengthy wait to order and be served, but it never happened. Even with ten people in front of him, he didn't have enough time to decide what would accompany his perennial link-sausage biscuit.

Five minutes later, the server magically appeared with a golden biscuit cooked to perfection, mouthwatering sausage hanging out both ends. Adam's very short prayer contained the words "Thank You" repeated three times.

"How's yours?" Adam asked Shane between bites.

"Heart attack on a plate and worth every mouthful." He swallowed a forkload of steak and eggs and sighed. "There's just nothin' bad about this place."

"I disagree," Adam said. "They're not open twenty-four hours."

Adam's attention was diverted to the parking lot, where an early-twenties white guy with a backpack approached a kid who looked seventeen. Both parties did the look-all-around routine to be sure no one watched. If Adam had been on the street, nothing would have happened. But given the sun's reflection on the window, he was invisible to the dealer and the buyer.

The guy thinks if he can't see anyone, then they can't see him. It occurred to Adam that he'd sometimes lived that way himself.

The dealer looked like a college student. He swung his backpack around to hang against his chest. He unzipped it and took out a rolled sandwich bag with a greenish cigar-size substance, then a couple of miniature ziplock baggies, one clear, one transparent green. The large baggie was marijuana and the smaller ones methamphetamines and cocaine. Adam sighed. He knew these deals occurred everywhere, all the time.

Shane looked too. "I saw that dealer in Hilsman Park a week

ago when I was there with Tyler. What's he doing at Pearly's? Sheesh. If you're looking for a hundred witnesses . . ."

Just then, as the buyer reached in his pocket for his money, Adam saw his face.

"Jeremy."

"You know him?"

"Jeremy Rivers. He's a friend of Dylan's. On the track team. Okay, this just got personal. Let's go, partner." Adam pulled Shane's arm.

Shane stuffed his last chunk of steak in his mouth, saying good-bye to the remnants of biscuit on his plate, which, in a perfect world, he would have licked clean.

"693c reporting a drug deal with a minor at North Slappey and . . . What am I saying? We're at Pearly's. Parking lot. Corporal Mitchell and I are approaching."

Adam stepped toward the suspects. "Hands out where I can see them."

Adam took the drugs from the young kid's hand and the money out of the dealer's hand. He said to Shane, "You take care of this guy while I talk with Jeremy."

When the kid heard his name, he raised his eyes from the asphalt and looked into the officer's face, where he recognized Dylan's dad.

This just got personal for him too.

CHAPTER TWENTY-THREE

THE SHIFT GATHERED in the muster room, Shane on Adam's left, Bronson across the aisle on their right, Nathan and David in front of them, as usual.

The sergeant gave way to the sheriff, who stood at the podium with a memo in hand.

"Men, starting today, I am implementing a new code of conduct for the entire sheriff's department. This is awkward, but we need to address it, so hear me out."

He had Adam's attention. *What's this?*

"No matter how you feel about another employee, I want you to keep your personal feelings to yourself. I don't want to hear about how much you love me or any other staff member. It's inappropriate. It's awkward. And it's unacceptable!"

Adam lowered his head. He couldn't remember ever feeling so embarrassed. The silence was interminable.

"And, Corporal Mitchell . . ."

The sheriff pointed at Adam, who looked up, horrified.

"I gotcha!"

The room exploded with laughter. Those near Adam

slapped him on the back. Adam blushed and shook his head. He turned and his eyes fell, as was statistically probable, upon Brad Bronson.

The planetoid put his palm to his lips and blew Adam a kiss.

Javier Martinez laid his new suit and tie, still covered in plastic, across his bed. It was the first suit he'd ever owned.

"Javy! It's perfect!"

"I don't know, Carmen. It was a great sale, and Adam insisted on helping, but I still paid for two-thirds of it. I can take it back."

"You're not taking it back. Put it on."

"Now?"

"Right now. I want to see you in it."

She picked it up and took the plastic off. Javier put on the slacks and shirt, then the jacket. He picked up the tie and put it under his collar, then stopped.

"What do I do next?"

"I used to do this for my father on Sundays. Here, let me try."

"There. Perfect," Carmen said as she patted his chest and smoothed his lapels.

Isabel and Marcos ran into the room. Their eyes got big when they saw their father. Isabel said, "You look handsome!"

"Is it yours, *Papi*?" Marcos asked.

"Yes," Carmen said. "This is Daddy's suit that he will wear to our special meeting. We will all wear our very best."

Javier turned to look at himself in the mirror. He smiled sheepishly, not wanting to be proud.

"I feel like a rich man."

Carmen took his arm. She looked tenderly into his eyes.

"Javy, you *are* a rich man. You have a strong faith, two children that love you, and a wife that adores you."

Javier's face contorted and his eyes misted as he looked down. "Stop it, Carmen. You'll make me cry in front of the children."

★ ★ ★

Adam and Nathan stood talking to David in an empty court-room adjacent to the sheriff's office. David leaned against a dark wood bench, gazed at the floor, and rubbed his sweaty palms along the sides of his dark-brown uniform pants.

"I want to do this, guys, but . . . I'm scared to death."

Adam said, "David, you know that little girl is your responsibility, right?"

"Yeah. I think about her all the time. God seems to have put my conscience into another gear."

Nathan leaned toward David. "You're a new person now. He lives inside you. He's convicting you to do the right thing."

"But this will be like dropping a bomb. Amanda hasn't heard from me for over five years. Olivia's never even met me."

"Then it's time to man up, isn't it?" Adam said.

David looked at both men and ran his fingers through his short sandy hair. He agreed. "When I'm alone, all the reasons not to do it take over. But it's hard to rationalize my way out of it while you two stand here."

"I hear you," Adam said. "Since I told you guys I'm deter-mined to cut back on television, I sit in the living room and think, 'I don't want to have to tell them I wasted another eve-ning.' So I turn it off. Maybe not the best motive, but it's a good result."

"It's peer pressure, isn't it?" Nathan supposed. "We never outgrow it. I told Jade the other night she's not the only one whose decisions are affected by those she hangs out with. Who Kayla and I hang out with affects ours, too."

"'Stimulate one another to love and good deeds,'" David offered.

Adam smiled. "There you go quoting Scripture. You're the man, David."

"This will be one of the hardest things I've ever done."

"The right things are often the hardest," Nathan said. "But when you act courageously, there's a huge payoff."

Adam, in jeans and a T-shirt, stood outside the open door. Sam Rivers's face looked like a skull with skin. All sheetrock, no insulation. On another face his eyes might have looked normal, but this was not another face. They bulged like eggs stuffed in Play-Doh.

"What do you want?"

"Mr. Rivers, when I talked with you before at the sheriff's office, it was as a cop. Now it's as a dad. My son, Dylan, and your boy Jeremy are friends."

"Yeah? So what?"

"Well, I'd want someone to talk to me if my son took drugs. So I'm talking to you."

"Okay. Then talk." Rivers poked at his iPhone. Adam barely resisted the urge to slap it out of his hand.

"There are signs to look for when your son is on drugs."

"I know the signs."

"You knew your son was on drugs?"

Rivers looked like he'd had his tooth pulled without novocaine. "Half the school takes drugs. His friends in sixth grade got him smoking cigarettes. Then weed. On the school playground—can you believe it?"

COURAGEOUS

STILL PHOTOS FROM THE MOVIE

all photos by Todd Stone

★ *Adam (Alex Kendrick, left) and his partner, Shane (Kevin Downes), carefully search a house where they've arrived to serve a warrant.*

★ *Sheriff's deputies chase a suspect who has taken off running through Albany, Georgia.*

The Hayes family looks ★
to God's Word for wisdom
in facing life's challenges.

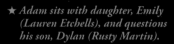

★ *Adam sits with daughter, Emily
(Lauren Etchells), and questions
his son, Dylan (Rusty Martin).*

★ *Derrick (Donald Howze, on ground) learns the hard rules of gang life.*

★ *Javier (Robert Amaya) and his wife, Carmen (Angelita Nelson), worry over a dilemma he faces at work.*

★ *Emily dances in the sunlight as her father, Adam, looks on.*

★ *Fathers in the film bow their heads in prayer, seeking God's help with the challenges in their lives.*

★ *Starting gun of the Father & Son 5K*

Adam Mitchell leads the men ★
of the movie Courageous *in resolving to be godly fathers.*

COURAGEOUS

BEHIND-THE-SCENES PHOTOS FROM THE MOVIE

★ *Members of the cast and crew gather for a morning devotional and prayer at the start of each day on set.*

★ *Donald Howze takes direction from director Alex Kendrick.*

Director of photography ★ Bob Scott captures the action.

★ *Preparing for a gripping chase scene on a lonely Georgia country road*

Robert Amaya (center, red ball cap) ★ *preps for shooting a construction scene, helping build a backyard shed.*

★ *The film crew captures Ken Bevel (Nathan Hayes) chasing a suspect on foot in an action scene.*

★ *A crime suspect crouches in wait, hoping to avoid sheriff's deputies.*

★ **Courageous** *cowriters Alex (right) and Stephen Kendrick watch shooting on the set.*

Crew members on a location shoot prep ★
a sheriff's squad car for the next scene.

★ Crew members film a confrontational scene between Ken Bevel and Donald Howze while Taylor Hutcherson (Jade) looks on.

★ Randy Alcorn (center), writer of the novelization, visits Stephen (left) and Alex Kendrick on the set.

Young talent takes a needed juice break ★ from working in the hot Georgia sun.

"And then it led to the other drugs. Marijuana always does."

"Not always."

"Jeremy bought meth too."

"Allegedly." Rivers looked at him. "You're off duty and you said you weren't talking to me as a cop. So this is off the record, right?"

"Right."

"So if you take anything I say and go after us, my lawyer will eat you for lunch. You got that, mister?"

As Adam stared into Rivers's bulgy eyes, he tried not to let his face know what his brain thought.

"My wife has prescription OxyContin. For pain. Totally legal. Jeremy got started on the Oxy. Then, when he couldn't get any more and he found out what it cost, he panicked. They told him he could get the equivalent amount of meth or cocaine for half the price."

"You seem pretty calm about it."

Mr. Rivers shrugged. "He'll grow out of it."

"What makes you think so?"

"I did. I mean, I don't do real drugs anymore. Just booze and a little grass once in a while." His eyes widened. "We're off the record—you promised."

Adam sighed. "Have you talked to Jeremy about it?"

"I told him don't buy drugs, okay, but if you do, don't be a moron and do it at Pearly's. Might as well rob a donut shop and not expect cops to notice."

"Did you tell him drugs will ruin his life?"

"I turned out okay, didn't I?"

"So you've given up on him?"

"It's not my job to interfere in my son's life."

"Isn't that *exactly* what your job is?"

He rolled his eyes like Adam clearly didn't understand what dads were for.

"Okay, he bought meth and powder cocaine. What about crack?"

"I don't know."

"Have you asked him? Have you looked in his room?"

"I respect his space, Mitchell. Right to privacy. Maybe you've heard of it?"

"Don't take the moral high ground when you're neglecting your son."

"Instead of arresting my boy, how about going after thieves and lowlifes, Barney? Thanks to you, we'll waste our time with the courts. I got a lawyer. We'll get my son off. It'll cost us, but hey, what are cops for? Never there when you need 'em, always there when you don't. I can get pizza delivered faster than I can get a cop to show up."

"Will you get drug counseling for Jeremy?"

"Like I said, he'll grow out of it."

"Lots of people never outgrow it. It can become a five-hundred-dollar-a-day habit."

"He can't afford that."

"Which is why he'll have to steal or sell to sustain it."

"You saying my boy's a thief?"

"He could become one. Especially if you don't get involved!" Adam's indignation at Sam Rivers embodied his thoughts toward all the out-of-touch fathers who had waved a white flag to the culture and given up their children as hostages.

"The lawyer will take care of everything."

"Jeremy doesn't need a lawyer. He needs a dad."

"Instead of passing judgment on me and my family, why don't you take a closer look at yours?"

"What do you mean? Dylan?"

"Yeah, Superdad. Have you talked to *your* son? Have you checked *his* room?"

Adam drove home. Dylan was at track practice and wouldn't be home for an hour. Adam went into his room and looked in the obvious places where he knew nobody with brains would hide something. And Dylan had brains. He thought of the dresser, but Victoria put away laundry.

He assessed the bookcase with more video games than books. He looked at the closet shelf filled with old shoes, old video games, and some boxes. Under the mattress? No, Dylan knew his mom stripped the bed to wash the sheets.

Adam looked around the room. If he were Dylan, where would he hide something? He remembered where he'd hidden things from his parents. At the bottom of a box of comic books at the top of his closet. It was out of his mom's reach. And she was indifferent to comic books; a perfect combination—she wouldn't throw them out, and she wouldn't look through them either.

So Adam reached for the thing Dylan knew he'd be least interested in—video games. He picked them up and opened them one by one. Finally he came to an old, worn Madden box, a video relic, and opened it. There it was. A baggie of marijuana with a few rolling papers and a roach clip.

He thought of Sam Rivers, the neglectful father, so out of touch with his son's world. The man's negligence as a father and ignorance of his son's life had outraged Adam. In an instant, Adam realized he himself was the man he despised.

CHAPTER TWENTY-FOUR

WHEN VICTORIA arrived home thirty minutes later, she found Adam on the living room sofa, head in hands.

"What's wrong?"

"It's Dylan. He's been smoking marijuana."

"What?" She nearly collapsed.

Starting with Pearly's, the arrest, Jeremy Rivers, and the confrontation with Jeremy's father, Adam told the whole story. She wanted to see the drugs. When she did, she cried.

"He'll be home anytime," she said.

"Because I confronted Jeremy and his dad and searched Dylan's room, I think maybe this should start as a father-son conversation. Does that make sense?"

She nodded.

Adam hadn't seen Victoria so frail since Emily's death. He realized this too felt like a death, a smaller one, but a grave threat to her only remaining child.

He talked with her in the bedroom until he heard Dylan come in the front door.

"I'll pray," Victoria whispered.

Adam walked to the kitchen while Dylan raided the refrigerator.

"Dylan?"

A pitcher of orange juice in his hand, Dylan turned and looked at the Madden box his father held, with a baggie protruding. The pitcher crashed to the floor. Orange juice splattered over their shoes and pant legs.

"You searched my bedroom?"

"Yes, I did."

"That's my private stuff."

"I'm not the one in trouble. You are."

"I don't go through your stuff. Maybe I will now."

"Don't mouth off to me, Dylan. I want some answers."

"What do you want to know?"

"How long have you been using?"

"A party at Drew Thornton's. When I was in eighth grade. Everyone was smoking weed. I didn't want to be alone."

"Last year? At the Thorntons'? I don't believe it! They go to our church!"

"Believe what you want. You always do."

"What's that supposed to mean?"

When Dylan looked away, Adam raised his hand to calm himself and Dylan. "Look, how about we clean up the juice and change? Then we can talk."

For the next five minutes, they mopped the kitchen floor with wet hand towels. Without a word, Dylan got up and went to his room. Adam changed his pants and sat on Dylan's floor.

"How much pot have you smoked?"

"Maybe a few times a month. I'm no teahead. It's not every day."

"I know what it smells like, Dylan. How come I've never caught a whiff of it?"

"I don't smoke it in my room. I'm not that stupid."

"What else have you used? Meth?"

"No."

"Cocaine?"

"No!"

"Prescription stuff? Like OxyContin?"

Dylan looked down. No denial.

"Oxy?"

"No. That's all over the place at school. Some kids just take it from their parents' medicine cabinet and pass it around. I don't use it."

"Dylan, you hesitated. I think there's something else, isn't there?"

"It's legal. It's nothing bad."

"What is it?"

He sighed. "The patch. I used it just once. After Emily died."

"You mean a prescription painkiller?"

"Fentanyl. You just need a doctor to get it."

Adam shook his head. "It's only legal for the person the doctor prescribes it to. It's against the law for you to use this."

"It's just a painkiller, Dad. How bad can it be? Normal people use it; it's not like being a crack addict on the street."

"Dylan, these meds work for people who are really in pain. But if you're not in pain, they mess you up. They're mind-altering drugs."

Dylan's look said it all: *That's the point.*

"You got the patch from Jeremy, didn't you?"

Dylan didn't answer. "Look, I'm not an addict! I mean . . . I don't smoke weed that often. Just sometimes when I'm stressed out, I really want something to help me forget."

Adam breathed deeply. If he lost his cool, the conversation would quickly go south.

"Give me names of people you smoke marijuana with."

"You'll just arrest them."

"Not if they don't deal it."

"But then you'll interrogate them. And tell their parents."

"Not interrogate. But tell their parents? Probably. Have you ever bought from an adult?"

Dylan didn't answer.

"That means you have. How many times?"

"Lots of kids buy from him."

"I want his name."

"No."

"You're in no position to hold out on me."

Dylan squirmed. One moment he appeared embarrassed, the next angry.

"Did you know your sister's dead because some guy took drugs?"

Dylan's face changed in an instant. "What do you mean? They said he'd been drinking."

"Yeah, but he also took cocaine."

Dylan hung his head.

"Son, all of this stuff is really bad. You'll have your driver's license soon. Just one high and you could kill somebody's daughter, somebody's sister."

Dylan didn't respond.

"You know how stupid it is to do drugs? It starts with marijuana, but it usually doesn't stop there. I see the results all the time. I see kids shoplift to pay for their habit. They steal from their parents and their brothers and sisters."

"I don't have a brother or sister."

Adam stopped. Tears found their way out. How had this happened? He looked up. Dylan was crying too.

"After she died, I smoked some more dope. Then Jeremy

sold me the patch. I wanted to die. Didn't want to hurt any-more. That's why I used it."

Adam got up and sat on the bed next to Dylan and hugged him.

"I felt like I wanted to die too, Son. I understand that part." Adam moved back. "Buddy, why didn't you tell me?"

"Tell you I took drugs? Oh yeah, that would have gone over *real* well."

"I would have helped you."

"No, you wouldn't. You would have made me quit track. You'd have taken away my video games. And you would have locked me in my room while you played Yahtzee with Emily!"

Adam took deep breaths, deliberately keeping his temper in check. Though Dylan's words stung, the last thing either of them needed was for Adam to lash out in his own defense. But after sifting through dozens of possible responses, none of them seemed adequate. Honestly, could he be sure he wouldn't have responded the way Dylan described? "We need to talk more. But my relationship with you is more important to me than anything I have to say to you."

They sat quietly. Finally Adam said, "Do you feel up to a run?"

Dylan considered his options. "Okay."

"Good. Let's go."

After their run, Adam and Dylan sat in the driveway and talked for another thirty minutes. While Dylan headed for the shower, Adam came into the kitchen and was pleased Victoria's color had returned.

"You and Dylan shouldn't consider housecleaning as a busi-ness," Victoria said, wiping sticky spots off the floor.

"Sorry. I told him he needs to tell you about the drugs. I'll be there too."

"I appreciate that."

His mom's tears moved Dylan. He apologized, then asked her forgiveness. The three of them hugged. Adam prayed.

Afterward Victoria leaned against the dresser in their bedroom. "How on earth did you know where to look?"

"I thought about where I used to hide things from my parents."

"Same place you hide things from me?"

"What?" Adam's face flushed.

Victoria opened the closet door and reached up on her tiptoes. She edged a box off the shelf. "So what's in here?"

"It's a gun box. You're scared of guns, aren't you?"

"Which is what made it the perfect hiding place."

She opened the box and removed what Adam had thought was safe. She held it up and waved it in his face.

His eyes dropped. "How long have you known?"

"Maybe two years. I check it a few times a week, and I see the stuff that comes and goes. Guess I should have checked on my son like I did on my husband."

He looked up.

She held it up in front of him again. "You had to hide this from me?" She took a bite of it.

"Hey, don't," Adam said.

"Not bad," she said. "What is it?"

Adam shuffled his feet. "A raspberry cruller."

"From the Donut Factory?" She took another big bite.

"From the office."

"Where do they get them?"

"Krispy Kreme."

She finished it, smacked her lips, and licked her fingers.

"You're a mean woman," Adam said.

"Is this all you're hiding?"

"Yes."

"Then I guess it's okay."

"It is?"

She grinned. "I've kept a stash of dark chocolate for years."

"Where?"

"Why would I tell you?"

"I told you about mine!"

"No, you didn't. I found it myself. And I never bother it either." She hesitated. "Okay, one time I had a maple bar."

"I knew I'd put it in there! I looked through three other boxes. Thief!"

"Then there was that bear claw, but I replaced it."

Adam smiled. "Apparently Dylan came by his hiding habit honestly. Well, maybe I should say *naturally*."

"Yeah, it's just that his stuff is a lot more dangerous. Not to mention illegal." She searched Adam's eyes. "He seems to be a casual user, not an addict, right?"

"I think that's true."

"Do you think we got through to him?"

"After we ran, he told me it's hard when so many other kids talk about experimenting with drugs."

"That makes sense. It's hard for kids to go against the flow."

Adam breathed deeply. "This is tough. Tougher than I bargained for when I wrote the points of the Resolution. One thing for sure, I can't do this without you."

After a few minutes of silence she asked, "What are you thinking about?"

"Honestly?"

"Yeah."

"That I'm trained in search and seizure. And I'm gonna take this place apart till I find your dark chocolate."

"You'll never find it."

"If I don't, I'm bringing home Chopper the drug dog. I'll have his handler familiarize him with the scent of dark chocolate. Chopper will find it before you can say *hot fudge*."

Victoria shook her head. "Not if I eat it first."

CHAPTER TWENTY-FIVE

WITH THE FLINT RIVER behind them, five men and their families mingled on a gorgeous manicured lawn, awaiting the Resolution ceremony. Everyone wore their best.

Adam approached his pastor. "Glad you came, Jon. If you hadn't encouraged me to study what the Bible says about fatherhood, we wouldn't be here today."

"I wouldn't have missed it. I love this Resolution! My kids are grown, but the principles apply to grandfathers and mentors of young men. This shouldn't just stay with the five of you. It should be presented to fathers everywhere."

"But how would we do that? We're in Albany, Georgia—not a likely place to reach dads around the world."

"And David the shepherd boy wasn't a likely choice for king either. But with God, nothing's impossible. I have some ideas about the Resolution that I want to talk to you about. But first, let's see what God does today."

Across the lawn, Nathan Hayes talked and laughed with his mentor of twenty years, William Barrett. William silently recalled how he'd almost given up on Nathan. It was hard

enough to raise his own family. And "that Hayes kid" hadn't
always looked like a great investment. In retrospect, his decision
was one of the most strategic he'd ever made—already affecting
future generations.

When the time came to begin, William Barrett solemnly
took his place in front of the group, next to a table with a white
cloth. On the table lay five documents, each with black frames
under them.

"I can't tell you what an honor this is for me," William said.
"To hear the stand that you men are taking for your faith and
your families overwhelms me. May God bless the commitment
you make today.

"Nathan Hayes, I'd like you to face me and for your wife and
children to stand beside me."

Nathan walked to the center of the semicircle of men and
their families. He wondered how many of William Barrett's
white hairs he'd caused. He considered how different his life
would be if this man had given up on him. Nathan knew
William had prepared him to believe in God the Father by
making the very word *father* seem welcome to him for the first
time in his life.

"Nathan . . . my son in the faith," William began. Nathan
could see how close Mr. Barrett's emotions were to the surface.

"I took joy in mentoring you as a young man. Today I take
joy in blessing you as a godly father. Are you ready to make this
commitment before God and your family?"

"Yes, sir, I am."

"Then I'd like you to repeat after me. . . ."

One by one, witnessed by their families and their God, the
five men stood before William and repeated the words of their
Resolution.

"I do solemnly resolve before God
    To take full responsibility for myself, my wife, and my
children.
    I will love them, protect them, and serve them
    And teach them the Word of God as the spiritual leader
of my home."

Adam stole glances at Victoria and Dylan as he made his pledge.

"I will be faithful to my wife, to love and honor her
    And be willing to lay down my life for her, as Christ
did for me.
    I will teach my children to love God with all their
hearts, minds, and strength.
    I will train them to honor authority and live
responsibly."

When Shane Fuller took his place, only his son was there to witness the promises he made. Shane gazed into Tyler's eyes and spoke the words of his commitment.

"I will confront evil, pursue justice, and love mercy.
    I will pray for others and treat them with kindness,
respect, and compassion."

When his turn came, Javier Martinez proudly stepped forward in the first new suit he'd owned. He was proud to face his family and vow always to be the man they needed him to be.

"I will work diligently to provide for the needs of my
family."

David Thomson felt honored to stand among these older men. No family was there with him, but for a fleeting moment, David imagined a woman and her daughter there, loving him and looking to him for leadership.

"I will speak truthfully and keep my promises.
I will forgive those who have wronged me and reconcile
with those I have wronged."

Each man repeated the entire Resolution in an air of seriousness and dignity.

"I will learn from my mistakes, repent of my sins, and
walk with integrity as a man answerable to God.
I will seek to honor God, be faithful to His church,
obey His Word, and do His will.
I will courageously work with the strength God
provides to fulfill this Resolution for the rest of my life and
for His glory."

Finally, on behalf of all, Adam spoke the Scripture he'd written beneath the Resolution: "'Choose for yourselves this day whom you will serve . . . As for me and my household, we will serve the Lord.'"

After the five men finished making this declaration, they moved as one to the printed Resolutions at the table. Each picked up an attractive wooden pen Kayla had selected. Each signed. Nathan was last, weighing every word before putting his name to paper. He looked longest and hardest at one particular statement: *"I will forgive those who have wronged me and reconcile with those I have wronged."*

William Barrett said, "Now that each of you has committed

to live by this Resolution, I bless you in the name of the Lord. May His favor rest on you and give you strength and grace."

The men relaxed, thinking the ceremony was over, but William spoke again, and everyone snapped to attention because of his serious tone.

"But I also have a warning. Now that you know what you are to do and have committed before God and these witnesses, you are doubly accountable. You may have confidence in your resolve now. But be assured, to keep it will require *courage*. And you will not be able to remain courageous without the help of God Almighty."

Back home at their kitchen counter, Adam asked Victoria to talk.

"Pastor Rogers said he didn't think we should keep the Resolution to ourselves. He said other fathers might want to sign it."

"I think he's right," Victoria said. "Anyone who witnessed what I saw today would feel the same."

Adam considered. "We won't be able to fulfill these promises without God's grace and power. And without each other's help. But it sure means the world to have my wife support me."

"It's true; you don't deserve me." Victoria drew him near.

She pointed to the Resolution. "Well, are you going to hang this?"

"Actually, I'd like to hang it right now—where it will be a reminder to me and you and Dylan."

"Today it felt like you were repeating your marriage vows. Only this time I think it meant more to me."

"Why?"

"We were sincere when we said our vows. But I don't think

back then we understood what they meant. 'For better or for worse' covers a lot of ground, doesn't it?"

He nodded.

"Sometimes I've thought, 'If Adam had known what marriage was really like, he wouldn't have made that commitment.' But you're doing this now with eyes wide-open. You've chosen to recommit yourself. I don't know how to say it, but . . . I guess you've made me feel loved. Thank you."

"I'm sorry I've been a selfish jerk and you had to doubt my commitment to you."

"Well, you haven't *always* been a selfish jerk."

"Thanks!"

She put her head on his shoulder.

Adam called for Dylan and pointed to the Resolution on the table. "This is what I want to do, Son. This is who I want to be. Sometimes I'll fail. When I do, please forgive me. With God's help I *will* be a better father. Would you sign here at the bottom as a witness to my commitment?"

Dylan signed.

Adam sensed his son's cautiousness about whether this was a real change.

Fair enough. He has the right to wait and see. Time will *tell.*

"Victoria?"

She signed it, then raised her eyebrows. "Does this mean I'm supposed to remind you of this commitment when I think you're not living up to it?"

"Yes. Preferably with respect and gentleness. I'll need your help with this. So I really *do* want you to remind me. You too, Dylan."

They agreed.

"Let's get it in this frame, and I'll hang it."

"You're putting it on the wall?" Dylan said.

"Yes, I am."

"Where? There's no room."

Adam took down a prominent wall hanging, then pointed to the space he had created. "Right there."

Dylan looked wide-eyed. "You're retiring *Steve Bartkowski*?"

"We'll just have to find a less prominent spot for Steve."

"Where?"

"I'm not sure."

"Can he move to my room?"

Adam started to say no. Then he said, "Sure, buddy. Steve would be honored to hang in your room."

Dylan smiled and immediately left with the photo.

"Smart kid," Victoria said. "He didn't give you time to change your mind."

"Actually, I feel pretty good he even wanted it. Bartkowski was my hero, not his."

"Keep it up and he may have a new hero."

CHAPTER TWENTY-SIX

ANTICIPATION WAS HIGH at the Hayes home as a feast of enormous proportions was prepared in honor of William Barrett and Nathan Hayes. Jackson, though too young to understand, caught some of the excitement of a day that would shape his life. Five-year-old Jordan just knew his mother was happy, that she was fixing a fancy dinner, and that his sister worked with her in the kitchen, too busy to be bothered if Jordan played with her things, which took the fun out of it.

Kayla was overjoyed to welcome Nathan's mentor into their home. She realized yet again that the greater part of her life as she knew it was due to this man's influence.

William Barrett had always reminded Kayla of her own father. So she decided to prepare an old-fashioned Southern dinner like her mama used to fix. Kayla shared her cooking secrets with her assistant chef, Jade, who enjoyed the experience but didn't admit it.

Kayla put ham hocks in the pot and poured in some bacon grease.

"Boy, oh boy! Those smells are enough to make me think I've died and gone to heaven." William Barrett and Nathan

Hayes inhaled deeply. This delighted Kayla, but true to tradition, she snapped a dishrag at the men, shooing them out of the kitchen.

Kayla showed Jade how to wash and cut the greens just like Aunt Flora used to do. Kayla mixed the cornmeal, then at the right time added the greens to the pot of ham hocks and bacon grease. Water drops sizzled, the grease started soaking up, and the scent was sensational.

When Kayla saw Nathan and William peek in again, she took up her mother's role. "Nathan Hayes, I declare! And William Barrett, what kind of example are you? Get your man paws out of my kitchen, and stop torturing yourselves!"

William Barrett grinned like a little boy. It pleased Kayla that he was so obviously enjoying himself. Kayla had prepared just about every food William loved best. She watched as he breathed in the aromas with conspicuous delight. Nathan's history of black Southern cooking had been shorter and not as rich, but she knew his mouth watered nonetheless.

When all was ready, Kayla paraded into the dining room with Mama's dressing, loaded with onions and peppers and celery, and positioned it in the center of the table. One by one, big plates filled the table—collard greens, butter beans, and crowder peas.

William Barrett leaned over the table. "Mm, mm, MMM!"

"Now there's a man with convictions," Kayla said.

Jade brought in a large side of macaroni and cheese, then candied yams. Kayla brought in a plate heaped with fried catfish, then smaller bowls of okra and corn.

William Barrett said, "This reminds me of Jackson, Mississippi, where the sign at Mama's Kitchen says, 'When You Can't Go to Mama's, Come See Us.' But, Kayla, my dear, this smells even better than Mama's!"

Nathan looked at his wife and smiled. The mention of Mama's made him think of his. She had died too young, worn-out from raising all those boys on her own. She'd have been proud of Kayla and her grandchildren. And delighted to know that William Barrett was still her son's mentor. He knew she had thanked God this man had taken an interest in Nathan. Mama had often said she wished there had been a William Barrett for each of her sons.

"Now, I went small on the fried chicken and pork chops," Kayla said. "But there will be plenty for you to take home, William. Hope you all like this meal because you'll be eatin' it the next four days!"

William looked like a kid in a candy shop. "Just fry it up and you can't go too wrong, Mama always used to say."

"Wait, I forgot something."

She marched back in with a basket, which she handed to Nathan.

"Hush puppies! I'm in hog heaven!"

Kayla stood at the table like it was a pulpit. "Now, when a Southern woman goes to the trouble of fixin' up a meal, you eat it till it's comin' out your ears, and when she asks if you want more, you say, 'Yes, ma'am,' and that's all there is to it."

They held hands, and Nathan thanked God for the beautiful ceremony and prayed that he would be a better husband and father than he'd ever been.

Then he asked William Barrett to pray. "O great God and Father, thank You again for the Resolution and for all it means. May it change the lives of these families. Thank You for my son Nathan and his commitment to his beautiful wife and children. And thank You for Kayla and Jade and their hard work preparing this food. In Jesus' name. Amen."

After he loaded up his plate, Nathan picked up corn bread

and mixed it with his fingers into the collard greens. The salty, grease-soaked greens attracted stray crumbs like a magnet draws iron filings. He licked his lips. This was eatin'. Then he looked at Kayla and mouthed, "I love you."

She looked back at him, and he saw in her eyes a love and loyalty so fierce that it nearly took his breath away.

CHAPTER TWENTY-SEVEN

ADAM AND SHANE walked up the front porch steps of a small, run-down house in southwest Albany. Nathan and David parked in the back. Nathan stood at the rear left corner of the house, and David stood in his line of sight at the right corner, at the bottom of the back porch steps.

"You ready this time?" Nathan asked into his radio, only half-joking as he remembered the Holloman brothers' house.

"That won't happen again," David whispered his reply, eyes riveted on the exit point.

Adam knocked on the front door. No one answered. He tried the knob and the door slipped open. He pushed it slowly, looked inside, then walked in cautiously. Shane followed close behind.

"Sheriff's department. We have a search warrant. Sheriff's department," he repeated. It helped in court if you could swear you clearly identified yourself twice.

Silence. He looked around the living room and noticed rectangular holes in the matted orange carpet where heating vents belonged.

Shane eyed the front and back doors.

A newspaper covered something on the couch. Adam removed it. An open shoe box held about ten small plastic bags of white powder.

"693c to S.O., we need an inspector at the 400 block of Wayland. House 419, narcotics."

"10-4, 693c."

Adam continued through the house; its few pieces of furniture looked like thrift store rejects. He approached the bedroom, prepared to point his weapon and shout a warning. All he saw was a dirty mattress, a worn blanket, and strewn clothes. He glanced to his left and right, then went out the back door to where David waited at the base of the steps.

"Seems to be clear," Adam said.

"You sure?" Shane said over the radio. "It doesn't feel right. I say they wouldn't leave the dope on the couch unless they were nearby."

"I checked, but I'll double-check," Adam said.

He stepped back into the house; Nathan waved David to follow.

Adam walked into the bathroom and cautiously approached the drawn shower curtain. A movie scene came to mind. Seemed like eerie music should be playing.

Dreading a reverse scene from *Psycho*, Adam took a breath, then flung open the shower curtain.

Empty.

David walked in the living room and looked down at the shoe box on the couch.

"Don't touch it, Rookie," Shane called. "Gotta photograph it first."

"Cocaine?"

"Yeah. I still say they wouldn't leave it out unless they're nearby."

"You guys checked everywhere?" David asked.

David reached for the hall closet door. As he opened it, something pushed back with great force, knocking him against the wall. A huge muscular man lunged out, grabbed David, and flung him down the hallway. David immediately jumped to his feet. He stood between the man and the door.

"I'm gonna tase you," Shane warned and fired the Taser just as the man pushed David back into the couch. The confetti with the Taser's ID numbers on it flew freely, but only one of the two probes hit, making it worthless.

The attacker grabbed a chair and threw it at Shane, who ducked, then loaded another Taser cartridge and fired again. He gave him the full five-second ride. But it just made the guy mad.

Adam jumped on his back, forcing him into the wall. Adam tried to put him in a headlock, but the man spun around. Adam's legs smashed into an old recliner.

"Tase him! Tase him!" Adam shouted. David drew his Taser, locked in, and fired just as the man turned. The tase hit Adam, confetti flying again.

Adam writhed in agony. "Not me! The other guy!"

The assailant knocked Shane onto a table, breaking it.

David fired his second tase, this time hitting him optimally, in the middle and upper back. Stunned, the man lunged at David and shoved him into Shane. All three hit the floor. The man screamed but got back to his feet and headed for the front door.

Nathan charged in and tackled him to the floor. The two wrestled, but when he broke free, Shane applied his Taser directly to his lower back and performed a drive stun. He spoke his warning right as he fired the Taser. The man screamed and hit the floor on his stomach.

Nathan jumped him, pulling his Taser. "Put your hands behind your back. No more movements or we'll tase you till the cows come home!"

The man scrambled to get up. Nathan squeezed the trigger and zapped him, sending him back on his stomach. This time he didn't move.

While Shane pulled one wrist back and Adam the other, David applied his handcuffs quickly.

"We got him?" Adam asked breathlessly.

"He should be a UFC cage fighter."

"I think he is."

"He could probably bench-press 350."

"Better get those estimates up." Shane leaned against the couch. "It took four of us to subdue him."

David nodded. "I'd say 450."

Adam grimaced.

"You okay?" Nathan asked.

"My back's out. The only thing worse is my neck. Where your partner tased me."

David used a chair to pull himself up. "I got the guy on the second round."

Nathan rose to his knees and reached for Adam.

Adam took his hand but moved gingerly. "Easy. Give me a second."

Suddenly Sergeant Bronson exploded through the door, a millisecond before his cigar odor.

He stopped and gave them a once-over. "What are you ladies doin' on the floor?"

"We had a fight," Adam said.

"You lost. Bad."

"We're not the ones in handcuffs."

"Looks like a Main Street parade with all this confetti. You the grand marshal, Mitchell?" He looked at the various confetti groupings. "Three Taser rounds? Four?"

"Four, I think," Shane said, groaning.

"My advice? Try one Taser, and if it doesn't work, warn him, and if he resists, shoot him in his center body mass. Tell yourself, 'I'm goin' home tonight.' If they make it a civil case, so be it. I'd rather be tried by twelve than carried by six."

"It would take more than six to carry him," Shane whispered.

Bronson put his fingers on the felon's neck, checking his pulse.

"This is quite a house you chose to have your little tea party in." He touched the sheetrock. "You could throw a cat through these walls. Maybe I better take this guy in, to be sure he gets there."

Adam shook his head. "No way are you getting credit for this bust."

Bronson knelt to examine the drug evidence spread out on the floor behind the couch.

Shane raised his eyebrows at Nathan. "We'll tase you *till the cows come home?*"

"An old expression of my mother's."

"Your mother used to tase you?"

"She'd say, 'I'll *spank* you till the cows come home.'"

"Did it work?"

"No."

Bronson, still behind the overturned couch, said, "She should have used the Taser."

CHAPTER TWENTY-EIGHT

VICTORIA SAT on the bed next to Adam, examining his swollen face. "You look beat."

"Only because I am."

"Sure you don't want to call off this evening?"

"No way. The Holts have been on the calendar for weeks."

Victoria held his hand. "You know what? I'm encouraged about Dylan. Since we discovered the drugs, it's like a load's been lifted off him. I'm so glad he was at the ceremony. He's proud of you. And you've set an example for him—given him something to live up to."

"Now's the real test, though. William Barrett was right. It will take courage. And we can't be courageous without God's grace and strength." Adam's eyes sought hers. "I'd like us to start praying together and sharing what we learn in the Word."

"Okay," Victoria said. "I guess that means I'd better learn something from the Word, right? When would we do this?"

"Could we try after breakfast, when Dylan's gone for school? If we're dressed and ready to go, we'll have thirty minutes before I leave for work."

"Every day?"

"How about Monday, Wednesday, and Friday?"

"Monday morning it is."

"You're smiling at me."

"I just realized something. If you're going to be the spiritual leader, you'll need me to follow!"

"Are you up for that?"

"Hey, if you're gonna man up, I can woman up!"

Adam looked like he wanted to say more.

"What is it?"

"You know how you've told me I've become more and more cynical as the years go on?"

"Yeah?"

"Well, that made me defensive."

"I noticed."

"You were right. I'm determined to get on top of it. But I do want you to understand why I'm cynical so you can help me."

"I think I understand, but please tell me."

"I see the worst in people's behavior. People lie to cops about everything. Eventually you assume everyone's lying. Remember how you used to say I was idealistic?"

"It's been a long time."

Adam winced when he leaned against the headboard. "Other cops made fun of me. I believed the best about people, but I gradually changed. When your expectations are low, you're not as disappointed."

"And other cops don't think you're gullible and naive."

"Exactly. Jeff used to say, 'In God we trust; all others are suspects.'"

Victoria shook her head. "Jeff stopped trusting Emma. He ran checks on numbers she'd called."

"When the Kellers first came to our church and invited Dylan over to spend the night, I ran a criminal background check. You think, 'What's the harm?' And what if I found out later the man's a criminal? When I'm cynical, there's no one at work to talk me down from it. Shane's more cynical than I am. We see the whole world through the lens of our job."

"Fathers should be protective, of course. But there's a limit. Like when the guy from the mariachi band touched Emily's shoulder. You nearly came unglued."

He pointed. "My ankle still hurts where you kicked me."

"But I had to get your attention. All these years when I've mentioned stuff like this, you've pulled rank, saying you're a cop, so you knew what people were like, and I didn't."

"You're right. I've done that. And I'm sorry. Forgive me?"

Victoria looked him in the eyes. "I do forgive you."

"Anyway, I've made a decision."

"You're retiring from police work to try out for the Atlanta Falcons?"

"No, but it feels almost as . . . unlikely. I've decided I'd like to talk to you more about . . . what's going on inside me."

"Sounds good. The Bible says I'm supposed to be your helper. I can't help when you shut me out."

"I did that when Jeff . . . died. And for a while after Emily died."

Victoria heard loneliness in Adam's words. "God put me here for you, Adam. We've talked about Emily now, and that's been good. But we never talked about Jeff. That was so hard on you. I wanted to help you. But you wouldn't let me in."

"I do want to talk to you about that. Not tonight, but soon. I mean, about Jeff's suicide and what the psychologist said."

Victoria blinked. "You saw a psychologist?"

"No. A police psychologist talked to all of us about cops and suicide, before Jeff's funeral."

"Why didn't I know about that?"

"Because . . . I didn't want to worry you. Anyway, on the cynicism thing, I think you can talk me down from it, remind me of the good around us—that God has a plan and one day He'll turn this upside-down world right side up."

"I have to remind myself every day. I'll put you in the loop."

Adam smiled. "It's funny—Nathan is the best cop influence I've ever had. He's a serious Christian. Still, he's a cop. But I've noticed when I'm around Javy, he energizes me. He's so . . . I don't know . . ."

"Childlike," Victoria said. "In the best sense—not immature, just kind of innocent."

"Exactly! You can be positive like that, Victoria. And you know me better than anyone."

"I'm really glad you opened up to me. What made you decide to?"

"I've been thinking about the Resolution. Yeah, I want to be a better husband. But I want you to be my best friend. And best friends tell each other what's inside, right?"

Victoria hugged him. "Adam Mitchell . . . the other day when you gave me roses, it meant a lot to me. But what you just said may be the best gift ever."

★ ★ ★

When Caleb and Catherine Holt arrived at the Mitchells' home, they sat down to a table heaped with comfort food. A platter piled with Southern fried chicken, mounds of mashed potatoes with butter dripping down the sides, and a big bowl of green beans cooked with bacon.

Adam touched his face. "Before we dig in to this feast, I want to clarify that it wasn't Victoria who beat me up. She's capable of throwing a sucker punch, but that's not what happened."

They all laughed as he told the story over dinner. After a

dozen cop and firefighter stories, Dylan excused himself to finish homework. The couples migrated to the living room. Catherine and Caleb sat on the love seat near the fireplace; Adam and Victoria settled on the couch.

Victoria fidgeted. "Adam and I regret that we never properly thanked you for the way you treated us at the hospital the night that Emily died. And then for coming to her funeral. Your support meant a lot."

"No need to thank us," Catherine said. "All of us on duty that day were deeply touched. We deal with crises all the time, but that day in the chapel at Phoebe Putney Memorial, a dozen people at a time prayed for your family. People prayed in the hallways and at workstations. I'd never met you, but Caleb said he knew you from the Responder Life breakfast."

Victoria said, "Caleb, when they told us you gave Emily CPR, I thought our little girl was in good hands before the Lord took her."

Caleb sat a little straighter. "Thank you. I wish we could have saved her, but God knows. She hung by a thread. As I worked on her, I felt like . . . I don't know . . . I felt like an angel of God was right there watching over her. It was very real. I told Catherine that night, it was a sacred experience. Emily was so . . . peaceful."

Adam squeezed Victoria's hand as tears streamed down their cheeks.

After he regained composure, Adam said, "We should have invited you over long ago."

"We thought about asking you over too," Catherine said. "But we didn't want to intrude. People are different. Some want to talk; some don't. When I was at the hospital that day, I've never seen so many people want to do something, anything, for Emily."

"I didn't know that," Adam said.

"After Adam and I finally left that emergency room, we didn't want to leave the hospital." Victoria paused. "We weren't ready to admit that Emily had died. It was wonderful how they set up that waiting room just for us, where we could just sit and be with our friends."

"That was Catherine," Caleb said.

"It was no big deal. I wanted you to have some privacy. We don't have children of our own. But if we did, I would want . . ."

Suddenly Catherine put a hand to her face. Caleb stretched his arm around her. Now it was Adam and Victoria's turn to wait.

Catherine finally laughed through her tears. "Well, I didn't expect that!"

Victoria said, "I take it you'd like to have children?"

Catherine nodded. "We've been trying a long time."

"The good news," Caleb said, "is that we're finally on a waiting list to adopt."

Catherine put her hands together. "In another few months we could get the call and suddenly fly off to China to get our child! We said we're open to one with special needs."

"That's great," Adam said. "Caleb, I know you'll be an excellent father."

Catherine looked at her husband. "Yes, he definitely will."

Victoria served them each a piece of lemon pie with whipped cream. They consumed a pot of decaf, and the evening went quickly. Hours passed like minutes.

Just after midnight the Holts stood to leave. Everybody hugged. Though they'd barely known each other six hours earlier, the combination of laughter, tears, prayers, and shared dreams sealed their friendship in a single night.

CHAPTER TWENTY-NINE

ALONE IN HIS APARTMENT, in jeans and an old red-and-white Valdosta State T-shirt, David Thomson sat with his laptop at the kitchen table, glancing every now and then at the Resolution on the living room wall. He didn't have to make room when he hung it—his walls were mostly bare. He'd selected a spot where he could see it from his beanbag chair and from the kitchen table.

He felt as if he'd signed the Declaration of Independence. David had won awards, most of them athletic, but he'd never signed a document and hung it on a wall.

For once, David did not feel alone. He was part of something bigger than himself. Part of a common cause with his friends, guys he respected, who meant the world to him.

He imagined himself in Philips Arena with 18,000 people watching the Hawks play basketball. Except this time *he* was on the court. And it wasn't just a game. It was *real* life—a battle of its own, far more important than any game.

He stared at his laptop's screen, squared his shoulders, then began to type.

Amanda,

I know it's probably a shock for you to hear from me. But I need to tell you what's happened in my life. In the last two years, I've become a deputy for the Dougherty County Sheriff's Department. The job is tough, but I work with some of the best guys in the world. Being a cop has forced me to see how one person's selfish decisions can hurt many others.

Recently I had a life-changing experience. I began a relationship with God through Jesus Christ. I've still got a lot to work on, but He's helping me make some sense of my life and become a better man.

For years, I've been afraid to admit that I have a daughter and have done nothing to help take care of her.

I know how wrong I've been. I'm ashamed of myself. I've asked God to forgive me. I'm writing this letter to tell you that I've decided to stop running.

If you are willing, I'd like to meet with you and begin the process of rebuilding your trust. In time and with your permission, I hope to meet Olivia and let her know that she has a father who cares about her.

I have no other expectations. I only ask for a chance to be a part of Olivia's life. I will wait for your response.

Until then, I'll pray for you and Olivia. I have enclosed a symbol of my commitment to help with her care.

Sincerely,
David Thomson

He printed the letter, signed it, addressed the envelope, and enclosed a check.

"Okay, God," he said softly. "Do whatever You want to do. I'm ready."

Amanda walked to the house and sat at her faded Formica kitchen table. Filled with curiosity and fear and a hope so distant she didn't recognize it as such, she read the letter. The check was for $500. She stared at it.

There must be some mistake.

She watched as Olivia played with her toys on the old coffee table. Amanda read the letter again.

What does this mean?

★ ★ ★

Adam knocked, then opened Dylan's door. "Hey, Son. What are you doing?"

"Just playing a video game."

"Got a question for you. Have you ever seen a movie called *Chariots of Fire?*"

"Don't think so."

"Well, it got the Oscar for best picture in 1981."

"What's it about?"

"Runners. And the Olympics. And a lot more. I picked up the DVD today. Want to watch it with me tomorrow night? Popcorn, Doritos, drinks are on me."

Dylan nodded, looking skeptical but polite.

"Okay, Son, so tell me about the video game you're playing."

"Why?"

"Because it's something that interests my son. So I want to learn about it."

An hour later, Dylan had taught his dad about preferred armament, ranged and melee attacks, "weapons-grenades-melee," hit points, recharging energy shields, and dual wielding. Adam tried the game, which caused both of them to laugh. But he picked it up quickly.

Adam told Dylan that some of it was like what he did as a cop on the firing range. Dylan seemed interested. Adam invited him to come and watch him at the range. Dylan said he'd like to.

Wow. I'll put in a request tomorrow.

Fifteen minutes after leaving Dylan's room, Adam sat in the living room reading. Dylan approached him, holding out a paper bag.

"That's all of it," Dylan said.

"All of what?" Adam opened the bag and found a small bong and some marijuana.

"I had another hiding place," Dylan said. "I haven't touched it since you found the other bag. But I figured I should give you the rest of it."

Kayla sat down with Nathan after the kids were in bed.

"At the center today, I counseled a girl from Albany High. She's Jade's age. Gave her the pregnancy test. She wanted to fail, but it was positive. I'm glad she came in, but, Nathan, I don't know what goes through these kids' minds. They don't think about consequences."

"Will she have the baby?"

"At first she said no. Just came for the free test, but if pregnant, her plan was abortion. We barely talked her into an ultrasound. When she saw it, the girl said, 'They told me it wasn't a baby. But look!' Once she saw the baby, she couldn't believe the lie. One of the staff is following up to help her decide whether she'll raise the child or place him for adoption. Nathan, I keep thinking, if only I'd gone to a center like ours nineteen years ago . . ." Kayla wiped her eyes.

Nathan hugged her, tight and long.

"It's tough out there," Kayla said.

"And the toughest part is, we've got to send our kids out into that world. Jade's not ready."

"We do our best."

"Do we? I don't know. But I meant what I said in the Resolution. I won't be a passive dad. Jade may not like it. Sometimes you might not like it. But I've got to be God's man and lead this family. I'll make mistakes, but I refuse to do nothing."

"Sometimes doing nothing is wise."

"Sometimes. But when that gangster drove off with Jackson, doing nothing might have cost us our son. And right now, Jade's heart is in danger of being stolen by a young man. And I don't care if that boy's an honor student or the Prince of Wales, I need to take hold of the wheel."

Kayla frowned. "You know I agreed with you about Derrick when he first dropped by. I was ready to write him off. But Jade told me that wasn't fair. I think she's right. I mean, he looks like a responsible young man, honor student, no police record, and they just want permission to hang out together with other kids there. It's not a one-on-one date."

Nathan shook his head. "It might not start one-on-one, but it would go there. I'm convinced it would be a mistake to let this go further. I think I should take the lead on this."

"Are you saying I should stay out of it?"

"No. I just think if God has made me responsible for this family, He's given me the authority to lead it. And, Kayla, I know young men, what's inside of them, way better than you do. The question is, do you really want me to lead? Because when I do, it means sometimes I'll lead us where you may not want to go."

Kayla shook her head. "I'm not so sure about all this. I think of myself as your equal."

"So do I. Always. You have equal value, equal wisdom, and far greater beauty and charm. In a lot of ways, you're smarter than I am. But remember, the leader answers to God. It's not an easy job."

Kayla gazed at him. "Well, I will say this. I *liked* that part about beauty and charm. Sometimes, Nathan Hayes, you have exceptional insights! *Sometimes.*"

"Yo, TJ, what's poppin'?"

TJ shook his head in disgust at Chewy, who'd been his most promising Gangster Nation soldier only a year ago. "You wasted, dawg. Where your teeth go? Why they let you in here?"

"Heard 5-0 collared Big Leon. It really take four 5-0s with Tasers to put him down?"

"Stop actin' like you still a player, man. You nothin'."

TJ looked Chewy up and down. Chewy used to be ripped. For a while he'd worked out with TJ, Antoine, and Leon. Now he looked pathetic. "You stink, sucka."

"Gotta have the rock, TJ."

"You gotta *pay* for the rock. Why you comin' to me? I sell to ballers, not junkies."

"I all cashed out, brah. You said you'd always take care of me."

"Only when you took care of me. You was one fine delivery boy, but you got bit by the product."

"Can't help it, man."

"Don't come whinin' to me. You ain't got no more bones."

"Need a place to crash, man."

"Go to your own crib."

"Mama kicked me out. Locks the doors. Sisters won't let me in either."

"'Cause you been stealin' from 'em, lyin', and cheatin', huh, tiny? You deebo yo mama's credit card?"

"How you know that?"

"It's what the rock does. It's da masta; you da slave. Price you pay. If people not payin' the price, TJ wouldn't be makin' the bank. You can't handle the big stuff, you shoulda just stuck with hood scratch, man."

"I keep crashin', man. Goin' through the jonesin'. Bugs crawlin' under my skin. Big ones. Freakin' me."

"You a sorry fool. Look at you, all raggedy and geeked up."

"Scared of everything now, TJ. Tired, man, so tired. They're comin' after me."

"Who's comin' after you, fool?"

Chewy hadn't stood still since he'd arrived. Now his fidgets and twitches became spasms. His hands moved constantly, scratching at his face and arms one moment and reaching out the next in shaky gesticulations as if to ward off something unseen.

"Spirits. With big mouths. Sharp teeth. They tryin' to swallow me up. Help me, TJ!"

"One day them demons with the big mouths and sharp teeth?" TJ grabbed a clump of Chewy's sparse hair and pulled him close. "They gonna eat yo flesh and pick their teeth with yo bones. Whachu think about that?"

"No! No! Help me, man! Please help me."

TJ threw him to the ground. "Time for you to bounce, fool!" TJ gestured to Antoine. "Take out the trash."

Emily stood on the lawn by the driver's side door of his truck. She held out her hand to her father.

"Daddy, come dance with me."

Adam wanted to follow her lead, but his arms were frozen.

"Please, Daddy! Just for this song. Come dance with me."

"Corporal Mitchell. Hey, Mitchell!"

Sergeant Murphy?

Adam found himself in the muster room; the other officers stared.

"I'm sorry. I . . . uh . . ."

Brad Bronson looked away, embarrassed for Adam. But Adam was embarrassed enough. He didn't need any help.

Murphy continued, "With the three arrested yesterday, that's sixty burglary suspects we've rounded up this month. Yesterday at McKinley Street, we arrested three suspects affiliated with the Gangster Nation. We confiscated a load of handgun ammo, shotgun shells, and two assault knives with nine-inch blades."

Shane nudged Adam. Adam gestured that he was fine.

He wasn't.

CHAPTER THIRTY

JAVIER MARTINEZ was filling spools at the thread factory when a custodian wearing coke-bottle glasses tapped him on the shoulder and spoke loudly into his ear. "Boss wants to see you."

Javier cringed. *Last time a boss wanted to see me, I lost my job.*

He walked down the hallway to the office of Frank Tyson, factory manager. Javier knocked. Mr. Tyson's assistant, Walter, opened the door, then stepped aside for Javy.

"Mr. Martinez, have a seat," Frank Tyson quietly commanded from his chair in the paneled office.

"Thank you, sir."

Javier tried not to fidget like Carmen said he did when nervous. He focused on the man sitting across the desk. Medium build, with thinning black hair and a quiet, confident air, Frank Tyson examined a sheet of paper on his desk while he spoke.

"I see you've been very productive in your first month here. You do good work."

Javier smiled. "I'm grateful to be here."

"Mr. Martinez, I need an additional manager to oversee inventory and shipping. It carries more responsibility and would pay more. Is that something you'd be interested in?"

"Oh *yes*, sir."

"Good. Before I make my final decision, I'd like you to take a shift next week in that department." Mr. Tyson took off his reading glasses and picked up another piece of paper, which he handed to Javier. "On this sheet, you'll see a list of seventeen crates. One of these crates will be taken to a separate warehouse. When you report the inventory, I want you to report that we received sixteen."

Javier stared at it, then looked up at Frank. "Seventeen will come in, but you want me to report only sixteen?"

"That's right. I have another purpose for the extra crate. But for your help with this, you'll get a $2,000 bonus. How's that sound?"

Frank paused. "You're on my team, right? Because I really can't use people who aren't on my team. Do you understand?"

Javier glanced at Frank, then at Walter, who stared at him soberly.

"I'll tell you what, Mr. Martinez. You think it over tonight, then let me know tomorrow. Come to my office at 10:00 a.m. I need to know whether you really want this job."

Javier stood. "Good evening, sir," he said. Shoulders slumped, Javier walked slowly back to his post.

That evening, after dinner with his family, Adam walked to the front room and sat. Bartkowski had relocated, but now Adam had established a new routine. Before leaving the house each morning, he would look at the Resolution, choose one line, and ask God to help him live it out. This evening he read it all.

Maggie saw him to the door when he left, just as she greeted him when he came home. He suspected her memories of life as an outdoor dog were growing dim.

Adam got on his knees and scratched her. He wished he'd entered Maggie's world while Emily was still part of it. But he was grateful for Maggie and the way she seemed like a conduit to memories of Emily. He patted her on the head one final time before he left.

Adam drove three miles up Westover Boulevard and parked across from the bank and by the big oak tree—the same place Emily had asked him to dance. He unwrapped a brand-new CD and slid it into the player. Emily's song began.

I'd like to sail to lands afar
out on a boat that's built for two.
Beneath the canopy of stars
that would be just like a dream come true.
Just to be with you.

As the song played, Adam closed his eyes.

He heard Emily's voice say how she loved this song. Adam opened the door, turned up the volume, and put his feet on the ground. Then he got out and went to the exact place Emily had stood. He heard Emily instruct him how to dance with her as if it had been just a moment ago.

"When you're ready to dance with me, this is what you do. First, you put your right hand around my waist like this."

Adam closed his eyes again and reached out his right hand. He could see her so clearly, it took his breath away. Emily was there with him. Wasn't she?

"Then hold your other hand out like this."

He held up his other hand as if to take hers.

"Then we sway back and forth to the music. And . . . we can spin."

Adam began slowly. He took small steps back and forth to

the rhythm. He turned as if to lead Emily in the dance as she twirled at the end of his hand.

As the song continued, tears streamed down his cheeks.

I'd like a castle on a hill,
where you and I could spend a day.
And I'd love to go where time stands still
and all that doesn't matter fades away.
You are here with me.

Smiling slightly, Adam kept his eyes closed and let the song play as he continued the dance he never shared with Emily.

When the song ended, Adam opened his eyes and drew his hands up to his face, fingers clasped together.

"Lord, thank You for the nine years I had with Emily. I'm so grateful." He hesitated, then said, "I don't know if I can ask You this or not. But would You tell her I did my side of the dance?"

★ ★ ★

A beautiful girl, eyes sparkling, put her little hand into the big hand of the Carpenter-King. He stroked her hair, then picked her up effortlessly. He smiled at her warmly, delighting in her as one delights in His most wonderful creation.

"One day, after the resurrection, you will sit with your family again at a great table, and we will all feast together."

Her eyes widened. "Will I dance with Daddy then?"

"Yes, Emily. You will dance with him in your new body on a new earth. Your father will cherish that dance as much as you will. It'll be my gift to him—and to you."

She squealed with delight. "I can hardly wait!"

He put her down. "Why don't you and I dance together now?"

He reached out to her. She placed her hand in His. She saw,

then felt, the great scars. But they didn't frighten her. Rather, they reminded her of the price He had paid, in the other world, to show His love and purchase her entrance into this world.

The Carpenter led Emily in the dance. She swayed, giggling, then laughed loudly as she twirled at the end of His hand.

She was at home, with the Person she was made for, in the place made for her.

Emily Mitchell had never felt so happy. Joy was the air she breathed.

★ ★ ★

Javier and Carmen sat across from each other at their kitchen table. Javier's face had been carefree lately. Not today.

"Javy, we need this job. For the first time in a year, we are able to pay the bills."

"I know. But Mr. Tyson made it clear that if I was not a team player, he did not want me there."

"But he's the manager. Isn't he free to handle inventory how he wants? Maybe it just looked wrong, but it's really okay."

"He asked me to record false information, Carmen. He asked me to lie."

"But surely he will not fire you if you refuse!"

Javier stared at the wall. "It sounded like he would."

"But we need this job."

It hurt Javy to hear her despair. She was such a good wife and mother. Something told him he owed it to her and the children to do what Mr. Tyson was asking. Something else told him he owed it to them and God *not* to.

"You know I would like to keep this job. But if I did this because you wanted me to, you would lose respect for me. And I would lose respect for myself. Carmen, how could we tell our children to do what is honorable when we have not?"

He pointed to the Resolution on the wall. "'I will . . . walk with integrity as a man answerable to God. I will seek to honor God.' I should not have signed that unless I meant it."

"When do you have to let him know?"

"Ten o'clock."

"Javy, promise me if he lets you go, you will call me as soon as you leave his office. If you do not call, I will know everything is okay."

He agreed.

"Javy . . . I don't want us to go back."

"I know. We need to pray. I think we should explain it to the children and ask them to pray with us."

"They are too young to understand it all. And if you get fired, they may not understand why God did not answer."

"God listens to the prayers of His children. And if they are to know our God, they must know that He answers prayer and that when He answers no, we should still trust Him."

The children joined them. They explained the situation and prayed together.

If I am so moved by the prayers of my children, Lord, surely You must be.

★　★　★

After five miles, Adam leaned over, hands on his thighs, catching his breath. "You know how good I always say it feels when I stop running?"

"Yeah?" Dylan said.

"Well, this was the first time I've ever felt good when I *was* running." He tried not to breathe too hard and spoil the effect of his words. "I think I was . . . in the groove."

"You mean in the zone? Runner's high?"

"Yeah, that's it. I could understand Eric Liddell when he

said, 'God made me fast. And when I run, I feel God's pleasure.'"

"Yeah. I get that. Except the part about God making you
fast."

Adam pushed his son's shoulder.

Dylan laughed. "I've thought a lot about Eric Liddell—how
he stood up for what he believed. I did that today."

"You did?"

"In science class I said something about intelligent design
I got from those videos you showed me. A couple of students
rolled their eyes like we must be idiots to believe in a Creator,
but I figured, so what? I mean, it didn't cost me a gold medal."

"That's good, Son. A man takes a stand for his convictions.
Truth is, I never spoke up like that when I was your age. If I had
it to do over again, I would."

"Can't you still do it?" Dylan asked.

"What do you mean?"

"Well, you're not in school, but you work around people
who don't believe in God, right?"

"Sure, a lot of them."

"Then you still have a chance to speak up, don't you?"

Adam looked at his son. "I guess I do. So maybe instead of
regretting the opportunities I missed, I should be taking the
ones I have?"

Dylan smiled, then took off running.

CHAPTER THIRTY-ONE

THE MEN SAT at the Cookie Shop, an Albany legend, happily downing homemade baklava and chocolate nut surprise and enjoying endless coffee refills.

Javier described his meeting at the factory.

"Frank Tyson wants you to lie?" Adam said. "He's a deacon at my church! He's the guy I asked about your job!"

"I was surprised. But Carmen said maybe that's the way they do business."

"But he'll hand you $2,000 to do it? That's a payoff!"

"Maybe you don't see the full picture," Shane said. "I know Frank Tyson. I don't think he's dishonest. Before you say no, hear him out. And a $2,000 bonus? Don't look a gift horse in the mouth. Or as Adam once put it, 'Don't kick a gift horse in the teeth.'"

Adam smirked but couldn't deny it.

Javy lifted his hands. "I need this job. I don't want to let down Carmen."

"But you've got to be honest," Nathan said.

"I still say let him explain," Shane said. "But sure, in the end, honesty's the best policy."

Adam wasn't so willing to let Tyson off the hook. The guy was a church leader. Where did he get off putting Javy up to something shady?

Javy said, "I would like to hear your opinion, David."

David looked at all the men, then back at Javy. "Well, I think you have to be able to live with yourself. I've been able to live with my conscience for the first time I can remember. Obviously my faith in Christ is a big part of it. But so is making things right with Amanda. Javier, you might think you should keep the Resolution about providing for your family, right? But if you violate the points about honesty and accountability to God, that would be wrong. So if you're a Jesus follower, shouldn't you say to your boss, 'Jesus followers can't lie like that'?"

Adam gaped. *Where did he get such insight?*

"You are a wise man, David," Javier said. "Thank you."

David swallowed hard. "You're welcome."

Adam looked at the young deputy. "You just spoke to me too, David. I remember something that happened when I was at the police academy with Shane and Bronson. A young man— in fact it was Brock Kelley, the football player from Shiloh Academy—asked how it worked for a Christian to be a cop. I answered, but I didn't have the guts to come right out and say *I* was a Christian. At the time it seemed wise. But the truth is, it was cowardly."

"Don't be so hard on yourself," Shane said.

"To keep the Resolution, we have to be hard on ourselves. A good athlete never trains easy. And when he competes, the hard work pays off. So, Javy, we'll pray for you. If you lose your job, so be it. We'll stand behind you and do everything we can to help. Including finding you a new job."

Adam looked at Shane and whispered, "And if Frank Tyson loses his job as deacon, so be it!"

★ ★ ★

Javier looked at the big factory clock and walked toward Frank Tyson's office. He paused to pray. After taking a deep breath, he knocked three times. The door opened and Walter let him in.

"Good morning."

Tyson kept writing while Javier stood across the desk from him. "Hello, Mr. Martinez. How are you today?"

"Fine, sir. How are you?"

"I don't know yet. Have a seat. I trust you thought about our conversation yesterday."

"Yes, sir, I did." Javier sat.

Mr. Tyson stopped writing and glanced up. "Well. What did you decide, Mr. Martinez? Are you on my team?"

Javier swallowed hard, then with a steady gaze said, "Mr. Tyson, I am very grateful to have a job here. But . . . I cannot do as you have asked."

Frank Tyson regarded him a moment, then leaned back in his chair. "And why is that?"

"Because it is wrong, sir. It would dishonor God and my family if I lied."

Frank studied Javier's face, then looked at Walter, clearly surprised. He turned back toward Javier. "Do you understand what this may do to your job here?"

"Yes, sir, I do."

Tyson slowly stood and held his hand out toward Javier. Javier was confused.

"Javier, may I shake your hand? Young man, you just gave me the right answer."

Javier rose and shook his hand.

"I've searched a long time for the right person to manage shipping and inventory. You were actually the last person on my list. But I need someone I can trust. Would you take the job? We would adjust your pay, of course."

Javier, bewildered, looked at Walter, who smiled and nodded. He looked back at Frank Tyson. "I would be honored, sir."

"Good. The job is yours. Walter will go over the specifics with you. I'll announce it to the staff next week." He started to sit down. "Oh, and, Javier? Thanks for your integrity. It's rare."

Walter shook Javier's hand and opened the door for him. "Well done. After six times, I was getting discouraged."

Javier thanked both men and stepped out of the office. There was a bounce in his step as he strode down the hall.

★ ★ ★

Carmen was working in the kitchen, grateful for every minute after ten o'clock. But at 10:10, the phone rang.

"No, no, no. Please, God. No." She tried to compose herself as the phone continued ringing. "Carmen, be strong for him," she said aloud. "Be strong."

She picked up the phone. "Hello?"

"Carmen."

She sobbed. "It's okay, Javy! It's okay, baby. We'll get through this."

"Carmen, no, listen to me. I . . ."

"The Lord will take care of us, Javy. We'll get through this."

"Carmen, listen, they—"

"I know you trust God. I will, too. You are a good man. A good husband and a good father. I am proud of you."

"Carmen, stop! You're not listening! They didn't fire me. They *promoted* me!"

Carmen froze. "What?"

"It was a test. They wanted someone they could trust. They made me a manager. And they raised my pay!"

"A test?"

"Yes, Carmen. I got a promotion. Everything will be okay."

Carmen held the phone out and screamed, jumping up and down. The kids ran into the room, terrified.

"What's wrong, *Mamá*? Please don't cry."

Carmen hugged both of them while holding the phone.

"Hello?" Javy said. "Is anyone there?"

"Yes! I am okay. We are all okay!"

"Tell the children that God heard their prayers. He gave us much more than we asked!"

"I'll tell them. I love you, Javy!"

"I love you, Carmen. Tell the children I love them too. I'll talk to you soon."

"Gracias a Dios," Carmen whispered.

CHAPTER THIRTY-TWO

ADAM, VICTORIA, and Dylan walked toward the Westover High School track. Dylan wore his uniform and carried a team duffel bag.

"We'll see you after the race."

Dylan jogged ahead while Adam and Victoria walked up to the fence and watched the runners stretch and warm up.

"You know this is a long shot, right?" Adam asked Victoria. "He's only running the 400 because one of the older students got sick. Billy Reeves is a senior, and he owns the district record. Every guy on our team is faster than Dylan—but maybe there's somebody from Monroe he can beat."

Victoria put her hand on Adam's shoulder. "That's only the third time you've explained it. You're as nervous as he is. He said he just doesn't want to come in last. But I say it's okay if he does."

"Let's get a seat."

Victoria looked at the mostly empty stands. "When you come an hour early, that's no problem."

Adam watched Dylan from the stands. Despite attempts to loosen up, Dylan looked very tight to Adam, who now knew his routines and habits. He seemed so young alongside the upper-classmen. The Mitchells spoke with other parents as the stands filled up and a few other events took place. But to Adam, these were preliminaries. His son's race was the main event.

Coach Kilian approached Dylan, gestured, and spoke. Though Adam couldn't hear exactly what he said, his attempt to lip-read yielded, "Just try to stay with the group."

"He'll be all right," Adam said.

Victoria wondered if Adam would be all right.

"I'm proud of him no matter what," Victoria said. "His grades are better, and he does his chores without my reminders."

"Well, I've been reminding him," Adam laughed. "But not as much. The key is, he's growing spiritually. He's really becoming a man."

"Does he know that's what you think about him?"

"Well, yeah, I think . . ." Adam stopped. "Maybe he doesn't."

Adam popped out of his seat and walked down the stairs toward the track.

Victoria reached out. "Where are you going? Are you supposed to . . . ?"

Warm-ups were over, and they were moments away from the lineup. Adam saw the disapproving stare from the coach. But he walked up behind Dylan and put his arm around his son's chest, startling him. Adam spoke into his right ear so only his son could hear.

"Dylan, I've watched you take more responsibility. I've seen you own up to your mistakes and be honest, and I admire you for it. I want to tell you that today I consider you a man. I love you. Your mother and I are proud of you no matter what. Do what God has gifted you to do. Run your race. God has made you fast, so when you run, just like Eric Liddell, feel God's pleasure."

Adam let him go. Walking briskly, he saluted Coach Kilian and hopped up the stairs back to his seat.

"What did you say to him?"

"I said what it was time for him to hear."

"What did he say to you?"

"Nothing. I just wanted him to know I believe in him."

Soon the announcer called the runners to their marks for the 400.

Victoria squeezed her husband's arm. "I know how excited you can get, Adam, but remember there are other people around."

"So I shouldn't embarrass you? I'll make no promises."

The gun went off. Runners sprinted down the track. Near the first turn, Dylan was seventh of the eight. As they went through the turn, Dylan picked up his pace and moved into sixth place.

As the runners swept around the turn to the back straightaway, Dylan passed another.

"He's in fifth!" Adam yelled. "Go, Dylan!"

"Come on, Dylan!" Victoria yelled—louder than Adam.

As they continued down the back straightaway, the lead runner, Dylan's senior teammate, extended his lead, but Dylan passed another runner.

"Fourth place! He's in fourth place!" Victoria shouted. She jumped up on the seat.

"Go, buddy! Go!" Adam yelled.

The runners got to the final turn and fought for position. Dylan edged to third.

Now half the crowd was on its feet, and people all around were yelling.

"That's it! Go, Dylan!" Adam and Victoria both screamed, felt their throats go raw, and didn't care.

As Dylan came around the turn, the lead runner, Billy Reeves, pulled out of reach, but Dylan gained ground on the second-place runner from Monroe. The entire Westover crowd cheered, and anyone who didn't have a favorite cheered for Dylan. Dylan and his opponent neared the finish line neck and neck.

"He's doing it! He's doing it!" Adam yelled.

"Go! Go! Go!" Victoria's voice went hoarse.

Dylan crossed the finish line a half step ahead of the runner next to him, taking second. His coach, teammates, and friends mobbed him.

Coach Kilian was astonished. "Where did that come from? You haven't run like that all year!"

Dylan fought to breathe while everyone patted him on the back and embraced him. He looked up in the stands to see his father and mother jumping up and down, celebrating his victory.

"Dylan, you're the man!" Adam shouted. He grabbed Victoria's shoulders. "My son is the man!"

"My little boy is the man!" Victoria yelled. Her voice gave out completely on the word *man*.

"Let's get down there," Adam said. He grabbed her hand and pulled her down to the track. They pushed toward Dylan.

"Way to go, Dylan," his father said, voice raw.

"You were terrific!" His mother mouthed the words, but no sound came out.

"What'd you say, Mom?"

The winner, Billy Reeves, back from his cooldown, approached the mob around Dylan and looked confused. "Hey, what's going on? I won the stinkin' race!"

Ninety minutes later, Adam, Dylan, and Victoria headed for the parking lot. Adam's arm was around Dylan. "So your mother doesn't want me to yell too loud and embarrass her, and pretty soon she jumps up on the bench and screams like a banshee."

"You were actually up on the bench, Mom?"

"I guess I got a little excited," she whispered.

"I was pretty excited myself," Adam said, "though I certainly held it together better than your mother. How are you feeling, Son? You must be on top of the world!"

"It was amazing. I kept thinking about Eric Liddell when he came from behind."

"So did I!"

Dylan tossed his duffel bag onto the truck's backseat. "I kind of felt bad for Billy."

"Billy always wins. He ran well, but it wasn't a personal best. He got first, but it was your night. Hey, let me pray right here. Father, You gave Dylan such a great night. Thanks! Please help him enjoy his success and be grateful to You and give You credit."

"I think Dylan should pick the restaurant." It took three attempts for Victoria to communicate this opinion.

Adam's eyes shot past Victoria, and he froze. About forty feet from their truck, a man in jeans and an old jacket watched them.

Victoria turned pale. "What's he doing here?" she whispered.

"Get in the truck. Both of you."

Adam walked toward the man, who looked down. When Adam got within fifteen feet, he stopped.

"Mr. Mitchell, I saw on the Westover website that your son was running today. I figured you'd be here."

Adam remained silent, but his eyes betrayed his intense emotions.

"My lawyer told me not to communicate with you or your family."

"Maybe you should have listened to him."

"I just can't stop thinking about what I did."

Mike Hollis tried unsuccessfully to find a safe landing site for his eyes. "I start my sentence in a few days. I'll be in prison a long time, but I wanted to tell you that . . ."

His eyes and Adam's finally met.

"I've got a little girl, too. She's seven, lives with my ex. It would kill me to lose her." He paused a moment and swallowed hard. "I guess I *will* lose her. I know I can't do anything for you, Mr. Mitchell, but I had to tell you . . . I'm sorry. I know you must hate me. I understand."

Adam braced himself. "Look, Mr. Hollis . . . Mike." Something changed when Adam stopped thinking of him as "the drunk" and called him Mike. "I don't hate you. I hate what you did. But hating you or trying to get even won't bring Emily back."

Mike looked down.

"There's just one thing you *can* do for me."

"What?"

"You can never touch alcohol or drugs again—not now, not when you get out. And go to your little girl while you still can and love on her. View every moment you spend with her as priceless. Hear me?"

Hollis wiped his eyes with his sleeve.

"And just so you know, God is your judge, not me. Jesus Christ forgave me. How can I not forgive you? I do. But above all, Mike, you need God's forgiveness."

"Thank you. But if you knew everything, I don't think you could forgive me. I . . . saw you at the Fun Park not long before the accident."

What does he mean? Adam hadn't been to the Fun Park for six months, when he last took Emily.

"I've felt the same way myself, Mike. I guess if we deserved forgiveness, we wouldn't need it. God's seen me at my worst and still loves me. He knows everything about you too. And if you ask Him, He'll forgive you."

Mike nodded. "Thank you."

Adam walked back to his truck, weighing what had just happened.

"What did he want?" Victoria whispered.

Adam closed the door and sat with his hands on the wheel. He took a moment to calm himself. "He said he was sorry. I told him God loves him and we choose to forgive him."

Victoria looked incredulous.

"We have to. Jesus has forgiven us for all our worst sins. He commands us to forgive others. Mike Hollis is no exception. That's the gospel."

Dylan listened from the backseat. "He's going to prison, right?"

"Yes, for a long time. And he has a daughter, who's seven."

Victoria looked at him, then stared straight ahead. She prayed aloud, barely audible, "God, give me the grace and strength to forgive. I want to, but I need Your help."

"He will help us," Adam said. "Each of us."

They sat in silence. Finally Adam said, "Dylan, you had an amazing night. And if Emily could talk to us right now, she'd say the same thing I think Jesus would—'Go out and celebrate!' So, Son, where do you want to go? You name it."

Dylan took a full five seconds to decide. "Bruster's Ice Cream. I want a turtle sundae."

"Hot fudge brownie for me," Victoria might have said; Adam wasn't certain.

"And," Dylan said, "I want a banana split with a pretzel rod and extra whipped cream."

"You got it, Son," Adam said, already picturing a Bruster's peanut butter cup.

Adam pulled out of the parking lot, spraying gravel.

"Way to peel out, Dad!"

"If I had the patrol car, I'd turn on the lights and siren."

The next evening Dylan and Adam stood in the driveway cooling down after a run.

"You're quiet," Adam said. "What's on your mind?"

Dylan stretched. "There's something I think I should tell you."

Adam leaned toward him.

"You asked me before if there was an adult I bought drugs from."

"You ready to tell me his name?"

"It's eaten at me ever since Emily died. I feel so guilty."

"We talked about that. God forgives us."

"This is something else, Dad."

"Why? Who sold you the drugs?"

Dylan put his face in his hands and mumbled a name.

"Who?"

"Mike Hollis."

"What?"

"If I'd turned in Mike Hollis a long time ago, if I'd told you he sold to high school kids, then—" Dylan sobbed—"then he would have gone to jail. And Emily would still be alive!"

Adam moved closer. "Dylan, you couldn't have known. If we had do-overs, we'd all choose differently. Maybe you wouldn't have done the drugs, but if you had and we had the kind of relationship that I think we're developing . . . then you could have talked with me. And then maybe Mike Hollis would have gone to jail. If anyone's to blame, it's me."

"Both of you are wrong." The voice came out of the dark-ness.

"I'm no eavesdropper." Victoria held her hands in the air as she approached from the side yard. "But when I go outside to find Maggie's chew toy and hear my husband ask, 'Who sold you the drugs?' I hope you understand why I kept listening!"

"Of course," Adam said.

"Then let's talk," Victoria said. "But it's cold; can we go inside?"

While the men showered, Victoria fixed decaf for Adam, hot chocolate for Dylan, and green tea for herself. They met in the living room, and Adam started a fire.

Maggie curled up at Victoria's feet. "Drink up and get your insides warm while I tell you what I think. Do you know how many what-ifs and should haves there are? I've come up with a hundred. First, I could have told Emily she couldn't go to the party. Or I could have insisted that one of us pick her up from school and drive her to the party. I could have even discouraged Emily from ballet class as a seven-year-old, where she first met Hannah. There's no end to it. But you know what difference I think all those things would have made?"

The question sounded rhetorical, so neither answered.

"Well, *do* you?"

"No," Adam and Dylan answered together.

"No difference at all. Because either God is in control or He isn't. And if God isn't in control, if our destinies are in the hands of birthday parties, traffic flow, demons, or a man who gets drunk and takes cocaine . . . then God is not God. Why worship Him?"

"But you believe God *is* in control, right?" Dylan asked.

Victoria nodded and opened her Bible to a marked spot. "Listen to this verse from Proverbs 16:9: 'In his heart a man plans his course, but the Lord determines his steps.' Did Mike Hollis have a choice? Yes. And he made a bad one. But Emily's life was *not* in his hands. It was in *God's* hands. God could have prevented that crash."

"Then why didn't He?"

"Dylan, I don't know. Here's another verse that might help. Genesis 50:20. When Joseph was maybe your age, his brothers sold him into slavery. But years later he says this: 'You intended to harm me, but God intended it for good.' He could look back in retrospect and see that what God *intended* triumphed over what his brothers intended."

Adam sat up straight. "You're right! Think about Good Friday. It was the worst day in history, but we call it *Good*. Why? Because looking back, we know that God used the worst thing to accomplish the best thing—our redemption."

Dylan turned to his mother. "You really think someday we'll see that God made the right decision when He let Emily die?"

"I couldn't say this a couple of months ago, but yes, I do. It's the only thing that keeps me sane. I believe that if she'd never met Hannah, she still would have died that day. I don't know why or how. But I *do* know this—God never lies. And He makes a promise in Romans 8:28—'In all things God works for the good of those who love him, who have been called according to his purpose.'"

Dylan shook his head. "I don't think I can believe that."

Victoria understood Dylan's struggle. "Your father knows this, Dylan, and I wasn't sure if I should ever tell you. After Emily died, I was really angry when someone quoted Romans 8:28 to us. I wanted to rip it out of the Bible. If He will work all things together for our good, the 'all things' must include the very worst thing that has ever happened to us—even Emily's death. Could I believe that, in the end, God will use it for all of our good? At first I couldn't. Yet, if it *isn't* true, then Romans 8:28 isn't true. And if it's *not* true, the Bible's not true."

"You really thought that?" Dylan asked.

"Yes. But finally I decided Romans 8:28 is as true as John 3:16 and every other Bible verse. I asked myself, even if I can't see God's purpose now, can I by faith trust Him that one day, in eternity, I will? By faith I choose to believe God is good and He loves me. With what He did for me on the cross, how could I ever believe anything less?"

Adam stood and put one arm around Victoria. Then he pulled Dylan up beside him, putting the other around him. Maggie pushed her head against their shins.

CHAPTER THIRTY-THREE

ADAM WALKED down to the sheriff's department evidence room, part of the county courthouse complex. Through the window he watched the evidence room custodian, Sergeant Smith, catalog entries. The room had rows of shelves filled with bins of bags and folders.

"Hey, Sarge, Bronson said the bags of cocaine we found on Highland have been logged in; is that right?"

He flipped open the evidence log and ran his finger down the page. "Yep. Sergeant Bronson turned them in. 4:30 p.m." He chuckled. "He ranted about the PIO getting some big award tomorrow night and wondered if she would fly in on her broomstick to pick it up."

"That's Bronson. Listen, he mentioned twenty-four bags, but I could have sworn there were thirty."

Sergeant Smith looked at the sheet. "It says twenty-four went to the lab. Sure you guys counted right?"

Adam thought about it. "Bronson should know since he turned them in."

Adam started to leave.

"Your shift has brought in some heavy hitters this month.

You had that bust on Hoffman last week and that shoe box with six bags of rocks."

Adam stopped. "There were *six* bags in the shoe box?"

"Yep. Says so right here. Keep this up and you'll put these guys out of business."

"I wish." Adam hesitated. *You can always say more later, but you can't unsay what you say now.*

Adam strode down the hall past several sheriff's department employees. He noticed Nathan and David walking by. "Nathan, hold up."

Nathan stopped and turned as Adam approached.

"I just need a second alone, David."

David left, casting an unsettled gaze on Adam.

"You know the Highland bust?" Adam said to Nathan. "You, David, Shane, and I were there; then Bronson showed up before the narcotics inspector came. How many bags of coke do you remember?"

Nathan thought about it. "Seems like . . . what, close to thirty?"

"The log says twenty-four."

"I don't think that's right."

"And the shoe box we found when we were all tasin' Big Leon and Bronson showed up at the end? How many bags were there?"

"I'd say ten."

"Six were turned in."

Nathan studied Adam's face. "Be careful, man. Before we start down that road, we better be sure it's the right one."

On an overcast afternoon, Nathan and Kayla watched three women enter the Planned Parenthood facility.

"You know why they all wear sunglasses, don't you?" Kayla asked Nathan, who stood beside her, uncomfortable at his first-ever visit to an abortion clinic.

"No," Nathan said quietly.

"For the same reason I wore them when I came to this place nineteen years ago. To hide the mascara stains from all my tears. And to be less recognizable if somebody I knew drove by."

Nathan put his arm around her. "I wish I could punch out the jerk who encouraged you to go to that clinic. But I wasn't any better when it came to advising my brother."

"My guilt is gone, Nathan. So is yours. Christ paid the price."

Nathan reached up to wipe a tear. Kayla noticed and pressed her head against his shoulder.

"You took time to see what I do at the Pregnancy Resource Center. And that means a lot to me."

"I should have come sooner, Kayla. To both places. If the sheriff's department knew children were being killed anywhere else in Dougherty County, they'd send us out, sirens blaring and lights flashing. Yet children die here every day, right under our noses."

Kayla nodded. "We're blind. But Jesus isn't. He cares about these children. Whatever we do for them, He says we've done for Him."

Nathan pointed to the doorway. "The children who die here all have fathers. Yet they're fatherless. If their fathers won't stand up for them, who will?"

A dark-cherry-colored Acura MDX pulled into the parking lot. A man drove. A woman sat in the passenger seat. Both stayed in the car.

"Pray for them," Kayla said. "When they don't get out of the car, I figure they're reconsidering this decision."

Finally the man got out. He looked tentatively at Nathan and Kayla, then leaned down and talked softly to the woman inside. At last she opened her door.

The woman wore large black sunglasses; her auburn hair was shoulder length. She seemed familiar to Nathan, but he couldn't place her.

The two walked toward the door of the clinic. Kayla moved toward them.

"Ma'am, my name is Kayla Hayes. I wanted to give you this brochure that shows you the development of your unborn baby. It also has a phone number where you can get a free ultrasound so you can see what your little boy or girl looks like."

The woman's face twitched as she took the brochure out of Kayla's hand.

"Why are you here?" the man asked. "It doesn't make things any easier."

"I had an abortion. And I've regretted it ever since."

"I really don't think—"

Kayla pointed at Nathan, who was ten feet away, still on the sidewalk. "Sir, that's my husband, Nathan Hayes. He has a story you need to hear."

"Hello." Nathan moved a little closer but asked, "Would you mind joining me over here?" Nathan didn't want to have to explain to the sheriff's department why he stepped on private property to try to save a life the law didn't protect.

The woman nodded to the man, and she went alongside Kayla to Nathan.

Nathan swallowed hard. "I'll be honest. This is my first time at this kind of place. But I have great regrets going back twenty years; I advised my brother to pay for an abortion. That child was my niece or nephew. I didn't stand up for that baby's life. I should have done everything I could, even offered to raise that child. Kayla and I both regret our decisions. We don't want you to have to live with that kind of pain."

"We already have two children. Our youngest is seven." The woman noticed Nathan's face for the first time. She studied him as if trying to place him.

"I work full-time now. We've got the house payments and . . . car payments." She looked at the Acura. "We just can't afford another child."

"But you already *have* another child," Kayla said. "Inside you."

"Look, sir," Nathan said. "I don't know you. But you want to be a good father to your children, don't you?"

The man eyed Nathan. He nodded.

"Someday you may have to explain to your children why you took the life of their brother or sister. I believe no child should have to die because he's inconvenient. Honestly, I think his father should be the first to defend his right to live."

"You don't know our financial situation."

"I know this," Nathan said. "If you will let this child live and you feel you can't afford to raise him, Kayla and I will help pay to place him for adoption in a home where he's wanted. It won't cost you a dime."

The woman shook her head violently. "I would never give up my own child for adoption! What kind of person do you think I am?"

Kayla let the words hang in the air for a few seconds, then said gently, "Then do you really want to have that same child killed?"

The woman looked at Kayla, then at Nathan again, and suddenly gasped. "I know who you are! I saw you thrown off the side of that truck on Newton Road! I was with my friend, and she pulled over. I jumped out to see if I could help you."

She took off her sunglasses.

"Of course," Nathan said. "I thought I recognized you."

She looked at her husband in disbelief. "Mark, this is the guy! The man who grabbed the steering wheel and wouldn't let go." She looked at Kayla. "When he was thrown off the truck, he wouldn't sit still and wait for the ambulance. I thought he was insane to be so concerned about his car. I'll never forget when he opened the back door and that little boy started crying."

Tears poured out now, and Kayla put an arm around her.

"Jackson," Kayla said softly. "Our little boy's name is Jackson."

Her husband looked at Nathan. "She talked about it for weeks. I'd like to think I'd have done the same for my children!"

And yet here you are, about to . . .

"Sir, you have the opportunity to do the same thing right now. Jackson's my third child, and I knew he was worth saving. This is your third child, and he or she is worth saving, too."

"But . . . I don't know how we could make the payments." The woman glanced at their car.

"Ma'am, do you remember what you said to me when I crawled over to see my son? You said, 'Sir, don't worry about your car.'"

She looked at her husband, and it was as if a searchlight suddenly penetrated the darkness. "Mark, what are we doing here?"

"I thought it was what you wanted."

"I thought it was what *you* wanted."

Her husband shook his head. "I don't think it's really what either of us wanted. It seemed like we had no other choice. But . . . we do."

She sobbed. "I want to get away from this place." She turned and hurried toward her car.

Nathan extended his hand to the husband and said, "Mark, let me congratulate you for hanging on to the wheel to save your child. I guarantee you won't regret the choice you made today."

CHAPTER THIRTY-FOUR

ADAM WANDERED into the living room, where Victoria sat with her laptop. "Busy?"

She looked up. "Just checking Facebook. What's on your mind?"

"I was just thinking about Tuesday breakfast with the guys to discuss the Resolution. For the first time in my career, I think my relationship with other cops is actually helping my family rather than hurting it."

"Speaking of family relationships, your dad's birthday is Sunday. If you write him a note, I'll send it."

Adam sighed. "You told me once that I've spent my life trying to please my father. I didn't like that. But I think it's true."

"Yeah."

"I mean, the guy got a Medal of Honor because he saved his platoon in Vietnam. Retired as a lieutenant colonel. How can I compete with that? Every time I see him, he says, 'Are you still a corporal?' Those two chevrons on my uniform are impressive to a slick-sleeve deputy, but they're nothing to him. If I was a sergeant, he'd want me to be a captain or sheriff. It would never be enough."

Victoria shook her head. "If you cared less about what your dad thinks about you, it would improve your relationship."

"I don't know about that. But I've thought about asking him to come fishing with Dylan and me. Or maybe even come for the 5K."

Dylan was about to leave for a run when he heard Adam say this. He sat down around the corner and listened.

"You know he doesn't like to travel. You may have to go to him."

"I'll write him that note, but I'll call him on his birthday too. I need to talk to him, man-to-man."

"That would be good for you both." Victoria studied Adam's face. "Something else is bothering you, isn't it?"

He paused for a moment, deciding how best to say it, then told her about the discrepancies with the drugs checked into the evidence room.

"What will you do, Adam?"

"I have to do what's right. If another cop steals drugs, I have to report it."

"But you're not sure who it is."

"Besides me, it could only be Shane, Nathan, David, or Bronson. The five of us were at both scenes. Different guys turned in the reports. If the drugs were stolen by someone else before the guy taking inventory saw them, no one would know."

Victoria leaned toward him. "Okay, it's not you. And Shane's honest, right?"

"So honest he admitted he didn't warn Holloman before tasing him. Sarge gave him the chance to tell one lie that would have avoided that reprimand."

"And I don't think you believe it's Nathan."

"I'm not sure what to believe. And that bothers me. Bronson showed up at two drug busts. Why? Unless . . ."

"Sure, Bronson's a hard-nosed jerk. But he's always been honest, right?"

"I think so."

"So what about David? Do any of the guys buy stuff or make payments they shouldn't be able to afford?"

Thoughts came into Adam's mind he didn't want to consider.

"I just don't think any of those guys would do it," Victoria said.

"I hope not. But we're all tempted sometimes."

"Have you been tempted?"

"Three years ago, I brought in some cash from a drug bust, when Dylan had that colon problem. Remember? The insurance should have covered it, but they refused. And I thought, 'This is drug money to be confiscated by the county and probably wasted on some fat cat's slush fund.' There were thousands of dollars in that bag. Nobody would have known if I'd skimmed a thousand."

"What did you do?"

"Nothing. I told myself I just couldn't."

"What made the difference?"

"I knew it was wrong. I'd like to say I did the right thing because I love God so much. But the truth is, it was because I knew He was watching, and I feared Him."

"Well, if it kept you from stealing, it was probably a good motive."

Adam put his face in his hands. "I don't want to go where this stolen drug thing is taking me, Victoria."

"I know." She squeezed his shoulder. "But you have to, don't you? Because you love God. And because you fear Him."

He nodded.

Dylan walked in the room at that moment. "You want to run, Dad?"

"Sure, buddy. It's a nice night."

Adam changed his clothes and joined Dylan on the front porch. They set off at an easy pace. While running, Dylan reached into his jacket and pulled something out.

Adam strained to see it under the streetlights. "What's that?"

"A baton."

"That's what I thought. What's it for?"

"Coach Kilian asked me to carry it when I run."

"Why?"

"He wants me to run on the 4 x 400 relay team."

"Dylan, that's great!"

"He said since I finished second in that race, I'd earned a shot at it."

"Are you excited?"

"Yeah. But . . . what if . . . you know . . ."

"What if what?"

"Well, if I do a bad job when I run on my own, I let down myself mainly. But in a relay if I drop the baton or I make a bad pass, I can ruin it for everyone. There's a lot at stake."

"You can do it, Dylan. I know you can."

"Coach showed me how to pass and receive, and tomorrow I'll try it with the team. But I've never done it while actually running."

"Can you show me?"

"I guess so. Why?"

"Well, while we run, we can practice. You take it from me; I'll take it from you."

"We could try it. It'll be like practicing in slow motion."

"No, I can run all out."

"Exactly."

Adam passed the baton to Dylan, who took it and turned on the afterburners. Adam was amazed at Dylan's acceleration. He knew his boy held back when they ran together. But he'd never seen this kind of speed. It made him try to run faster whenever he put the baton into his son's hands.

The next thirty minutes were start and stop, give and take. They brought out the best in each other.

As they made their way up the driveway, Dylan said, "Thanks, Dad. That really helped. I think I'm ready for tomorrow."

"No problem, Son." Adam smiled. "Hey, what are dads for?"

It was a black-tie event in a large banquet room at the Albany Civic Center, and Diane Koos was slated to receive the annual Albany Award for Courageous Community Service.

Tonight Koos outdid herself. Perfect hair, professional makeup, fresh French manicure, shantung strapless gown, and four-inch patent pumps. She glittered and shimmered and was ready for every angle a camera could find. Her smile showed no signs of fatigue. How she could walk in those heels—let alone afford them—was a mystery.

The honorary presenter was Darrin Gallagher, Koos's cohost for fourteen years on the WOIA-TV evening news. A *GQ* cover wannabe with his sprayed-on tan and every hair in place, Gallagher wore a suit that looked like it had materialized on his body straight from the hanger.

He addressed the audience. "I can't think of anyone who deserves this award more than Diane Koos. During her stellar career, she put herself on the line day after day. She covered the stories most important to the city of Albany, whether it was breaking news on police corruption or brutality, or scandals in city government. She was the voice of the people.

"We miss Diane at WOIA, but we are grateful that she

now serves as the people's watchdog at the Dougherty County Sheriff's Department. We sleep a little better at night knowing she is on the job doing her part to keep us safe. On behalf of the WOIA family and the people of the great city of Albany, it's my honor to present this prestigious award to my longtime colleague and coworker in journalistic excellence, Diane Koos!"

People applauded warmly. When the CEO of WOIA-TV stood, WOIA executives and employees followed. Then the sheriff and his staff stood. People still seated and self-conscious about it stood, so eventually everyone participated in a not-quite-spontaneous standing ovation.

Darrin Gallagher handed Diane Koos a heavy rosewood plaque. Her name was beautifully inscribed on its twenty-four-karat gold plate.

Diane gave a speech that would make Toastmasters proud—short, pithy, and clever, with the sort of credit-dispensing humility any community pillar could be proud to possess.

When the event concluded after countless photos, fawning hugs and handshakes, and multiple rounds of celebratory cocktails, it was 11:30 p.m. and time for Darrin Gallagher to escort Diane Koos to his car. They took the elevator to the parking garage. Darrin had one arm around Diane and one hand on his remote to open her door.

Out of the shadows stepped two young white men dressed in flights and thick-soled, heavy-laced black boots. One man was short and wiry, the other tall and beefy. Both had crops, and swastika tattoos covered their well-muscled arms.

The big one pushed Gallagher to the ground while the other grabbed Diane's purse.

"Your wallet, man, and your car key. Quick!"

Gallagher tossed his key at the young man's feet and pulled out his wallet, which he tossed as well.

Diane Koos wasn't so cooperative. She pulled back on her purse, and the slim strap broke.

Her wiry assailant shoved her viciously against a concrete pillar. "Gimme the necklace, the bracelet, and the ring."

"No!" she shouted. "Help! Help!"

The man punched her in the jaw. She staggered backward, but when he came at her again, she swung the heavy gold-plated plaque. Its sharp corner drew instant blood, leaving a gash in his cheek. The plaque fell to the ground. He reached for her necklace. She lashed at his face, digging her fingernails into his flesh.

The man screamed, one eye injured by a razor-sharp nail.

The taller perp ran to aid his injured comrade. Darrin Gallagher sat on the asphalt, stock-still. When it was clear he'd been forgotten, he snuck out to the street, where he pulled out his cell phone and punched 911. Just as someone answered, a patrol car, lights flashing, pulled into the parking garage. He jumped out of the way.

The car screeched to a stop, and a huge but nimble driver jumped out. By this time, one of the men held Diane Koos in a choke hold while the other had yanked off the necklace and bracelet and tried for the ring. She managed to bite his finger, and he drew a knife.

At breakneck speed, the massive officer grabbed the assailant's shoulders and picked him up a foot off the ground, then smashed his forehead into the smaller man's. He fell with a violent thud.

The wiry man put his knife to Diane Koos's throat.

Without hesitation, the officer pulled his big Smith & Wesson and pointed it at the assailant's forehead. "Drop the knife or you're dead," he growled.

The assailant, voice breaking, said, "Throw your gun toward the street, and I'll let her go. If you don't, I'll kill her."

"No, you won't. Because you don't want to give me any more reason to put a bullet in your left eye, followed by a bullet in your right eye and one more in your mouth as you drop to the ground. You want some white power, bucko? I'll give you more than you can handle!"

"I'll cut her throat!"

"You draw one drop of blood, you Aryan Nation lowlife, and you'll be dead and in the fires of hell before you can say, 'Adolf Hitler's birthday.'"

The man, hardened in the school of hate, looked into the officer's eyes and knew without the slightest doubt that the brown-uniformed colossus was ready, if not eager, to kill him on the spot. He looked at his buddy on the ground with the dented skull and dropped his knife.

"Good dog. Now let her go. Down on your face, Nazi boy, and kiss the asphalt like it was Hitler's feet."

He quickly obeyed.

"Hands behind your back." Despite his bulk, the cop swiftly handcuffed the two men and called dispatch.

"693a. I've got two wannabe Aryan Nation street punks in custody here in the Civic Center parking garage. And I've got an injured woman; she needs an ambulance."

"I'll be okay," Diane Koos said.

"The paramedics will decide that. They beat you up pretty good, lady." He looked at the guy on the ground with the shredded face. "But obviously he got the worst of it."

Diane Koos looked at him. "I thought you worked day shift."

"I do. Frashour was sick and I volunteered since I had to miss my own shift."

"Why's that?"

"Got a memo ordering me to attend an all-day sensitivity

training session. They told me it was a recommendation from the PIO."

"Well, it's lucky for these guys you came fresh from your training."

Darrin Gallagher came forward out of the shadows. "Diane! Are you all right?"

"I guess so."

"Man, that was just crazy! Those guys were *nuts*."

"You might have stayed and helped the lady," the officer said.

"They could have been armed!" Gallagher said.

"Right. They could have killed her, armed or not. Looks like they made your makeup run."

Gallagher touched his cheek unconsciously. "I went to call the cops. That's what we're supposed to do."

The cop stared at him. "Someone else called first. You called as I drove in. Or did you call the TV station to get a film crew?"

The officer bent over and picked up the gold plaque, read it, then presented it to Diane Koos. As she reached for it, he saw that four of her fingernails were broken; globs of drying blood stained her fingertips.

Koos asked the officer, "Have you met Darrin Gallagher?"

"No. Seen him on TV, sides of buses, and in a couple of latrines. First time I've seen him with his makeup smudged, though. I recall his investigative report on police brutality. In fact, I believe I may have been in it."

"I thought I recognized you!" Gallagher stepped back.

"Yeah, I'm a little hard to forget. Well, we both did our jobs tonight, *Darrin*. Yours was to run like a coward. Mine was to come and assist the only one of you two with guts. This is a brave lady; you might want to learn from her so I don't have to come charging to your rescue if you ever get mugged by a gang of third-grade girls."

"That's uncalled for. And abusive!" Gallagher pulled out his smartphone and typed furiously with his thumbs. "You're digging a big, fat hole for yourself. I'm filing a complaint with your superiors!"

"Take a number," the cop said.

Koos glared at Gallagher. "You file a complaint, Darrin, and it'll come to me. And when it does, I'll tell the sheriff *everything* that happened tonight. And I'll spread multiple copies around WOIA."

The officer stared at the award-winning former news anchor with her torn dress, bruised face and neck, disheveled hair, and totaled fingernails. "Ma'am, is this cupcake your date?"

"No! I mean, well, he brought me here and planned to take me home."

"The two of you make a good match. One of you could wear the pants in the family, and that same one doesn't look half-bad in a dress."

Both Gallagher and Koos stared at the cop with radically different expressions. Gallagher conjured images of features, exposés, firing, a civil lawsuit, and talking sense into his former coanchor.

Diane Koos reached out her bloody right hand and put it on the cop's arm. "Thank you, Sergeant Bronson."

He looked at her long and hard.

"Just doin' my job." He paused. "And, ma'am, it was my pleasure."

CHAPTER THIRTY-FIVE

ADAM WALKED to where Tom Lyman waited at the Whispering Pines Retirement Center.

"I've looked forward to meeting Victoria and Dylan for a couple of months now. Help me get this coat on, would you?"

As Adam assisted Tom, he asked, "Where's the guy who always sat in that corner?"

"Andy Worthington? Andy passed away on Saturday."

"Really?"

"I'm sorry to say I don't think he was ready to go. He'd become bitter. Thought his kids didn't care. Never even met most of his own grandkids."

"That's sad."

"Yes. But I told Andy a half-dozen times, you can't change other people. The only life we have the power to change is ours, and even then we need God's help. I could never get him to think about Jesus. He refused to seek the one thing that could have brought him joy and hope."

"I'm glad you cared enough about Andy to share the gospel with him."

"This is where God has put me. As surely as he's put missionaries in Africa and you at the sheriff's department."

Adam marveled at Tom's wisdom. What he could glean from Tom, others—Dylan included—could glean from him. Godly men would pass the baton to one another, generation after generation. Adam was determined never to drop his again.

"Acts 17 says that God determined the times and places where each of us would live. It's no coincidence that I'm here, Adam. God has determined the time set for Tom Lyman and the exact place he should live. And He's done that so that I and those around me can seek Him and find Him. That's my life's calling."

As Adam rolled him out the front door, Tom asked, "You plan to throw me in the bed of your truck?"

Adam laughed. "I borrowed a friend's van with a sliding side door. It should be perfect."

Adam lifted Tom into the backseat, then handed Tom his Bible.

"A couple of visits to a chiropractor and you'll be fine," Tom joked. He fell silent for a few moments, framing his words while Adam loaded the wheelchair and slipped into the driver's seat.

"Adam, in your journal notes you dropped off last time, you said part of your grief is never being able to hug your daughter again. I've wanted to talk to you about that. Don't you believe in the resurrection?"

"Well, sure."

"But the resurrection means that God will raise our bodies and join them with our spirits and that we'll live forever with Him. I'll tell you, nothing has been a greater encouragement to me. And once we're reunited with the people we love, I'm eager to talk with Marianne again, walk with her, dance with her."

"Dance with her? You think so?" Adam's voice croaked at the thought. "I guess . . . I haven't thought of it that way."

Tom grinned. "Well, why *wouldn't* we dance?"

"I do what you suggested—remind myself that while Emily's body is dead, Emily is alive with Jesus in heaven. That helps a lot."

"Exactly. And one day Emily's soul will be reunited with her body. That's the resurrection. So, Adam, I'm profoundly grateful for the time I had with Marianne here. But I'm also grateful for the eternity we'll share in God's presence. Your relationship with Emily hasn't ended; it's been interrupted. Take every precious memory you had with her here and remember those are only the beginning."

Adam wiped his eyes.

"One day the thoughts in your journal will be a treasure for you, Adam. Sometimes I go back and read what I wrote the first year after Marianne died. It's been fifteen years, and I still miss her, but I see how much God has done in me. I've learned to trust Him."

"I want to trust Him. But I still don't understand."

Sometimes, Adam noticed, Tom would sit quietly before responding. He'd mine the caverns of his memory, which held treasures, some of them long hidden. He was old in a culture that valued the young, athletic, and glamorous—those who hadn't purchased wisdom with decades of selfless living, courage, and compassion. Tom Lyman would never be featured in a magazine, secular or Christian. And yet . . . he was perhaps the closest likeness to Jesus that Adam had met.

Tom touched his Bible affectionately. "In Isaiah 55, God says as high as the heavens are above the earth, so high are God's ways above our ways. If we could always understand God, it would mean He is as dumb as we are."

"Well, I'm grateful that's not the case."

They both laughed.

In Adam's driveway, he unfolded the wheelchair and helped Tom into it.

Victoria opened the front door. Adam tipped up the chair and wheeled Tom over the threshold, where Victoria waited, ready to hug him.

"What an honor to meet you, Victoria," Tom said. "Where's Dylan?"

Dylan shyly appeared from around the corner.

"So this is the track star! Your father told me about how great you're doing. He's so proud of how you took second in the 400!"

Dylan smiled.

Victoria served up a beef stew with corn bread muffins and a leafy salad loaded with cheddar cheese, tomatoes, onions, and homemade croutons. Before Adam prayed, Tom reached out to Victoria and Dylan, who in turn reached out to Adam.

"Father, thank You for Tom. Thanks for all the wisdom he has brought into my life. And thank You for Dylan and for Victoria and the work she has put into this meal. We are so grateful for You, Lord. In Jesus' name. Amen."

"Amen!" Tom looked at Victoria. "Adam told you I like beef stew?"

"Yes, he did."

"When he mentioned how good your beef stew is, I dropped a few hints, but he doesn't always get it; you know what I mean?"

"I know *exactly* what you mean."

Tom smiled broadly. "What a blessed man you are, Adam Mitchell! To have such a beautiful and charming wife and a strong and intelligent son. And how blessed they are to have a man who loves God and loves them. Now, if the rest of this beef stew lives up to the first bite, I'll have to request deliveries to the retirement center!"

Dylan and Victoria seemed delighted to answer Tom's many

questions, and Adam was stunned at how much he'd learned about both when Tom finished.

"Now, I have a little bit of beef stew left and half a muffin. I understand there is a family member named Maggie. I would like to meet her."

"Can I let her in, Adam?" Victoria asked.

"Sure, why not?"

Maggie ran in the back door and trotted straight to the stranger who held a bowl for her. She polished it off it in ten seconds as everyone laughed.

The family retired to the living room, where Maggie sat at Tom's feet; her head rested on one of his knees.

"I know it's been difficult for you all since Emily died."

"It has," Victoria said. "But God is faithful."

"Yes. He's not always easy to understand, but always faithful. When I took a bad fall six years ago, I told myself I would never walk again. I was miserable. Then one day I read about Christ's resurrection, and God turned on a light."

Adam watched Victoria and Dylan as they listened carefully to Tom's words.

"I realized, 'Well, of course I *will* walk again.'"

He turned to Dylan. "After the resurrection, I'll race you, young man, and it will take everything you have to keep up with me!"

"Yes, sir!"

Suddenly Tom teared up. "Victoria, I look forward to introducing you to Marianne. She will really like you. And I look forward to meeting Emily too."

Victoria couldn't talk, but she smiled. She went to the kitchen and five minutes later brought back warm peach pie with French vanilla ice cream. Tom ceremoniously offered Maggie the remains from his dessert plate.

Victoria looked down at Maggie, head resting on Tom's ankle. "I'm pretty sure Maggie thinks she's in heaven right now!"

After Adam and Dylan returned from the retirement center, Adam told Victoria, "Tom was a huge hit tonight. And not just with Maggie. Dylan told me how much he liked him."

"He's quite a guy, isn't he?"

"I told Tom about my tendency to believe the worst about people."

"Like Frank Tyson."

"Yeah. For starters. Well, it dawned on me that at the one drug bust when we had that brawl with the big guy and the couch got turned on its side, how hard would it be for a few bags to fall down one of the open air vents?"

"It's possible."

"On the other hand, I have to be sure I don't ignore the evidence. One of the guys may be stealing drugs. But this could cost my relationships with other cops."

"Why?"

"Because cops who snitch on other cops aren't popular."

"I wouldn't want to be in your shoes."

"Neither would I."

CHAPTER THIRTY-SIX

ADAM ARRIVED at Pearly's fifteen minutes early.

The guys' preferred table was taken, and while drawing his weapon would have cleared it, he looked for an alternative. He was headed for an empty table when he heard a woman's throaty voice say, "Corporal Mitchell!"

He turned to see the perfectly made-up face of Diane Koos.

"Ms. Koos. Hello. What brings—?" He stopped in mid-sentence. His peripheral vision sent a message too bizarre to comprehend. Namely that Diane Koos shared a table—a comparatively small fraction of it—with none other than the human planetoid.

"Mitchell," the cement mixer rumbled.

"Sergeant," Adam said weakly. He made contact with Bronson's bloodshot eyes. "What are you two . . . doing here?"

"That's our business," he growled.

Koos laughed and swatted Bronson's arm. "Oh, Brad. Don't be a cave troll!" She looked at Adam. "I told Brad breakfast was on me. When I asked where he wanted to go, you know what he said?"

"Pearly's?"

"He said, 'When I'm at Pearly's, I'm happier than a pig in slop.' Isn't that hilarious?"

"Uh . . . yeah."

"Go ahead, Brad; show him what's in the bag."

Bronson reluctantly pulled out a heavy gold-plated plaque. It said, "Albany Award for Courageous Community Service." Diane Koos's name was crossed out. Right beneath, in bold engraved lettering, it said, "Brad Bronson."

"I had that done for him because of what he did for me."

"See the corner of the plaque, how it's banged up?" Bronson said with a hangman's grin. "That's where Diane whacked the punk in the face."

"Yeah, I heard the story."

Koos smiled. "Have you met Brad's rottie, Marciano? I brought him a pound of ground round and a bag of Cheetos. We're friends for life."

Brad said brightly, "The peanut butter cookies didn't hurt your cause either." He looked at Adam. "And guess what Diane named her Jack Russell?"

He assumed it wasn't Toto.

"Otis Spunkmeyer!" Bronson laughed so hard it went into a cough.

The phrase *Now I've seen everything* took on new meaning for Adam.

Uncomfortable in this no-man's-land between the twilight zone and the outer limits, Adam said, "Listen, I need to find a table for the guys. Uh . . . have a nice day."

From where he now sat, Adam could still hear Bronson's voice: ". . . he charged at me, and my forehead met him halfway. He dropped like a rock. I went in and cleaned house, threw his punk buddies out on their keisters. I left that drug boat so clean you could lick mashed banana off the deck."

Koos giggled and leaned close to murmur something to Bronson. Adam got up and found a table in the far corner, beyond earshot.

Today's *Albany Herald* in front of him, he bypassed the front page and sports and turned to section C, the classified ads. To keep his fingers on Albany's pulse, he looked at 596, legal notices, which went on for eight pages. The first notice was from Dougherty County Juvenile Court. It began with the initials of two children, their birth dates, and it was addressed to three males, first names Ronnie, Ernest, and Willie, followed by "and other individuals who might be the biological father of said children born to Gail Edwards."

A petition had been filed by a named caseworker—"Petition of deprivation of the above referenced children."

Adam saw another similar notice, and still another and another. He shook his head.

Javy and Nathan arrived and pulled out chairs, sitting down at the same time.

"Who won?" Shane sat next to Adam.

"I'm reading legal notices. Children's services is asking possible fathers of children taken into custody to claim their kids in court."

"Like I always say," Shane said, "Rome is falling."

"We can't give up. I won't give up." Adam looked up to see David arrive with coffee and plop down in the remaining chair.

"It's gettin' bad," David said. "Last night I dreamt about Pearly's."

Shane said, "Yeah, I heard they've named you employee of the month. Pretty good since you don't even work here."

"Should make it easier to find a parking spot."

David sipped coffee to find his voice. "I found out something about Amanda that's pretty hard to take."

"What's up?" Nathan asked.

"I really don't know how to say it."

They all waited.

"Well . . . she's a vegetarian."

Silence.

Adam finally spoke. "Does that make Olivia a vegetarian, too?"

"I'd think so," Shane said, "unless she has a cash source and transportation to Burger King."

Adam leaned in. "When did you find out?"

"When I brought her and Olivia some dinner."

"From where?"

"Jimmie's Hot Dogs."

The group emitted simultaneous groans of empathy. Shane asked, "Did you let her know you're a baconatarian?"

"She told me she had a bumper sticker that said, 'Meat is murder.'"

"If meat is murder, David, you're a serial killer. What would Amanda think if she knew how many steers have given their lives to make you happy?"

"Quite a few pigs, too," David added.

Shane nodded. "I'm not sayin' it would be grounds for divorce, but it'd be a compatibility issue if you considered marriage."

"Under most circumstances that might be true," Nathan said.

"What do you mean?" David asked.

"Well, the two of you had a child together. That means unless there are overwhelming reasons not to, you should be married."

David cleared his throat. "And her being a vegetarian doesn't qualify?"

"No."

"Even if it means I could never barbecue a steak for her?"

"Even if you could never barbecue a steak for *you*," Nathan said.

David winced. "Commitment can be tough, can't it?"

"Believe it or not, David, sometimes it's even tougher."

"Seriously, guys, I've spent some time with Amanda. I respect how she's raised Olivia. I couldn't have done what she's done. Amanda's . . . amazing."

Adam asked, "David, if you had to choose between eating meat the rest of your life or being with Amanda and Olivia, which would you choose?"

David thought long and hard. "Honestly? I think I'd choose Amanda."

Javy became the group spokesman: "He's in love."

After the combination of congratulations and wisecracks that followed, Adam got serious. "Here's what I think—" he tapped the newspaper in front of him—"nobody talks about the plague of motherless children. Just fatherless children. Yeah, moms struggle, but it's dads who don't step up to the plate. I'm really proud of you, David, for the choices you're making. It's not too late to make things right."

"Reminds me of what I've been reading in the Word," Nathan said. "In Ephesians, there's a command given specifically to men: 'Fathers, do not provoke your children to anger, but bring them up in the discipline and instruction of the Lord.'"

Adam grew more animated. "In my case, that was exactly the problem. Ever since Dylan became a teenager, I've sent him negative messages. He's only heard me say no or tell him to get home sooner or do his homework or stop playing video games. I made him angry because I never encouraged him."

"That's something I need to watch with Marcos," Javy said. "I constantly tell him to stop it or to slow down. I need to find a way to say yes to him."

"I track with the need to be more positive," Nathan said. "I talk with Jade about getting off the phone, not texting so much, staying away from the wrong kids. But I don't ask her to share her favorite music with me or tell me what she's reading. If I need to tell her I don't approve of something, I will, but I don't want to discourage her. Like you said, Javy, I don't want to say no to her without finding a way to say yes about something God likes."

"When Dylan was growing up, I put him in baseball and basketball camps. It's like I resented that he had his own dreams instead of mine. I became just like my father, and Dylan got angry at me like I did at my dad! He loved running, and since I didn't, it meant I didn't approve of him. Why did I try to make him another me instead of helping him become the man God wants him to be?"

"So you go to all his track meets now?" David asked.

"Three in a row. I'm a Westover High track dad now. Go Patriots! I'm in his world. We invite his track buddies over to our house. What better way to know what goes on? Last night one of Dylan's friends said, 'Mr. Mitchell, what's it like being a cop?' So I asked if any of them wanted to go on a ride-along. Then Dylan looks at me and says, 'Can I come?'"

"You'd never invited him before?" Shane asked.

"He'd never shown any interest. I should have asked him years ago, but he had his world and I had mine, and the house was just a hotel where we spent the night, then returned to our separate worlds. It's like I had blinders on."

"I think a lot of us do," Nathan said.

"The home is supposed to be the base of operations," Adam said. "Deuteronomy 6 says to post Scripture on the walls, tell your children about God, and talk with them about spiritual stuff in the evening and the morning and as you walk around. Or in my case, as we run."

Adam pulled a folded paper from his pocket. "I brought a list of questions Caleb Holt uses in a men's accountability group so no one slips through the cracks."

Adam unfolded the paper and pointed at it. "They share at least one memory verse they've learned that week, like we do. But then they ask some questions, like: How are you doing with God? How are you doing as a husband? As a father? What temptations are you facing, and how are you dealing with them? How has your thought life been this week? Have you been spending time in God's Word and prayer? How can we pray for you and help you?"

"Good questions," Nathan affirmed. "It's been fun for me to talk with you guys about something more than sports and cars."

"That relates to a verse I memorized this week," Javy added. "Proverbs 27:17—'As iron sharpens iron, so one man sharpens another.'"

Adam nodded. "We have to say 'My life is your business, and I want it to be.' We can't be afraid to ask each other tough questions."

"William Barrett used to say to me, 'Nathan, my job isn't to help you *feel* good. It's to help you *be* good.'"

David jotted that down.

"But by helping me *be* good, Mr. Barrett showed me the way to *feel* good."

When the meeting ended, as Adam went out the door, he heard laughter over in a corner. He watched as Bronson bid a fond farewell to the woman formerly known as the Koos.

Just when you think you've got life figured out . . .

Four hours later Adam had things to take care of at the sheriff's department, so Shane was on his own for lunch. As he finished his vending machine sandwich, Shane said hi to Sergeant Smith as a few deputies entered the break room. He left and walked into the hallway adjoining the county courthouse and the sheriff's office.

"Fuller," Sergeant Murphy called, standing just outside a courtroom. He held a clear bag of white drug cookies.

"Hey, Sarge. What's up?"

"They're still doing motions in here and I've got to testify. Mind dropping these by the evidence room for me?"

Shane raised an eyebrow. "No problem."

Shane took the bag, and Sergeant Murphy walked off.

Weird. Sarge is usually a stickler for chain of custody. And he didn't even ask me to sign for it?

Shane came to the evidence room. "Anybody here?"

He checked his watch. The evidence room was low traffic, especially at lunch hour.

Shane looked outside, saw it was clear, then sat at a table with a small lamp. He turned it on and set the bag of crack-laced cookies down, then opened a drawer and pulled out gloves. He looked at the doorway before putting on the gloves and opening the bag.

Shane transferred two crack cookies into a separate bag, which he put in his pocket. He took a marker and wrote on the bag, altering the information.

Shane worked swiftly and efficiently. And, he thought, smartly. He never saw the hidden camera.

He heard movement behind him. He whipped around, knocking over his chair as he turned.

"What are you doing, Shane?"

"Adam . . . ?"

"It was you? So this is what you've been doing?"

"What are you talking about? I'm just rechecking the count before I turn it in."

"Don't lie to me! You've got drugs in your pocket right now."

Shane stared at Adam a moment, then slowly pulled out the bag and put it on the table. His expression hardened. "You won't turn me in. It'll just be an ugly mess and embarrass the whole department. Besides, it would be your word against mine."

"No, it wouldn't." Nathan stepped into the room.

"Oh, I see. Two cops camp out to bust their friend."

Adam's neck veins swelled. "What have we been talking about for the last month? What did you commit to?"

"Don't throw that in my face! I work hard, and thirty-six thousand a year doesn't cut it! I risk my life every day to protect people who don't appreciate it enough to pay me a decent wage. Figured it wouldn't hurt anybody if I gave myself a little raise from money that doesn't belong to anyone."

Outraged, Adam moved toward Shane, who backed into the wall.

"Does your word mean nothing to you? You signed the same Resolution we did, and you throw it down the toilet for what? An extra thousand a month?"

"Adam." Nathan tried to calm him.

"You've lied to all of us, Shane! To your friends, your son, to God." He took another step.

"Adam!" Nathan stepped between them.

Adam moved back and looked at Shane like he didn't know him.

Shane glared at Adam. "I'm a fellow officer and your friend. You do not want to do this."

"You're right. I don't."

Sergeant Murphy, Sergeant Smith, and Riley Cooper walked quickly into the room.

"Turn around and put your hands on the wall," Murphy said. "Shane Fuller, you are under arrest."

"This is a mistake!"

"We got it all on camera," Murphy said.

"This'll burn all of us. Is that what you want? Is that *really* what you want?"

Adam stood wearily as they cuffed his partner of thirteen years and walked him out. Shane's words haunted him. How could this have happened?

Nathan put a hand on his friend's shoulder. "We all agreed, Adam. We are *doubly* accountable."

CHAPTER THIRTY-SEVEN

WHILE ADAM GRILLED burgers, Dylan came to talk.

"Six burgers? Two for you, two for me, one for Mom. Somebody else coming over?"

"Nah." Adam poured on some Worcestershire sauce and gave a generous shake of Lawry's seasoning salt. The flame-grilled aroma and the sizzle were much-needed therapy.

"Dad, what'll happen to Mister Shane?"

"They'll separate him from the general population in the Dougherty County Jail. Private cell. He wouldn't be safe around inmates, especially the ones we put there."

Dylan heard the discouragement in his father's voice.

"Maybe in a couple of months he'll be sentenced, then moved to prison. Probably be federal charges, too. We're talking major prison time."

Adam flipped the burgers.

"What about Tyler?"

"I told Shane I'd look out for him." Adam's voice cracked, and he wiped his eyes, pretending it was the smoke. Then he realized his pretense and stopped hiding the tears from his son.

"Dylan, I know Tyler's just twelve, but . . . would you mind if he comes over sometimes and hangs out with us?"

"No problem."

"I haven't seen much of him since Shane and Mia split up. But he seems like a good kid."

"When he was maybe eight and I was eleven, I guess, we had that vacation together, remember? Waterskiing?"

"Maybe he could go camping or fishing with us. Or just watch a movie."

Dylan nodded.

"You could be a good role model to him, Dylan. He could use a big brother. His father's choices have already scarred his life. Unless someone helps him . . ." Adam's voice broke again.

"We can help him, Dad. I'm in."

"That means the world to me, Son."

Victoria joined them with potato salad and iced tea. After they sat down to eat, Dylan noticed his dad slip a hamburger patty under the table to Maggie.

After dinner Victoria cleared the patio table while Adam cleaned the grill.

Dylan hung around. Finally he asked, "Dad, how did Mister Shane get messed up?"

Adam shook his head. "I don't really know. I keep thinking about his question 'Is this what you want?' Of course, it wasn't. Obviously, it's not what *he* wanted either. Yet he's the one who made his choices, the little compromises."

"They were big compromises, weren't they?"

"In the end, yes. But the big slide begins with small choices. Each one leads to the next. Unless you stop, the little rocks become an avalanche." Adam looked at his son. "It wasn't just that hidden camera that got Shane. He didn't realize that there's a hidden camera on everyone, all the time."

"What do you mean?"

"God always watches us, Dylan. There's no such thing as a private moment. Our choices have consequences. We don't get away with anything."

"That's scary."

"Yeah. But remember how He cares about us, so much that He died for us. He's seen us at our worst but still loves us. Since He knows how bad we are, that's pretty encouraging. He forgives us when we ask Him. We just need to remind ourselves we can't keep secrets from God. That will keep us from pretending like Shane did. I wonder how real Shane's faith is."

"He usually went to church, didn't he?"

"Sure, but that's not the same thing. I used to think it was. Now I realize my relationship with Jesus wasn't very deep before Emily died."

"Haven't you always been a Christian?"

"My parents raised me as a Christian and took me to church, but there's more to it than that. The apostle Paul calls on people to follow his example. I'd like to be an example for you, Dylan. But I haven't always been a good one. So I want to ask your forgiveness. I haven't paid good attention to you. I haven't always treated you with respect. I want to change that."

"You *have* changed, Dad."

They went inside and continued their conversation in Adam's office. When the time seemed right, Adam said, "I've been thinking that you and I should memorize some Bible verses together. We could talk about them sometimes while we run."

"Memorize?"

"Yeah. It was new to me, too. Are you up for that?"

"What verses?"

Adam picked up a list with a dozen verses on it. "Here's the first one, John 3:3. 'Unless one is born again he cannot see the kingdom of God.'"

"I've heard that before, but I never really knew what it meant."

They talked for another hour. Adam didn't watch television. Dylan didn't play video games. Neither of them noticed.

"Whassup, girl?" Derrick took a seat across from Jade in the high school cafeteria.

Derrick eyed Jade's friend Lisa, who said, "I'll leave you two alone." She picked up her tray and vanished.

"Did you talk to your mom about us?"

Jade nodded. "She's sort of open to us spending a little time together."

"What does that mean?"

"Well, she knows you're a good student."

"That's cool," Derrick said.

"She still thinks you were rude when you dropped by our house."

"Your dad was rude. I was just mindin' my own business."

"You know how he feels."

"Well, girl, you need to decide how *you* feel. I like you, Jade. But I can't just wait around for you a couple of years until your daddy lets his little girl out of the nursery."

"We can talk here at school. And we can still text."

"Does your dad know we're havin' lunch and textin'?"

"No. I guess he doesn't have to know. I mean we're not datin' or anything."

"But I *want* to be datin' you."

"Yeah, but . . ."

"Then let's do it, Jade. Tell your parents you're spendin' the night at Lisa's Friday. I'll pick you up from her house."

"But . . . I don't want to lie to them."

"What's the big deal? There's nothin' wrong with us having a good time together, right? They don't own ya, girl."

"No. But . . ."

"You need to decide. I been holdin' out for you. You can't expect me to sit on my hands and not have a girl for another year. I'm movin' up in the world. I'd like you to move up with me. Don't you want that?"

"Yeah, I do. But . . ."

"You keep sayin' *but*, girl. Your daddy's got a problem. Don't let his problem be your problem. I'm livin' my own life now, makin' my own choices. You need to live your own life too."

CHAPTER THIRTY-EIGHT

"FRIED GREEN TOMATOES?" Adam asked as he sat at Aunt Bea's, joining Nathan, Javy, and David.

"Kayla's got me back on them," Nathan said. "I've been thinking. Here we are—a black man and a brown man and two extremely white men—sharing this table as brothers. That is exactly what Martin Luther King dreamed about."

"An Albany diner?" David asked.

Nathan smiled. "In one of the greatest speeches ever made—Washington, DC, 1963—King said, 'I have a dream that one day on the red hills of Georgia, the sons of former slaves and the sons of former slave owners will be able to sit down together at the table of brotherhood.' Well, I'm a descendant of slaves. You two both grew up in the South, so you're likely descendants of slave owners."

"Really?" David had never thought of that. Of course, he could never know who he descended from on his father's side.

"My mother's great-grandmother was a slave," Nathan continued. "Paul says in Ephesians 2 that Christ has broken down the barriers that divide the races. If Jews and Gentiles can be one, then blacks and whites and Hispanics and Asians can be one. The Flint River divides Albany, but it doesn't have to divide the people of Albany. You know, Adam, William Barrett told me that your church was the first one to help his when the last flood hit. And they've never forgotten that."

Adam nodded. "It was just a few years ago I heard that Martin Luther King was arrested in Albany, then run out of town. The police carried out their orders. I'd like to think I would have refused on the basis of principle. But given the times, I doubt I would have. That bothers me."

They talked awhile longer. Thanks to the jukebox, they had to raise their voices over the Beach Boys, Herman's Hermits, and Three Dog Night. Eventually the conversation turned to the Resolution.

Nathan asked, "It's just plain hard work, isn't it?"

"You're telling me," Adam said. Each man nodded and laughed, relieved to get it out in the open.

"It's tough," David offered. "But I like the challenge. It's kind of like football. Sometimes I find myself thinking like I used to, and I have to remind myself I'm a new person now. 2 Corinthians 5:17 says that."

"And without God's strength, we won't make it," Adam said. "Our own resolve isn't enough. Shane signed the Resolution just like we did. It humbles me to realize that on my own, I'm no better than Shane. I could go down, maybe in some other way than he did, but I could definitely go down."

"We all could," Javy agreed.

Nathan nodded. "I heard Shane say that Rome is falling and the barbarians are winning."

"He said that often. But I've heard the Romans' own moral corruption took them down. If they hadn't let themselves become morally weak, they wouldn't have been defeated by the barbarians. And if we're not careful, we could self-destruct too."

Nathan folded his hands on the table. "We can't surrender to the culture. We've minimized the role of fathers, so we've created a generation of barbarians—children who become men without growing up. They stay in boyhood through their twenties and thirties, sometimes their whole lives. They think of themselves first, indulge in pornography, do what they feel like, and leave their wives and culture and churches to raise their children."

Adam said, "Unless we stand up and win back some turf, guys, we'll lose this war. Maybe we can't turn around the whole culture—we *can* take hold of our own lives and families. But we need each other's support to press on."

Nathan said, "You know, four of us have talked about our fathers. But, Javy, we haven't heard much about *your* father."

Javy hesitated. "I feel nervous saying this . . . My dad was a great father."

"Why are you nervous?"

"Perhaps because you have all said your fathers were not there or that they frustrated you. And I am the only one at this table not carrying a weapon."

They laughed.

"My father was not perfect. But he loved me and Jose and Charro."

"The Snake Kings?" Adam asked.

Javy laughed. "We were the toughest brothers in northern Mexico, so we thought. Our father was kind and fair. He disciplined us, but only when we deserved it. He would tolerate no disrespect for our mother. He showed us what it meant to love a woman. If I am any good as a husband or father, it is because of my *papá*."

The table was quiet. Each man hoped that one day his children would say the same of him.

"Did your father listen to you?" David asked.

"Always. And he asked me questions to find out my dreams and plans. He never discouraged me. When I told him I wanted to come to America and work to send home money to help the family, he told me I was an honorable son."

David had trouble imagining what such a relationship would look like.

"When did he find all that time to talk with you?"

"He worked alongside us. When you work together, you talk together."

Adam nodded. "Like you and I did, working on my shed."

"Yes. He showed me how to work with my hands. And to take pride in what I did. It wasn't just about money. You did your best for your family and for others."

"I can vouch for how well he taught you to work," Adam said.

"Thank you." Javy lowered his head. "We had fun together too. He took us fishing. And always he took us to church. Some of my friends, their mothers were godly, but their fathers didn't go to church. And those friends are not followers of Jesus today."

Nathan nodded. "I read that if boys grow up with mothers who attend church and fathers who don't, a huge percentage stop going. But when the father goes to church, even if the mother doesn't, the great majority of boys attend church as adults."

Javy hesitated a moment, then spoke again. "One day my father came home discouraged. He drank too much and got angry. He didn't hit any of us, but he yelled at our mother and us. Charro cried. So did my mother.

"The next day my father sat us down and got on his knees and wept before us. He told us he had begged forgiveness of our mother and she kindly forgave him. And now he asked our forgiveness. He wanted to hear it from each of us. Never once did he bring alcohol into the house again. He knew it was a problem for him and didn't want to take a chance."

There was a long pause. Nathan said, "God can even use our failures for good."

Javy said, "I have heard people here in Georgia talk about growing up dirt-poor. I am not sure they know what that means. But my father does. To this day his life is not easy. But it has helped the last month that I have been able to send most of my check down to my parents."

"*Most* of your check?" Adam said. "That must have been quite a raise."

"It was. We have more for ourselves now, but I will not have more unless my mother and father have more."

"'Honor your father and your mother,'" Nathan said. The Scripture required no explanation. Javy was its commentary.

David volunteered to take Javy back to work. Nathan had to get to the station, so Adam took him. David and Javy talked as they rode and continued their discussion outside the Coats & Clark factory.

"When you told us about your dad drinking that night, it really hit home. The alcohol thing, I mean."

"You're brave to admit you have a problem, David."

"I thought it would just go away when I became a Christian. It's better, but . . . some nights it's still difficult."

"Some things remain temptations as long as we keep them near. In his moments of strength, my father removed from the house what would have ruined him in his moments of weakness."

"That makes sense."

"I know some churches have group meetings for this. Talk with one of your pastors. They will know how to help you."

"Thanks, Javy."

Javy extended his hand to David. "I hope one day I can introduce you to my father."

CHAPTER THIRTY-NINE

KAYLA SAT on the couch reading a piece of paper.

Nathan sat in a chair opposite her. "What do you think?" he asked.

"I know she's fifteen, but do you think it's time for this?"

"Kayla, one thing I believe is that we've got to have our children's hearts. Adam's winning Dylan's heart back. I've got to go after Jade's. If her dad doesn't have her heart, it's an open invitation to a string of boys to try to take it."

"I just want to make sure a fifteen-year-old will take care of it."

"And that her little brother won't put it down the garbage disposal."

Kayla winced. "You had to put that picture in my mind, didn't you?"

"Jade's becoming a young woman. I believe she'll take care of it. Besides, the biggest thing isn't the symbol itself. It's what it symbolizes. And that's something even Jordan can't heist."

Kayla nodded. "Okay. I'm in agreement."

"I'll go invite her now."

"I did tell her she could spend the night at Lisa's Friday."

"How well do we know Lisa?"

"Jade says she's a good girl."

"Is Jade the best judge of that?"

Kayla frowned. "We have to trust our daughter. Otherwise she'll rebel."

"Well, I'd prefer Friday, but if not, we'll do it Thursday."

"Why not Saturday?"

"Because . . . I don't know. I just don't want to postpone it."

Jade was texting in her room when she heard a knock on her door. "Go away, Jordan."

"It's your father."

Jade came to the door, cell in her hand. "Everything okay?"

"Yeah, I just want to ask you about something."

Her phone beeped. Text message from Derrick.

"Jade, would you please turn off your phone for a few minutes while we talk?"

"It's okay; I won't look."

"No, I'd rather it was off." He pulled his cell phone out of his pocket, raised it in the air, and pressed the Off button. "Join me?"

Jade reluctantly complied.

"May I sit down?"

"Yeah."

"Jade, I want to invite you out on a date with me Friday night."

"But . . . what do you mean, a date?"

"Dinner at a really nice place. Just you and me."

"But Mom already said I could spend the night at Lisa's Friday."

"I know; maybe that could be Saturday night instead. Then Lisa could go with you to church Sunday morning."

"Why couldn't you take me Saturday?"

"I already made reservations for Friday night."

Jade thought about it. "Dad, I really need to be at Lisa's Friday night. A commitment is a commitment."

Nathan nodded. "Okay, I'll respect that. Would you go with me to dinner on Thursday?"

"Okay."

"Thank you."

Nathan walked out of the room, looked back at her and smiled, then closed the door.

Jade exhaled. Friday's plans were still together. Not that Lisa would have minded since her plan was to go out with her boyfriend Damon while Derrick took Jade to dinner, the mall, and a late movie. Jade dreaded the thought of telling Derrick he couldn't pick her up at Lisa's Friday afternoon because she was going to dinner with her dad. He would have been *really* mad.

Victoria looked at Adam. "You took Maggie to the vet?"

"She wasn't feeling well."

"I had the flu a week ago and you didn't take *me* to the doctor."

"You didn't look at me with soulful eyes or I would have."

"And you made her *waffles*?"

"Comfort food. She appreciated the butter too."

"I smell bacon."

"You can't have waffles without bacon."

"You put waffles and bacon in her dog dish?"

"Not exactly. I . . . hand-fed her."

"You hand—"

"She wasn't feeling well!"

"She seems fine now."

"Did it occur to you that maybe she's fine now precisely

because I took good care of her? Okay, I'll make *you* waffles and bacon Saturday."

"And hand-feed me? You're on."

They laughed; then Victoria asked, "So when will you get a new partner?"

"I hope it won't be soon."

"Why?"

"Because I'm afraid who it'll be. They replaced Jeff, so Riley Cooper's covered. Now who's the only cop on my shift, besides me, who's missing a partner?"

"Bronson? But he's a sergeant."

"Top brass think they need to get Bronson a partner who will keep him under control."

"Could you do that?"

"Iron Man couldn't keep Bronson under control. I'm telling you, Victoria, the man . . . he just . . ."

"What?"

"He *scares* me. There are things he needs to hear but . . . I'm afraid to tell him. That's not easy for me to admit."

"It takes courage to admit fear." She leaned toward him. "But you said Bronson rescued Diane Koos, right? And they're on good terms?"

"To the point of sharing sweet nothings together at Pearly's and being on a first-name basis with each other's dogs. But that doesn't change Bronson's record. Koos is only an adviser. The sheriff's senior staff will make the call whether he gets a partner."

"They wouldn't put a sergeant and a corporal together, right?"

"Stranger things have happened. Though I can't think of anything stranger than having Bronson as a partner."

"Who knows? Maybe that's God's plan."

Adam's face deflated. "Thanks. Just what I didn't want to hear."

★ ★ ★

Late at night, after he tucked Isabel and Marcos in, Javy said to Carmen, "I need to write a letter to my *papá*."

"*Por qué no escribes a tu madre?*"

"*Mamá* hears from me often. I ask her to greet *Papá* for me. But this time I want to write directly to him."

"That will mean a lot to him. Good night, *mi amor*. I'm going to bed."

Javy sat down at the kitchen table and took out a writing tablet and pen. Javy scrawled, feeling the pleasure of writing in his mother tongue.

> *Dear* Papá,
>
> *I meet often with the* amigos *I have mentioned to you and* Mamá: *Adam and Nathan and David are honorable men. As I told* Mamá, *they are deputies. Please explain to her that no, I did not meet them by being arrested. Rather, I met them through something miraculous that God did. God's ways are amazing!*
>
> *We have talked about our* papás. *I was surprised to learn that none of them have a relationship with theirs that has brought great happiness.*
>
> *But I was very proud to tell my friends about* mi papá.
>
> *You taught me the importance of working hard and taking pride in my work. You taught me to honor* Mamá *and love my brothers. Above all, you taught me and Charro and Jose to love God.*
>
> *I know,* Papá, *you will tell me that you were just doing your job. And while I would say the same thing, the fact is that if not for your example and your words, I could not say it.*
>
> *Mi Dios has blessed me far more than I deserve. Just*

when I think that Carmen could not be a better esposa, she continues to amaze me. Isabel is beautiful. The photos Carmen has sent you do not begin to do her justice.

Marcos is a boy who wants to conquer the world! I think he may give me as much difficulty as I gave you. If I can be half the padre you were to me, Papá, then my son will be privileged.

I told you about my job and the promotion and raise. I am honored to share with you and Mamá from the dinero I am paid. I know you use some of it to help your neighbors and the church. I am glad for that. Please buy yourself a new fishing pole.

Mr. Tyson has told me that as long as his factory is open, he will have a place for me. So after many years of dreaming of this, I have something I wish to propose. I want to send dinero for you and Mamá to take a bus to Guadalajara. I will buy the tickets to fly you to Atlanta, Georgia, where I will pick you up at the aeropuerto.

I know you and Mamá have never flown in a plane. But it is a great adventure that I think you would enjoy.

And it is not only for you. It is for Carmen and los niños. And it is for me.

And when you are here, I will take you to the factory to meet Mr. Tyson and to our church, where our services are en español. Then we will introduce you to all my new amigos and their families.

Por favor, Papá, say yes. Tell Mamá that her grandchildren await her hugs.

Muchas gracias, Papá, for being the man my friends wish their fathers had been.

Your grateful son,
Javy

CHAPTER FORTY

BRAD BRONSON DROPPED by Harveys Supermarket on North Slappey. His mission was to storm the front doors and capture items from all four primary food groups—frozen pizza, beer, ice cream, and bacon. Then there were nature's finest—the canned foods. Unfazed by shoppers' reactions to the clatter, he let gravity do the work as he flipped Dinty Moore beef stew and SpaghettiOs cans from the shelves into his cart.

Had to get Sweet Baby Ray's and Cheetos, or he'd answer to his rottweiler. Marciano was persnickety about his bacon, and Harveys had his favorite. Bronson also picked up a carton of eighteen eggs.

Since the vet had declared Marciano lactose intolerant, Bronson was careful in the dairy section. Ice cream didn't count as dairy since it was in the freezer case, so Bronson got rocky road for himself and butter pecan for his sidekick.

Multiple plastic grocery sacks dangled from each hand as he stepped into the parking lot. He paused a moment to let his eyes adjust to the dim light. Ten feet from the car, he reached for his remote, unlocking his gray Tundra 4x4 that towered over the wimpy vehicles crouched around it.

Groceries still in hand, his peripheral vision registered movement. A large, shadowy image approached. Just as Brad turned, a blow hit the right side of his neck all the way to his throat.

He crumpled to the asphalt. Chili cans rattled as they rolled away. Bronson wasn't sure if the cracking sound he'd heard was his skull or the dropped eggs. He looked up to see a black bandanna-covered face like the one that had attacked David at the theater. And he would recognize those biceps anywhere. In the assailant's gloved right hand was a baseball bat.

"Still awake, fat man? Was goin' fo' the back of your skull; lucky you turned. This time I'm gonna crush yo head in."

The right side of Bronson's face throbbed, and the back of his head didn't feel much better.

He wanted to reach for his gun, but he was so dizzy, he knew he could kill a bystander. Instead he reached up to the door handle.

As TJ drew back the baseball bat, Bronson opened the door.

Cujo's worst nightmare leaped out of the truck and lunged at TJ.

TJ swung at the 140-pound rottweiler, who yelped when the bat connected. Undeterred, Marciano bared his teeth at the gangster, positioning himself between TJ and his master.

"What's going on?" called someone exiting the store.

TJ drew a gun, pointed it at Bronson, and in a flash Marciano was on him again, clamping down on TJ's right arm. The shot fired into asphalt, a foot from Bronson. The gun flew out of TJ's hand.

TJ ran. Marciano took off after him. As TJ got to a fence, Marciano bit his calf. TJ screamed. One hand on the fence, he swung the bat at Marciano with the other, but not hard enough to keep him down. He climbed the fence, and the dog jumped to the top, nearly making it over and snarling viciously as TJ disappeared into the darkness. The threat gone, Marciano bolted across the parking lot to Bronson.

A man and woman stood over Bronson. Marciano—hackles raised—growled. They backed off. He turned to Bronson, whined, and began licking his face.

"It's okay, boy. I'm all right."

The man said, "You are *not* all right!"

The side of Bronson's face was a mess of blood and deep purple bruises. He had the mother of all headaches.

As Bronson, still on the ground, leaned against his truck, Marciano licked his head wounds, then crawled into his lap. Marciano was a lot of dog for a lap. But Bronson had a lot of lap.

The store manager stepped out. "An ambulance is coming."

At that moment everyone heard a loud bang from the street. The store's front window shattered. Three more explosions followed. One bullet tore into Bronson's Tundra, the other into his left shoulder.

People panicked, ducked, and ran back into the store. Pandemonium reigned for a wild minute.

Soon sirens blared, lights flashed, and an ambulance pulled into the parking lot. Two EMTs jumped out.

"Nobody said anything about gunfire!"

"It happened after I called," the store manager said.

The first EMT, whose name badge said Paul Martin, hurried toward Bronson. Marciano stepped between them, growling. Every time he tried to take a step toward Bronson, the dog's growl intensified.

Bronson called to the EMT, "In those sacks there's a bag of Cheetos. Open it."

"Sir, you're in shock; you need to—"

"Feed the dog or he'll help himself to your backside."

Paul Martin didn't care to participate in that prophecy's

fulfillment. So he opened the bag and offered it. Marciano delicately removed a single Cheeto, ate it, then tore into the rest of the bag, which dropped open onto the parking lot. The lifespan of the remaining Cheetos was approximately seven seconds.

"Okay, you can come over."

Cautiously both EMTs approached with a stretcher.

They took Bronson to the ambulance.

Marciano's growl became a whine.

"I won't leave without my dog."

"Wait. That dog's bleeding." A pool of blood had formed on the asphalt.

"Help him!" Bronson yelled with panic his voice box had seldom felt. Now that Marciano's adrenaline had leveled, his condition became apparent. Paul Martin approached him.

"He's been shot in the neck. It came through the other side."

"Get him in here!" Bronson said from the ambulance.

"We're not equipped to take animals—"

"Put him in the ambulance *now*." He placed a hand on his holster.

Guiding Marciano up the ramp since he was too weak to jump, they complied.

Bronson awoke, alarmed by the daylight. Adam and David stood near his bed.

"How long?"

"You went through surgery and you've been out cold for maybe eight hours."

Bronson reached for his shoulder. "Only a flesh wound."

"You're a mess," Adam said.

"Main thing's my head. When the bat hit me, I heard it break."

They cringed.

"The bat, not my head!"

Bronson's eyes showed sudden alarm. "Where's Marciano?"

"He spent the night with the vet. Keels from K-9 took him to your house an hour ago. It's his day off. Says he'll stay there as long as needed."

"My dog's wounded."

"Marciano's fine. The shot went through cleanly, didn't hit his windpipe."

"Marciano took a bullet for me. Get Keels on the phone."

"Sarge, there's no need to—"

Bronson's eyes locked onto Adam's like a missile system. "Now."

Adam handed him his cell. "Keels? Bronson. Never mind me. How's my dog?" He listened. "Good. Good. Okay, turn on 93.9 FM, would you? Yeah. He likes the classics. And do me a favor. I've still got some eggs and half a pack of bacon. Fry up three eggs over easy, salt but no pepper. And five strips of bacon. Yeah, *for the dog*. You think I was talking about the mailman? And don't give him milk, okay? He's lactose intolerant."

This went on for another three minutes and included instructions about closing the shades in the afternoon because Marciano liked to nap on the couch. Bronson insisted that Keels put the phone to Marciano's ear and not listen. Adam and David stepped back a few feet while he whispered into the phone.

After hanging up, Bronson looked at Adam and David. "They got his gun, right? Marciano ripped it out of his hand."

"Yeah," David said. "Guess what. It's my Glock 19C."

"I knew it was the same guy. He wore gloves. No prints, right?"

"Right."

"What about the bullets?"

"They ran ballistics on the bullet in your truck. It's a .357. No provenance. But obviously it's the same guy."

Bronson's eyes burned. "What kind of a man would shoot a dog?"

"He shot you too, Sarge."

"That's different. This was Marciano."

An hour later Bronson awoke with a start. He heard the clicking of heels just as Diane Koos burst into the hospital room.

"He deserves a purple heart, so I brought one . . . along with a few kidneys, a liver, and half a dozen link sausages." She held up a large paper bag from Carroll's Sausage & Meats.

"The meds are messin' with my appetite," Bronson growled. "But thanks."

"This isn't for you; it's for Marciano. He took a bullet in his neck. You only got winged!"

Bronson stared at her, then slowly smiled.

"I wanted to visit you before we relieve Keels. But Otis Spunkmeyer's in the car, so I can't be long. We'll stay with Marciano until you get home. He won't go hungry."

She planted a quick peck on Bronson's billiard ball and disappeared.

An unfamiliar feeling akin to thankfulness welled up within him. *She's taking care of my dog.*

A slight tear came to his eye.

He contemplated what he could give her to express his gratitude. Perhaps a daddy Glock for her bedside drawer. And a baby Glock for her purse.

What more could any woman want?

CHAPTER FORTY-ONE

THURSDAY NIGHT Jade and Nathan sat at a table for two at Mikata Steak House. Nathan hadn't been there in years.

He'd stopped by earlier in the week to scope out the menu and prices, calculating how many trips to Jimmie's Hot Dogs could be made for the same price.

This is the right place.

It wasn't opulent, but the atmosphere was warm and classy, with soft music in the background. Jade wore her best dress, a dark-brown knit, and Nathan wore his suit and best silk tie. He'd successfully negotiated a "cell phones off" accord.

"Order whatever you want, Jade. I mean it."

"But, Daddy . . . this place looks expensive."

"You're worth it to me, sweetie."

The waiter approached. "The filet is excellent, and our special tonight is the shrimp Alfredo."

"Jade, would you like to try the shrimp?"

"Yes, please."

"And I'll have the filet, medium well, with vegetables."

The waiter took their folded menus. "I'll be back in a moment with your appetizers."

Jade looked around. "Daddy, I can't believe you brought me here."

"The first time I brought your mother here, I asked her to marry me."

Nathan took a sip of water, then leaned forward and looked into Jade's eyes.

"Tonight's a special night. Jade, I brought you here because I wanted to tell you how grateful I am that God entrusted you to me. I see my daughter becoming a beautiful woman, and I can understand why any young man would be drawn to you. But I also want you to know that as your father, I want the best for you. No man on earth loves you like I do. One day I will give you away to another man, but I want that man to love God more than anything. Because if he does, then he will love you."

For the first time in recent memory, Nathan saw Jade sit with her eyes fixed on his, taking in every word.

"Jade, I know how young men think. They want to win your heart, but they don't know how to treasure it. So I'm going to ask you something."

"What?"

"I'd like to make an agreement with you. If you'll trust me with your heart and allow me to approve any young man that desires to have more than a friendship with you, then I promise to take care of you and give you my full blessing when God shows us both who the right one is."

She kept her eyes on him and smiled.

"Jade, will you trust me with your heart until God shows us the right man?"

Jade nodded. "Okay."

"Thank you, sweetheart. I hoped you would. I got you something that will help us remember tonight."

He reached in his coat pocket. Jade watched intently as

Nathan set a small black box in front of her. He slowly opened it. Inside lay a gold ring with tiny diamonds in the shape of a heart.

She stared at the ring, wide-eyed.

"Jade, may I have your left hand?"

Jade placed her hand in Nathan's. He slid the ring on her finger.

"Daddy, is this real?"

"Yes, it is. This is meant to be worn until the day it is replaced with your wedding ring. It speaks of our agreement and your commitment to purity to save yourself for your husband."

She looked at the ring, mesmerized.

"I love you, sweetie. You are priceless to me, and from this night on, I am determined to treat you as the young woman you are."

Tears filled her eyes.

"I love you too, Daddy. Thank you so much." She looked like his little girl again. "Do you have a tissue?" she asked.

Nathan searched his pockets. "I'll be right back."

He walked toward the bathroom, hardly believing what had happened. It had gone exactly as he hoped. When he found tissue in the bathroom, he grabbed a handful for Jade, then looked in the mirror and quickly used three himself.

After Nathan composed himself, he returned to the table. The next two hours were sacred. They talked about nothing and everything, laughed about things that mattered and things that didn't.

They drove home at nine thirty, finally silent. He had been able to speak to his daughter about something incredibly important. No texts. No Facebook. She had been there for him 100 percent—probably because he had been there for *her* 100 percent.

When they entered the house, Jade ran to her mother to show her the ring. Kayla walked with Jade into her bedroom and didn't come out until after eleven.

Jade texted five friends to tell them what her daddy had done for her. And at midnight, she lay on her stomach in bed, staring at her ring in the moonlight.

★ ★ ★

"Good morning, Daddy." Jade hugged him tight.

"Morning, sweetheart. I could get used to hugs like that. How did you sleep?"

"I didn't sleep much, but that's okay."

Kayla turned to Jade. "You weren't up late texting, were you?"

"A little." For the first time she could remember, Kayla felt good about what she figured her daughter had been texting to friends.

When Nathan took a call on his cell phone, Jade asked her mother, "Do you wanna see my ring again?" She held it out for Kayla, who was peeling an orange.

"I saw it the first three times you showed me. But I'm glad to look again. Yes'm, looks just as good."

"I love it. I can't wait to show Tasha and CeCe."

"Jade, I'm glad you'll show your friends, but make sure you don't do it so they're jealous. That ring represents a promise between you, God, and your daddy. And me too. It isn't just bling."

Suddenly Kayla covered her face.

"What's wrong, Mama?"

"I was . . . thinking how my life as a young woman might have been different if my daddy had done for me what yours did for you last night." Kayla wiped her eyes.

Nathan returned to the table. "You okay?" he asked Kayla as he sat next to Jordan and picked up a box of cereal.

"Yeah. Peeling oranges just makes me emotional." She laughed. "Hey, do those cops you work with know that you eat Cap'n Crunch?"

"What's wrong with that?"

Kayla turned to Jade. "Okay, Lisa's mom takes you after school. So what time should we pick you up at Lisa's tomorrow?"

Jade looked down. "I'm not going to Lisa's."

"What? You've been looking forward all week to spending the night. What happened?"

"I decided I'd rather stay home."

"But, Jade, your father changed his plans so you could go to Lisa's tonight. And now you've canceled?"

Nathan stood and put his arm around Jade. "You know what? Last night was perfect for our dinner. And I think tonight would be perfect to have the family home together."

Jordan piped up. "Why not now? Do you have to go to work today, Daddy?"

"I do, little man. But I'll be home in plenty of time for a movie and Bible story time. Okay?"

"Are you gonna stop the bad guys today?"

"I'm gonna try."

"Will you wear your vest?"

Nathan glanced at the newspaper and saw the weather forecast. Ninety-one degrees. "It's gonna be hot today."

CHAPTER FORTY-TWO

ADAM, IN JEANS and a casual shirt, parked his truck at the Dougherty County Jail, an imposing 1,244-bed prisonlike facility with two on-site courtrooms operating seven days a week. When Adam looked around the waiting room, he saw two dozen forlorn and nervous faces. He exchanged pleasantries with the female deputy running the front desk and got clearance.

The jail doors opened. Adam went through a metal detector, but the full search was waived when the sleepy deputy recognized him. Adam walked down the tunnel-like corridor of white cinder blocks and polished concrete floor.

Shane Fuller was held in protective custody, in the E building's Echo 400, far back in the jail's bowels. Steel doors opened, and a deputy escorted Shane into the visiting room. Adam took a seat across the glass from Shane, who looked down.

"Hey, Shane."

"Adam. Thanks for coming. I . . . can't tell you what it's like to be on this side of the glass."

"Shane, I'm sorry."

"You did the right thing. It took me a while to admit it, but

I deserve this. I knew what I was doing. I guess I just thought
I had a free pass."

"What happened, Shane?"

His old partner, with whom he'd had a hundred adventures
and a thousand laughs, looked him in the eyes. "I ask myself
that every day. Remember when we talked about hanging on,
not letting go of that steering wheel? I guess somewhere along
the way I let go." His voice cracked. "Now my life is over. I
couldn't get it back even if I wanted to."

"Your life doesn't need to be over. But you've got to get right
with God. Then you need to get right with your son."

"I've lost him, Adam."

"No. Tyler's hurt, but you haven't lost him. I've talked with
him. It's not too late."

Shane leaned forward. "You have to help me with Tyler. He
needs someone to look out for him."

"Dylan and I discussed this. We'll keep an eye on him. You
have my word. In fact, we already invited him to run with us
in the 5K."

"I was gonna do that with him. Thanks."

"Shane, can I ask you something?"

"Yeah."

"Why did you choose to tell the truth about not warning
Jamar Holloman before you tased him?"

Shane sighed. "I knew that if I claimed to have warned him
before turning on the Taser, they'd go back and study the foot-
age to determine whether that was possible. If they looked at it
again, I was afraid they'd notice."

"Notice what?"

"The bag of crack was right there. It had to be in the camera's
field of view. And while he was on his stomach, I grabbed it,
poured half the rocks into a baggie, and stuffed it inside my shirt.

Maybe fifty rocks, a thousand dollars. Internal affairs studied the film for the tasing, not the drugs. But if someone checked the report and looked back at the video, they could have seen there were twice as many rocks in Holloman's bag as I turned in."

"So you took a reprimand rather than risk the felony."

Shane hung his head. "We were partners, friends. Please forgive me."

The guard stepped in behind Shane and nodded to Adam that their visit was over.

"I forgive you, Shane."

Shane looked up with haunted eyes. "Adam, I've really let you down. Even worse than you know. I'm so sorry."

The guard took Shane's arm.

"Don't let go of the wheel," Shane said.

Adam nodded. "Never."

Adam watched Shane as he was taken away and the door closed behind him.

He walked out of the room and down the long hallway that separated the captives from the free. Yet, Adam pondered, some in prison were free in their hearts while many outside were slaves to their appetites.

On his lonely walk from Echo building back to the free world, Adam asked himself, *What did Shane mean when he said, "Even worse than you know"?*

Adam's patrol car wouldn't start, so Murphy assigned Adam to ride with Bronson. Neither was happy about it. Adam feared he'd be swallowed up in the black hole of Bronson's infinite gravity. Since it was Bronson's first day back after the shooting, Adam volunteered to drive. Bronson gave him a look that suggested he would die or kill before letting someone else drive his car.

They parked a half block from a notorious drug house and watched customers go in and out. Bronson ate his second Jimmie's hot dog, "all the way" with mustard, chili, and onions on a toasted bun, more slaw than you could shake a stick at, and some specialty sauerkraut Bronson kept in the car. The kraut was reason enough for Adam to keep his window rolled down.

"Is this how you spend your lunch hour?" Adam asked him. "Have you ever considered reading a book or listening to the radio?"

"Have you ever considered stoppin' your yakkin' and lettin' a man eat in peace?"

After ten minutes, a man carrying a blue lunch cooler climbed the steps to the porch and opened the door without knocking.

"He's carried that same cooler three days in a row. I don't think he's buying. I think he's delivering."

Soon the man left again, cooler still in hand.

"It frosts me, Mitchell. We know where the drug houses are, and we have to wait around until we get a warrant. I say we just go in and put them out of business today. We know what they're doing. What's to stop us?"

"Well, there's the law. And the Bill of Rights. And also the fact that you're asking for someone to blow your head off."

"They're not blowin' *my* head off."

Adam sighed, remembering what Dylan said about opportunities to speak up. "Look, we deal constantly with death. It should make us more aware of our mortality, not less. Even if we retire and live another twenty years—which, despite our stellar dietary habits, most of us won't—we'll all die. You know that, right?"

Adam studied Bronson's profile, searching for a way to penetrate that thick skull.

"I've cheated death dozens of times."

"Brad, come on, you want lightning to strike you? Do you know how close to death you've come in the last couple of months? Especially at Harveys Supermarket."

"Marciano saved me."

"Yeah, he did. Then they opened fire on you, and one round hit you in the shoulder. Could have been your heart. That's twice you could have died that day."

"Okay, *I'm gonna die.* There, I said it. Happy?"

"Then doesn't it make sense to be prepared for it?"

"Prepared for what? Being eaten by worms? How much planning does that require?"

"You're created in God's image, Sarge. You will exist someplace forever."

"Do I look stupid?"

Adam wisely withheld his answer.

"Because I don't believe that for a minute."

"Your disbelief doesn't change reality. You are who you are, and God is who He is. And Jesus did what He did for you on the cross. Nothing you think or say will ever change that. You and I don't get a vote."

Bronson stared at him like a wolverine at a rabbit. "I pay my own way. I don't want your religion; it's for thumb-sucking fools who need a crutch. Do I make myself clear, Corporal?"

Adam returned Bronson's stare. "You know, Brad, I'd rather be judged a fool by you for the moment than be judged a fool by God forever. And please don't say you'd rather pay your own way. You may get your wish. It's called hell."

"Mitchell, get your mind off that hocus-pocus and do your job. Otherwise while you see visions, some street punk's gonna blow you to heaven sooner than you intended to go."

"I do my job fine. But life is more than the job. And if

someone does blow me away, I'd rather be blown to heaven than to hell. How about you?"

Adam squared off with Bronson eye to eye, awaiting the next eruption of belittling sarcasm.

Bronson blinked first.

"You know, Mitchell, I don't agree with you. But I'll say this for you—you must really believe this nonsense to fight for it when you knew I'd fight back on every point. I always thought you were a wimp. You showed me somethin' today."

Bronson started the car.

They pulled very slowly toward the drug house. Bronson flipped on his lights, no siren. Adam watched several people turn and head the opposite direction or walk right past as if they hadn't planned to stop. He saw someone peek through the blinds.

Bronson spoke over the loudspeaker, the cement mixer coming through loud and clear. "I know who you are, Gerald Ellis. There's a bed with your name on it at the Georgia State Pen. Flush those drugs. Burn them now while you got a chance. I'm comin' back for you."

He finally turned off the lights and headed toward Jackson Street.

"Where we going?" Adam asked.

"I could use one more hot dog from Jimmie's. Watching drug dealers gives me an appetite."

At the end of an eight-hour shift that felt like two days in a jail that smelled like sauerkraut, Adam marched straight to Sergeant Murphy's office.

"Tell me you're not going to make me Bronson's partner."

"That's not your call, is it?"

"I just spent one day with him. I couldn't handle five days a week."

"Maybe he'd grow on you."

Bronson *grow*? That was a scary thought.

"Please, Sarge." Adam hoped he didn't look as pathetic as he sounded.

"Sorry you feel that way, Adam. I'm surprised you have less consideration for Bronson than he has for you."

"What do you mean?"

"Well, you know those thirty days of paid leave donated to you after Emily died?"

"Yeah?"

"Ten of them came from Brad Bronson."

CHAPTER FORTY-THREE

THIS WAS ONE trip Nathan Hayes knew he had to make alone.

He stood with the warm sun on his back. A light breeze rustled the leaves of the oak trees that dotted the serene landscape. The grass beneath his feet smelled freshly mowed. He looked at a card in his hand and read aloud:

"'My name is Nathan Hayes, and I am your son. I've wasted too much time being angry with you, asking why you were never there for me. I've always felt that I needed to prove myself to you, wondering if I was worth being loved. I now realize I have a heavenly Father who loves me, even though my earthly father did not, and that has made all the difference. My Father God is more than enough. Because of Him, I have forgiven you. He is your judge, not me. I live with the hope that you gave your life to Him while you still could so that one day I will finally meet you face-to-face.'"

Nathan placed the letter next to a small, neglected tombstone etched with the name Clinton Brown. He walked away and never looked back.

★ ★ ★

Three days after Adam's stint in Brad Bronson's patrol car, Bronson approached him at the end of their shift. Adam noticed something was different. His usual intensity seemed ratcheted down.

The cement mixer cleared his throat. "We found out about Shane Fuller's middle man."

"Shane told who he sold the drugs to?"

"No. The buyer confessed. We knew he was a dealer; we just didn't know he sold stolen police evidence. We already had the guy—bound for jail on another charge."

"What charge?"

"Vehicular manslaughter. Under the influence. Alcohol and cocaine."

Adam stared at him. "Are you telling me . . . Shane sold evidence room crack to *Mike Hollis*?"

"Yeah."

Adam pondered it. "So Shane sold to Hollis, knowing Hollis would deal it on the streets. To kids. But where did Shane pass the dope to Hollis?"

Bronson growled, "You won't believe it. The All American Fun Park."

"You're kidding. I dropped him off there one day when his car was in the shop. It was the same day I drove him to the bank with Emily." *The day she danced.*

Adam smashed fist into palm. "That's when Mike Hollis saw me in the parking lot at the Fun Park!"

"What are you talking about, Mitchell?"

"Shane brought a bag of stuff that day. Said he'd bought a couple of Bulldogs T-shirts for Tyler. I asked to see them; he didn't let me. He was taking cocaine to Mike Hollis in my truck with Emily there. Maybe the same stuff Hollis was on when he . . ."

Adam turned and walked away.

★ ★ ★

After dinner, Adam and Caleb sat in the Holt's family room while the women remained in the dining room, talking.

"I saw Dylan run past the fire station one day and waved him down. He tells me the two of you run together."

"It's been awesome. A great way to spend time with my son. We talk about everything."

Catherine and Victoria joined them, coffee in hand. A knowing glance passed between Catherine and Caleb. He said, "Catherine and I have something to ask you and a few things to tell you."

"You planning to move a trailer into our backyard?" Adam asked.

"No, but thanks for the offer," Caleb said. "We'll consider it."

Victoria looked at the guys with mock disapproval. "What did you want to say, Catherine?"

"Well, it's official—we're adopting a little girl from China!"

Victoria got up and hugged Catherine. "That's wonderful news!"

Caleb grinned. "She's three years old. It'll probably be another few months before we can fly over and get her."

Catherine said, "What we want to ask you is this. I hope you don't mind, but . . . well, how would you feel if we named our little girl . . . Emily?"

Victoria stared at Catherine, then covered her face with both hands.

"I'm sorry," Catherine said.

Victoria shook her head. "No. I'm just . . . We would be honored, wouldn't we, Adam?"

Adam looked at Caleb and Catherine. "Yes, we would."

They celebrated this for several minutes. Then Caleb smiled at Catherine. "Now, we have something else to tell you. We just found out today. Except for family, you're the first to know."

"Know what?" Victoria asked.

Catherine smiled. "It turns out we'll get two children!"

Victoria clapped her hands. "Siblings?"

"We're just adopting one. The other one is already with us."

"What does that mean?" Adam asked.

Victoria looked at Catherine. "You're *pregnant*?"

"Yes!"

Victoria shrieked and threw her arms around Catherine a second time.

Adam laughed. "I haven't seen Victoria so excited since Dylan finished second in the big race! But I thought you guys couldn't . . ."

Caleb shrugged. "Apparently the doctors were wrong!"

"Wow."

"So it's like we're having twins. Except one's from China and three years older! I'm sure glad we didn't know Catherine would get pregnant."

"Why?"

"Because we wouldn't have adopted Emily. God wants us to have both children, and He worked the timing so it would happen."

Adam nodded. "Sometimes we're better off not knowing His plan in advance, aren't we?"

Adam scanned the group in his living room, meeting there because some items of conversation might be too private for Pearly's. Five men. Shane was gone, but his place had been taken by a figure of immense proportions.

While Adam knew Bronson's opinion about everything, he'd

begun to realize he knew little about the man behind the opin-ions. For reasons Adam didn't grasp, Brad Bronson had invited himself to this meeting.

Since their conversation in Bronson's car outside the drug house, Bronson had made occasional references to his mortality. Though Adam knew Bronson thoroughly disliked everyone, it occurred to him for the first time that maybe the sergeant hadn't granted himself an exemption. Maybe someplace below the surface—even if *way* below it—he knew that he needed to make some changes before he left this world.

The pervasive scent of a burning tobacco plantation was not Adam's main concern, though he wondered what Victoria would say about the smell on the couch. Bronson looked around sullenly at the other men while Adam handed him a Bible. Touching it only with his fingertips, he muttered, "I feel like a pork chop at a bar mitzvah."

"Guys, Brad and I agreed that we'll do things just like we would if he wasn't here. He can listen and participate when and if he wants."

"Good to have you, Sarge." Nathan extended his hand, as did the others.

Bronson didn't actually touch anyone, but he nodded, an unusually effusive display of warmth.

"An honor to meet you, sir," Javier said.

Bronson looked at Javy. His voice boomed, "Are you legal?"

"Yes, sir."

"Good."

"You don't have to call him sir, Javy," Adam said. "Sergeant Bronson will be fine, but actually we've said rank doesn't mat-ter here, so Brad or Bronson is better. That okay with you, Brad?"

"I don't care if you call me Little Bo Peep. I just hope we're not gonna sit around and whine about the stork dropping us down the wrong chimney."

"Well, we normally don't whine, and we believe in God, not the stork, and God knows His chimneys pretty well. But other than that . . . we're on the same page."

Adam studied the guys' uncertain faces a moment, then jumped in. "First, I wrote down something Tom Lyman said to me the other day." Adam opened the flyleaf of his Bible and read: "'At the end of his life, no man says, "I wish I had spent less time with my children."'"

Nathan nodded. "The regret is always the opposite, isn't it? Wishing they'd given less time to work or golf or projects or a dozen other things and more to their children."

Adam said, "I want to read something from Charles Spurgeon's *Morning and Evening*. Spurgeon was a nineteenth-century British pastor. It's old-fashioned English, but it's still relevant:

"Fearless of all consequences, you must do the right. You will need the courage of a lion unhesitatingly to pursue a course which shall turn your best friend into your fiercest foe; but for the love of Jesus you must thus be courageous. For the truth's sake to hazard reputation and affection, is such a deed that to do it constantly you will need a degree of moral principle which only the Spirit of God can work in you; yet turn not your back like a coward, but play the man. Follow right manfully in your Master's steps, for he has traversed this rough way before you. Better a brief warfare and eternal rest, than false peace and everlasting torment."

Bronson leaned forward. "This guy Sturgeon was a preacher?"
"Spurgeon. Yeah."

Bronson propped his chin on a fist. "Always thought church was for women and sissies. Fearless? Courage of a lion? Be a man? I like this guy. Even if he *is* named after a fish."

★ ★ ★

Jade's long braids spilled over the shoulders of her blue- and white-striped tee; she sat next to CeCe, a church friend. The school cafeteria buzzed, students everywhere.

Derrick Freeman made his approach with a self-aware swagger and planted himself across the table. "'Sup, Jade? Hey, why don't you answer my calls?"

"After I canceled the get-together at Lisa's, you were pretty mad, remember?"

"I forgive you. But you should answer my calls."

"I told you I don't answer my phone or text after ten now. And besides, I have an agreement with my dad. He has to approve of a boy before we spend much time together, even at school."

Derrick almost made a comment about Jade's father but refrained.

"Well, I been thinkin' about you a lot lately, Jade."

"Yeah?"

"As a matter of fact, I picked up somethin' for ya."

He pulled out a thin gold bracelet and draped it over his fingers. "Looks real, don't it?"

"Where'd you get that from?"

"My cousin gave it to me. Now I'm givin' it to you."

He assumed she would fawn over it. He'd seen what the girls did when TJ iced them out with the bling.

"I can't take it."

"Why not?"

"Because we're friends, Derrick. That's all."

Derrick stared at her, then pulled the bracelet back. "Well, you're the one missin' out."

Jade raised an eyebrow.

"Hey!" Derrick noticed her left hand. "Where'd you get the ring?"

"My daddy gave it to me." She glanced at CeCe and smiled as she looked back at Derrick. "Looks real, don't it?"

Derrick lifted the bracelet, glittering under the cafeteria lights. Several girls saw it and stared. "You sure you don't want this?"

"I'm sure." She fingered her ring.

Derrick's phone vibrated. He looked down at a text: **C U in 2**.

"My ride's here," Derrick said, standing. "Gotta go."

"You leaving early?" Jade asked.

"Personal field trip. Later."

Derrick strutted off, thinking he might shop a little more to find the fortunate girl who would receive the 'jacked bracelet. Jade didn't know what she was missing. She'd be sorry.

CHAPTER FORTY-FOUR

DERRICK WALKED out the high school's front door. While he tried to look like he didn't care who watched, he scoped out the spectators, wanting them to see the righteous dudes who picked him up.

Derrick got in the back of TJ's tricked-out dark-green Cadillac DeVille. Antoine rode shotgun.

"Wassup, D?" Antoine asked.

"Hey, little bro," TJ said. "We just picked up the mother lode. We gotta get it to the house and meet Tyrone. We got some serious weight here."

"How much?" Derrick asked.

"Forty stacks, dawg!"

"Forty stacks? TJ, that's crazy, man!"

"We ain't playin' Little League, D. We goin' prime-time. This is more benjamins than you can count, math whiz. Dawg, I got two keys in the trunk."

"Two kilos?"

"That's right. All we gotta do is cook it up."

"That's four hundred benjamins."

"Cash money. You help me get this done and you gonna be ridin' phat for a while."

Derrick smiled. *Ridin' phat.* Maybe he'd buy Jade a diamond bracelet. That would change her tune. He imagined her in the backseat of a car with him, proudly wearin' her bling. And if not Jade, then Lisa or Doniece. He smiled wider. Life was gettin' good.

At that moment, Nathan and David drove the outskirts of Albany.

David, a look of terror in his eyes, said, "I'll stand up there with you guys, but public speaking's my biggest fear. Dying is second."

"Javier won't do it either. He wants to be there; we all do. But the Resolution was Adam's idea. He should speak."

Nathan answered his cell phone. "Adam. Hey, we were just talking about you."

"Where are you guys?"

"We're comin' up on Denson."

"I'm three miles behind you. Listen, we need to talk about this Father's Day deal. Can you guys come over sometime this week?"

"We already talked about it. We decided that since you came up with the Resolution, you're gonna be the spokesman."

"That's only fair," David called.

"No, no, no. We didn't agree to that. We gotta vote."

"We already voted. David and I chose you, and you know Javy will side with us."

"Man, standing in front of a whole church? Look, if I do this, you guys owe me dinner. At Campbell's Steakhouse with all the gals, including Amanda. Tell her they have lots of salads!"

"You're on, man! I'll cover David and Amanda." Nathan's eyes narrowed. "We'll talk about this later. I've got a green Cadillac with a blown taillight." He ended the call. "Hey, light 'em up for me, David."

"Got it." David flipped on the blues.

TJ saw the lights in his rearview mirror. "Hold up! What this cop doin'? I ain't even speedin'! We can't do this, man."

Antoine turned to TJ. "They bust us this time, that's an automatic ten years."

Derrick looked behind them to see the sheriff's car. "Ten years? Whatchu gonna do, man?"

In the squad car, Nathan frowned. "What's he doin'? He'd better pull over soon or I'll get him for more than a busted light. Go ahead and call it in."

David reached for his radio to inform dispatch of the situation.

TJ set his jaw. "I'll take him out before I go back to jail." He reached between the front seats and pulled out a sawed-off shotgun.

Derrick stared at the shotgun. "Take him out? You gonna *shoot* him?"

TJ whipped his head around toward Derrick. "Look, you wanna go to prison? Huh? 'Cuz if he searches this car, that's where you goin'.

"I got my three pieces under the seat," TJ said to Antoine. "The deuce-five auto's right under you. Trey-five-seven under me, and the revolver's here." He patted the seat by his right leg. "Grab what you want, solja."

Antoine reached under the seat.

"You got that nine I gave you?" TJ asked Derrick.

"No way, man. I came from school!"

TJ finally pulled over but kept the engine running.

Nathan stopped ten feet behind him and took out his ticket book before he and David exited the car.

Ahead of them, inside the Cadillac, Derrick said, "Wait, man, I can't do this. Can't shoot no cop!"

"We ain't got no choice, D! Be cool. I'll get rid of him; then we'll make the drop and ditch the car."

Derrick, sweating profusely, turned to see Nathan and David get out. "There's *two* of 'em, TJ! You can't shoot both!"

"Shut up, man! You do what I tell you."

TJ looked in his side mirror and saw Nathan lift his sunglasses as he noted the license number.

"Oh, man, I know this cop. He's 'bout to get what he got comin' to him." He eased the shotgun into his lap and chambered a round.

Derrick saw who it was. "TJ, that's Jade's daddy!"

TJ put his right index finger on the shotgun's trigger.

David had a bad feeling. He and Nathan still stood behind the car. "He hasn't turned off the engine," David said. "You want me to take this one?"

Nathan shook his head and walked toward the driver's side door but stopped a few feet short. "Sir, I need you to turn off the vehicle and place your hands on the wheel."

TJ left the shotgun on his lap, out of Nathan's view. He switched off the engine and placed his hands on the steering wheel.

Nathan walked up to the window. "I pulled you over because—"

TJ grabbed the gun and raised it in a flash.

The instant before TJ fired, Derrick got both hands on TJ's right bicep and pulled back with all his strength. Then came the deafening blast.

"Nathan!" David screamed as his partner fell backward into the road directly in front of an oncoming pickup.

The driver punched the brakes. The truck skidded toward the deputy's head. Nathan lay motionless, curled into a ball.

David, the explosive shot still in his ears, thought Nathan had been hit. But he drew his .40-caliber Glock 23 and trained it on the back of the Caddy.

"Go, go, go!" Antoine yelled as TJ hit the ignition and gunned the engine.

TJ yelled back at Derrick, "I'm gonna lock up with you, tiny!"

Nathan grimaced as he lay on his side. He felt a numbing pain in his left bicep.

At that moment David found his range and fired a round through the Caddy's back window. David let loose six more rounds in succession, four of which hit the car.

"No!" Derrick shouted, covering his face and pressing himself down on the seat.

Glass fragments covered Derrick's prone body.

Nathan sat up and fired three rounds, one of which hit TJ in the left shoulder. TJ screamed, and the car turned sharply to the right, veered into a shallow ditch, and hit a fence.

"Back up, back up!" Antoine yelled, his side of the car now exposed to David and Nathan. TJ gunned it. Gravel and dirt sprayed everywhere, but the car didn't budge. Antoine extended his right hand and fired off three shots from his nine, all of which pierced the windshield of the truck. The driver ducked just in time.

Nathan shouted at the driver, "Stay down, sir! Stay down!"

Realizing their car was bottomed out, Antoine yelled, "We can't stay here; we gotta move! Get out! Get out!"

TJ opened his door and fell to the ground while Derrick did the same. Antoine continued to fire from the passenger seat.

Two other cars pulled up behind the pickup truck, then hit reverse as they heard shots.

David grabbed his radio off his left shoulder. "This is 693d. Shots fired, Denson Road! Backup, repeat, we need backup!"

Adam was less than a mile away when he heard the message. "693c in route!"

Antoine launched himself out the driver's door and fired from the car's far side.

TJ was on top of Derrick, right hand on his face with a vise grip.

"Whatchu think you doin', man? You crazy? You tryin' to save a cop? You ain't nothin'. I should kill you myself!"

He grabbed the shotgun, stood, and opened fire on the cops. The shotgun's backlash against his injured shoulder caused him to recoil and cry out in agony. A barrage came back at him. As he stooped, he pounded the car door with his elbow and shrieked with pain and frustration.

Two more cars came down the road from behind the cops. Nathan waved and yelled, "Stay back, stay back!"

David pulled a fresh clip from his belt and reloaded. He heard a siren blaring from behind him and took a deep breath. "Adam's coming, Nathan!"

Adam barreled ahead at high speed, finally spotting Nathan and David crouched behind the vehicles and firing toward the Caddy. He floored the pedal, swerved around the truck, braked, and spun the car sideways to provide more protection between the gangsters and the officers.

As Adam ducked and crawled out the passenger side door, TJ and Antoine fired several rounds into the side of his car, which now blocked TJ's view of David and Nathan. Glass shattered as the squad car was hit by the shotgun blast.

Nathan apprised him as they crouched on the ground behind the car. "Three guys, one has a shotgun, a 9mm. I'm almost out of ammo."

"Antoine!" TJ held his shoulder and winced. "Come here, man. You gotta shoot this for me!"

"We gotta go! Give it to me." Big Antoine grabbed the shotgun while TJ pushed Derrick down to the front of the car. "Get out of our way!"

The gangsters looked for an escape, but a fence ran down the road on the right side, an open field beyond it. The land was all flat and open on the left until it came to a house where a young black girl, maybe nine years old, watched, three hundred feet away.

Antoine shot his last two shells.

Adam heard an explosion of glass and metal overhead. Mirror and metal flew through the air like skeet.

TJ pointed down the road. "'Toine. The girl! We need leverage. Let's go!"

Antoine cried, "I'm out; I'm out," dropped the shotgun, and ran after TJ toward the girl and the house.

Adam yelled, "I got 'em," then saw the girl and realized he couldn't fire.

"Goin' after that girl. Stay with me!" Adam yelled.

"With you," Nathan said.

David ran alongside them.

"Front of the car, front of the car," Adam called.

Derrick screamed as they rounded the side of TJ's car.

"Show me your hands," the cops yelled, guns drawn. Derrick waved his hands frantically.

David pointed toward the girl and the gangsters. "I've got him. Go!"

Adam and Nathan took off in pursuit of TJ and Antoine.

TJ chased the girl while Antoine hid behind a massive tree, waiting.

Adam ran beside Nathan, surprised at his own speed and

endurance. He thought of Dylan, the only person he'd ever run alongside at this pace. Just as Nathan pulled in front of Adam, Antoine lunged and tackled Adam.

TJ pursued the girl, who climbed the wooden ladder of a tree house. TJ climbed behind her and grabbed her ankle. She screamed, paralyzed with fear. Nathan jumped up and grabbed TJ, pulling him down. The gangster fell to the ground, Nathan on top of him.

"Daddy! Daddy!" the girl screamed.

Adam fought with Antoine. He pulled his Glock, but Antoine knocked it out of his hand. Antoine exchanged punishing blows with Adam, each connecting to the other's jaw.

TJ landed two pile-driver blows on Nathan's cheek as he had several months ago when Nathan hung on to the steering wheel.

Nathan was nearly overcome when out of nowhere someone slammed into TJ, knocking him off Nathan. Then came screams of sirens and the screech of tires as more patrol cars pulled up. Two of the officers ran for Antoine, who was still pounding Adam's face. They tackled him and finally handcuffed him.

Two other officers jumped TJ and subdued him. The girl's father left the officers to finish TJ. He went to the base of the tree house and reached for the terrified girl, who lowered herself to the safety of her father's arms.

Adam lay on the ground, face bruised and bloody. One of the officers came over. "You all right, Adam?"

"Get the girl. Help the girl!"

"She's all right, man. She's with her dad."

Adam, head on the grass, caught sight of the girl, now secure in her father's arms. He saw the look in her eyes and thought of Emily. And somehow, beaten half to death, he felt incredible relief, even happiness.

Ten minutes later, after TJ, Antoine, and Derrick were taken to separate patrol cars, Nathan walked gingerly over to Adam, who sat under a tree, still wiping blood from his face.

"You okay?"

"That dude was strong."

He assessed Adam. "You're lookin' like I'm feelin'."

"I'm feelin' like I'm lookin'."

Nathan extended his hand to Adam. "Thank God for backup. None of us could have done this alone."

"Just be glad you fought the small guy."

"The *small* guy?"

"What's that on your arm?" Adam pointed to just below Nathan's left sleeve, where a bloodstained bandage wrapped his upper arm.

"An object lesson."

"What do you mean?"

"You know how Jordan pesters me to wear a vest?"

"Yeah, I've mentioned it a few times myself."

"Well, when my gangster buddy, who has now remodeled my face twice, let go with the sawed-off shotgun, I thought I'd been hit. I was so close I could feel the force of all that shot exploding out of the barrel."

"Yeah?"

"So a few minutes ago when all my pains registered, I felt this awful sting in my arm. And there, implanted in my skin, was a single piece of shot."

"One?"

"*One.*" He pulled the little piece of metal out of his pocket. "It's not a heavy gauge, but I'll tell you my arm hurts like crazy. Had I been just a foot closer, I'd have gotten dozens of them at least. If he'd gotten off a straight shot, I would have taken maybe a hundred in the chest, point-blank."

Adam cringed.

"So I figure God fired me a warning. True, the vest wouldn't have protected my arm. But if I'd taken it in the chest, the vest would have saved my life. *If* I'd worn it. I'm going to tell Jordan he was right and I was wrong."

Adam looked at Nathan. "Glad you're okay."

"Likewise."

As Adam pulled his cell out and called Victoria, Nathan approached the patrol car where Derrick, handcuffed and bent forward, stared at the floor. Nathan opened the door and leaned down. Tears streamed down the young man's face.

"Derrick, what are you doin'? Why were you with these guys?"

He shook his head like he wondered the same thing. "I ain't got nobody, man. I just ain't got nobody."

Nathan remained silent but put his hand on Derrick's shoulder.

Meanwhile Adam approached David, who leaned against his bullet-pierced patrol car.

"You did good today, David."

"You mean, for a rookie, right?"

Adam shook his head and slapped David on the back. "You're not a rookie."

CHAPTER FORTY-FIVE

HUNDREDS OF MEN, ages six to eighty-six, took their places on Third Avenue, one of Albany's most beautiful streets. Lined with massive oak trees, sun and shade were dappled in the leaves of late spring; it was spectacular.

A big banner stretched across the street: *First Annual Father & Son 5K.*

Grandfathers and mentors were invited too. Ten minutes before the race, Adam stood between Dylan and Tyler.

Adam spoke softly. "Dylan, feel free to break loose. I'll stay back with Tyler. We'd slow you down."

"That's okay, Dad. Let's run together. There'll be other 5Ks."

"You sure? I appreciate that, buddy. I really do."

He turned to the twelve-year-old boy with black hair and almond eyes. "Tyler, we're really glad you could join us."

"Yeah, man." Dylan slapped hands with Tyler. "This'll be fun."

After they took off and the runners spread out, Dylan stayed by Tyler and Adam, but just a few steps ahead to set the pace and squeeze the best performance out of them. Both Adam and Dylan were impressed with Tyler's ability to keep up.

There was something magical about running with all these

men and being cheered on by grandmas, wives, daughters, and sisters.

Dylan said to his dad as they ran, "I feel like rooting for everyone around me, like we're all on the same team."

Familiar faces surrounded them: Riley Cooper with his dad, Caleb Holt with a high school boy Dylan knew from Young Life.

The more Tyler ran, the more he hit his stride, eyes on Dylan, determined to stay with him.

At about the 4K mark, they spotted Victoria and Mia waving and holding out drinks. "Adam!" Victoria called. As he veered over, she handed him something he didn't expect.

He smiled, turned, and waved. Victoria and Mia both laughed.

"What is that, Dad?"

"Well . . . it's a raspberry cruller from Krispy Kreme."

"How do you know it's from Krispy Kreme?"

"Trust me, Son. I know."

He ripped off a third and handed it to Dylan and gave another third to Tyler. No cruller had ever been more quickly consumed.

The more Adam and Dylan encouraged Tyler, the faster he ran. Though the run was short, Adam was so sore from the Denson Road incident, he had to push himself. They finished in the first quarter of the pack, much faster than Adam or Dylan had anticipated.

When they crossed the finish line, Adam and Dylan both slapped hands with Tyler.

"Tyler, good job!" Dylan said. "You should definitely go out for track!"

Wave after wave of men and boys crossed the finish line. As they regained their breath, they laughed and talked like old friends. It was a spontaneous fraternity meeting on the streets of Albany. City streets sometimes plagued by the consequences of fatherlessness had been reclaimed to celebrate fatherhood.

Adam had never experienced anything like it. He thumped Dylan on the back. "Aren't you glad I talked you into running this 5K?"

They met Victoria and Mia and went to the Cookie Shop on North Jackson. By the time lunch was over, Dylan and Tyler agreed to meet twice a week at Westover High's track.

Dylan said to Adam as they were leaving, "I'm just warning you, Dad—our next race is a 10K."

Adam stretched out in his recliner that night—given recent events, he figured he'd earned it. Over popcorn and sweet tea, he and Dylan and Victoria talked and laughed for an hour about the 5K and the raspberry cruller and anything else that came to mind.

When Adam got a call from Sergeant Murphy, he braced himself to leave for work; rare to be called out on a Saturday night, but not unprecedented.

"Adam? I have good news for you."

"What's that?"

"The paperwork's done, and as of Monday morning, you've got a new partner."

"Anybody I know?"

"Fresh out of the academy. Nice kid. I think you'll like him."

On Monday, Adam, still feeling stiff from the race and the Denson Road episode, entered the sheriff's department and headed to the muster room. He saw the familiar face of a big young man seated on a bench.

"Brock Kelley?"

"Hey, Corporal Mitchell." Brock stood, and they shook hands.

"Call me Adam. I see you're wearing the proud uniform of the Dougherty County Sheriff's Department."

"I'm reporting for duty."

"That's great news," Adam said. "Have they told you who your partner is?"

"No, sir. I'm in the dark."

"Get used to that." Adam grinned. "But stop calling me sir. It's Adam."

"Okay. Adam."

"Coming in for roll call?"

"Sergeant Murphy told me to stay out here until he sends for me."

"See you inside."

As Adam walked to the muster room, he couldn't help but smile.

Thanks, Lord, for answering my prayer. I'll be able to help Brock as a cop and as a Christ follower. And he'll be great for me. Dylan will like him, too. And he'll be impressed that his dad's new partner is the local football legend!

Adam sat behind David, drinking coffee and waiting for roll call.

"How'd your dinner go with Amanda and Olivia?"

"Great! Awesome!"

Adam grinned. "Sounds like you had a good time, David!"

"I just keep feeling . . . closer to Amanda, closer than I could have imagined. And Olivia's like . . . I can't describe it." David swallowed hard. "I met a family at church, in that home Bible study group I go to. They rent out a nice little apartment."

"Yeah?"

"So I checked it out. The rent's the same as what Amanda's paying now, and it's a better setup. And . . . it's three minutes from my place."

Nathan entered and sat just before Sergeant Murphy stepped to the front. After a few announcements, the sergeant said, "We have a new rookie. Let's give a warm welcome to Brock Kelley."

"State championship," Adam heard someone whisper.

Lord, use me in this young man's life.

"And Deputy Kelley will have the distinction of being the partner of . . ."

Adam smiled.

"Sergeant Brad Bronson."

What?

Bronson groaned audibly and glared at Brock like he was an IRS auditor with leprosy.

Snickers mixed with looks of surprise and pity.

Murphy smiled wryly. "All we can say, Deputy Kelley, is 'Good luck' and don't expect Bronson to be impressed with your police academy credentials. Or your football accomplishments."

"Or pretty much anything else," Riley Cooper added.

"So welcome your new partner, Sergeant Bronson," Murphy said, obviously enjoying himself. Brock followed Murphy's pointing finger, walked over to Bronson, and extended his hand. Brad grunted and nodded at the chair next to him.

Adam was stunned. It never occurred to him they might sacrifice the newbie to Bronson.

Brock, seated between Adam and Bronson, whispered to Adam, "I remember Bronson from the academy. I take it he has issues?"

"No," Adam whispered back. "He has the whole subscription."

"Now," Murphy said, "we have a second vacancy to fill. I

want to introduce Adam Mitchell's new partner, also a rookie, just graduated from the police academy. Welcome Bobby Shaw."

Adam froze when he saw the skinny kid walk in, the one the trainer said would have flunked out if there'd been more candidates.

Adam's heart sank. If they faced a crisis, this was the person he would entrust his life to? That's what Adam *thought*. What he *did* was shake Bobby's hand, then lead him to the seat to Adam's left.

Adam Mitchell, sitting between two rookies, looked at Bronson's scowling face and determined that for Bobby Shaw's sake, he was not going to let his face know how the rest of him felt.

★ ★ ★

That evening Adam and Victoria sipped decaf in the living room.

"After Sergeant Murphy calls and tells me I'm getting a new partner, I show up, and Brock's there waiting. What else was I supposed to think? I could have been his cop coach. Like Grant Taylor was his football coach."

"Maybe God wanted to teach you about disappointment and trust."

"A guy can still whine a little bit, can't he?"

"Yeah, as long as he doesn't abuse the privilege," Victoria said. "You've been praying for Bronson, right?"

"Right."

"Well, if Brock is a solid Christian, doesn't that make him a good choice to influence Bronson?"

"No one's a good choice for Bronson."

"Sounds like you've given up on him."

"No. I'm just sayin'—"

"And I'm just sayin' maybe God thought it was better to answer your prayer about influencing Bronson for Christ than about you influencing Brock. And doesn't Bobby Shaw need a partner who can show him the ropes and be a spiritual role model?"

"I guess, but I'd sure rather put my life in Brock's hands than Bobby's."

"Who's more ready to meet God, you or Bronson?"

"Well, I am, but—"

"Then maybe that's another reason Bronson should have Brock and you should have Bobby."

Adam sat up in his recliner. "Cop wives are *not* supposed to say things like that!"

"You know I'm concerned for your safety. I just believe you've been put with Bobby Shaw for his good and for yours. Romans 8:28, remember? You told me the trainer at the academy said Bobby grew up without a dad. Maybe you're the father figure he's always needed."

"After one day with him, I can tell you he's not much of a cop."

"Neither was David. But when he's spent a year with you, I'll bet Bobby Shaw will be as solid as David has become."

Adam smiled. "When I griped to David about my new partner, you know what he said?"

"What?"

"He said, 'Maybe you'd better man up!'"

"I *love* that young man."

"Me too. But I'm not telling the sheriff."

"Adam, you've become a mentor to your own son. What you do with Dylan will help you with Bobby. And what you do with Bobby will help you with Dylan. And Tyler too."

"Thanks for your honesty. And your encouragement."

"I love you, Adam Mitchell." She crossed the room and wrapped her arms around him. "And now there's something I want to talk to you about."

He looked at her suspiciously as she stood there beside his recliner.

"What I'd like to say may seem a little crazy, but I'd like us to pray about it."

"What?"

"You know that evening we spent at the Holts? When they told us Catherine is pregnant?"

"You're pregnant?"

She laughed. "No. But I'd like to consider adopting."

Adam jerked to the front of his chair. "A child?"

"No. An orangutan." She shook her head. "Of course a *child*. I know another child won't be Emily. But what would you think of adopting a little girl?"

Victoria sat down, and Adam came up with a dozen reasons why it was impractical. He was forty. Kids were a challenge. They took a lot of energy and money. But when he ran out of practical objections, he thought about what it would mean to have a daughter. He could hold her, wipe her tears, and dance with her in the park.

"I agree there's only one Emily," Adam said. "But another girl would be special too. And maybe I'd have a second chance to be a better dad to my daughter."

Victoria stood again and walked toward him. "We'd need to talk with Dylan. This child could require more work—we'd have to take it on together. There'd be sacrifices."

She put her hands on her hips, her face filled with adventure. "But I think I want to do this. Will you pray about it with me?"

Adam gazed into her eyes and saw inside her. "Yes, I will."

★ ★ ★

The church parking lot filled up quickly the last ten minutes before the service.

Pastor Jonathan Rogers stood in his office with Javier and David. Adam walked in with Nathan.

"Adam," Pastor Rogers said, "every father should be encouraged to fulfill these Resolution points. That's why I wanted you to present them to the church today."

"If it helps men understand how to step up, then we're glad to do it, right, guys?"

"As long as I don't have to open my mouth," David said.

"*Sí.*" Javy smiled and nodded.

"Fortunately we've got Adam to do that," Nathan joked.

None of these guys could dread being up front as much as I do, and here I am, the spokesman. How did this happen?

Jonathan led them into the auditorium and stepped to the pulpit. Adam, Nathan, David, and Javier stood behind him and to his left.

"For the last six weeks, I've preached on God's design for fathers. To be teachers, protectors, and providers. I read to you a Resolution for fathers that was written and signed by the men who stand behind me. The principles of this Resolution come from God's Word. But instead of talking about these men, I want Adam Mitchell to come and speak to us."

Adam walked to the pulpit. Besides informal classes at the police academy, Adam had never spoken in public. He hoped he didn't look as nervous as he felt. He gazed out at the packed auditorium, a sea of faces. His stomach hosted a swarm of butterflies. He tried to take a deep breath but barely managed a few shallow ones. He hoped he wouldn't pass out.

Adam looked down to his right and saw Victoria.

She gave him a warm smile, pretending she wasn't nervous about what he might say. Next to her sat Dylan, who looked curious. On Dylan's left was Tom Lyman in his wheelchair, signaling a thumbs-up.

Adam's hands trembled slightly as he opened his notes, looked at them a moment, then gazed at the congregation.

Okay, Lord, it's up to You.

"As a law enforcement officer, I've seen firsthand the deep hurt and devastation that fatherlessness brings on a child's life. Our prisons are full of men and women who have lived recklessly after being abandoned by their fathers, wounded by the men who should have loved them the most. Many of these children now follow the same pattern of irresponsibility that their fathers did. While so many mothers have sacrificed to help their children survive, they were never intended to carry the weight alone.

"We thank God for these women," Adam continued, "but research is proving that a child also desperately needs a daddy. There's no way around this fact."

Behind him, Nathan prayed for his brother, that God would use him to speak especially to the men.

"As you know, earlier this year my family endured the tragic loss of our nine-year-old daughter, Emily." Adam's emotions threatened to incapacitate him, but he pressed on.

"Her death forced me to realize that not only had I not taken advantage of the priceless time I had with her, but that I did not truly understand how crucial my role was as a father to her and our son, Dylan."

He glanced at Dylan, his enormous love for his son prevailing over his nerves.

"Since her passing, I've asked God to show me through His Word how to be the father that I need to be. I now believe that

God desires for every father to courageously step up and do whatever it takes to be involved in the lives of his children. But more than just being there or providing for them, he is to walk with them through their young lives and be a visual representation of the character of God, their Father in heaven. A father should love his children and seek to win their hearts. He should protect them, discipline them, and teach them about God."

As Javier listened to Adam's impassioned speech, he silently thanked God for his father, who had done those very things in his life. All the while, Javy's eyes never left Carmen, Isabel, and Marcos. He didn't want to look anywhere else.

"He should model how to walk with integrity," Adam said, "and treat others with respect and should call out his children to become responsible men and women who live their lives for what matters in eternity."

Adam's voice took on an almost-otherworldly strength. It surprised him and all who knew him. "Some men will hear this and mock it or ignore it, but I tell you that as a father, you are accountable to God for the position of influence He has given you."

David scanned the room until he found the pretty young woman near the back, with their four-year-old daughter on her lap. Seeing David's eyes move to them at last, the woman whispered in her daughter's ear, and the little girl suddenly smiled and waved. David smiled back and moved his hand.

"You can't fall asleep at the wheel only to wake up one day and realize that your job or your hobbies have no eternal value, but the souls of your children do. Some men will hear this and agree with it but have no resolve to live it out. Instead they will live for themselves and waste the opportunity to leave a godly legacy for the next generation."

Adam thought of Shane in his cell and all the regret his former partner was feeling. He could have been standing here with them today. Adam paused a moment, his heart crying out to God to restore Shane and fix his brokenness.

"But there are some men who, regardless of the mistakes we've made in the past, regardless of what our fathers did not do for us, will give the strength of our arms and the rest of our days to loving God with all that we are and to teaching our children to do the same. And whenever possible, to love and mentor others who have no father in their lives but who desperately need help and direction.

"We are inviting any man whose heart is willing and courageous to join us in this Resolution."

Adam's surge of intensity commanded attention.

"In my home, the decision has already been made. You don't have to ask who will guide my family because by God's grace, *I* will. You don't have to ask who will teach my son to follow Christ because *I* will.

"Who will accept the responsibility of providing for and protecting my family? *I* will. Who will ask God to break the chain of destructive patterns in my family's history? *I* will.

"Who will pray for and bless my children to boldly pursue whatever God calls them to do? *I am their father; I will.*

"I accept this responsibility, and it is my privilege to embrace it. I want the favor of God and His blessing on my home. Any good man does. *So where are you, men of courage?* Where are you, fathers who fear the Lord? It's time to rise up and answer the call that God has given to you and to say, I will! I will! *I will!*"

Electricity jumped across the auditorium.

First one man stood. Adam saw William Barrett join him. Then two of Adam's own pastors. He watched as Riley Cooper and other deputies from the Dougherty County Sheriff's Department and officers from Albany Police stood. He saw firefighters he knew, including Caleb Holt. Even Tom Lyman pushed his arms down against his wheelchair and, with great effort, rose to his feet.

Throughout the room, some men wanted to stand but couldn't bring themselves to. Others wanted to be anywhere else in the world. Adam caught the eye of a huge bald man who rose to his feet in the back row, a foot taller and two feet wider than anyone around him. No sooner had Brad Bronson stood than he appeared to realize he had done so. He walked to the back of the church as if to leave, then turned and stood against the wall.

Most of those who stood remained standing, their resolve growing. Some had yet to grasp the extent of commitment and dedication this decision would require, but no one doubted that something remarkable had happened.

For many men and their families, it marked a new beginning. A fresh chance to win a battle worth fighting and gain a treasure worth keeping.

After the service, people lined up to thank Adam and speak with him. He was so aware of his weakness and inability and his terror at speaking that he wasn't even tempted toward pride. What had happened in that auditorium had been God's doing. Yet in his heart he sensed God saying to him something he didn't recall his earthly father ever saying: "Well done, my son." It felt good to be content, not proud, yet not disappointed in himself.

As he made his way out the door with Victoria, Dylan, and Tom to join the other families for dinner at Campbell's Steakhouse, he suddenly envisioned Emily's approving smile. Maybe he was being sentimental, but he sensed it so profoundly he wondered if it was more than his imagination.

CHAPTER FORTY-SIX

ALMOST A WEEK LATER, on Saturday, Adam walked into the Dougherty County Jail and went to the check-in line, only to see a familiar face in front of him.

"Nathan! How was your week off?"

"Great family time. And feelin' a lot better. Nice of the doctor to recommend time off after my arm was still killing me and I was shuffling around to serve warrants. I needed some recuperation!"

"You visiting Derrick?" Adam asked. "How's he doing?"

"His heart's open. Reads everything I give him. Before this is over, I think he'll be a Jesus follower."

"No kidding?"

"There are some good men in this jail. Solid Bible studies. Lots of temptations, sure, but Derrick goes to the chapel services and meets with the chaplain. I told Derrick I'll help him, but he's got to take the initiative."

"TJ and Antoine are in maximum security, right?" Adam asked.

"Oh yeah. And Derrick's in medium. When I met with the

warden and told him how Derrick betrayed TJ to save my life, he assured me they'd never be near each other."

Adam put his hand on Nathan's shoulder. "You said Derrick saved your life, and now you're saving his. Your part will take a lot longer. But the results will last for eternity. I told Victoria something that really struck me—you ran a prominent gang leader off the road twice. The first time, when you grabbed the wheel, you saved your son's life. The second time, when you shot him in the shoulder, you saved Derrick's life. Two crashed cars, both driven by TJ, two young men saved."

"You sayin' I should crash more cars?" Nathan laughed. "Anyway, we'll see about Derrick. You know, at first Jade really liked him and Kayla didn't, but she changed her mind. I was the hard guy dad who kept Derrick at a distance. Then, once they found out what he was into, Jade and Kayla wrote him off and wonder why I'm so interested in him now."

"What do you tell them?"

"The grace of God. William Barrett reached out to me. I'm reaching out to Derrick. He said he's got nobody—well, now he's got me. It's too early to say, but who knows? One day he might be a son to me like I am to William. Meanwhile, I get to teach my family about grace. We don't help people because they deserve it, but because God tells us to love others as He loves us. Hey, maybe someday I'll visit TJ or Antoine."

Adam blinked. "Wow. That thought never occurred to me."

"Stranger things have happened when God's unleashes His grace. How's Dylan's Bible study with Tom Lyman?"

"Great. You should hear him go on about it. Two of his buddies come with him now. They memorize Scripture. If you'd told me six months ago my son would ask to spend two hours a week with an old man at a retirement center, I would have said you were nuts. But Tom's like a grandfather to him."

"Makes sense—he's become like a father to you. You and Bobby Shaw doing well?"

Adam nodded. "He's slowly coming out of his shell. Once he trusts me, I think we'll be fine. Javy and Carmen and the kids came over last night. Yesterday he signed up for a naturalization class to help him become a US citizen!"

"Fantastic!" Nathan slapped Adam's hands.

"And Frank Tyson's paying for the class! You know, I keep thinking about last week at Pearly's when Javy read us the letter from his father telling him he'd be honored to fly up here and visit his son. When Javy cried, we all lost it."

Nathan nodded. "I wasn't prepared for the effect on our newest group member."

"Yeah. Did you ever imagine you'd see Brad Bronson cry like a baby?"

"He said it was allergies."

"And Brad told me the other day he's thinking of reaching out to a son and daughter in their thirties he's been out of contact with for years. Amazing."

The visitation deputy looked at Nathan. "You can go in now, Deputy Hayes. That's D building; here's your pass."

Nathan put his arm around Adam, who reciprocated.

Just then a strong, deep voice said from behind, "If you two would finish with your public display of affection, we could get this line movin'."

Adam turned . . . Sheriff Gentry.

"I was just . . . never mind. Good to see you, sir."

Gentry nodded. Then smiled—tentatively.

Nathan was just a few steps ahead of Adam when the visitation deputy asked, "Who are you here for, Corporal Mitchell?"

Adam said, "Mike Hollis."

She looked at the charts. "He's in D building, too."

"Wait up," Adam called to Nathan. "We're headed the same way."

One at a time they spread out their arms as security patted them down and checked their weapons in lockers.

Nathan looked at Adam. "Mike Hollis? No kidding? I figured you were seeing Shane."

"I saw him a few days ago. As for Mike, you raised the bar for me by visiting Derrick. I can stand back and watch you, or I can get in there and try to jump higher myself."

The two men walked toward D-block in the dim cinder-block hallway, a sterile land bridge between two worlds.

Nathan Hayes came to visit a young man who'd had designs on his daughter and whose allegiance had been to the gang leader who'd abducted Nathan's son, beat up his partner, and tried to murder him with a shotgun.

Adam Mitchell came to visit the man who'd sold drugs to his son and, under the influence, killed Adam's daughter.

It took courage for them to walk this hallway to extend grace to these men. But it was easier to walk it side by side than alone.

In the silence punctuated only by their footsteps, both men thought not of themselves but of a Man who once made a long, lonely march up a hill, who in the world's worst hour did the most courageous thing ever done.

At the end of His climb, He spread out His arms and permitted guilty men to drive nails into His hands and feet. He endured untold agony to give undeserving men—like Mike Hollis, Derrick Freeman, Nathan Hayes, and Adam Mitchell—a second chance.

To most people, none of this—not what these men were doing now, nor what He did two thousand years ago—made sense.

From the outside, grace and truth, honor and courage, seldom do.

BE STRONG AND VERY COURAGEOUS.

JOSHUA 1:7

CHOOSE FOR YOURSELVES THIS DAY WHOM YOU WILL SERVE . . . BUT AS FOR ME AND MY HOUSEHOLD, WE WILL SERVE THE LORD.

JOSHUA 24:15

Acknowledgments
FROM RANDY ALCORN

A special thanks to my wife, Nanci, who made many personal sacrifices in the four months of seemingly endless work I poured into this project. Without your partnership, friendship, and encouragement, I would be lost. My daughters, Karina and Angela, and their husbands, Dan and Dan, discussed with me different aspects of the book along the way, and I appreciate their help.

My thanks to Stephen and Alex Kendrick, the writers of the *Courageous* screenplay, which provided the framework for this novel. About 20 percent of the book comes directly from the movie; the other 80 percent I had to invent to make this into a novel. So if there's something the reader doesn't like, chances are it's my fault.

I am deeply grateful to Captain Craig Dodd, who drove me through the streets of Albany and shared many insights into gangs, drugs, street crime, and the consequences of fatherlessness. Craig kindly received many phone calls about police and jail procedures. Craig, sorry I couldn't use more of the priceless information you provided me. When I did use it, I hope you'll find it mostly accurate and that you'll enjoy the story.

As always, thanks to my friends at Tyndale, including Karen Watson and Ron Beers. And to my Tyndale editor, Caleb Sjogren.

I could not have completed this project without the tireless help of Doreen Button, my colleague at Eternal Perspective Ministries, who worked countless hours, including way into the night and on a number of weekends, making editing suggestions. Doreen, I am profoundly grateful to God for your help.

Thanks to Stephanie Anderson, who made herself available on short notice to help reduce word count on drafts. And to Bonnie Hiestand, premier typist, who can read my handwriting sometimes even when I can't. And to my assistants, Kathy Norquist and Linda Jeffries, without whom I would never have time to write a book.

Tim Newcomb and Steve Tucker looked over the first draft and offered helpful comments. Bob Schilling assisted with some research. I appreciate your help, my brothers.

A special thanks to my cop buddies Jim Seymour, Claudio Grandjean, Brandon Gentry, and Dave Williams, all part of my church. Jim, you went above and beyond, dropping by my house in your police cruiser and showing me on my front porch how the Taser operates. Thanks for not actually tasing me, Nanci, or our dog Moses.

Bill Leslie and Tom Skipper were my Spanish-speaking helpers, who assisted me with portions related to Javy. Thanks to all my go-to friends who helped with fact-checking in their area of expertise. They include Doug Gabbert, who made a crucial car recommendation for the story line. Thanks also to Sawyer Brown Rygh and Chase MacKay.

Words can't express how much it meant to me to have our EPM prayer partners praying for me during the long and difficult writing process. God knows who you are. I trust that He answered and will answer your prayers and reward you for participating in this book and whatever impact it may have.

Others who helped, some probably without remembering, include Ron and Ione Noren, Tom and Donna Schneider, Don and Pat Maxwell, Rod and Diane Meyer, Steve and Sue Keels, Chuck and Gena Norris, Rick and Amy Campbell, Jay Echternach, Todd DuBord, Tony Cimmarrusti, Mark Kost, Paul Martin, Gregg Cunningham, Kress Drew, Robin Green, Stu Weber, and Scott Lindsey.

Far and above all others, I thank my Lord and Savior Jesus Christ, who sustained me through the unusually difficult process of this book, especially in the latter stages. As Psalm 107:1 says, "Oh give thanks to the Lord, for he is good, for his steadfast love endures forever!" You are good, Lord, and even when times are hard, I praise You for your steadfast love to me.

Acknowledgments
FROM ALEX AND STEPHEN

Christina and Jill (our wives)—your patience and support is wind in our sails. We cherish you dearly!

Joshua, Anna, Catherine, Joy, Caleb, Julia, Grant, Cohen, Karis, and John (our kids)—may you grow in faith and strength and become mighty in your influence for Jesus. He is Lord and He loves you! So do we!

Larry and Rhonwyn Kendrick (our parents)—for over forty years you have loved us and cheered us on. Thank you for training us up to know the Savior and to seek Him!

Jim McBride and Bill Reeves (agents)—You guys have taken the hits, handled the headaches, and been amazing partners and friends. May God bless you many times over for your faithfulness.

Randy Alcorn (writer)—Keep writing, serving, and giving. Your ministry impact will no doubt continue to grow. There are not many like you.

Karen Watson and Caleb Sjogren (editors)—Thanks for believing in us and taking this journey with us. Your help, insight, and partnership has been a blessing.

Sherwood Baptist Church (home base)—You make the harder road seem sweeter and the challenges more bearable. Thank you for loving Jesus. We are blessed to be a part of this family!

A Personal Message
from the Kendrick Brothers

THANK YOU for reading *Courageous*! We hope you were encouraged and inspired by the journey of these fathers and their families. Now that you have read the novel, we want to boldly challenge you in your own spiritual journey. How will the story of *Courageous* influence you? Will you allow the message of faith and love to penetrate beyond the pages of this book?

If you do not have a relationship with Jesus Christ, we want you to know that He is the real deal. We're not talking about religion but a *relationship* with Jesus. He alone has proven to be the missing link to God that people are longing for . . . and desperately need. One that you need.

His entire life demonstrates His uniqueness as God in the flesh. His virgin birth, sinless life, powerful teachings, amazing miracles, unconditional love, sacrificial death, miraculous resurrection, and impact on the world are all unique to Jesus Christ alone. Try reading Matthew, Mark, Luke, and John in the Bible and see for yourself what those who were with Him witnessed firsthand. He not only is qualified to forgive your sin, but He can change your heart and make it pleasing toward a holy God. It is foolish to trust in your own goodness to get into heaven. Only God can make us clean through Jesus Christ.

The Scriptures say that all of us have fallen short of God's righteousness (Romans 3). We've all broken His commands. Each of us has lied, lusted, and hated. That's why we could never stand before Him. We are guilty of many sins. He requires righteousness to enter heaven.

That's why He lovingly sent Jesus. His death on the cross was necessary to make things right between us and a holy God. He didn't have to do that. That's just love in action . . . personified.

Regardless of where you are, let us encourage and challenge you, on behalf of Christ, to do what David Thomson did and surrender your heart afresh to God. Romans 10:9 says that if you confess with your mouth Jesus as your Lord (Master or Boss), and you believe in your heart that God has raised Him from the dead, then you will be saved.

If you are already an obedient follower of Christ, then we want to encourage you further in your spiritual journey. We challenge you to let the faith and integrity that Christ brings influence your relationships, children, daily habits, and work environments the way Adam, Nathan, and Javier did. Do you model honesty and the Golden Rule in how you treat others? Have you dedicated your personal ethics and work environment to God? Are there people you need to get right with that you have wronged in the past? Don't wait any longer. Do it!

We encourage you to refocus your passions toward the higher purpose of glorifying God and not living for your own temporary fulfillment in this life. Start your days in the Word of God and in prayer. Pray that people will be wowed by the changes that Christ has made in you. And let your commitment be independent of others. People will fail you, reject you, and let you down. But don't be discouraged. Don't let anything or anyone cause you to stop loving Him. Find a group of believers at a local church who share this passion and who will join you in this great adventure! Then let's plan to rejoice together as we watch God glorify Himself through our lives and do more than we can ask or imagine! May your life in Christ be courageous!

God bless you!
Alex and Stephen Kendrick

Discussion Questions

1. Which characters or events in this novel resonate with you? How has your life been similar?

2. Discuss some of the differences between bad parenting, "good enough" parenting, and effective parenting. What are the marks of excellent parenting? Why do many people settle for good enough?

3. In the very first scene Nathan refuses to let go of the steering wheel, risking his own life to rescue his son. What in your life is worth that kind of risk? What are some sacrifices God might ask of you for the sake of people you love?

4. Have you had a positive father figure in your life? If not, how can you seek out and cultivate that kind of relationship even now? If so, what can you do to express your appreciation for that person's influence?

5. Where was the breakdown in the relationship between Dylan and Adam? What did each do to bridge the gaps between them?

6. Why is Adam reluctant at first to share his faith with Bronson? How does Bronson's outlook eventually change? Who is someone in your life who needs to hear the truth?

7. How does Javier reflect his faith in God's provision and sovereignty? In what situations does he live out his faith well or not so well?

8. Name and discuss some of the characters in this story who receive grace, compassion, or forgiveness. How does it affect these characters' lives?

9. Were you surprised by Shane's actions at the end of the story? Why do you think he made the decisions he did? In what situations is it easy to make excuses for our wrong-doing?

10. David finds many second chances through the course of this story, including an opportunity to truly become a father to his daughter. But consider if Amanda had not invited David back into her and Olivia's life—how could David still have fulfilled his Resolution?

11. Discuss the truths of Proverbs 22:6. What does this verse say about child rearing? What does it say about children who leave the faith?

12. In what ways did the men in *Courageous* maintain their Resolution? In what ways did they fail to keep it? How can a man make sure his Resolution is more than just an idle promise?

About the Authors

RANDY ALCORN is the founder of Eternal Perspective Ministries (EPM). Prior to starting EPM, he served as a pastor for fourteen years. He has spoken around the world and has taught on the adjunct faculties of Multnomah Bible College and Western Seminary in Portland, Oregon.

Randy is the bestselling author of over thirty-five books (4 million in print), including the novels *Deadline*, *Dominion*, and *Deception*, as well as *The Chasm*, *Safely Home*, and *Courageous*. His nonfiction works include *Heaven*; *If God is Good*; *Managing God's Money*; *Money, Possessions, and Eternity*; *The Treasure Principle*; *The Grace and Truth Paradox*; and *The Law of Rewards*. Randy has written for many magazines and produces the popular periodical *Eternal Perspectives*. He's been a guest on numerous radio and television programs, including *Focus on the Family*, *The Bible Answer Man*, *Family Life Today*, *Revive Our Hearts*, *Truths that Transform*, and *Faith Under Fire*.

The father of two married daughters, Randy lives in Gresham, Oregon, with his wife and best friend, Nanci. They are the proud grandparents of several grandchildren.

You may contact Eternal Perspective Ministries by e-mail through their website at www.epm.org or at 39085 Pioneer Blvd., Suite 206, Sandy, OR 97055, (503) 668-5200. Visit Randy Alcorn's blog at www.epm.org/blog. Connect with Randy also at facebook.com/randyalcorn and Twitter: twitter.com/randyalcorn.

ALEX KENDRICK is an associate pastor at Sherwood Baptist Church. In 2002, Kendrick Brothers Productions in association with Sherwood Pictures began work on the first movie, *Flywheel*, which Alex wrote, directed, produced, and acted in. After the overwhelming response to the film, Alex and his brother Stephen again partnered to write and produce *Facing the Giants*, which was picked up and distributed by Provident Films, a branch of Sony Pictures. Alex directed and acted in the film, which went on to gross more than $10 million in box office receipts. The DVD was released in thirteen languages, in fifty-six countries, and sold more than 2 million copies. Alex and Stephen followed that hit by writing and producing *Fireproof*, the highest-grossing independent film of 2008 with over $33 million in box office sales. Alex directed the film, which has since sold more than 3 million DVDs. To date, Alex has received more than twenty awards for his work, including best screenplay, best production, and best feature film.

Alex and his wife, Christina, have been married for seventeen years and live in Albany, Georgia, with their six children.

STEPHEN KENDRICK is an associate pastor at Sherwood Baptist Church. Kendrick Brothers Productions in association with Sherwood Pictures has released four films. Stephen has cowritten, produced, and held key roles in all of the Sherwood Pictures movies. He has also worked with Provident Films to develop marketing and Bible study resources for each picture. In 2007, the Georgia House of Representatives and Senate passed a resolution honoring Sherwood Pictures for its ministry success and positive impact.

Alex and Stephen coauthored *The Love Dare*, a nonfiction title based on the *Fireproof* plot, which quickly became a number one *New York Times* bestseller and stayed on the list for more than two years. With over 5 million copies sold, it is an international bestseller with translations in thirty-two languages. The Kendricks also coauthored (with Eric Wilson) novels based on the screenplays of *Flywheel*, *Facing the Giants*, and *Fireproof*, and wrote *The Love Dare Day by Day*, a 365-day devotional for couples, and *The Love Dare Day by Day: Wedding Edition*.

Stephen and his wife, Jill, live in Albany, Georgia, with their four children.

FOR COURAGEOUS PARENTS

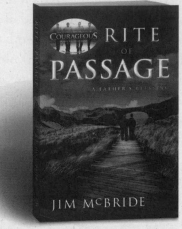

Live Courageously.

978-1-4336-7122-7

978-1-4336-7401-3

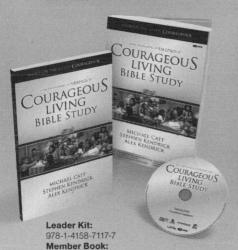

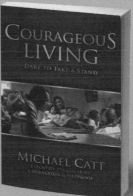

Leader Kit:
978-1-4158-7117-7
Member Book:
978-1-4158-7119-5

978-1-4336-7121-0

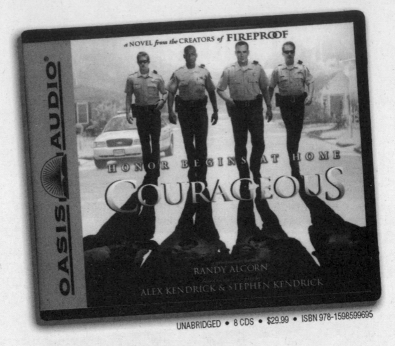